TWO DIFFERENT WORLDS

TWO DIFFERENT WORLDS

Skeet Will

TWO DIFFERENT WORLDS

Copyright © 2025 – Skeet Will
ISBN: 979-8-9986565-8-3

JK Press

JK Press
Oregon, USA

DEDICATION

To Tom and Sally.
Thanks for help when I needed it.

BOOK ONE

CHAPTER ONE

"We should be able to hit the pier on this course with the wings out."

Manny Fry moved to the other side of the tiller and watched his crewmate secure the jib halyard to the opposite cleat. With the boat settled on this course the wind was directly behind them, so the mainsail filled out on the starboard side of the boat and the jib sail did the same on the port—thus, 'wings out.'

Bobby Josephson stretched his long legs across the small cockpit and propped his feet up on the seat opposite.

"So, it doesn't look like you're going to join the Navy, at least for the next little while," he said, looking at his friend.

Manny smiled ruefully. "Not this year anyway. Maybe I'll have to join as a sailor."

"Where's this other guy from?"

"He's from the Oakland side of the Bay. His family knows the Senator well so he got the call. Each Senator and Representative has two appointments a year so Mister Henry will become a plebe this year instead of me. Maybe I could find someone else to appoint me but I'm not counting on it."

He looked up at the sail. "If the wind holds, we should make the landing on this course all right."

Bobby had been looking at the dock where they were heading.

"Is that your dad?"

Manny could see a figure waving at them and he wrinkled his forehead wondering what was so important his father would be waving at him across San Diego Bay. "Looks like it," he replied. "I wonder what he wants."

"I bet we'll find out in a minute."

The boom and mainsail swung quickly across the boat and Bobby ducked just in time.

"Sorry, I wasn't paying attention."

Bobby grinned at him. "I'm used to it. They did it on the Bay just to make sure I was awake." Bobby had crewed on a sailboat working in San Francisco Bay the previous two summers.

Within five minutes they were dropping the sail and Johnny Fry was manning the line to pull them in to tie up.

"Hi, Papa. I thought you were in Sacramento," Manny said to his father.

"I just got off the train and they handed me this. Saved the telegraph messenger a trip all over town looking for you."

He handed the telegram to his son and nodded a greeting to Bobby while Manny tore it open and read the flimsy.

When he finished reading it he handed it to his father, who read it and handed it to Bobby.

"It seems I might be going to Annapolis after all," he said. "Joe Henry's father died in an accident, and he's had to withdraw. I need to be at a doctor's office in San Francisco Monday morning. If I pass the preliminary physical, I'll be on my way."

One nice thing about the prevalence of the new telephone was how easy it was to get in touch with people when you had something important to tell them, like when your son was going away to school and you wanted to have a family celebration. That night the entire family was seated around the table to wish him well in what they all knew was going to be a completely different life for him for the next four years and beyond.

Of course, his only blood relation at the table was his older sister, Teressa. The two of them had been adopted when they were six and four but all the people at the table were family because they did what families were supposed to do, provide love and support when needed.

"You'll have to leave tomorrow to make a doctor's appointment in San Francisco Monday morning," said Lemuel, his father's business partner.

"I'm all packed and ready. I'm not taking much. From what I hear, when you get there most of what you bring with you goes into storage until you leave. I guess it's sort of like suddenly being a new you."

"From what I've read since you started talking about Annapolis it sounds like that's the case," said his father. "Everyone around you will be strangers when you arrive but by the time you come home, we'll be the strangers and the people there will be closer to you than those of us you left behind."

His mother drew him out of his chair and pulled him into a warm embrace. "You won't forget us, will you?" She spoke close to his ear then held him at arm's length and gazed at him. She shook her head. "It won't be the same around here without you," and there were tears in her eyes when she said it.

"No, Mama. The next time you see me I may look a little different, but I'll still be Manny Fry, and this will still be my family."

He had been hugged, had his hand shaken many times and been kissed by every woman and girl in the house, including the servants, when, later that night, he opened the door to the bedroom he shared with Bobby while his friend was in town. The light was already on and his sister was sitting at the fireplace talking with Bobby, who stood when he entered and said, "I know you two want to talk. I'm going to take a walk."

When he closed the door behind him, she said over her shoulder, "Turn out the lights and let's sit by the fire and talk." He did so and sat waiting for her to speak but she continued to stare into the fire.

Finally, she gave a deep sigh and said, "We've never been apart like this before." She looked at him with a sad smile playing reluctantly around her lips. With the moving, changing shadows the firelight cast on her face, it was almost mesmerizing to look at her and he marveled at how beautiful she was.

She was unquestionably Mexican. Dark, lustrous hair, brown eyes, her skin a light coffee color, but unlike most Mexican women, she was tall. When she smiled her teeth sparkled and her eyes could challenge or invite but never without thought. She was never careless with her affections or her beauty.

The day after their mother died their father had disappeared and suddenly, they were alone. Annaliese Fry had been their mother's doctor and had taken them into her home and raised them as her own. They knew they weren't but loved her more because, to her and Johnny, it didn't matter.

At school she was always a leader, and her self-confidence was an essential part of what she was, though she was never overbearing or condescending. She was friendly with everyone but enamored with no one. Well, maybe Bobby.

They had grown up together, she and Bobby, and been friends since either could remember. She always treated him a little differently from anyone else, but he seemed oblivious and for years, had no interest in anything but sailing. To Bobby she was a sister. He would be leaving in a week or so as a crewman on a schooner headed to Hawaii and thence to the South Seas, and it's all he could talk about.

The boys and men in Teressa's life worshiped her and were almost overpowered by her beauty and strength but realized she was different, and few would hazard the rejection they knew would come. And reject she did because, more than any girl Manny knew, she didn't seem to need a man to feel complete.

She was what he would miss most while he was away. She had always been there for him while they were growing up, a shield when she could protect him and someone to talk to about things when she couldn't.

"I'll miss you most," he said. She nodded and continued looking into the coals.

"When can you come home for the first time?"

"After the end of the second year. We take a cruise that summer and after that, get a month's leave. Maybe if Bobby's back by then you two could hop a train and meet me in Kansas City."

"That's a thought, but we'll probably just wait here. Of course, he may not be back by then. Who knows?"

She looked at him for a long moment then said, "So this is how you want to spend your life. In the Navy." It was a statement, not a question.

He nodded and said, "I think so. Course, it's not an irreversible choice but it's what I've always wanted so I'll try my best and see how it fits."

"I'm the older sister and still haven't decided what to do with my life. Maybe your leaving will help me make up my mind."

She stood and pulled him into an embrace then pushed him away and held him at arm's length. "When I see you again, you won't be my little brother anymore. You'll be a man." She was crying; no sound, just tears running down her face. "I won't go to the station with you in the morning, but I'll be thinking about you."

He nodded. "I understand." She disappeared into the dark and he heard the door close behind her.

His bags were aboard, and he embraced his father, shook hands with Bobby then swung onto the back steps as the train pulled away. His father raised his hand and shouted over the noise of the train, "Remember, if you hate them back, you lose."

He settled into his seat and thought about this parting bit of advice. The night before, after the dinner was over, he and his father had sat in Johnny's office up under the eaves and talked about him having to deal with being the first Mexican American to attend the U.S. Naval Academy.

He knew there would be those who would hate him reflexively because he was different and looked foreign. He was determined not to hate them in return but to accept them for what they were.

Since the day his mother died and his father disappeared, Manny and his sister had lived with a foot in different worlds. At home they were surrounded by Mexican servants, and their mother was the doctor for the Mexican community in the county. These people all spoke Spanish to them while most of their family and friends were Anglos who spoke English.

From the beginning Annaliese and Johnny had tried to understand the things that shaped their lives as adopted children who looked so different from their parents. Manny remembered little of his parents and life with them, but Terresa had some memories and sometimes he'd come across her sitting by herself crying quietly and he understood.

All his life, he'd had to face problems when he was brought into contact with the Anglo world outside the family and had learned to deal with them, sometimes letting them pass and other times confronting them.

He had developed a way of slipping punches, either rhetorical or physical, and dealt with things as they arose. He carried no grudges and refused to become bitter over the abuse, preferring to react to situations rather than the person facing him. He'd continue to do that at the Academy and hoped it would help him succeed.

He glanced out the window only occasionally. This trip to San Francisco was rather routine. He had come up and down the great central valley of California many times, but his pulse quickened a little when he thought of the novelty of the trip east. He had never been beyond Sacramento, and the idea of the towering, snowcapped Sierra Nevada excited him.

Beyond them were the great deserts of Nevada and Utah, then the Rockies and Great Plains. He would be following the route his father and friends had traveled when they came west in the 1880s. He had heard many tales of their adventures while growing up among the people who had made that trek. Now he would see it for himself.

His father, Johnny Fry, had come west from Kansas, met and married his mother, Annaliese, in Salt Lake City, where she was his nurse when he was injured. He followed her to San Francisco where he and a friend had opened a bookstore while she attended medical school.

Upon graduation she purchased a practice in San Diego, and Johnny had opened another bookstore. Two years later they adopted Manny and his sister. The family they joined was more of a circle of friends than people related by blood but the love and support these people provided always made the children feel they belonged.

He found himself breathing deeply when the train left Sacramento and began to climb into the foothills of the Sierra Nevada two days later. He had dreamed of this trip many times over the years since he first began to envision himself as a naval officer. Now he was taking the first step toward that future and found he was a little nervous. He suspected the closer he got to Annapolis the more nervous he'd become.

The physical exam the previous day had been easy enough, though his weight just barely cleared the bar for the Academy. He was of average height but had been so thin growing up that his sister teased him she could see his heart beat under his ribs. He had put on some muscle since then but was still almost slight, though wiry and deceptively strong.

Bobby had told him the thing you do on a long trip is look at the scenery and think. At first Manny looked in awe at the snow-capped peaks the train wound among, the waterfalls wherever he looked, and one stream after another that had led man through these awesome mountains. But eventually, he began to think.

He was leaving the only home he'd ever known and everyone in the world important to him. In the future his life would be controlled by impersonal forces, rules and regulations, traditions and forced acceptance of men he didn't know as his superiors.

Be they just and fair or malevolent and capricious, he must obey. He was sure he would make enemies as well as friends, but he was entering a world where he would have no choice but to accept things as they were because it was that or failure and failure would be the end of a dream.

In Carson City, he stretched his legs on the station porch, watched the lights of the city come on and thought about his father. As a boy coming into manhood Johnny had been forced into a gunfight here and killed a man, watched him bleed out on the floor of a dingy saloon and wondered if his life would ever be the same because of what he had just done.

Over the years they had talked about that episode at different times because, as he grew older, Manny had different questions about it and Johnny wanted to make sure he understood. Johnny always wanted him to understand everything. He believed he was failing his son if the boy went to bed with a question unanswered. If Johnny didn't know the answer they would find it together in the bookstore.

The bookstore was where Manny went to learn. It was built into the house and most times it was how he entered and left his home. He had been raised around books. From an early age he had helped at the store and his parents had always encouraged him to look for books on things that entertained and interested him. When he first talked about a life in the Navy his father had found books that helped him decide whether or not it was an idea to build his life around and books that would help him achieve his goal once he decided.

In his home the word family had an almost unique meaning, and he had grown up surrounded by people he loved and trusted, though he was related by blood only to his sister. The dining room table at home had fifteen chairs and most nights were full of intelligent well-read people whose only connection was one of love and trust rather than blood. On many nights growing up his hopes for the future had been heard by all present and their support was important in helping him make his choice.

The train had stopped for coal and water at night in Salt Lake City and in the morning, climbing slowly up into the Rockies east of the city, he thought about his mother. This was where she grew up, adopted also, had worked with her father, the man she called 'the Doctor,' became his trainee, his nurse, his assistant, and finally, after medical school, his colleague in their medical practice.

Not long after they came to San Diego, a friend and patient had asked if Annaliese could help her daughter find out what it was like to be a doctor. She took the girl, Grace was her name, and tried to give Grace what her father had given to her when she was growing up in his house. She was present when Grace graduated from medical school in San Francisco as a doctor.

A year or so after she started working with Grace, her Mexican housekeeper asked if she could do the same thing for her daughter and thus began what became a constant in his mother's life.

Henceforth she would always have young girls working with her, working toward becoming doctors themselves, and always one of them was the daughter of one of her Mexican patients. So far, he knew of three of these women who were now practicing medicine in California, and Grace was a doctor in Hawaii. He had dated one of the girls working with her when he was in school.

Manny was always amazed when he thought of how much his mother had given the world by helping these women achieve their dreams and knew she would continue to do so as long as she was a doctor.

The sun was climbing over the horizon as the Great Plains unfolded around him. He remembered his father's reverence for them and when he saw them understood it. All that day they followed the muddy Platte to a change of trains at Omaha, and it was getting dark when they crossed the Mississippi River. The next morning, he awoke as they were leaving Pittsburgh, and he marveled at the industrial power he saw in the hills outside the city.

All that day, he sat at the window mesmerized by what was passing. He had never seen anything like the green pastoral beauty and soft, round mountains they passed. Late that evening in Baltimore, tired but excited, he found a hotel room near the station and arranged to catch a train to Annapolis the next morning.

The next morning at the station, there were a dozen boys his age waiting for the train, and they all managed to avoid looking at each other. He knew instinctively they were like him, prospective plebes who would become ship captains and admirals of the fleet. He studied them somewhat covertly, knowing some would be friends and others not so much.

Most of the seats were taken in the last car when a short, stocky, dark-haired fellow carrying a large grip stopped and asked Manny, "Anyone sitting here?" When Manny shook his head, he swung his bag onto the rack above and held out his hand.

"I'm Jack Higgins," he said. "Are you headed for the Academy?"

Manny nodded. "Yes, and I'm a little nervous about it."

Jack glanced around the car and chuckled. "I'll bet you're not the only one. Do any of us know what to expect when we get there?" Several of the other boys in the car laughed nervously.

He sat across from Manny and asked, "Where are you from?"

"California."

"I'm from Boston. Never thought about going to college but the chance came up and here I am." He put his hand on his stomach and said, "Kinda gets you in the gut a little, doesn't it? Trouble is I don't know if I'm excited or just scared to death."

"Just how I feel," replied Manny, grinning ruefully at him. Jack's good humor was infectious.

"You must have been on this train a long time coming all the way from California."

"Three days plus a little more but there was a lot to see and a lot to think about. I'm like you. The closer I get the more butterflies I get."

Jack looked at the two boys sitting across the aisle. "And you are…?" he asked one of them. They answered and soon there was a circle of young men sitting or standing around them, talking and getting to know one another.

Manny watched a tall, slender blonde from Ohio and a short, freckled redheaded fellow from Missouri talking to Jack and thought, "This is the beginning. We'll do this a lot before it's over. Just talking to one another."

CHAPTER TWO

Teressa was taking a train ride to her future much like her brother. She was going to San Francisco to talk to someone who would help her realize a dream but unlike Manny, she hadn't reached out for it before. Now she would.

When the cab dropped her at the mansion, she sat on the front porch swing and gazed out at the city below for a few minutes before taking a deep breath and pulling the doorbell. She was steeling herself to take this final step to see if she could find a way to make her dream happen.

"What are you doing out here?" asked Tony, the butler, who answered the door.

She smiled at him. "I wanted to look at the view for a minute before I came in."

Madame and Sarah considered her family, and she usually came in through the kitchen which was why Tony was surprised to see her at the front door.

Madame and Sarah were having tea in her upstairs parlor with a stranger someone Teressa recognized even though she'd never met her. Madame smiled at her and Sarah stood to give her a hug while Tony positioned another chair for her.

Sarah was Bobby's grandmother and Madame (accent on the second syllable) was her longtime companion. She had gotten the name when she ran the best brothel in the city during the Gold Rush of the late forties and early fifties. She later married a wealthy man and when he died, she was left to console herself with all his money.

The stranger was the reason Teressa had come. Madame introduced her but she already knew the woman's name.

Emily Bancroft was a legendary figure in the world of theater. At age eight she had begun appearing with her father and mother as they traveled the nation seeking and sometimes finding audiences for their art, such as it was. Later she worked with a number of traveling companies touring the nation and spending time in Europe, all while perfecting her craft.

In her late twenties she attached herself to a prominent producer and their marriage opened doors that she passed through to acclaim that continued even after he drank himself to death.

Now in her fifties, she had been off the stage a few years but still looked good enough to return whenever she liked. In years past when she played in San Francisco she and Madame had become friends and when Teressa heard she was visiting and staying for a while it seemed like a rare opportunity.

Since she was a child Teressa had wanted to be an actress. Her brother's departure had forced her to face the future, and she had to decide whether to give up her dream or reach out and grasp it before it slipped away, maybe lost forever. She hoped this would be the first step toward grasping it firmly.

Living all her life over a bookstore had given her the opportunity to learn about everything and learn she did. What fascinated her most was the theater. Her childhood performances for friends and family had been more than just enjoyable child's play but also a way for her to keep the dream alive and learn all she could about it.

In addition to reading plays she read magazines and newspapers, learning about stars, stage managers, stagecraft, and recently, the new concept of producers and directors. When theatrical troupes were in town, she would talk to the people who worked behind the scenes and learn the little things that made it all work.

San Diego was not a major stopping place on any theater tour but every once in a while when there was a play in town she would beg Annaliese and Johnny to accompany her.

"You just caught us," said Madame after the introductions. "We're going to dinner with some friends and then to the theater after. If the production wasn't sold out, I'd invite you along."

"Actually, I heard Mrs. Bancroft was here and I'd like to talk to her when you return or tomorrow will be fine. Can you put me up for the night?"

"Of course. You're family. Come and go as you like."

"What did you want to talk to me about?" asked Mrs. Bancroft. "It had to be the theater because that's all I know anything about."

"Yes, it is. But it can wait till morning."

She had stayed at the mansion many times over the years and when she was settled in, she wandered down to the kitchen to see what was cooking. Geppetto was sitting at the kitchen table talking to his mother, Carlotta, Madame's personal maid. Geppetto had grown up in the house where his mother and father had worked since they came to San Francisco fifteen years before. He and Manny were the same age, and he was getting ready to attend the university across the Bay.

Madame had never had a family, so the servants and their children had been adopted and wherever Madame traveled, Carlotta and Tony and Geppetto were never far away. Teressa had known them for years. She was welcomed and soon was eating a nice dinner while they talked.

"I hear Manny's gone to join the Navy," said Geppetto.

"Yes, he left Monday for the Naval Academy. I think he'll be there tomorrow. It feels so strange without him around to talk to."

She was quiet for a moment then said, "I think the reason I'm here is because he left. Since we came to the family, I think I've felt responsible for him as his big sister. Now he's gone. When he comes home, he'll know his classmates better than he knows his family." She sighed and leaned her chin on her hand. "I guess now I've got to figure out what to do with my own life since I don't have him to take care of anymore."

The next morning, she was seated in Madame's sitting room when the ladies came in for breakfast.

"Aren't you the impatient one?" said Madame. She sat down and took a sip of her coffee. "So, if it's not a secret what did you want to talk to Emily about?"

"Manny left the other day and he's on his way to a new life. I suppose I've decided it's time for me to do the same. I've always wanted to be an actress, and I think maybe she can help me decide the best way to begin."

From the doorway Emily asked, "And what is it you wanted to know?"

While Teressa was thinking about her answer, Emily seated herself, was served coffee, and looked at her inquiringly.

"I've always wanted to be an actress." She looked at Sarah and Madame. "Remember the shows we used to put on for the family?"

"Oh yes," said Sarah. "I'm just surprised you've waited this long. What do Johnny and Annaliese think about it?"

"I think they believe I'll get it out of my system, or I won't. They've always let us go where our interests lie. I know they'll be there for me if I fall on my face."

She looked at Emily and said, "So how do I begin? From what I've read at the store I've learned a lot about what the life is. Now I need to take the first step to get things going. But what's the first step?"

"I don't think you can say 'the first step.' I think it's 'a first step.' It's different for everyone. Many begin as children, usually with parents who are already in the trade so it's what they've known all their lives. Others get into it from all different directions. You come from a settled home so it will all be new and strange to you.

"Sometimes it's a lonely life. There's usually not a place you live so much as which a hotel you're staying in tonight. Cast members come and go so long-term friendships are not common. The men begin drinking when they first appear on the stage, probably because all the other men do it and it usually gets worse.

Of course, there are plenty of women drunks too."

She looked at Teressa and shook her head. "They're going to be around you like flies at a picnic. Can you handle that? Many of the actors you'll meet are smooth-talking and suave and the idea will be to get you into bed as soon as possible and then 'we'll see.'

"Among many important bits of advice you will get I will tell you one rule you should never break. Never lend, or give, for that matter, money to an actor. When it comes time to repay it they can come up with some amazing stories, many of them tragic, why they can't."

She glanced at Madame, then back at Teressa. "If you really want to learn, I'd love to have you work with me. You'd learn the business inside and out and I could help you learn the basics of acting and theater. When you're ready I can help get you a place in a company or a theater. Or," she looked at Teressa significantly, "maybe you can make your first appearance with me at the new theater? Madame and I are going to open sometime later this year around the corner from here."

Teressa's mouth fell open in astonishment. "Really! You're going to open a new theater? When?"

"Would you be interested in working with Emily?" asked Madame. "It won't be acting for a while. We have a lot to do to get the building ready for an opening. Might be some hard work."

"I think it would be a dream come true. I was just hoping to talk to her, but this would be perfect. I need to go home and make some arrangements, but could I begin next week?"

For the next hour Emily answered her questions, and they talked about her ideas for the new venture. She also told stories of her years in the profession. "We can work on the theater in the daytime, and, at night, you can read for me and I can tell you many stories about my years on the stage."

As Teressa was getting ready to leave for the station, Emily said, "The way I see it by the time you step on the stage for the first time you should know a lot about what it takes to make it all work." She held out her hand. "I think this will work for both of us."

After the girl left Madame said good night to her friends, and as she was opening the door, she turned and said to Emily "Don't forget, she's family. That means something to me."

After she left, Emily sat quiet for a while and finally asked Sarah, "Do you know what she means by family?"

"I think so. She has no kinfolk. Her first husband died young and left her alone in what became San Francisco. No children. The people you see around here are her friends from the old days when she was a working lady. They helped her when she needed it and she remembers. The maids and butlers, gardeners and stable men you see around here don't have much to do, but she knows they'll be here if she needs them.

"I know you've heard Madame and I talk about Johnny and Lemuel and their families. A few years ago they opened The BookSeller down on Chestnut, and over time it became the center of a circle of people. She sees many of these people as family for the same reason; she knows they'll be there if she needs them and her loyalty runs both ways."

"Do I know any of these people?"

"Rebecca and her daughter, Beth, I think. I can't think of anyone else. Have you met Woman?"

"Oh yes. She's hard to forget. I met her years ago. Is she still around?"

"She's family, and so is her man. They live in San Diego now. If you stay around here long you'll meet most of them."

"I'm assuming she told me that for a reason?"

Sarah smiled at her. "I'd say so. She wants you to know that young lady is important to her and she wants to make sure you understand what that means."

"It sounds like you might have struck gold with this lady," said Johnny. "It seems she might be the kind of person who can open doors for you, help you find your feet in a new world."

"I had no idea she would reach out to me like this," said Teressa. "It feels like she's opening a curtain for me. If I join her, I might find what I've wanted since I can remember."

Annaliese sat down beside her and took her hand. "I don't want you to feel we were against you on this. It's just that we've heard so much about the perils of the life, we were a little afraid of where it would take you. It sounds like this will be a great opportunity for you. Try it and see. We'll be here if it isn't what you hoped."

She was alone in her room later that night when someone tapped on the door. When she opened it she was glad to see Maggie, one of her mother's partners in the clinic and a friend since childhood. There were things she could talk to Maggie about that were not so easy to bring up with her parents. The bookstore was closed so they sat with tea in chairs in the bay window in the front of the store and talked. The only light was from the streetlights outside that cast shadows across them.

"This is all very sudden, isn't it?" asked Maggie. "Have anything to do with Manny leaving?"

"That and Bobby heading off to Hawaii and then, God knows where," answered Teressa. "Suddenly the people I grew up with are gone. Not all of them maybe, but my two closest friends. It's made me think about what I want in my life."

"And that is?"

"I want to try acting. I wanted to see Mrs. Bancroft to see if she could point me toward a place to begin and she offered me what seems like a perfect way to get started."

"Really?"

"It seems Madame owns a theater and the company who's been renting it has decided to go on the road so suddenly it's vacant. She had it up for sale for a while and when Mrs. Bancroft came to visit they talked about it. Since she retired from acting Emily has wanted to try her hand at producing and maybe directing a play just to see how she likes it.

"They worked out a deal then I walked in the door and suddenly I'm her new assistant and a 'student of the profession,' as she says. She says it will take some work to get the place ready, but with Madame behind her, she'd like to start from the ground up and make it something special. Give the city something to be proud of."

"Anyone who's watched you grow up will not be surprised by this," said Maggie. "This has been your dream for as long as I've known you. When do you start?"

"When I get back. I catch the train in the morning."

A month with Emily was a constant education for Teressa. She had read about the theater for years but now she was involved in turning a drafty old barn into The Crown Theater, a beautiful venue where the people of the city could enjoy well-written, well-produced theater with performances by the finest actors from America and abroad.

She was Emily's eyes and ears, listening to ideas, checking deliveries and receiving and passing on messages. It was not acting, but it was theater in depth, and she loved what she was doing, all that she was learning. She watched the progress of the remodeling of the theater and kept a diary so they could estimate when it would be ready and begin to plan for their first performance.

She was sitting in the small room near the back of The Crown she had set up for an office, writing in the diary when one of the carpenters stuck his head around the corner and said, "Someone out front to see you, Miss Fry." With all the vendors and construction workers in and out this was not unusual but when she came out on the stage she was surprised to see her father sitting in the center of the front row.

"Papa! What are you doing here?"

They embraced, and he kissed her on the cheek.

"Lemuel comes up every once in a while to check the bookstore up here and I thought I'd come with him this time and visit so I can report back to your Mama about how you're doing. Can we go somewhere, get some coffee and sit for a while?"

"Of course. Let me lock up the office and we can go to Harry's. It's just down the street."

When they were seated and had ordered he asked, "So, how are things going in the big city? It looks like the place is a while from being ready to open."

She took a deep breath, rolled her eyes and shook her head. "We still have a lot to do but Emily and Madame seem to be satisfied with how things are progressing. She's already beginning to talk to people about getting the stage crew together. She says it won't be long until we get a play in hand and begin to line the actors up for rehearsals."

"Never thought I'd see you with sawdust in your hair," he said. "Looks like you've picked up Maggie's idea about wearing pants when you need to." He blew on his coffee before he took a sip. "This doesn't seem much like acting. On the other hand, your smile tells me you're happy about something."

"I'm happy to see you, Papa. Is everything all right at home?"

"Everything's fine. Your Mama would have come but she's pretty busy at the clinic right now. We're staying at the mansion, so why don't you and Emily join us for dinner? I'm anxious to meet her."

"Three or four evenings a week, we sit in our flat, and I read different parts in different plays to her." She and Johnny were sitting on a porch overlooking the lights of the city later that evening. "She's very exacting with me and sometimes makes me read lines again and again until I deliver them to her satisfaction, with just the right emotion or intonation."

"One evening a week, we go to a performance in the city. She has a copy of the play and the night before she chooses a part for me to learn. While we watch the play, I'm to focus on the one who has my part and later, back at the flat, we sit and critique her performance. I say her, but one night she had me watch a man the same way. First thing after breakfast every morning I think about what I've learned that night and write about it in a diary I keep." She smiled at her father. "That diary's already getting pretty big."

Johnny grinned at her. "Any romance in that diary yet?"

She snorted. "I don't have time for any of that. Between the work at the theater and the time I spend working with Emily, I stay pretty busy."

"Are you living with her, then?"

"Yes. We have a two-bedroom flat just down the street from work. It's enough for now. We come up here a lot to talk about things at work and just to visit and we eat here quite often. Madame is interested in what we're doing but she doesn't interfere. She just likes to be apprised of what's going on."

He stood and held out his hand. "Let's rejoin the others," he said. "It sounds like this is working out beautifully for you, but if you need our help, we'll be here."

She hugged him and said, "I know. That's one reason I can enjoy it so much. That and Emily. She's a wonderful teacher, and we really enjoy doing things together."

"Emily told me Madame told her I was family and that was important to her." She kissed him on the cheek. "Thank you for that, Papa."

CHAPTER THREE

Bobby Josephson would always remember the sight of Diamond Head rising from the ocean as the beginning of his life in the South Pacific.

"Well, Bobby, how do you feel about your first time in Honolulu?" asked the captain as they stood watching the harbor come into sight. The captain's name was Peter Atwell, but to the eighteen-year-old Bobby, he was Cap'n Pete.

"I'm hoping to have time to look around a little," he replied. "A friend of my parents is a doctor here, and I'd like to stop in and see her."

"I don't know about that. You'll have to stay on board while Rudy and I take care of some business in town and we'll be leaving day after tomorrow. That is, unless I find a cargo or a passenger. Cookie also has to buy supplies and that leaves you to look after things on the boat while we're gone."

Rudy was the mate, a morose, taciturn man who rarely spoke except when necessary to operate the boat. Cookie was a native Kanak from New Caledonia who had served with Atwell for years. The four of them made up the crew of the schooner. These were the men he would live and work with as long as he was aboard.

"There have been some problems with boats that were stolen or robbed when they were left unmanned in this harbor."

Bobby's brow furrowed. "What do I do if someone tries to come aboard while you're gone?"

"There's a pistol hanging in the galley. If you let 'em see that it should solve the problem," the captain replied. "Remember, no one comes on board if I'm not here." Behind him, the mate and Cookie were already in the dinghy. The captain joined them, and with Rudy manning the oars, they were soon on their way to the dock.

In the distance, Bobby could see the lights of the city beginning to come on. He had a few chores around the boat but finally settled himself in the cockpit to wait. Already on the voyage from San Francisco, he'd learned patience.

On the boats he'd worked in the Bay, they were never far from some kind of contact with the shore, but Diamond Head was the first land they had seen in the last three weeks or so, and night watches had usually been quiet unless there was a squall or a change in the wind and something needed to be done to the sails.

Because he was new on board and had never sailed on a schooner, he wasn't familiar yet with the sail plan and how each sail affected the boat in a given situation. The captain had to be notified before anything significant could be done.

Sometimes the captain would remain on deck after being roused for a change in the wind and they would talk. Peter Atwell was a small, weathered, wizened man with a proper British accent who had been sailing the oceans for some thirty years, most of it in the islands of the South and Southwest Pacific. He loved to talk, so during some of these night watches, he talked, and Bobby listened and learned things he needed to know.

Atwell was also curious about a crewmate he would be sailing with for God knows how long, so sometimes they talked about Bobby and how he had come to be a sailor.

A friend of the family owned a bookstore in San Francisco, and when he was nine years old, Bobby read *Treasure Island*. Appetite whetted, he devoured everything he could find by Stevenson and later Melville, and then everything he could find on sailing and the South Sea.

While there were probably seafarers among his Swedish forebearers, his father, Handy, had grown up on a Minnesota farm, the youngest of five and surrounded by a migrant community of mostly blood relatives. He once told Bobby he could stand on his father's farm and look at family farms as far as he could see in any direction.

Visiting family in Kearney, Nebraska, Handy met Johnny Fry traveling across the country by horseback and fascinated by the idea, asked to join him. On the ensuing trip, he met and married Bobby's mother, and later the two of them joined Buffalo Bill's western show and spent six months traveling and performing. They came to San Francisco for Bobby's birth and eventually bought a horse farm north of the city.

Bobby had enjoyed an unusual childhood. His father, remembering his own mother and her loneliness on a farm distant from any neighbors, had encouraged his wife to visit her mother in San Francisco as often as she liked and that had evolved into a week living at the ranch in Mill Valley, across the Bay and twenty miles north of the city, and a week at the Mansion in San Francisco with his mother, grandmother, his grandmother's lady friend, and all the servants. Most winters, the family spent in San Diego with other family

On the ranch, he was sometimes on a horse from morning till night with other children or his parents. He worked with Handy and his pardner from the time he could walk, exercising horses, repairing tack, blacksmithing, and helping wherever he could. He learned to fix things and tinker with whatever new thing he came across.

This last trait was one of the reasons Atwell had signed him on. While on board craft in the Bay, he had learned how to maintain and repair the small gasoline engine that was becoming more and more common on sailing vessels as an auxiliary for better-controlled handling at piers and maneuvering at close quarters.

At six and a half feet tall, he had grown into a gangly giant at age eighteen, but his broad shoulders and deep chest and the hard work around the boat made it easy to believe he would grow into a very large, strong man, much like his father.

While he had his father's frame, there was a lot of his mother in him too. He had her black hair that he kept cut in a mop that covered his ears, her warm brown eyes and a slightly reddish tinge to his skin from her Indian heritage. Her father had been a Sioux warrior who was killed in a raid by another tribe. Her mother had been a captive who escaped during the raid and returned to her family in Wisconsin. Eventually, she married and moved west, following her children to San Francisco.

In San Francisco and San Diego, Bobby spent time sailing when he could and watching other boats go about their daily tasks came to see his future as spent beneath a sail of one sort or another. Winters in San Diego, he and Manny Fry spent much time together, usually sailing the bay by themselves or with other friends.

At sixteen, with his parents' reluctant permission, he signed on board a ketch odd jobbing around San Francisco Bay and learned how to sail for a living. His hiring as a hand on *Mirabelle II* came about because he'd been prowling the docks and shipwrights along San Francisco Bay looking for a berth just as the refurbished boat needed a new hand when it was ready to relaunch.

When he hired on, part of the deal was that Atwell would teach him celestial navigation, how to use the sextant, do the calculations and chart a course past and future. His experience with sailing, to this point, had almost all been on the protected waters of San Francisco and San Diego Bays, so learning navigation wasn't a priority so much as learning the navigational hazards of the Bay.

Now, however, he was on the world's biggest ocean, and it was imperative he learn how to find out where he was and how to get to where he wanted to go. The Captain's love of talking translated into being a good teacher, and he enjoyed watching Bobby's face as the boy learned and digested something new.

To this point they had been north of the Equator, so navigation revolved around the North Star, the only fixed star in the constellation. But once they crossed the Equator all the stars would course across the sky nightly and he would need to learn the movements of each as signposts to tell him where he was and guide him where he wanted to go.

Sitting in the cockpit on a beautiful evening, the lights of the city shadowed by the mountains behind them, he gazed up at the stars, brilliant in the moonless night, seeing them as friends who would guide him into his future. He was excited about being here and where he was going.

This was the path he had set his foot on when, as a nine-year-old boy looking through books at the BookSeller in San Francisco, he had first seen a picture of a schooner and marveled at its beauty. That year, Handy bought a small sailboat for him and they learned to sail it together. He had been sailing by himself since he was ten.

Mirabelle II was a refitted 68-foot island schooner. It was replacing one Atwell had sailed for years. The original *Mirabelle* had been torn from its mooring by a typhoon and smashed on some rocks in the harbor at Noumea in far-off New Caledonia. The refitted boat was unusually clean and fresh and Atwell was anxious to get back to the trade of the islands.

He had sailed from Bristol on a bark in 1871, jumped ship, and hidden in the hills of New Caledonia until it sailed away. He joined another Englishman as a working partner a few years later and sailed the islands carrying anything that needed carrying for the intervening thirty years. He never got rich, but it was easy to see he desired no other life.

The pistol was in easy reach and Bobby had settled himself in the cockpit to await the return of his crewmates when he saw a faint shadow against the lights of the town. He sat up and strained his eyes to see if he could make it out and finally saw a dinghy creeping across the water toward him.

"Ahoy the boat," he called, but there was no answer. He reached into the cabin and took the pistol from its holster. When he cocked the hammer, the mechanical sound reached across the water and the boat paused in its stroke, then began again, bringing the boat closer.

A hoarse voice called. "Take it easy. Just want to talk," it said. "Can I come aboard?"

"No," answered Bobby. "Capt'n's ashore. He told me no one

is allowed on board until he returns."

The boat kept moving closer and Bobby raised his voice. "I've been shooting rabbits with a six-gun since I was ten years old. Are you sure you want to come any closer?"

"Why are you so jumpy? We just want to talk."

Off the bow, out of the corner of his eye, he saw the white water from a mishandled oar.

"Mister," he said, conversationally. "Unless you want to pay for a funeral, you better tell that man trying to sneak around to my other side while you keep me busy talking, to feather his oars. If he comes any closer, I'm going to shoot him, and then I'm going to shoot you. You know, it'd be a while before they found your bodies out here. At least you wouldn't have to pay for a funeral that way."

There was a pause but no reply, so Bobby pointed the gun in the general direction of the second boat and pulled the trigger. The shot hit the water close aboard, and the boat stopped.

"I'm not going to warn you again. I won't miss next time." The quarter moon had begun to peak over the rim of the ocean, and he could see the boats a little more clearly. After a moment, he saw them back the oars and turn away.

He raised his voice to make sure they heard. "I'm going to be watching. If you try it again there may be a price. You've been warned."

Bobby was cleaning the pistol a couple of hours later when the crew returned.

"Did you have to use it?" asked Atwood.

"A warning shot is all," replied Bobby. "A couple of boats working together tried to sneak up on me, but I warned them off."

The captain joined him in the galley and sat smoking his pipe, watching Cookie and Bobby stowing the supplies and talking.

"It would be a good thing if you paid attention to what he's stowing. It's good to know what all we have aboard and where it is." This was an example of how he was teaching Bobby the little things he needed to know about how to keep a boat functioning so it could complete its job, whatever the job was.

Though she was refitted and refurbished, *Mirabelle II* was a tramp just like her predecessor. She would pay her way, taking whatever she could find wherever it needed to go. Sometimes cargo, sometimes passengers, sometimes mail. Over the years, the old girl had paid her way quite well and now it was time for the new girl to take over.

As Bobby learned what was necessary to keep the boat afloat and sailing, he also learned about his crewmates. Rudy was from somewhere in the Balkans, had been imprisoned for debt, escaped to France and eventually worked his way to the South Seas. The man didn't talk much but was a good hand, did his share of the work without complaint and he and Bobby worked well together.

Cookie was from Noumea, had grown up there and had worked with Atwood as a cook, both on the boat and when they were at home on Grand Tierre. It was the largest of the dozens of islands that made up the archipelago of New Caledonia, a French possession since the mid-19th century. His sister, Marie, was Captain Pete's housemate when he was at home, and in years past, had sailed with *Mirabelle* a time or two. They had been with him since they were children.

Bobby had some trouble understanding Cookie at times. He spoke a mishmash of French, English, the pidgin of the islands, with some of his native tongue thrown in, but his mood seemed to be consistently sunny, and one way or another, they communicated well enough.

A few years before, a friend of his father's had taught Bobby to watch the way a horse moved and how to tell if it was injured or wasn't feeling good. Since he'd been sailing, he'd learned to assess his crewmates the same way. Watching the captain move around the boat, he could see the man was becoming clumsy and seemed weaker than he had when they had left San Francisco just three weeks before.

When he mentioned this to Atwood, at first, he avoided answering but eventually said, "I wanted to go to a doctor I knew here, but he's gone off to another island to work on a plantation. Didn't you say you knew a doctor in Honolulu?"

"I guess she's still here. Her father owns a shipping line, and she married a fellow who works for him."

"Her? She's a woman?" Atwood looked at Bobby with a furrowed brow. "Never been to a woman doctor before."

"I don't know much about her as a doctor, but I always liked her. She trained with a family friend for years and then went to school for it. I guess she knows what she's about."

Atwood sat quietly for a minute, clearly thinking. "What's her name?"

"She was Grace Spreckels then. I don't know her husband's name but if she's still here she shouldn't be hard to find."

"Spreckels? Is that John D. Spreckels' outfit?"

"I think so. I met him one time at a dinner in San Diego."

"I'll bet it was a nice dinner. He's one of the richest men on the West Coast."

"That's what I've heard."

"Reckon you could come with me tomorrow and we could try to find her?"

"You're the Cap'n, so I imagine we could."

The next morning, they tied the dinghy up to the pier in town and it took less than ten minutes to find Grace's office. They took a seat in the waiting room and after a short time were shown into a room to await the doctor.

She was smiling when she opened the door a few minutes later and the smile blossomed into a grin when she saw Bobby.

"Bobby, what are you doing here?" She embraced him, then held him at arm's length, looked him up and down and exclaimed, "You've grown up since I saw you last. You're almost as big as your father."

"Papa's still got me by a couple inches," he replied. "Grace, this is the captain of the boat I'm on. The doctor he wanted to see isn't here right now, so we decided to see if we could find you instead. It was easier since you still use your family name."

She turned to Atwood, and he introduced himself. "Were you looking for Dr. Bauserman?" she asked. When he nodded, she continued, "He's over on the Big Island. One of the plantations over there had an outbreak of typhoid. I don't know when he'll be back."

"Well," he said. "Can you take care of me since he's not here? We'll be leaving in a day or two."

She smiled and said, "I'll do my best."

The city of Honolulu looked to be a little bigger than San Diego and because he only had a short time before they sailed, Bobby had accepted Grace's invitation to meet at a local restaurant for coffee and talk. Since the captain had things to do after he left the doctor's office, they went their separate ways, planning to meet on the dock later in the day.

When they were settled with coffee before them, he and Grace began to talk about things back home and how she liked living in the islands.

After he had filled her in on what was going on with everyone from home, he asked, "Do you like it here?"

"I love it, though I don't know if I can build a practice big enough to stay." She shrugged. "Women doctors and all that stuff. Many of the people here won't go to a woman doctor. I guess it's almost a cultural thing with some people from the Orient. There were enough doctors for the white population before I got here. So sometimes I spend a lot of time reading and waiting for patients that never show up. I've taken to writing just to have something to do."

She smiled ruefully, then brightened and asked, "So, where are you bound? I remember you always used to talk about the South Seas."

"I guess it depends on what the captain can scare up as a cargo. He was going to a factory here to find something to carry. The captain's home port is Noumea in New Caledonia so that's where we'll probably end up but where to before that, God only knows."

"When are you leaving? I'd like you to meet James, but he's on Maui checking a plantation the company has over there."

"We were supposed to leave tomorrow, but it seems he's got a lead on a passenger going to Samoa. We go where there's a cargo, from what he says."

"Well, I'm glad you found me. I don't see many people from home out here."

They embraced, and she returned to her office while he wandered along the waterfront until time to meet the captain to go back on board.

"Well," the Captain said while Bobby was pulling toward the boat, "it looks like we got a missionary to take to Samoa, and he's taking a printing press with him. We'll load the machine in the morning, and he's to be on the pier with his dunnage by noon."

The captain watched Bobby and Rudy secure the dinghy to the stern and led the way to the galley for dinner.

"I've had more than a few missionaries on board over the years," he said between mouthfuls of stew. "Some were good people, and I enjoyed sailing with them. On the other hand, some were self-righteous fools. Don't know about this one. He's young so maybe he hasn't learned how to be a self-righteous fool yet."

CHAPTER FOUR

Though most probably don't realize it the first time they see it, for most cadets who make it through Bancroft Hall will likely become the symbol of the four years spent at Annapolis on the Severn. In the early years of the twentieth century, many didn't make it through. By graduation day, some 40% of those who began with hopes of future service in the Navy will have fallen by the wayside, victims of academic, disciplinary, or fitness failure. But even those who fail will remember the Hall.

It was constructed from 1901 to 1906 and Manny and Jack Higgins, his new friend from the train, belonged to the first class to spend their lives there. Every graduate of the Naval Academy since has followed where they led, sleeping there, eating there, seeing a doctor or dentist there, buying uniforms and books there, even getting their hair cut and their laundry done there and, at one time or another, seeing every other student member of the brigade of cadets there.

There was one thing about the brigade in those days of the early twentieth century that made it different from the present, but at the time seemed completely normal. It was composed of fit, young, white, American males. The idea of a negro, oriental, Hispanic, or foreign male or a female midshipman didn't occur to anyone.

This particular requirement put people like Manny, with his Mexican heritage, and Jack, an Irish Catholic from Boston, on the edge of this society and led to some difficult situations, especially since at that time, it meant any upperclassmen could harass and belittle them under the guise of accustoming them to the discipline necessary to become an effective military officer. This was the practice known as hazing, and it had been a part of the Academy since its inception.

Manny was an American citizen, born and raised in the country, as was Jack Higgins but to many of the citizens of the country during that day and time they weren't the right kind of American citizen.

All candidates for the Naval Academy in those days had to file through the same rooms and talk to the same people as they made the step from candidate to Midshipman but not all at the same time. Manny and Jack were among the first and were well into the system while others of their year were still arriving or being tested. Many of the class had attended prep schools aimed at sharpening focus on things necessary to succeed at Annapolis, and they had to be academically tested to see if they qualified for final admission to the Academy.

All the candidates were soon plugged in and moving through the system. First, a final and very detailed physical exam. Next, they signed a commitment to serve eight years in the Navy and an affirmation that they did so with the permission of a parent or guardian. Then they were given the oath of office and became members of the Brigade.

Next, they went to a clerk who relieved them of any money in their pockets, noted it in a ledger, and gave them a receipt. Plebes were not only not allowed to have any money when they entered but were also forbidden to receive any from home. Whatever they needed from here on the Navy would provide.

The rest of the day was spent getting their hair cut, being measured for uniforms by tailors, and being issued hats. These hats, which were to be worn whenever they were outside, were the only part of their uniforms they were issued. They would wear them until their uniforms came from the tailors and thus felt conspicuous, since the hats, with their civilian clothes and newly shaved heads, clearly marked them as plebes.

At the end of the first day, Manny and Jack were finally alone in their room on the lower deck of the Hall looking at one another with wry smiles at their newly shorn heads.

"We took a big step today," said Manny.

"That we did," replied Jack. "More than one, it seems."

Manny was stowing his things in trunks and drawers. The room had the smell of newness and was clean to a fault, but the furniture had been in use for what looked like a long time.

Jack held out a drawer in two pieces and said, "They must have run out of money when it came time to furnish this place."

"The desks look pretty sturdy," said Manny. "We'll spend a lot of time sitting at them before it's over."

"I guess that's what worries me the most," said Jack, sitting down on his bunk and bouncing to assess it. "I had no idea of coming here until this year. My Pap was a councilman back home and went to work for a new congressman. He found out about the appointment and asked. I probably wouldn't have gone to college if I hadn't got into this place. Never really studied much in school, but I do seem to be good at mathematics. Don't know why, it just comes easy to me. Other than that, I'm a bit of a dunderhead."

Manny was wrestling with the only window in the room. He finally got it up. "Not much of a view from this floor," he said. He leaned out and assessed the granite outside the window, then turned to the stove in the corner. "I'll bet it'll be hot in the summer and cold in the winter in this place. We don't have much winter in San Diego so I bought some long johns in San Francisco before I caught the train."

He sat down on his bed and looked across at his new friend. They were roommates because their names had been close together on an alphabetical list and now they were joined at the hip, so to speak and if they survived, would probably be like brothers after four years together.

"Are you going to need some help? I hear some students

volunteer to help others who need a hand with their studies."

"Maybe. Guess I'll just have to see."

"Do you read a lot?"

"No. Never have."

Jack shook his head. "I took this as a lark as much as anything. I'm finding out there may be a lot more to it than I thought. How about you? Are you worried?"

Manny smiled. "No. I think I'll do alright. My father owns a bookstore and he got me reading when I was young. Got to be a habit. I read a lot. Always got a book lying around.

"When I decided to apply, Papa got me books that would help me with what I needed to know. There were no schools out there to help me prepare so we worked out a plan and I studied what I thought I'd need. Know something about most of the things we'll need to learn."

"Like what?"

"Mostly marine things. Naval engineering, gunnery, seamanship. Things like that. Plus, I did well in my regular studies. I've had my own sailboat since I was ten and I worked one summer on a sloop hauling stuff around the Bay so I'm at home on the water. Also, I've had a mathematics tutor for the last two years."

"Think you can help me if I need it?" asked Jack.

"Can't see why not. Papa always told me the best way to learn anything better is to teach it to someone else so helping you will be helping me, too."

There was a sharp rap on the door and it opened to reveal three stern-faced, fully uniformed upperclassmen, to be specific, third-classmen, also known as 'youngsters.' These three had spent the previous year as plebes and carried with them the memories of the indignities they had suffered at the hands of the 'youngsters' of the year before.

They filed into the room. Manny, recognizing what was about to happen, immediately sprang to attention but Jack smiled at them and continued to sit on his bunk.

"On your feet, Mister," bellowed the one in the lead. Jack threw a startled glance at Manny and recognizing the situation leapt to his feet.

"You always stand in the presence of a superior officer," said the leader, whose face was inches from Jack's. "What is your name, Mister?" he shouted.

"Jack Higgins."

"You will answer, 'Higgins, Sir.' Do you understand?" at the top of his voice. He turned to his companions, both stone-faced, and introduced them as Midshipman Henry and Midshipman Grace. "I am Midshipman Fosbury."

When he turned to look at Manny his eyes narrowed for an instant. It was something Manny recognized. He had seen it before. "What is your name, Mister?"

"Fry, Sir."

"Where are you from, Mr. Fry?"

"San Diego, California, Sir."

Fosbury continued to look at him for a moment and then turned back to Jack.

Over the next half hour, the plebes were put through a series of ridiculous paces, including standing on their heads in a basin of water and having to repeat the word 'sir' between every word of any answer to any question.

These things would have seemed comical but for the serious demeanor of the Midshipmen watching. By the time they left the room both plebes were duly impressed by the necessity of maintaining a straight face and reacting to nothing no matter how outrageous or trivial it seemed.

This was known as 'running' plebes. It was, in essence, a mild form of hazing but since hazing was against regulations, anyone caught hazing a plebe could be discharged. If a plebe wanted to, he could, under the regulations, refuse to allow himself to be 'run' or even hazed, and there was nothing official that would be done as a result. Unofficially, though, the plebe would be 'cut' by others of his class and by all the upperclassmen and thus would be an outsider and eventually destined to 'bilge' out of the brigade.

Last through the door, Midshipman Fosbury paused and said, "Fortunately for you two, all upperclassmen are going aboard the three battleships you see moored in the bay tomorrow and will be gone for a month or more. This is our summer cruise and part of our education. When we return, we depart for a month's leave." He paused and said meaningfully, "Unfortunately for you, we will be coming back to help guide you through your first year."

He looked at Manny for a long moment before closing the door behind him.

They had joined the new Navy, the product of the strategic ideas of Albert Thayer Mahan joined to the dynamic personality of Theodore Roosevelt. Mahan's *The Influence of Sea Power upon History* was published in 1890 and embraced by Roosevelt when the two men met in 1893.

When he was appointed Assistant Secretary of the Navy in April 1897, Roosevelt brought Mahan's ideas to bear on the conservative, complacent, and rather indolent John Davis Long, President McKinley's Secretary of the Navy. In Davis's many absences from the office, Roosevelt assumed total command. He moved the Pacific Fleet to strategic positions relative to the Spanish Fleet, appointed commanders, and generally acted as though he was the boss.

When war broke out in the Spring of 1898, Commodore Dewey pounced on the Spanish Fleet and crushed the Dons in Manila Bay a week after war was declared. At the same time, the U.S. Atlantic Fleet blockaded the enemy in their Cuban harbors and destroyed them when they ventured out to fight. Roosevelt had been right; the Navy was ready to fight and in the right place to be the most effective. This was the only instance in the nation's history where the Navy was ready to fight a war the politicians had gotten us into.

Roosevelt believed in a strong Navy. When he became President upon McKinley's assassination, the nation began to flex its industrial muscle in that direction and the new Navy was the result.

In December 1907, when the "Great White Fleet" sailed from Norfolk Harbor, twelve of the sixteen battleships underway had been laid down during Roosevelt's administration. Because this new navy had new ships they needed officers who could handle the engineering challenges that came with the steel-hulled, coal-fired, screw-driven, four hundred fifty-foot-long monsters with crews of eight-hundred men.

This is the mission of The Naval Academy: to educate and train the men necessary to command these ships, these modern marvels, and lead them into battle.

Of the 230 men in Manny's and Jack's class, more than a hundred would fall by the wayside, but the ones that remained would learn what they needed to know and go on to lead the greatest Navy in the history of the world through the greatest war in the history of the world.

One dynamic of any group of young men is that leaders will come to the fore, gain a reputation for some reason and others will look to them when decisions and leadership are needed. Some men seek these leadership roles; others have these roles thrust upon them by people who see in them something they don't see in themselves.

Manny made his reputation in a strange way. Indeed, you might say he inherited it from his father.

One afternoon their section was standing in loose formation waiting their turn on the pistol range. In the distance, they could hear firing at the rifle range a little way down the road.

"I'm a tad nervous," admitted Jack. "Don't know much about guns. When Ma was alive, she wouldn't have one in the house. Pa never said much about it. He had a pistol, but I don't know if he ever fired it."

They were surrounded by classmates, and someone behind him said, "My Pa and I used to go hunting with some friends. Never used a pistol, though."

"What about California?" someone said. "They must have a lot of guns out west like that. Is that right, Manny?"

Manny smiled. "My Papa taught me to shoot a pistol when I was ten," he said. "Most weeks since then, we try to practice. I guess you could say I know my way around with a pistol."

Back in formation, they listened to a series of instructions about safety and mechanics and then began to move into positions on the range. Manny and Jack were on the far right of the line, and Manny was the last to receive his weapon, a single-action, short-barreled Colt .45. He felt right at home. There was one just like it hanging in a holster on the hat rack back home.

Range attendants, one between four men, moved along the line, observing and instructing each man who fired, so Manny and Jack could watch the others and see how they fared.

The targets were raised from a trench by hand, then lowered and marked, and raised again after each plebe shot. Instructors moved between students, assessing the targets and instructing as needed.

When the instructor came to Manny's position he leaned forward and said in a low voice, "Rumor has it that you're from California and have been shooting since you were a kid. That right?"

"Yes, sir," said Manny, nodding.

The instructor nodded his head at the target in the distance and said, "Well?"

Manny assumed the position instructors had been placing the other plebes in and carefully squeezed off five evenly spaced shots, cocking the Colt smoothly between each one. Even from that distance, the grouping could be seen in and around the bullseye.

From behind him, the instructor said, "Reload, I want to see you do that again. This time stand any way you want."

When he finished reloading, Manny flipped the loading gate closed and looked at the instructor for a long moment. Then he turned quickly, dropped into a slight crouch, and triggered three shots so close together there was but one long rolling sound.

He held the pose for a moment, gun extended, like a finger pointing. As the sound died away, he turned to the instructor, reversed the pistol, and handed it to him. The man was looking out at the target, mouth open. The three shots were centered in the bullseye. By the time he went to bed that night, Manny's reputation in the brigade was already in place.

Jack made his reputation a little differently.

All Academy students must engage in organized athletic activity as part of their education. The concept of teamwork is vital to any military organization. Team sports help create the idea of collective action to achieve goals. They are a part of any military force in the world.

"Which sports are you going to pick?" Manny asked one evening after study period. "I guess we can pick something we're good at and try to get better or else try something new and learn."

"I never played sports at school, but we played everything in the neighborhood. What I'm best at is football. It looks like there are a lot of chances to play with different teams here. And there's an intercollegiate team. I might try that."

"You'd have to be pretty good to play for the school. Are you that good?"

"I don't know. Never played in a league before. Or with rules, actually. We just got together and played. Organized on the spot. Sometimes we'd clear a vacant lot of rocks and stuff and play whenever we could. If they'd run us off, we'd go find someplace else." He smiled at the memory. "Scored a lot of touchdowns playing back home."

He walked to the window and stood looking out. "And it kept us out of trouble," he said. "I grew up in a rough neighborhood. More than a few of my friends went bad. The neighborhood was all immigrants and very Irish. Mass every week and going to school wasn't my favorite pastime."

Blocky was one way to describe Jack. He was a couple of inches shorter than Manny with broad shoulders and a deep chest. With the typical plebe haircut and short, slightly bowed legs, he looked like a wrestler, but it only took the Navy football coach a couple of practices to realize he was good, very good.

As a runner he had a low center of gravity, which made him hard to knock off his feet and also appeared to give him an almost inhuman ability to avoid being tackled in the open field. He could change direction quickly and dramatically, accelerate rapidly and his fakes caught defenders flatfooted. He was also a good blocker and absolutely fearless on the field.

Within two weeks, the freshman football coach was designing the offense around him, and his reputation was born.

CHAPTER FIVE

"How would you feel about getting a cat?"

Emily looked up at her and Teressa smiled impishly. They were in their small sitting room just beginning an 'after the theater' repast. This was something they did when they came home from a new production. In the play they had seen that night, a young girl had asked her mother for a cat and that had put the idea in Teressa's head.

"I hadn't thought about it. Why, suddenly, do you want a cat?"

"My Papa always had a black cat. In fact, he had Jinx with him when he rode horseback from Kansas to Sacramento in 1884. I think Jinx lived to be about seventeen. We always had a cat around the house when I was growing up."

"So you know how to take care of one?" When Teressa nodded, she said, "Well, I've never had a pet." She sat thinking for a moment, then smiled. "Let's do it. Where do you find cats when you want one?"

"I saw a lady yesterday with some in a box she was trying to find homes for. One of them was a little black male. Would that be alright?"

"Sounds like it'll be interesting. Why black?"

"That's what Papa always had. It will remind me of home."

The maid came in with a pot of tea and poured some for each of them.

"What do you think about that, Estella?" said Emily.

"About what?" she asked.

"Getting a kitten," said Emily. "You'll have to take care of it when she's not around."

"Kittens are fun. Old Jose has some cats in the stable at the mansion. I think they keep the mice and rats down." She shrugged. "It'll be company when you two are out at night."

They named him Othello, the Black Prince. He was just off his mother when she got him and within a week he was bouncing around the sitting room like a furry ball, climbing everything, including her leg, pouncing on anything that moved, and generally learning to be a cat. He made them smile and laugh a lot.

He was a lap cat from the beginning, had a loud purr, easily activated and the first time she put him on her shoulder, he seemed right at home. She smiled whenever she thought about her Papa's reaction to her new furry friend. Thello, as they decided to call him, looked enough like Jinx to be a reincarnation.

She celebrated his three-month birthday by taking him to work with her. She set up a place in her office with a bed for him and it was soon a given; when she was at the theater so was he. He had a cat door but seemed to prefer exploring the theater and meeting the crew. He was a 'rub against your leg' kind of kitten and soon a favorite with all.

Besides being Teressa's cat, he was the theater's cat, except of course, on nights when there was a performance scheduled. A play is, by nature, a structured venue, no place for a curious, unstructured kitty cat.

Emily's idea for using Madame's investment wisely was to organize it into two areas: managing the theater itself and producing the plays that would be performed there. In the beginning Teressa's part was to help organize and oversee the everyday things that had to be done.

First, they had to make the building, inside and out, ready for use. She checked invoices, talked to suppliers and craftsmen, ordered things, monitored progress, stacked lumber, paid bills, and if necessary, swept the floors. The acting part of it couldn't happen until the stage was ready.

As the theater began to take shape, her job changed. They hired a crew and began to organize what was necessary to make it all come together on opening night. Emily insisted she learn the business end of things before all else.

"Bad management and not paying attention to detail has ruined many theater enterprises. Know what's happening on the business end of it or you may not be in the business very long." Teressa worked with the bookkeeper setting up a payroll and a system to manage the money, pay bills, and order what they needed.

In addition to working with crews that designed and built the sets, she also learned how the sets were positioned and organized so they could be moved quickly as necessary between scenes. She worked with the tailors who made the costumes and the ladies who applied the make-up and she even worked the catwalks above it all, learning the ropes and lifts and what each did in the scheme of things.

There were times when she felt like her head was spinning from all she was learning, that it was so full there wasn't room for any more. And then they would sit round the stove in the evening in the small flat they shared and they would talk and Emily would explain, and it would all seem to make sense.

Three months in, they were ready to invite auditions. Now Teressa's pulse quickened when she went to work every day. She understood Emily's plan to give her a grounding in the whole concept they were working on, but now it was time for acting to begin and she relished it.

She watched every audition, studied every script till she knew it almost by heart. She rarely commented but when she did her questions were contributions to an assessment.

Many evenings they sat together at their flat or at the mansion and talked about the play and the players they had just seen. Sometimes Madame and Sarah and Sarah's daughter Rebecca and her daughter Beth were involved in the conversations and when they stayed too late, they had a place to sleep and coffee and a newspaper in the morning. They were family.

One reason Teressa enjoyed staying at the mansion overnight was having breakfast with Geppetto. Not every morning. Some nights he stayed across the Bay in Berkeley with Este and Roy, also members of Madame's family. Este had worked with Annaliese in an internship of sorts for four years before attending and graduating from medical school. Roy had lost his voice in the accident that killed his first wife. They had recently married and were attending a sign language school together in Oakland. They gave Geppetto a place to hang his hat when needed.

Geppetto was the son of the maid and butler at the Mansion, and he had been raised to think of Madame as his "Auntie Mad." Growing up, Bobby and Geppetto had spent a lot of time at the bookstore and in the house above it. He was the kind of friend she could relax and be herself with.

Even in her short time in the world of the theater she had found herself putting up a shield when she came in contact with actors. Somewhere in the back of her mind, she always kept them at arm's length, not able to really trust someone who made a living pretending to be someone else.

Emily had warned her about actors and their ways, and she had heard many stories. She was friendly with them but there was a line. So far no one had tried to cross it. Geppetto, she trusted like she trusted the others in the family.

On this beautiful sunny day in October, she helped him get the sail up and with the wind abeam, they were soon on their way across the Bay. Not only was it a nice day for it, but she wanted to meet the young lady he was sparking in Oakland, and she needed someone to talk to about something.

"Do you like going to college?" She was at the tiller, and he sat with his legs across the cockpit tending to the mainsail halyard.

"Some parts of it better than others," he said. "I like history and English, but not so much math and science." He grinned at her. "Maybe I just don't want to work that hard. I enjoy reading history and some literature, mostly English writers, but math?" He made a face. "Now that's hard work. Science can be fun sometimes though."

"Any ideas about what you'll do when you finish?" She used her hand to shade her eyes and watch a larger boat pass across their bow.

"My grandpa thinks I should learn another language and try the foreign service. I speak Italian well enough and English and Spanish. If I could learn French it would help. He has a friend at the Italian Consulate, and he talked to me once about a job with them. It would give me a chance to travel and sounds like something I'd like."

"Speaking about working hard, I'll bet Manny is working hard at Annapolis," he continued. "Have you heard from him?"

"I got a letter this week. He didn't know my address so he sent it to Madame knowing I'd get it. He said it's pretty much like he thought and he likes it so far. Likes his roommate too, which is nice.

"I can't imagine just meeting someone and then living with them in one room all the time. I guess it's part of the education. On a ship, you're all crowded together and live for months in cramped quarters like that. If you don't learn to get along with people, it could be bad for everyone and everything involved."

She grinned at him. "Speaking of living in small spaces with someone you don't know, have you ever met Emily?"

"I met her at the mansion. Can't say I know her."

"She and I live together. We have a small place near the theater. We each have a bedroom and there's a small sitting room between. Your friend Estella comes in as a maid and cooks during the week."

"You like it?"

"Yes. I love it, actually. The theater's pretty much finished and we've put out a casting call. So far we've heard from people as far away as New York City."

"Am I going to be seeing you on stage anytime soon?"

She gave a deep sigh and rolled her eyes. "Let's get the boat docked and then we can talk about that."

Geppetto watched her walk across the street. She'd had to visit the ladies' convenience and watching her coming to join him made him feel good. It always made him feel good to watch her do whatever she was doing, or when she was doing nothing, for that matter. The soft curves of her face were blended into a perfect picture, and when she smiled or laughed it made you want to smile and laugh too.

Her figure was full and round in the places where round looked good, and she had an unusual gait that caused her to sway in a very appealing manner. In the summer sunshine with just enough breeze to ruffle her hair, he was a happy man just being around her.

She took his hand, and they walked along a path toward town for a while before she spoke. "I read somewhere about the 'impatience of youth,' and I guess that's what I'm feeling right now. I want to be an actress. I want to act, and instead I'm paying bills and watching carpenters build things."

He could tell she needed to talk, so he just listened.

"On the other hand, I love working with Emily and she's taught me so much already. I know if I stay with her she'll help me get where I want to go." They stopped walking and she looked at him in silence for a moment, then shook her head.

"But," he said, drawing out the word.

"But I want to act. I've gotten an offer to join a troupe. It's a good group with a good reputation. I'd be working with professionals and with some good parts. It would be traveling around and learning by doing."

"But," he said again, grinning at her.

"Emily is like an older sister to me already. We sit at night and I read for her. She teaches me how to speak and stand, and little things like putting my hand on my hip to draw the audience's eyes to me or using a certain kind of make-up to look a certain way under the lights. I'll never, ever have a chance to be around someone like her again, or Madame, for that matter. She's backing the whole thing and I'd feel terrible about leaving them in the lurch."

Another deep sigh and a moan. "This is one of those crossroads you read about. Do I take the new path that will take me to a different life right now, one I feel I badly want, or stay on the path that makes people I love happy and promises the most for me in the long run?"

She closed her eyes and shook her head again. "I think this is going to be one of those times that no matter what I choose, I'll regret what I didn't."

On the way back across the Bay on a beautiful summer afternoon, they talked about how much she liked Abigail, Geppetto's friend and how he liked school and things she'd been doing. Everything, in fact, but what was really on her mind.

Finally, when they were saying goodbye in the kitchen at the mansion that evening after dinner, he asked, "Made up your mind yet?"

"Oh yes," she said. "And for a very selfish reason." He looked a question at her. "There's nowhere else I can learn so much that I need to know," she said with an ironic smile. "I'll always wonder about the other path, but this is the right one for me," she paused. "And for the people who are counting on me."

For the next few months, her life fell into a comfortable and occasionally exciting routine. She and Emily usually began the day with breakfast together, sometimes at home and sometimes at the mansion with Sarah and Madame. While Emily read the paper with her coffee or talked to the ladies Teressa was somewhere writing in her diary.

She wrote about plays they had seen and parts she had read for Emily, about some of the people who had joined the company (they were calling it a company now), about what she'd learned in some of her talks with Emily and others in the company and many tales of what Thello had done to make her laugh.

She also wrote about the future she saw in the life she was leading. Emily had outlined her ideas for Teressa's future education and they pushed steadily forward with ideas and activities to open her eyes to the theater, all of the theater.

She watched every rehearsal for every play she could and some of the performances again and again from different places in the auditorium, including standing just offstage and watching from the wings. She found the different positions made for different points of emphasis and helped her see things from points of view she had missed before.

In rehearsals, she usually stood quiet and would ask any questions of actors or others only when it was convenient for them, making sure it didn't interfere with their work.

Since Thello was with her a lot while she was at work, he became a sort of good luck charm for the company and they all loved to pet and play with him, even the few curmudgeons that seem to be in every company or troupe. They all learned to ignore him, even when he sometimes appeared in a scene during rehearsals where there wasn't a cat in the script.

She also wrote about personal things, such as her sailing day with Geppetto and the time a bold young actor pushed her into an alcove and kissed her. He didn't get the part.

She also read her diary once in a while. It made her think again about things that needed to be thought about again, pondered for a while, as it were.

Her first holiday season away from home was a revelation. One truism in their business was that holidays were workdays. She was kept busy from Christmas to New Year's working evenings and attending 'after the show' holiday parties given by people 'in the trade' several times during the week. The people she met and talked to were the people she'd be working with in the future.

One night, she and Emily had attended a party where probably thirty-five men and women spent an evening meeting old friends and making new ones.

"You know, as a guess, I'll bet that by the time you're my age you will have worked with half of the people that were there tonight, maybe more." Emily was sipping tea before the fire in their small sitting room.

"Really? That many?" asked Teressa.

"Oh yes. It's a small world, really, the theater that is. Each city has its clique of practitioners but one thing you can say about theater people, they don't like to spend much time in the same place. Which means they like change and considering how few people are in the business, it means a constant flow of these people and others like them in and out of your life.

"It's a good thing to stay in touch at a distance because it's a part of your profession and that's what these parties are about, but you need to be careful about trusting people too much in this business."

She sat for a while gazing into space. "It took me a while to figure that one out," she said. "Remember, there's always someone trying to sell you on an idea they've got that's a sure thing."

She looked meaningfully at Teressa. "Don't be buying what they're selling. Decide for yourself what's best for you. You don't have to hitch yourself to someone else's wagon."

She wrote that in her diary. 'Don't be buying what they're selling.' She never forgot it.

One of the most exciting days in her life was the day Emily handed her a manuscript and said, "I think we've got a play for you. It's called *The Mysterious Woman*."

Teressa dropped into a chair and looked at her open-mouthed.

"Yeah," Emily said, nodding. "It's a mystery by a fellow from upstate New York. He's a veteran, so he's going to look over my shoulder for a while during the time we're putting it together. If we get started this week, we can probably have it ready in April sometime. He's bringing the script by tomorrow."

She didn't sleep much that night.

Over the next months, until the spring opening, she was in a daze half the time. She'd be sitting with Emily during an interview and catch herself staring over everyone's heads at nothing, her mind miles away. There were new costumes and rehearsals and changes in the script and more rehearsals and hair and make-up decisions and more rehearsals.

Two nights before the opening, her family came to town to see her debut. They put up at the mansion, but to her chagrin, she almost had to ignore them because she was busy tending to last-minute details that always popped up before any opening.

Later that night she stood in her room holding a placard that read,

The Mysterious Woman
Starring
Hannah DeMarco and Harold Rains
Introducing Teressa Fry as
The Mysterious Woman
Crown Theater on Broadway Apr 18th 8:00 PM

Tomorrow her career would begin. With Emily's help she could go anywhere, and this was where it started.

In the night, Thello woke her, yowling and crying. She turned on the light and eventually found him on a shelf in the closet. She got him down and was sitting on the bed petting him when the building began to shake.

CHAPTER SIX

She woke by degrees. She lay for a while, wondering where she was and why her face hurt. She touched her cheek and could feel where the skin was broken and the hot, sticky liquid around it made her realize she had been bleeding. Suddenly, she remembered where she was and that she was trapped. Where was Thello? She remembered the shaking, roaring and crashing around her and things hitting her on the head. Then the lights went out.

The darkness around her had given way to a dusty gray and in the gloom she could discern shapes but had no idea what they were. She heard Thello meow from somewhere close but couldn't see him. Above her was something dark and solid-looking. She reached up to touch it and found there was just room to sit up. Whatever it was, it was just above her head. She found she could move, but it didn't take long for her to realize there was nowhere to go.

To one side of her, there seemed to be a pile of wreckage that was ceiling-high and almost up to the edge of the bed; on the other, a wall that hadn't been there when she went to sleep. Her bed seemed to be covered with pieces of something she couldn't see well enough to identify. Apparently, one of these pieces had hit her in the face. Actually, she couldn't see much of anything, and what she could see wasn't familiar.

She heard Thello again, closer this time and then she felt him rub up against her and push his head under her hand. With the cat's touch she suddenly thought of Emily.

"Emily!" she cried or tried to cry. Her mouth was full of dust and it came out as a croak. She desperately needed a drink of water and that's when she remembered, realizing she was trapped but had no idea how it happened. She sat, trying to use saliva to cleanse her mouth and then tried again. "Emily! Can you hear me?!" She listened for a moment and began to notice muffled sounds, now shouts and the shrill cries of horses, coming from somewhere above her and off to one side. There was an occasional sound like an explosion and she thought she heard thunder.

Suddenly, she heard what could have been a muffled voice. She sat immobile, listening. Then she heard it again, could distinguish words. After a moment, she raised her voice again.

"Emily! Is that you?"

She heard a "yes," and it sounded closer than she'd first thought.

"Are you hurt?"

"I seem to be trapped. There's something across my legs, and I can't move them. But no, I'm not hurt, I just can't feel my legs." She paused and then asked, "Are you hurt?"

"I've got a cut on my face and some other cuts and bruises. I can move alright but I'm not sure I can get out of here. I don't see a door, and the window is gone. From what I can see, I'm in a sort of box. Thello is with me and he seems to be ok. He found a way in here, so it is possible I can get out. I really can't see very well, though it seems to be getting lighter."

"So, what do we do? How are we going to get out of here?"

Teressa smiled a little in spite of the situation. Here, the whole world had fallen in on them, and Emily sounded the same as always, calm and in control.

"The problem with trying to dig our way out is that shifting this stuff around may cause more of it to fall," said Teressa. "We may just have to holler and hope someone hears us. I can hear people outside."

"What should we say when we holler?"

Teressa thought for a moment. "Let's just make it 'Help!' We can call out three times together and then wait a while and do it again."

"Sounds like a good idea. Let's go, on three."

Several hours later, they had been calling for help until they were hoarse, but no one had come.

An earthquake is the result of subterranean events that occur far below the surface of the Earth. The definition of an earthquake being caused by 'a slip on a fault' probably creates the best mental image of why it happened. The fault in question is the San Andreas fault. In the language of tectonic plate theory, it is where the North American Plate meets the Pacific Plate. These two huge plates are moving slowly in opposite directions, and tremendous energy builds up when and where they come together and their movement is checked. When the place the edges meet suddenly gives way to this pressure and 'slips,' you have an earthquake.

This slip cost some 3,000 lives and between 250 and 400 million dollars in damage (at 1906 prices), and it lasted only forty seconds. With the fire that followed and raged for three days, 80% of San Francisco, some twenty-eight thousand buildings, were destroyed. Two hundred and fifty thousand people were left homeless overnight. Out of a population of four hundred thousand, there were more people homeless than not.

Some slip.

Johnny was sitting on a side porch at the Mansion, looking out at the sleeping city shortly after five that morning. The rich meal from the night before had made it difficult for him to sleep, but regardless, he had enjoyed the meal. The table in Madame's large dining room had been full, and he had enjoyed being surrounded by many of his old friends.

They had all gathered for Teressa's opening performance on the stage, and they talked about that and times old and new. The guest of honor was necessarily absent due to last-minute production issues but they were all excited for her and there to wish her well.

Madame and Sarah were present to greet all the visitors.

Their rooms were ready, and when the servants called them for dinner, the talk was loud and friendly. They were family.

Far and near, he could hear many dogs barking and horses moving restlessly, neighing and snorting in stables and corrals.

Suddenly, the porch began to shake. Taken by surprise, he tried to stand but fell to his knees and cut his hand trying to hold on to the swing. As suddenly as it had started, the shaking stopped. In years past in San Francisco, he had felt quakes, but none quite as strong as this one.

He regained his feet, but as he turned to go back into the house, the floor moved sharply under his feet and he fell again, this time catching the porch railing. He lowered himself to the floor and sat waiting for the shaking to stop, but it didn't stop. It went on for what seemed like a long time. From inside the house, he heard things crashing to the floor and felt the porch lurch and sag on one side.

When it finally stopped, he sat still for a while. After a time, it seemed like it was over and he cautiously stood, opened the screen door and looked inside at the main hall. In the dim light, he could see pieces of what looked like plaster on the floor and several pieces of furniture had turned over, one of them a cabinet full of curios, some of which were broken and scattered on the floor.

The lights flickered, came on again and then went off, and he was standing in darkness. He felt his way into the dining room and in the dim light, opened the curtains and let in the beginnings of dawn. In the process, he found out that most, if not all, of the windows in the house were broken. In the house around him, he could hear loud voices, people calling out.

He raised his voice so he could be heard throughout the house and said, "Let's all meet in the dining room. The lights don't work, so open all the curtains and put on shoes. There's broken glass on the floor."

He made his way carefully along the hall and up the stairs, picking his way past broken light fixtures and chunks of wood and plaster. He opened the door to his bedroom and saw Annalise standing at a large window set in an alcove that looked out over the city. The glass in the window had fallen outward, and the smell of things burning came in with the morning air.

Without turning, she said, "Look. Look at this."

He crossed to her side. What he saw made his jaw drop, and he gaped in amazement. It was a scene he had seen many times, but he recognized nothing, and what he could see looked distorted, broken. Only by looking for clues, such as the color of a pile of bricks or a horse trough at the curb, could he identify houses he had seen standing there for years. The air was filled with dust, and in the distance, he could see three different columns of smoke and realized what it meant for the city.

He was an experienced city administrator. As a city commissioner back home in San Diego, he looked after the water and sewer departments. Part of his job was professional communication with other cities, and he knew the clay-piped water systems beneath this city wouldn't stand the strain of an earthquake like this. They would break into pieces and as a result there would be little water with which to fight all these fires.

While he watched, two more plumes of smoke began to rise in different places. He was seeing a disaster unfold before his eyes.

One of these columns of smoke was near where The BookSeller stood. He and Lemuel had opened that bookstore almost twenty years before. It had grown into the house next door and both buildings were made of wood—wood covered with many coats of paint over the years which would burn quickly and completely and books burn. Every other building in the neighborhood was equally flammable.

As they left their room, Lemuel came into the hall next door. "What should we do about the store?" he asked Johnny.

Johnny shook his head. "There are already buildings burning close in that neighborhood. I don't think anyone can do anything to save it. I need to get to Teressa's place. That's top of the list right now. I'll worry about the store when I have time."

"I understand," said Lemuel. "Do what you have to." Kate joined him and they followed Annaliese to the dining room. With Tony, the butler, behind him, Johnny was already out the back door headed to the stable.

Annaliese and Maggie left the mansion just behind Johnny to go to the hospital and see where they might help. As soon as they were gone, Lemuel and Roy began to assess damage to the house to see if it was safe to continue to live there.

Madame's late husband had built the Mansion in the years after the Gold Rush. Unlike almost any other building in the city it had a foundation under it and fortunately, it had been built on two very large lots. With no other houses close, it was much less vulnerable to fire. Two of the servants' cottages along the back line of the property had collapsed and there were several injuries, none serious.

It was two hours before Johnny got to the building where Teressa lived with Emily, normally a ten-minute ride. Many streets were blocked by collapsed buildings or fallen power poles, and they were forced to detour a number of times. Several times the pavement was torn asunder with huge cracks in the ground, and it was dangerous to try to pass. Twice they came to areas that were burning and got so close to the fires they could feel the heat on their faces. Fortunately, the wagon had two horses, and they were able to force their way through when they needed to.

From one block to the next, streets were lined with collapsed buildings or houses leaning against one another. Most of the construction in San Francisco at that time dated back to the previous century, and most houses were built without foundations. That plus construction of brick or wood facades over wooden framing simply could not withstand the stresses generated by the earthquake.

Another feature that contributed to the destruction was the value of land in the city. On a peninsula land is a finite resource and many of the Victorian homes were built almost side by side so that if one was damaged or burned the ones on either side would also suffer. Besides, from all the ash and smoke in the air, Johnny thought, even the rubble might not last very long.

The noise was so prevalent and persistent they had to raise their voices to be heard on the wagon seat. Men shouting, children crying, women screaming, horses neighing and snorting, fire bells in the distance and around the corner, the sudden rumble of a falling wall, the occasional blast as something exploded, and over it all, the steady roaring of flames and burning coming closer.

When they finally found the place, it was only because Tony remembered two small stone lions that had stood on the front steps. The rest of the building was just a pile of bricks, lumber, and pieces of plaster. The strangest thing he saw that day was a window, including the frame, completely intact standing in the rubble of a house they passed on the way. He didn't believe there were many intact windows left in the city that morning.

Johnny stood staring at the pile of rubble that was where his daughter had lived and wondered if she was still alive. Finally, he shook his head, took a deep breath, and looked at Tony.

"Any idea where to start?"

"No, I'll just follow your lead."

"Let me sit here and think for a minute," he said. He sank down beside one of the lions and put his head in his hands. But he couldn't focus. His mind was spinning, and whenever he reached for a thought, it slipped away.

He opened his eyes and got the shock of his life. A black cat had crawled out of a hole in the rubble and sat looking at him. It looks just like Jinx. Mouth open he stared at the cat wondering if it was really there. Then he noticed a small gold locket on a fine gold chain around the cat's neck. It took him a moment of staring before he realized he recognized that locket. He had given it to his daughter on her eighteenth birthday.

The shock of seeing the building and the black cat was suddenly gone and he slowly approached the animal and reached out to him. The cat slid his head under Johnny's hand and rubbed against it. He ran his hand over the cat's head, slipped his hand under the locket, bent, and looked at it closely.

"You're Thello, aren't you?" he asked. He could hear purring, and he took that as a sign.

"Is that hers?" Tony had knelt beside him.

"Yes, it is."

"What do we do now?"

Johnny looked around at all the people and horses and motor

cars around him and said, "Well, since we can't ask them all to shut up, I guess we'll have to improvise."

He looked at the cat steadily for a moment then picked him up, set him to one side and laid down on his stomach with his mouth as close to the hole in the rubble as he could get it. "Hello!" He spoke loudly but didn't yell, then turned his head so that his ear was at the hole and covered the other ear with his hand.

From fairly close, he heard, "Is that you, Papa?"

"Yes, it's me. I found the locket. Are you all right?"

"I think so. Is Mama with you?"

"No. Where is Emily?"

"I don't know. I can hear her, but she says her legs are trapped under something."

"Teressa, I'm going to stand up and talk to Tony and maybe the constable and see what they think is the best way to go about this. I need you to be patient."

"OK, Papa, I will. I love you."

When everyone was congregated in the dining room, Madame spoke to them.

"It looks like everyone's here. Is anyone hurt?"

There were some cuts and bruises, but nothing serious.

"For those of you from out of town you can stay as long as you like and if there are those from around here that need a place you've got it as long as the house doesn't fall down around us.

"Looking out the window, things look pretty bad around the city and it's probably going to get worse. I just want you all to know that we will be here until we're not needed. We all need to look around to see where we can help and help where we can."

She stood for a moment, looking around at them all, and finally said, "Something like this changes things for everyone. We can get through it working together and then we can see what's changed and what we need to do to get things back to normal. "I didn't say get things back to the way they were. That won't happen. We just need to get through it, see what's left and move on. This is our city. Let's help put it back together."

Annaliese and Maggie's trip to the hospital was a wandering

odyssey through a landscape of disaster. Everywhere buildings had collapsed, bricks coming apart like pieces of a jigsaw swept from the table. Fires burned unchecked while men stood watching helplessly with empty pails and hoses.

Annaliese and Maggie sat in the buggy surrounded by a cacophony of noise and tried to make sense of what they were seeing. They were able to see the hospital in the distance and as they watched a wall collapsed sending up a shower of fiery sparks.

"So now what?" asked Maggie.

Annaliese sat quietly for a minute mesmerized by the scene before her. Finally, with a start, she took a deep breath and said, "If the rest of the city looks anything like what we've seen, we can't do much to help here and now. I think we should go back to the mansion and assess things. We need information. Right now, we're operating blindly and accomplishing nothing."

She managed to get the buggy turned but returning the way they had come was blocked by something new at every turn. What was normally a fifteen-minute ride turned into an hours-long journey they would never forget. It was stop and go amongst crowds of people and when they could move, it always seemed like the wrong direction.

Something large and loud blew up close enough for them to feel the heat and threw a thick, black cloud of smoke over their route forcing them to wait until they could see again. They were only a few blocks from home when they were forced into a long detour by a flooded street where a water main had burst.

When finally they were sitting in the stable yard at the mansion trying to catch their breath, one of the servants called from the kitchen. "Dr. Fry, Mrs. Bancroft is here. She's hurt."

As she followed the girl up the steps Annaliese officially declared this as the worst day of her life.

"OK, Teressa, we're going to begin digging you out. I suggest you wait until we get to you. Don't try to move anything in there. We don't want to make things worse. After we get you out, we can get Emily."

Because the noise around him hadn't abated he was down at

the hole in the debris with one ear covered again.

"All right, Papa. I'll be here when you get here."

He heard a muffled voice in the background, "Me too."

CHAPTER SEVEN

Johnny was covered with dust, gray dust, mostly, with a tinge of brown. The first thing he did when he got out of the trench he was carefully digging into the debris of the building was stand up, take off his mask and breathe deeply.

Digging was not really the word for what he was doing. He was pulling pieces from a wall of debris and watching dust and more debris fill up the hole he'd just created. It was frustrating work all the more so because there was a fire burning on the edge of his sight and heading this way. Yet he had to be slow and careful to make any progress. From the sound of things she didn't seem to be too far in but he felt as though he was taking two steps and sliding back one.

He was afraid. His daughter and her friend were somewhere underneath all that stuff and their safety, even their very survival, was in his hands. He felt an edge of panic looming over him and willed himself to be calm and rational.

He looked around for Tony. He'd sent the butler back to the mansion to get some tools and some extra hands to help with the digging and moving the debris as they dug it out.

Back in the hole, he was talking to Teressa and Emily easily now, hardly needing to raise his voice. It seemed like they were close, but every time he moved something expecting to see his daughter's face, he was disappointed. As he stood contemplating how far there was to go, Tony pulled up with the wagon and two men from the mansion.

"Making any progress?" Tony shouted over the surrounding noise. "Looks like the fire's coming this way. We'd better hurry." He stood up and looked at the columns of smoke moving toward them from three different directions, shook his head and climbed down from the wagon.

He turned to one of the men with him and indicated the wagon. "Spread the blankets in here and make a couple of beds. We'll need to be ready to move fast when we get them out." He muttered under his breath, "If we get them out."

"Want me to dig for a while?" he asked Johnny. When he'd taken Johnny's place in the trench he talked while he worked. "Had to go way out of the way because of fire and collapsed buildings. Some of the streets are all broken up. It looks like the tracks have been bent out of shape and made big holes in the street."

"We shouldn't have far to go in there," said Johnny, stretching his back. "We were talking a while ago and she sounds really close. We should get things ready in the wagon and bring the tools over here."

As Tony dug and removed rubble he piled it behind him where Johnny shoveled it out of the way.

Fortunately, there were work gloves in a tool kit kept in the wagon. The rubble consisted of many sizes and shapes of lumber and a lot of it had nails in it. There were also shards of glass that were hard to see and could cut the skin easily.

Under the rubble Teressa was talking to Emily, ensuring her that rescue was at hand but knew she was trying to convince herself as much as her friend. Her father sounded so close It seemed like she could touch him and she had to close her eyes and summon patience.

The dust had settled in her little pocket and she was careful moving around so she didn't stir it up again. She'd finally stopped coughing and cleared her throat but her mouth still felt as though it had paste in it. She had no idea how long they'd been trapped but she noticed it was getting darker, and the smell of smoke was getting stronger.

She saw her diary lying on the pillow next to her. She had been writing in it before she went to sleep. Now she picked it up and sat looking at it thinking about what was written in it. If what had happened to her and Emily was happening around the city then the hopes and dreams she'd written about were gone, swept away by something that lasted less than a minute.

Before she had time to dwell on that depressing thought, she saw the rubble move and a hand came groping forward into her little cubbyhole.

She screamed with relief. "I see your hand."

Tony's voice came in through the hole. "It will take us a while to widen the hole so you can get out. We don't want to get impatient and make a mistake." There was a pause and he continued. "We'll have to wait until we get in there to see how to go about getting to Mrs. Bancroft. Did you say she can't move?" "She says something's across her legs," Teressa replied. "But she sounds alright. It doesn't sound like she's very far away." After a moment, she said, "I think I can crawl out OK, but I don't know what it will take to get Emily out."

"OK. Well hang on. We'll have you out of there as soon as we can."

Johnny could see the reflection of the fire in the gathering dusk. A building several blocks east of them, where the street ended in a 'T,' was already burning, and through the windows of the building, he could see flames climbing toward the roof. When it got there it would jump to the next building and so on until it was upon them. The air was very smoky, and everyone he saw had a mask of one kind or another.

He was working feverishly moving shovels full of rubble when he saw his daughter exit the path through the wreckage, straighten up and take a lung full of smoky, dusty air. She was holding Thello in her arm, and in an instant, he had them both in a tight hug. When they separated he asked, "Are you all right?"

"Yes. I've got what feels like a bad cut on my cheek. I need to clean and put a bandage on it, but other than that, I'm OK. We need to get Emily out of that place as soon as we can."

It was difficult and took longer than they thought, but eventually, they carried Emily out of the rubble. The place they had to work in was small, so Johnny had to wait outside but he took the end of the litter from Tony and helped carry it to the wagon. Teressa was waiting for her and took her hand when she was safely aboard.

They could feel the heat from the fire as the wagon pulled away and could see flames licking over the roof of a building just down the street. By the time they turned the corner, the building was engulfed in flames.

Teressa rode with Emily back to the Mansion but was not free of anxiety about her friend until she saw her between clean sheets in one of the main floor bedrooms.

"I knew you'd come." Teressa was looking out the window. She said it softly, almost a whisper and he could just hear what she'd said. She turned and came to sit on the bed looking at Johnny sitting in a bedside chair. They sat and looked at each other for a while and finally Johnny asked, "Is that why you put the locket around his neck?" Thello was lying in Johnny's lap and he was stroking a very contented cat.

She nodded. "Since Jinx died, whenever you see a black cat, you stop to look at it." She paused and looked at him. Her hair was pulled back, and a bandage swathed the right side of her face. "I knew you'd come."

He heard someone in the next room and Annaliese called, "Johnny, are you in there?"

"Yes. I'm talking to our daughter."

Annaliese came in and joined Teressa on the bed.

"How is she?" Teressa asked.

"She has some small injuries here and there. Nothing serious. The back injury is serious, however. She seems to have transected her spine in the lower back when the chifforobe fell on her. She has no feeling in her legs because her spine is injured. She also has no control of her legs at this point. Whether that will be permanent or not, I can't tell right now. We'll have to wait and see if she regains control or feeling. It could come back gradually or not at all. That's something only time can tell us."

She reached up to check the bandage on Teressa's face. "I'm sorry I have no material to stitch the cut on your face. It's not deep, but it looks like something scooped a chunk of skin out of your cheek. It's going to scar, I'm afraid."

Teressa hugged her mother. "I'm alive and I'm not hurt," she said. "I'm one of the lucky ones."

The morning after the earthquake Madame awoke from a fitful sleep. She lay for a while trying to piece together what had happened to her world the day before. Since her days as a successful bawdy house operator during the gold rush in the early 1850s, through her marriage and widowhood, she had never had to worry about money. It had always been there and someone else took care of it. She pretty much took it for granted. This morning, for the first time in many years, she had to wonder.

The night before she had watched the financial district of the city consumed in fiery splendor and this morning wondered how much of her fortune had been destroyed in the conflagration. Written records burn and one had only to look at the shell of City Hall to demonstrate how completely. One thing for sure, there would be no way of finding out today or probably for many days to come.

The important thing was to manage today and tomorrow and the day after that until things got back to something near normal. Then they could look around and see what was left. The important thing on this day was that the city was still burning.

Even in the areas that had been burned out there was danger in the smoking ashes. Many of the walls that remained were solitary with nothing holding them up. There was no way of predicting when one of them might fall. With every aftershock, walls would tumble, and unaware people had been crushed by suddenly falling masonry. Sometime that morning an army artillery unit would begin dynamiting most of those walls and buildings to use as fire breaks or safety measures.

A great deal of what used to be her wealth was probably in the ashes floating around the burned-out hulks she could see from her parlor window.

She turned over and kissed the lady lying beside her.

"Come on you," she said. "Can't sleep the day away and pretend the world's not there."

Sarah opened one eye. "Why not? We can just pretend the city's not on fire. Turn over and go back to sleep." She stretched, threw the covers off and went off to tend to business.

They passed each other in a familiar dance as they got ready for the day and together walked to the breakfast nook, seated themselves and rang for breakfast.

"Today's the last day we'll be able to do this," said Madame. "Life's going to change for a while, maybe forever." She gestured out the window. The day before when it appeared the fire was headed away from the mansion Lemuel had found an unbroken pane of glass in a workshop over the stable and installed it in Madame's sitting room. Today, at least, they could enjoy tea and breakfast as always, one last time.

"Have a seat and let's talk," said Madame. She and Sarah had been joined by Annaliese, Johnny, Lemuel, and Kate.

"From what Lemuel tells me the house weathered this thing in decent shape. Some damage but nothing that needs to be addressed at present."

They all looked at Lemuel. "Most of the damage was broken windows which will be near impossible to replace right now. Doubt if there's many unbroken panes left in the city," he said, looking at some notes. "We'll have to board up the empty windows in the rooms we're using. All the ceilings seem to be intact. We shouldn't use the gas until they tell us it's OK. I've turned it off where it comes into the house. We have enough kerosene lamps for a while.

"The only real structural damage I saw was several cracks in the foundation. That will have to be fixed but not right away. We can live here with no problems." He looked at her and nodded.

"From what little I've heard from people," said Madame, "and what I can see out the window we have one of the few intact houses in this part of the city.

"I have a number of friends who've worked for me at one time or another over the years and have become important to me. If possible, I'd like to offer them a place to stay with their families if they need one. When I was young and by myself many of them gave me a hand, in some cases a place to sleep and food to eat. I like to pay my debts.

"I realize there are going to be thousands of people left destitute and I also realize I can't help them all, but I would like to take care of family if I can and these people are family. "The problem is I may need help to hold on to what I have. You are all here and this has happened. I need help. Can I count on you?" She looked around the room and was not surprised to see them all nodding.

Lemuel scratched his chin. "Do you have any guns in the house?" he asked. "I wasn't counting on something like this or I'd have brought my twelve gauge."

Madame looked a little startled at that but finally nodded her head. "I hate it but I can see it might be necessary."

"Speaking of that," said Johnny, "Maybe I should slip up to Handy's and get the ten gauge. Who knows. Might need some artillery. Probably a good idea to get Handy while I'm at it."

"I bet a dollar he and Rebecca are on the way," said Lemuel. "Probably with that big gun on his shoulder."

"I think you're probably right," said Johnny. "First let's thrash out what has to be done around here and how and where to begin."

"Now, in answer to your question," said Madame. "Yes my husband had a gun room. Tony takes care of it. I haven't been in that room for years and have no idea what's in there. Talk to Tony."

"I'd say the first thing is to find out who's going to be working with us," said Lemuel. "Then we can point them toward what needs doing. Why don't you ladies round up everyone in the house, and while you're doing that, Johnny and I will see what's in the gun room."

It turned out to be quite an arsenal. Some of the long guns in two locked glass cabinets looked like they'd never been fired. Besides a rack of rifles and one of shotguns, there were pistols in glass cases, some finely tooled leather gun belts and enough ammunition to fight a small war.

Back in the dining room everyone who remained in the house was there seated at the table or standing around the walls.

When everyone was quiet Lemuel spoke. "A little while ago Madame said to us, this happened and you're here. Will you help?" He looked around the room. "We're going to help and it seems I'm the one who's got to try to make it work.

"The city's on fire but we seemed to have been spared, at least for now. Since that's the case, we need to see what we have and figure out where to get what we'll need. Make no mistake, this is a disaster of epic proportions and thousands of people will be homeless. We surely will have to take people in but Madame will decide who.

"As we begin to fill up, we will have to adjust. We'll need everyone to help us with that. Go out of your way to adapt and adjust and accept what has to be, and one day it'll be over, and you can go back to being as ornery as you were before."

He smiled and looked down at a paper in his hand. "Between guests and employees, there are twenty-one people in the house. Many of the people who have worked here over the years will probably end up here if they have nowhere else to go, which means even as big as the house is, eventually things will be a bit crowded. So the first thing is we try to make the best use of what we have.

"To start, why doesn't everyone pick someone to share a room with? Then we can figure out how much space we have. This could mean you'll be sharing space with people you hardly know, living in close quarters even. With no water in the house it could be dirty and smelly but it's the only way it will work. If we ask you to let a strange family sleep on the floor in what used to be a private bedroom, you'll understand. If you can't accept such things, I suggest you look out the window at all the people who have nothing, not even a place to sleep out of the weather.

"As I said, it looks like the water's not working. We may have to ration it and the food too until we know when and where we can get more. I know Madame would appreciate it if you could chip in to help foot the cost of food and supplies until this is over. As far as tomorrow goes, to get there we need to work together. If everyone accepts that fact then we've got a chance to make it through."

He was quiet for a minute, looked around the room, then continued. "We'll do the best we can with what we have and try to be fair. One thing that won't help is complaining, so please don't. We won't ask you to do anything we wouldn't do ourselves, and we'll all share equally in everything.

"Now, I've got things that need doing. I'll see each of you today sometime and we can talk."

"Oh, and by the way, trying to get somewhere in the city right now is near impossible. If you go out for anything, be prepared for problems and let us know before you go."

"Can I get you anything?" Teressa was sitting on a cot that was near Emily's bed. She looked down at her friend and took her hand. Emily smiled wanly up at her. "No. Well, maybe a glass of water."

"I'll have to ring for that. The taps aren't working. The earthquake seems to have disrupted the water supply."

"Don't worry about it then. If need be, spit will have to do." She patted the bed. "Sit. Let's talk."

She closed her eyes for a moment. "It seems as though our lives have suddenly been, as the British say, 'knocked into a cocked hat.' Have you thought about that yet?"

Teressa shook her head. "I've been in a daze since I crawled out of the rubble and saw Papa."

Thello jumped up on the bed but when Teressa made to put him down Emily said, "Leave him be. I feel better when I hear him purr."

Teressa reached out to pet the cat. "I guess I've tied my life to yours since I came here. I'm really at a loss. What do you think?"

"Do you still want to be an actress?"

Almost reflexively Teressa's hand went to her cheek and the bandage there. "Mama tells me that I'm going to have a scar on my face when it heals. Nothing she can do about it."

"That doesn't answer my question. Do you still want to be an actress?"

When Teressa didn't answer right away, Emily went on. "Something like this changes you, changes your life." She looked down at her legs, lifeless under the blanket. "I know it's changed mine. Everything I own is buried under a pile of rubble and everything I was working for is burned up in this damn fire. On top of that, I can't walk and may never again, according to what your mother says. So, I'll ask again, do you still want to be an actress?"

Teressa looked at her in silence for a long moment. "I have my diary," she said finally.

Emily's eyes widened. "How did that happen?"

"I was writing in it last night before I went to sleep. It was still on the bed this morning and I made sure to get it out."

"Do you have it here?"

"Yes. It's on my bed." She gestured at the cot that had been set up for her.

"Why don't you read it to me? Maybe we can figure out the answer to the question together."

CHAPTER EIGHT

This was the third time that day Bobby had climbed the steep, sunbaked path up a good-sized hill to a small house that sat on a cliff overlooking the bay where Mirabelle II was anchored. Whenever the path took a turn he stopped to catch his breath and look down at the schooner, again marveling at its beauty and that it seemed to be right at home where it was. He had never seen the blue of the water around her anywhere else.

He turned to face the house. Here, halfway around the world from the Midlands of England, stood a proper English cottage. The thatched palm roof and the shaded porch in the rear, positioned to catch the breeze, were nods to local necessities, but it wouldn't have looked out of place in Yorkshire.

An attractive black woman came onto the porch as he came around the house.

"Make this the last trip today," she said. "Sit down and cool off. He'll be out in a minute." She held out a glass of tea. He took it gratefully, sank into a wicker chair and looked out at the bay below. Cap'n Pete loved to sit on this shady veranda and watch over his beloved Mirabelle. He closed his eyes and savored the evening sea breeze. When he opened them, Pete was sitting there looking at him, with a grin on his face.

"Did you get it all?" he asked.

"Every last bit," replied Bobby. "Do you always bring everything off the boat when you come home?"

"No. Usually just things I need up here, but this time it's different."

Pete was looking out at the bay, toward the Coral Sea beyond, and he sat quiet for a moment, breathing deeply.

"This is the only life I've ever wanted. Over the years, Mirabelle and I made it happen."

He turned to Bobby and sat looking at him for a moment stroking his scraggly goatee.

"I never told you what your friend Dr. Spreckels told me back in Honolulu. She said I have a heart condition that will probably kill me if I don't change the way I live." He looked at Bobby meaningfully. "I had a lot of time to think on the voyage out here, when I wasn't talking to you and I made some decisions I need to talk to you about and see what you think."

"I knew something was wrong. Rudy told me you weren't the same the last little while."

Pete shook his head. "Over the years, building this house, keeping Mirabelle afloat and working, I've not saved much, especially if I decide to live a few more years. As a result, I've had to come up with a way to have a little money coming in from time to time." He paused and then said, "I'd like to sell you the boat."

Bobby's eyes widened and his jaw dropped. "What?" he stammered.

"You heard right," said Pete. "I've thought it out and I want to make you an offer. I've gotten to know you these last few months and I like what I see. If you're interested, I'll lay it out for you."

"I can't imagine not being interested."

"That'll do for starters, I guess." He called over his shoulder. "Marie, can you bring me that paper lying on my desk?"

She handed him a folded piece of paper. He unfolded it, looked at it for a second, then looked at Bobby. "To me, it looks like you want to get somewhere but don't know how to go about it. I was the same way when I was your age. I think you want to build a life down here and what I propose is to help you do that and at the same time make a few francs so I can live the rest of my life comfortably.

"Over the years I've developed a close relationship with the man who's my factor. A factor is a man you'd go to if you wanted something carried to another island. The missionary we picked up in Honolulu we got from a factor.

"Degarde, my factor, is a displaced Frenchman who came out here years ago and figured out how to make his living without raising a sweat. He knows all the boats around and people know that. They come to him, and he comes to us. He's kept me running for years.

"I want you to meet him. You'll impress him the way you impressed me, which means he can help you make ends meet. You see, it's not just the boat you'd be getting but the business I've managed to build over the years."

Bobby held up his hand. "Wait a minute. You can't really be thinking of turning me loose in this place with the schooner. I'd be on a reef before the first day was over."

"You think I don't know that?" asked Pete.

"So how do you propose to get around the fact that I don't know much of anything about sailing a schooner in the Coral Sea, where being ignorant can get you drowned in a hurry?"

"Well, we're going to teach you."

Bobby had a broad grin on his face. "You're going to teach me?" he said in a tone of disbelief.

"No, not me. I won't be going down that hill for a while, if ever. No, I have someone else in mind. There was a note here from an old friend when I got home. He wants to go back to sea. His name is Henri. He was my mate for 20 years and he knows the islands as well as I do, probably better. I want you to go to work with him and learn how to sail these islands."

Bobby's astonishment was written on his face. "How long will that take?"

Pete shrugged. "However long it takes," he said. "I think you're a quick study but it took me a few years to learn enough when I first came out here.

"We're going to be here for a while. I need to arrange some things, and we'll need to talk a lot over the next few months. Sorta like a school, I guess. I'll teach you up here what I know about the islands and Henri will take you sailing."

He was looking out at the ocean again. Finally, he turned to Bobby. "Let me show you where you'll be sleeping tonight. Cookie will be up in the morning and then you and Rudy will have to alternate sleeping aboard while we're here. Henri will be here in the morning, and I want you to meet him. He'll be an important person in your life for the next little while, probably a few years." He held out his hand and Bobby took it. "I think you and I will be important to each other for the rest of my life, however long that is."

For the next two months, he learned about the boat from Henri and about the islands from Pete. Henri taught him how to set the sail for what weather, how to handle the schooner when passing through the reef breaks, how to care for the woodwork, the sails, and the ropes. From Pete, he learned about the people he would meet on each island, the different port regulations for each of the many nationalities he would encounter, and on and on.

In the latter part of the nineteenth century, European nations began to value islands in the South Pacific as coaling stations where stockpiles of coal could extend the range of a nation's coal-fired ships and therefore its power and influence. This meant a half dozen European nations plus the United States and Japan had simply taken possession of islands for this use and in each case, had imposed restrictions on traffic and commerce in and out of the island.

Pete had kept logs and diaries of his travels in the islands, and wherever Mirabelle touched land, he wrote of things he saw and of his relationships with some of the men and women who lived there. These logs and diaries were Bobby's textbooks. Pete was a good writer and wrote with a fair hand so the books were legible and readable.

He had bound them, and they sat on a shelf behind his desk. Most every evening, either on watch in the boat or sitting on the veranda, would find Bobby absorbed in one of these volumes. For years, he had dreamed of living the life Pete had lived for thirty years and here in his hands was the story of it all.

The only problem he saw was he didn't know the terms of the deal. Pete said he was drawing up a contract, but Bobby hadn't seen it yet. He loved the days when he and Henri and Rudy would take the schooner out through the reef and let the wind take them where it would while he learned what he needed to know about Mirabelle, the ocean and the beautiful, treacherous Coral Sea.

He talked to Rudy and found the man had no ambitions to own a boat like this. Said he didn't need the headaches. Said he was happy doing what he was doing and would be happy to keep on doing it with Bobby. It was funny, with all that talk about being happy, he'd never seen Rudy smile.

He had a certain place he sat during his 'lessons' with Pete and one morning when he sat down on the veranda there was an envelope on the table waiting for him. Pete had seen him arrive, joined him and when he was seated said, "I made three copies of the agreement, which is why it took so long. I wanted to get it just right. I expect you to read it carefully and I'll answer any questions you have. You can bring it back when you've made up your mind.

"I want to make sure you know as much as possible about the islands. Each one of them has its own society with their own rules about what's right and what's not. To them, a taboo is not a suggestion. It's part of their belief system. Over the years, I've made it my business to study these people and I recommend you do the same. If you're going to live among them you need to respect them and to do that you need to know who they are."

He handed Bobby one of his diaries. "Read what I had to say about 'blackbirding.'"

"What's blackbirding?"

"Read it and we'll talk. I think tonight is your night to sleep on the boat and tomorrow Henri is going to take you sailing again. So, I'm going to give you the day off. Think about it." He gestured at the envelope Bobby held. "It's a long-term commitment. Think about the future you see for yourself and see if it fits. If it does, sign it and bring it back up here."

He slowly got to his feet and reached to squeeze Bobby's

shoulder. "I feel a little under the weather this morning, so I'm going to take a nap." It was the first time Bobby had seen him with a cane.

At the bottom of the hill he sat on a fallen log and opened the envelope. Inside were several sheets of paper. The first couple were a contract between them then what appeared to be a will and finally a page for signatures.

The contract was straightforward, and it was between the two of them. Bobby would get one-half ownership in Mirabelle and would operate the business and share the profits with Pete. Half of the net profit from each trip would be paid to each of them as long as Pete lived. Upkeep, maintenance and repair costs were to be paid before profit was shared and Bobby was responsible for contracting and supervising all work done on the boat.

When he finished the first page he sat looking at the occasional patches of green on the red dirt hills that rose above the small bay but not really seeing anything. The terms were clear and simple and also fair and incredibly generous. He felt an emotional surge of excitement or maybe even joy when he pictured the life he would lead if he did this.

But there were costs. If he did this, it would likely mean he would never see his home or his parents again. Sailing the schooner to San Francisco from most of the places he would be took a long time. This part of the world was remote, and travel to and from it was a major investment in time and money.

Of course, he'd known where he was coming when he signed on back in San Francisco, so this wasn't something he hadn't thought about before.

The second sheet was equally simple and direct. Bobby was to be Pete's sole heir. He was given the boat and the house on the cliff on the condition that he allowed Cookie and Marie to continue working with him and living in the house while he was away.

This was another consideration. He would be committing to a long-term thing. Did he want to be responsible to two human beings for the rest of his life? It would be like replacing one family with another.

He thought about Marie. She was a pretty woman, dark brown

skin and a beautiful smile, a warm and pleasant lady. It was hard for him to judge, but he thought she was in her early forties.

Cookie was her younger brother but looked ten years older. He was constantly smiling and spent much time humming to himself. He moved slowly at work but steadily and always had the job done on time. Bobby had liked him from the start.

Henri was special. He had crewed for Pete for twenty years and they were as bonded as brothers. When Bobby was learning something new he was conscious of the man watching him carefully as though he expected something and wondered what Pete had told him.

As a teacher he was patient but Bobby had an idea that even though Bobby was technically the captain, if Henri saw the need he would step in and take control. That's what this period was; he was learning, and they were his teachers. What they taught him would help him survive until he knew enough to survive on his own.

The next evening, Bobby climbed the path after a long day on the ocean. It had been his first time taking the boat into the lagoon through a break in the reef. It had been a good day. He had learned how to spot the break in the reef even when he had no chart and wasn't sure how to reach the calm, smooth waters of the lagoon, any lagoon. Some atolls had no break, and he learned how to spot that too.

While he sat waiting for Pete, he closed his eyes and thought about home. Wondered how Teressa was doing and if Manny had made it through his first year at Annapolis.

He heard a clink and opened his eyes to see Marie setting a glass of tea before him. "He wants you to come into the house. He's at his desk."

Pete was waiting for him under a slowly revolving fan that did little to alleviate the heat, just moved the hot, moist air around a little. He gestured at a chair, and Bobby sat.

"So what do you think? Do you have any questions?"

"No," Bobby replied. "It's all pretty straightforward and simple. I don't think we really need a contract, do we? Can't we just shake on it?"

Pete smiled. "The first captain I ever worked with told me, 'It's okay to trust but make sure you get receipts.' If I were to die suddenly and someone contested your ownership of this place, or the boat, how would you prove it was yours? If everything's on paper you don't have to worry about such things."

"M. Cherou, my attorney, and Henri will be here shortly and they will witness the signatures. Then he will put the papers in a safe place where you can lay hands on them if you need to. Then we will have a drink, they will leave us alone and you and I can talk a bit."

In the next few minutes the lawyer arrived with Henri and they sat and talked, then signed the papers. Later when Bobby and Pete were alone sitting on the veranda Pete asked, "Did you read about blackbirding like I asked you to?"

Bobby nodded. "Is it still a problem?"

"Yes. Probably as bad as it ever was. It's somewhat like the American South and the Caribbean before the British outlawed slavery in the 1820s. There was always a labor shortage for farmers and plantation owners, mainly in Australia and New Zealand and there's a bit of it done here in New Caledonia too. The natives don't want to work in the fields. The farmers find answers in the whip and the gun. Blackbirders swoop down on an island and round up whoever they can catch. They take them west, sell them to farmers and they rarely make it home again."

"If it's against the law how do they get away with it?"

Pete shrugged. "Britain's halfway around the world and their navy doesn't cruise these waters too often. And remember, there's no law on the ocean so they can pretty much get away with it. Once in a while, the islanders put up a fight and a time or two, they've been run off but they always come back.

"The planters and miners do what they can get away with, and you can't dig stuff out of the ground or plant crops without someone to do it. No one close wants the job so they go where they have to for labor. This is the closest place where nobody's paying attention.

"These blackbirders have been getting away with it for so long they don't pay any attention to the law. Not just that law either. Any law. They're dangerous, like pirates and it's best to stay as far away from them as you can.

"They may approach you about joining them. A couple of times over the years, they tried to talk to me about it, but mostly they leave me alone.

"I know of a couple of islands where they've taken all the men and even some of the women. You can't imagine what that does to the people they leave behind."

He was quiet for a minute, then said, "I've talked to Henri, and he thinks it's time for you to spread your wings. Degarde has a couple of jobs for us so we'll buckle her up and be ready to weigh anchor for Samoa Wednesday on the morning tide."

Bobby sat still for a minute, thinking about that, then asked, "Do you think I'm ready?"

"I trust Henri's judgment. I think you will too after a while. Just let him guide you and you'll probably make it back safe."

The morning Mirabelle departed Pete was sitting on the patio at the edge of the cliff watching his beautiful, beloved schooner ease away from her mooring, slide through the break in the reef, and out into the Coral Sea. He watched until it was out of sight then, using his cane, walked slowly back to the house.

CHAPTER NINE

Manny was not studying and that was unusual for him. For some, reading and studying was a chore. For him, it was a joy.

Jack had come into the room and looked over his shoulder. "What are you writing?"

"Years ago, I read where Ben Franklin would write down the pros and cons of an idea then add up both sides and see what it looked like. I was just doing that with the last year of my life."

Jack sat down on the bed. "The good and the bad, hmm. What do you have so far?"

Manny picked up a piece of paper from his desk and turned his chair to face his friend.

"Hard work but I don't know which side to put that on. The classes take a lot of study and a lot of work. Of course, I don't mind that too much. Been doing that all my life. Advantage of growing up over a bookstore.

"But then there's the panic you feel when you realize what they expect of you and you're constantly worrying you don't measure up. We've both seen a lot of people bilge out of here for one reason or another, but academic failure was the biggest reason."

Jack snorted. "I didn't think you ever worried about that. I'm the one cruising along with a 2.7. You're in the top five in the class."

"But still, you always worry. There's so much to know."

Jack began to change his clothes, and Manny went back to his writing. After a few minutes Jack said thoughtfully, "I guess friendships are the most important thing on the positive side of the ledger. First time in my life I've felt really a part of something worthwhile. Back home there was the family and not much else but here," he spread his hands, "you've got people you trust and count on wherever you turn."

"When we walked in the door that first day, we were asking the Navy to make us into new people and they have," said Manny. "We are now people who'll spend our lives protecting something, serving something much larger than ourselves. How many times did you stand on your head in a bowl of water before you became a 'Middie'? Yet you did so whenever ordered to for the last year.

"That's discipline and if you remember that's one of the first things this place taught you. Because you want to be a part of something you do what it takes to gain admittance and acceptance. This place is set up to run that way. It's important to the Academy that a certain number fail to measure up. This makes the rest of us feel good about ourselves and the group we're a part of."

"So, do you like what you've become, this new you?" asked Jack.

"Yes, without question. Occasionally I miss what I was but I'm proud of what I am now, proud of what I've accomplished and where I'm headed." He paused and looked off into space for a moment. "When I was a boy, I had a dream and I can feel myself growing into that dream."

"What about the bad side of the ledger?"

Manny's forehead wrinkled and he smiled ruefully. Within the brigade, there had always been a curiosity about him. Not many people knew a Mexican and among the ones that did there was an undercurrent of racism and, in some cases, antagonism. Most of this kind of thing had happened early in the year when most were still learning what he was and how he conducted himself. In essence, he had proved himself worthy to his classmates.

"I feel accepted by most of them." He shook his head. "No, that's not right. I'd say almost all of them but there are a couple." He let the sentence trail off.

Jack knew who he meant. From that first day, Midshipman Fosbury had made it clear he didn't think Manny belonged and went out of his way for most of the year to make that apparent.

He understood that discipline underlays the hazing that was practiced in the Brigade but with Fosbury it had a personal edge to it. Fortunately, now he would soon be a Junior and contact between the two would be limited.

Manny had handled it the way he had handled it all his life. He didn't let it bother him. That kind of thing would cause him a problem, and he didn't think Fosbury, or anyone like him, was worth that. If in the future it needed to be dealt with he would. But now wasn't the time.

"Are you excited about the cruise?" asked Jack.

"Oh yeah! I can't believe we're actually going on board and beginning to learn how one of those things works.

"I hear we'll be shoveling coal and scrubbing the decks."

"There's that but look at how much we'll learn. This is a long step toward a place in the Navy. Knowing how a ship that big gets from one place to another and how to fire the guns is important, but if we stay in the Navy we'll be learning new things like that for the rest of our working lives."

"Mail call." The cry rang down the hall.

Within a minute, Jack was back with several letters in his hand one of which he handed to Manny. It was from Teressa and he put it aside. He always read her letters just before bed.

"Ha!" Jack slapped his leg. "Colleen is coming with her. That's great."

"Coming with who?"

"My girl, Molly. They're coming down for the Hop." The Hop was the first benefit of their new status as third years or 'Youngsters.' They had now learned enough about duty and honor to be trusted with the fair sex. It would be held shortly after the school year had begun. Scuttlebutt had it that the third year was as difficult in the classroom as what they had just suffered through. The Hop was a way to start what was going to be a long, tough year on a positive note.

"So who's Colleen?"

"She's my cousin. Our families grew up together. Out of the bunch, twelve kids, she's the brightest and has a sharp tongue to boot. She's always fun to be around especially if you like smart women. I'm glad she's coming. Hey! You can take her to the Hop. That way we can all have fun together."

About once a month, Manny rode a horse out to the pistol range. After the way he'd shot his first time at the range the range superintendent sought him out and they talked. That first meeting led to others and they became friends.

Conley Taylor, CT to his friends, was an Annapolis Graduate who had been injured on a ship shortly after he graduated and lost his leg from the knee down. Both the Navy and Ensign Taylor were loath to lose their investment in his education but it looked like the end of his career.

After deliberating for several months it was decided to make him a pensioner of sorts, that is, offer him a menial job at the academy that would pay enough to keep him out of the poor house. Fortunately, he had friends among the faculty who campaigned on his behalf and arranged a living situation he could accept, where he was happy and paid a living wage.

It meant he could live on the campus he loved and be amongst the Brigade he still felt a part of. He was a happy man and one who came to know the Academy better than anyone, including what was happening and to whom. In the process, he made many friends and, over the years, became an institution of sorts at Annapolis.

In his capacity as range superintendent, he was an expert on pistols and a crack shot but Manny's speed and skill amazed him. When Manny came out on Sunday afternoons they sometimes engaged in competitions of one kind or another to see who was best with different weapons.

Sometimes they sat in his office by a potbellied stove and talked about guns and shooting, sometimes about the teachers and the difficulty of their studies, sometimes about the Brigade and the people in it and sometimes about the future but with all that, one thing Manny was sure of, the importance of what he learned from his friend.

He learned much about the ins and outs and people of the Brigade, his classes and the history and traditions of the institution from a man who'd made it his life's work to study and understand the people around him.

"Have you thought anymore about the idea I gave you the last time you were here?"

"No. We've been busy with end-of-term exams and getting ready to go on the cruise."

"Know what ship you'll be on?"

"The Missouri."

"She's been around for a while. They don't last as long as they used to. The iron rusts, and they change so fast. We built up the Navy with all these new ships since the war and now the British have gone and built one that can take any of them in a gunfight. They call it Dreadnaught. I hear it's the future. Everything else is out of date. You young men have to learn what it takes to operate these ships, and they're going to get bigger with engines and guns more powerful than you can imagine.

"This is one reason I suggested the aeronautics club. If you start it you're going to attract people who look to the future and wonder about possibilities. Some of the people I talk to feel aviation is adaptable to military uses, and I think their reasoning is sound. Aeroplanes will change the future of naval combat and the Navy itself and if you want to go somewhere in this man's Navy it will help to be on the leading edge of that change."

"I said I haven't thought about the club, but yesterday I was walking down to a baseball game and I saw an airplane. Remembering what you said about the club, I looked at it differently than the few times I've seen them before.

"Actually, it reminded me of a box kite my Papa and I built to fly off Coronado Island. It looked like someone had put several of them together as the basic body of the whole thing."

"Manny, while you're on the cruise try to work out the parameters of what you think the club should be and how to organize it. Pay close attention to the first people who respond to your call for members. They will be the ones who think about new things about what's possible and how to shape those possibilities for the future.

"Have some notices ready to put up around campus and as soon as you get permission to form the club hit the ground running. I know you'll be working hard next term but make this important. I think time will show you just how important it will become. Some of those men you work with in the club for the next three years will be the admirals who will make air power work in the Navy."

That evening Manny was writing a letter to his sister when, for some reason, he thought about what CT had said. He put the letter aside and sat thinking about the idea it had generated in his mind.

This was a new technology whereby man had risen from the earth, not in a balloon or a glider, but with control and most importantly with survivability. Man had landed and flown again. The military implications of this were glaringly obvious and the Navy's interest was almost obligatory.

CT was telling him to become a part of that future, help it grow and be what it could be. How could he not?

He finished the letter and as he turned out the lights he was thinking about the first steps to organize the club.

When the launch pulled alongside the ship all the newly minted 'youngsters' stood looking up in awe at the huge steel wall rising above them. Almost 400 feet long and 72 feet wide with guns large and small wherever they looked, the idea they could master all the details of its operation seemed laughable. Yet they would eventually. Naval practice at the time required an Academy graduate to serve two years at sea and then sit for exams before he rated a commission as Ensign.

They began by shoveling coal and learning the most efficient way to get fuel into the massive boilers. Next they learned how important water was and how to regulate it so the ship could move and its crew could have the necessities of everyday life.

From these beginnings they would take what they had learned in the classroom and apply it to learn how to move the massive ship safely from one place to another and make its guns go boom when they needed to among thousands of other things. It would be three years, on their first-year cruise, before they would be allowed on the bridge of a battleship under strict instructions to touch nothing.

One of the best things about Manny's education at The BookSeller back home was learning to understand schematic drawings. Because you have seen a system laid out on a page in a book and understand it you're better able to see a system of pipes and valves snaking their way around a boiler room and understand their function in the scheme of things. They learned the movement of water and steam to places in the ship that provided power for all the things that needed to be done so the ship could do what it was designed to do.

They worked hard, slept well and ate good Navy food. On the morning of the third day, they shouldered their way from the Chesapeake Bay into the ocean and sailed to England across the stormy north Atlantic.

When he wasn't on duty Manny roamed the ship learning things and asking questions of people who were doing things he didn't understand. Jack was with him sometimes but there were times when he was by himself and would stand or sit near a group of crewmen who were talking just so he could listen.

One thing his father had taught him was the joy of learning. Manny was happiest when he was learning something new and seemed destined to spend his life trying to understand new and different things. Since there were so many things he didn't know on a ship this size, he smiled a lot.

After two days of liberty in Plymouth, Endland they touched at ports in France, Portugal, Spain and Italy. The great majority of the young men in the class had never been abroad and they spent much of their liberty in these places in wide-eyed wonder at the strange foods, modes of dress, strange customs and for the most part, non-English-speaking natives making strange, incomprehensible noises to one another.

As an experiment in Naples, Manny and Jack spent a day wandering around neighborhoods trying to eat and drink at places the locals were. Though the language issues led to some hilarity all around they enjoyed themselves and tried it again with great success in the Azores on the voyage home.

On the last night of the cruise Manny was sitting in the mess hall writing a letter when he looked up and was startled to see a first-class man standing at the table looking down at him. He jumped to his feet and stood at attention waiting for the man to speak.

"At ease, youngster. You are Manny Fry aren't you?"

"Yes sir."

"Do you mind if I join you?"

"No sir."

"My name is Ray Spruance, and I'd like to ask a favor of you. I understand you're a whiz at engineering and seamanship problems and among the top in your class. Is that right?"

When Manny nodded, Spruance continued. "Many plebes and quite a few Youngsters have problems with seamanship and engineering recitations and with mechanical drawing. As a result, we lose some good men who just need a little help to make it through.

"There are a group of us who work with them when we can by tutoring them and helping them get a grip on things they might be a little shaky on." He smiled. "When you help a good man stay the course it's a nice feeling. I know what your studies are like this year so if you don't think you can handle it, I understand. But next year when things ease off a bit, keep it in mind."

Manny had heard of Spruance. It was said he rarely smiled and even more rarely laughed but he was an officer in the brigade for a reason. He was smart and worked hard. Manny thought he was the kind of man he'd want as a superior officer.

"Let me get a look at what I have to deal with this year, Sir. I'll get back to you after the first month or so and see if I feel it's something I think I can handle."

Spruance extended his hand and Manny took it. "There's something I'd like to talk to you about if you have a minute," said Manny as Spruance rose to go. "I've been watching what's happening in aeronautics in the last couple of years and I think I'd like to start a group that focuses on flying and how it might apply to the Navy. Do you know anyone in your class who might be interested?"

Spruance sat looking at him in silence for a moment and Manny got the impression he was starting to smile again. "Yes, there are a couple of 'aeronuts' as we call them but actually some of them are second-class men. They'll be sore they didn't think of it first. I'll tell them to get with you when we get back in port."

Manny watched him walk away and smiled. This was a good start. He knew Spruance would tell his friends and they might tell theirs and then the club would be off and running. Yes sir, a good start.

The first thing he noticed was the way her red hair shone in the sun, just like his mother's. He came down the steps of Bancroft Hall behind Jack and watched him greet the shorter of the two girls emerging from the automobile. Jack grasped both her hands and they stood looking at each other, smiling.

The other girl met him at the bottom of the steps and held out her hand.

"Hi, I'm Colleen," she said, taking his hand. She gestured toward Jack and her friend. "They take a long time to say hello, so I thought I better introduce myself or we'll just be standing here looking at one another. You must be Manny." When he nodded, she continued. "Jack tells us you're the smartest one in your class. Is that right?"

Trying to keep from smiling at her directness, he replied, "Well, I think there are a few who might dispute that, but I do alright. Jack says you're the smartest one in your family. Is that right?"

"I just ignore what Jack says. He's such a liar. Besides, he doesn't like smart girls."

"You grew up together?"

She laughed. "Yes, and he's been sand in my sheets since I can remember."

Jack and Molly had finished saying hello and Coleen turned and gave him a hug then pulled away from him. "They've put some weight on you. Looks like they feed you good."

She gestured to Manny. "Since you didn't have the good

manners to introduce me to your friend, I did it myself."

Jack rolled his eyes at Manny then introduced Molly's mother who was the chaperone for the young ladies while they were at the Academy.

Later, as he and Jack watched her escort the girls to the inn where they were staying, Coleen turned and gave Manny a little wave of goodbye. To his friend, Manny said, "I think this is going to be a nice weekend." Jack grinned and slapped him on the back.

That night, the four of them were on the terrace talking as the last dances were danced and Coleen leaned over and kissed him on the cheek. "Thank you for a wonderful evening. I don't think I've ever enjoyed one more."

They sat in silence for a while both feeling the awkwardness that comes early on a first date. Finally, she asked, "How do you feel about smart girls? Do they intimidate you?"

He looked at her and slowly shook his head. "No, they don't intimidate me but I've never heard anyone ask so many questions. Do you always get answers?"

"Not always, but most of the time I do."

"My mother used to hate it if you went to bed with an unanswered question."

"Sounds like I'd like to meet your mother."

"Be careful, she might turn you into a doctor."

"What? Why do you say that?"

He didn't answer her right away but finally said, "It's a long story."

She smiled at him. "Will you take me the next time they have a hop?"

His mouth fell open, then he laughed.

"Oh, I know," she said. "I'm a forward hussy. In this case, it's because I really want to know. Close your mouth. You look silly."

"Of course. After tonight, I can't imagine asking anyone else."

They were in a shadow, and she couldn't really see his face when she asked, "Would you like to kiss me?"

He was expecting the kind of kiss he'd gotten from the girls back home, but this was different. She opened her mouth and her tongue found its way between his lips. It was something totally new to him and when it was over, he didn't want to stop. Indeed, he felt a little dizzy and there was a definite swelling against the buttons of his pants.

She reached out and ran her finger across his lips, then snuggled down against him. "Now tell me about your mother."

It was the furthest thing from his mind.

One night after classes began, he was studying in his room when Jack came in and dropped a letter on his desk.

"It's from Colleen."

Manny turned it over and could see it was still sealed with no return address.

"How'd you know that?"

"I know what she smells like."

He raised the envelope to his nose and grinned. "Oh yeah, me too."

It was the kind of letter he read just before he turned out the lights. When he unfolded the paper he was taken aback and shook his head slightly. "What is this?" he said. Jack looked over his shoulder and read the single sentence.

Send me your mother's address. Colleen.

CHAPTER TEN

Jonas Burke stood on the front porch of the mansion and looked out at the city spread out below him. He felt a little strange because so many of his visits here over the years had been through the servant's entrance that led through the kitchen.

In the six years since he married and stopped dating Sarah he hadn't been back to visit. With his wife and stepson dead in the earthquake, their bodies were never found, he had no desire to create the impression he wanted to rekindle an old flame. But he needed to talk to Johnny Fry, so here he was.

Like everyone else in the city his life had been torn apart the day the earth began shaking. He had been in Sacramento at the time and arrived home in time to find his house collapsed and in flames and his wife and son dead in the wreckage. His office, like everything in City Hall, was destroyed. The entire building was a charred hulk, and not even a piece of paper from his twenty-year career as a member of city government had been saved.

His wagon yard and much of his freighting business were also destroyed in the fire, though most of the rolling stock and livestock had been saved. There wasn't much left of his life besides what he'd carried to Sacramento and back.

So now the city he loved was piles of burned or wrecked buildings, collapsed homes, and destroyed lives. He had no idea how many had died. No one did. Many people died or were trapped in collapsed buildings and burned to death if they weren't already crushed lifeless by falling bricks. They would never find all the bodies and many times those they did find were unrecognizable.

As if all that wasn't enough the responsibilities of his position in city government had multiplied to the extent that he was sleeping very little and still not getting it all done. He had lost several of his office staff in the quake and fire and several more had left the city in the stream of refugees that fled to the east side of the Bay.

With a skeleton crew he was trying, and so far failing, to keep up with it all. With so many people leaving the city he couldn't find anyone to help. He knew Johnny had been a city councilor in San Diego for the last ten years and hoped he might have some ideas about anything that might help him solve his problems.

He could hear the maid announce him through the door to the sitting room and he had to grin.

"A Mr. Burke to see you, Madame," said the maid.

"Jonas Burke?" asked Sarah incredulously.

"I believe so, ma'am," replied the maid.

Silence. "It looks like this is going to be an interesting day already," said Madame. "Show him in, Consuela."

"Well what can we do for you, Mr. Burke?" asked Madame when he was seated. "I'm assuming this isn't just a social call although we're glad to see you in either case." She looked at Sarah. "Aren't we, dear?"

Sarah, red spots on her cheeks, nodded at him with a small welcoming smile then sat quietly and watched as he and Madame talked.

"No. Not just social. I'd like to talk to Johnny Fry if it's possible. Lemuel too if he's here."

"He and Kate left yesterday. It seems the city council down there has noticed her absence and called her home. You caught Johnny though. He and Annaliese are staying till next week. If you want to join us for lunch, they'll be there and you can talk then, unless it's private."

"No," he shook his head. "Not private. We're getting ready to begin a big job and I wanted to talk to him about it."

They sat and talked about the city and how the recovery was progressing. People were shaking off their dazed lethargy and had begun to join in the cleanup and budding, though disorganized, efforts to begin rebuilding.

The Army was omnipresent. The streets were cleared for the most part, and increasing traffic and its control had given the soldiers one more thing to do, along with feeding, housing, providing healthcare and sanitation for the roughly 200,000 people left homeless by the disaster.

Sarah mostly listened, letting her eyes linger on Jonas occasionally but looking away if he noticed. There was no reason for her to feel embarrassed or nervous but she did, though by the time they went in for lunch she at least had stopped blushing.

They had dated for fifteen years and he had proposed to her many times but she loved her life at the Mansion and spending most of her time with Madame so they had never taken the final step.

His letter telling her of his decision to marry had stunned her and for a few days, she was distracted, sitting around quietly and in a brown study. Madame noticed and as always, let Sarah mull it over for a while before she mentioned it. Their discussion had helped her put it to rest as a problem but there was always regret at the loss and his sudden appearance today had triggered an emotional response in her.

Most of the people staying at the mansion were working, doing their part to make the city livable again, so just a few were at the table when they sat down to eat.

Johnny and Annaliese greeted Jonas warmly and Johnny sat down across from him and asked, "So what's the big job you want to talk about?"

About that time the dining room door opened and Teressa came in pushing Emily in her new wheelchair. This was her first time with them at mealtime since she was injured and everyone stood to greet her.

"Thank you," Emily said. "That's more applause than I got in my last play." Her smile was rueful and a bit wan.

Everyone laughed and when they were seated again, Emily continued to Johnny. "What's this you were saying when I came in, something about a big job?"

"Emily, this is Jonas Burke. He's a city commissioner and he was just going to tell us when you came in." He nodded at Jonas. "You were saying?"

"It's not the job itself," said Jonas. "The city is going to build a whole bunch of small houses to get people out of tents. The Army's going to do most of the work on it and they'll be supervising any construction contractors they bring in. My problem is I need help. I lost some people since the quake and the ones still here already have their hands full.

"Though the Army's going to do the building, I have to set up a system to manage the job. They also want me to devise requirements for who gets a house when they're finished and staff a place where people can apply. I've got to keep track of all the material and labor costs and make sure what we've ordered actually gets here. What I need is someone to help me organize the whole shebang, then help me administer it when the houses are ready to be lived in."

"Is Sun Li still working with you?"

"No. I wish she was. Right now, she's working with the Chinese, helping them get settled in their camps. I'd love to have her, but I understand that situation. When she feels she can she'll be back which will be a big help. It's rare I ask that girl a question about the city she can't answer."

Sun Li Redbird and her husband Jason were friends who had operated The BookSeller in San Francisco before the quake, but like much of the city, the store was nothing but ashes and pieces of charred wood. Jason had been helping Johnny and Lemuel at the mansion, but since their home had been spared, they didn't live there.

"The plan is to get people out of tents and into some kind of housing. We're going to build about five thousand small cottages for people to move into. They'll be sited on the various parks around the city and set close together, almost side by side."

"The army's really saved our bacon here in the city," said Madame. "Housing, sanitation, food, clothing, and keeping everything in order. You know, if they hadn't stepped in a couple of hours after the quake things could have gotten out of hand real quick."

Jonas nodded vigorously. "The Relief Corporation and the Red Cross have joined with the Army to take care of the people who need help and given us a breather while we figure out what needs doing to get our city back. First few days people were talking about it being gone and despaired of any rebuilding. Mayor Schultz is leading the boosters among the survivors and it's amazing what all's been getting done."

"But back to my problem," said Jonas. "I was wondering if you could help me organize this new project and maybe help me find some people?"

"I'm sorry, Jonas," Johnny shook his head. "Annaliese and I are leaving in a couple of days. We've been here six weeks and more and we need to get back home."

"I wish I'd have come sooner but I've been so busy." He shook his head and took a deep breath. "I just don't know what to do. I hate to admit I can't get it done but that might be where I am at present."

Emily spoke up. "Mr. Burke, while I was traveling as a performer, I met some people in New York, and they talked about a new position created by the need to organize and administer the ever-larger companies headquartered there. The people who did these jobs were called 'executive assistants.' Sounds to me like that's what you need."

"Call me Jonas, please, Emily. It sounds like that's exactly what I need, but that doesn't solve my problem. Where can I find an executive assistant?"

"When we were working to get the theater ready, I had more things to do than I could keep track of so I hired someone to fill that kind of position for me." She paused and deliberately pointed her finger at Teressa. "She did a wonderful job for me and I believe if you told her what you needed done, she could help you figure out how to do it."

With everyone looking at her, Teressa looked around and stammered. "I wouldn't know where to begin something like that."

Jonas was looking at her now, his eyes narrowed in concentration. "Hmm, I was looking for a man but since there don't seem to be any available, why not? I could tell you what I need you to do and help you set up the system, then I'd just step back and let you do it. Are you willing to give it a try?"

"Well," Teressa said slowly, "I'm helping Emily right now and she still needs someone at least for a while yet."

"There are plenty of people here who can help Emily," said Madame. "Why don't you give it a try? What do you think about it?" She was looking at Annaliese when she asked this.

"I'd say it was up to her," said Annaliese. "I've never seen anything she couldn't do if she put her mind to it."

"We'd have to decide where to put you in the system so I'd know what to pay you. I don't think anyone around here ever had an 'executive assistant' before." He looked at Teressa. "If you're willing to try, we can start you tomorrow."

Teressa looked a little taken aback by the suddenness of it all but finally shrugged. "I suppose I could try and if I can't do it, you can always fire me. Where would I be working?"

"We'd have to work that out. Since the quake and fire I'm staying with one of my staff at his home and I more or less work on the fly since there aren't any city offices around at present."

"Would she be working in an office?" asked Madame. "The reason I ask is that we've had people leave and we have room for you here if you want. That way, she wouldn't have to go to an office somewhere else and you would be around here a lot if she needed you."

She glanced at Sarah and then continued. "We have room for you now if you want to move in here until you find something more permanent."

She smiled. "Of course, you'd have to keep us informed about what's going on around town. We could set the two of you up in an office, and we have plenty of space if you wanted to bring someone else in to help her."

For the next hour, Madame showed him the rooms she envisioned him using for his project and they talked about the specifics of the arrangement. He was on his way to the front door to leave when, in the dim light, he saw Sarah standing a little way down the hall apparently waiting for him.

They stood quietly looking at each other for a moment and then he said, "She didn't ask if this arrangement was alright with you, did she?" When she shook her head, he said, "If it makes you uncomfortable, I won't."

"It doesn't. I imagine I can get used to it without too much of a problem."

They were quiet again and finally, she said, "I still have the letter you sent. I opened it on New Year's Eve."

"Were you shocked?"

"Yes, actually, I was more surprised than anything. You never mentioned the possibility, so I didn't expect it."

"My career at City Hall and in politics was becoming such that I needed a wife and she was interested." He looked at her in that special way she remembered, a look that was usually followed by something warm and exciting.

She reached out and touched his face and then they kissed.

He held her and spoke into her hair. "I never loved her the way I loved you, but she said, 'Yes.' At that time, I needed to hear that yes."

"And now?" she whispered into his shoulder.

"She's gone and I still love you. Is that what you wanted to hear?"

"Yes. That will do to be going on with but I still don't want to get married."

He kissed her passionately and afterward looked into her eyes and smiled. "I'll take what I can get."

She smiled at him coquettishly. "If you're too busy right now, I guess we can wait. After all, it's been six years and I've forgotten what it feels like."

He grinned at her. They kissed again and she walked him to the door.

"Actually, I haven't forgotten at all," she whispered to herself after he'd gone.

She wondered what Madame would say, and by the time she resumed her seat at the window in the sitting room she'd decided she really didn't care what Madame said about her other lover. She knew she would only care that Sarah was happy, which was one of the reasons she loved her.

CHAPTER ELEVEN

When Rudy came to relieve him, Bobby went forward and stood at the bow, looking for a light in the darkness. Tomorrow they should be home and though he felt sure of his calculations as to their position, a light ahead would send him back to the chart looking for a mistake. There was no light.

Tomorrow they would swing south and come in through the reef and coral heads leading into Prony Bay and he would see the house on the cliff. But first he must get through the reef, and that made him nervous. Very nervous. Henri believed he'd learned enough to make it through but Henri's confidence didn't relieve the knot he'd been feeling in his stomach all day.

When he went below Henri was sitting in the galley reading a book and sucking on his pipe. He only lit it when he was on watch and the ocean breeze would blow the smoke away.

He looked up and smiled at Bobby. "It will be nice to be home tomorrow. I always miss talking to Pete when I'm away."

"I'll sure be glad to see him." Bobby poured himself a cup of coffee and sat down at the mess table.

Henri looked at him with that curious half-smile he had and asked, "So, my friend, do you still wish to sail the South Seas for a living? This has been a good voyage but they're not all like that. This life has its hard knocks like any other. But even for that I'd rather do it than anything else. Of course, I haven't done much of anything else most of my life so I have little to compare it with but I am content."

"I like what I'm doing so far, but there's so much about it that I never anticipated. Dealing with things ashore can be frustrating. I guess they have reasons for what they demand of you but they don't make it easy."

"They are not in the business of making it easy. They're like bureaucrats everywhere. Their god is record and routine, but like the reefs, they are hazards you must navigate around. I must say you seem to be fairly good at it. You don't let them make you angry and that's the key."

"Of course, there are compensations, like a night watch under a full moon with the trades behind you. Or some of the women of the islands." He brought his fingers to his lips in a typically Gallic gesture.

Bobby smiled dreamily. "Looking up at that moon, I was just thinking about that girl on Nuku Hiva the night of the last full moon. I can still see her smile."

They had seen each other just once in the village, but she was on the dock as they pulled for Mirabelle and when she raised her hand in farewell, he had stopped rowing, throwing Henri into a crab with the other oar. Seeing what had happened, Henri leaned on his oar, and after a moment, she disappeared into the shadows and they began to row the boat again.

They were quiet for a while, then Henri said, "You'll see many more just as beautiful in the next year."

Bobby grinned a little sheepishly. He started to take a drink of coffee but paused and set the cup down. "Maybe," he said. "But she's the one I'll dream about."

"You sound like a Frenchman. A little advice, my friend. Don't give your heart away on one of these islands. Mirabelle needs your heart and your soul for a while. Playing is one thing, but a woman is an anchor for a sailor. You must leave them where you find them and sail away."

"Have you ever been married?"

Henri smiled grimly. "Several times. Twice to the same woman, in fact. It takes a special kind of woman to be married to a sailor. I had one like that long ago and let her go. Tried two other times before I ended up back where I started. The second time we were smarter."

"Are you still with her?"

"Oh yes. When I'm in port, she comes to Noumea and we have good times. When I leave she goes back home. We're happy."

"Any children?"

"Two. A boy and a girl. She's fifteen, and I think he's about twelve. I see them once in a while. They live with her parents. One big happy family. She's much better off than if I tried to settle down. We'd both be miserable. We learned that much the first time around." He shrugged. "I'm a sailor. Apparently, she'd rather have me on my terms than not at all."

Bobby grinned when he thought about it. That sounded like a good thing to him but he couldn't picture any girl who would put up with it.

The motor made it possible the next day. Without it, passage into the lagoon and the bay would have been impossible for him. It gave him an ability to maneuver he would probably never achieve with just the sails. Using a chart and what Henri had taught him about how to identify the danger in a shadow in the water here or a ripple there, they slowly crawled through the maze.

Henri was at his shoulder the whole time, giving advice and information when asked, able to step in to ensure their safe passage if needed. But he didn't need it.

In the two months since they left Grande Terre Bobby had gradually become aware of what the captain of any craft on any ocean in the world comes to know; that he is part of the boat, and it is a part of him. Any injury to it causes him pain. The scrape of a coral head along the hull would be like a laceration on his own skin. That was part of the job.

It was quiet, the only noise the occasional slap of a wave against the hull or a groan from the boat responding somewhere below. He'd sent the crew off to do some things and Henri would return to stand watch the first night of their return. There were four of them and they took turns so that Mirabelle was never alone.

Then he would climb the trail to the house on the cliff, and for the next few days, he would relax and unwind. He was looking forward to seeing Pete. They had covered a lot of distance and made some money, enough to pay the bills and be comfortable for a while.

Sometimes it had been what he had dreamed about, and sometimes it had been difficult and frustrating but he had learned, gotten to know his crewmates and began to know the stars in the southern sky.

Even the bad had its good points. Days when they had to unload a cargo and ferry it to a dock under the tropical sun might seem bad until you took a breather and looked around at the green mountains of Samoa or a beautiful anchorage in the Marquesas or felt Mirabelle running before the trades in the evening of a beautiful day.

And then there was the paperwork. He never envisioned himself sitting at a mess table, trying to list and calculate operating costs, income, and repairs. It wasn't something he liked doing but it was necessary to calculate what share Pete was due, and Bobby's reverence for his benefactor was boundless. No matter what, he wanted to be fair to Pete.

He also didn't much care about dealing with most of the officials on the various islands they visited. In addition to complex regulations and rules that were different on each island there were sometimes language difficulties and finding an interpreter wasn't always easy. Time and time again he blessed Pete for his notebooks that dealt with almost everything he encountered, including some amorous and fetching beauties who seemed to be enamored with the tall, dark-haired American.

Time and time again, he was fascinated by native customs and practices and grateful for the several blank notebooks Pete had given him to begin his own set for future use. With the basic education Pete and Henri had given him to dampen him, he felt like a sponge soaking up new experiences every new day and the things he learned made it easier to learn more.

"Ahoy the boat." It was Henri returning for his watch. Bobby steadied the dinghy while Henri sprang on board.

"Well, my friend, it looks like you've recovered from your ordeal."

"Did it show?"

"Oh yes. I have stood in those shoes. Felt the fear. One of the bad things about water so clear is what you can see on the bottom. I know what these reefs can do."

"Does it ever get easier?"

"No, never easier but you become accustomed to it. And you learn. You become a captain and feel your boat as a part of yourself." That smile again. "You know Mirabelle's alive, don't you?"

Rowing to the landing, he thought about what his friend had said and realized he was right. Mirabelle was alive and the coral that could rip open her bottom was part of his life now just like Nuku Hiva and Tahiti, sunrises out of sight of land and beautiful women. It was something he had to live with, but he must never take any of these things for granted, especially the coral and the women.

Coral could tear the bottom out of any boat made of wood and do a lot of damage to any other kind. If he figured to stay in these waters he knew that today's trial was like many he would face as part of what he'd chosen to be and where he'd chosen to be it. Pondering the future, he could understand why Rudy was happy where he was, letting someone else worry about the coral.

At every turning in the path up the hill, he stopped and looked out at the bay and Mirabelle and every time loved what he was seeing. The green forest around the bay, the red dirt of the cliffs with Mirabelle floating on the clear blue water below, made him wish he was an artist and could preserve what he was seeing.

Marie had seen him coming and had a drink ready. He sat on the shaded terrace, drank a sip of tea and closed his eyes to enjoy the cooling breeze coming off the bay. He heard Pete ease himself into a chair and opened his eyes to see his friend looking at him, a smile on his face.

"Welcome home. From what Cookie told me, you had a good voyage."

"Yes, I think we did. Made a few bucks and learned a lot."

"Well, is it the kind of thing you want to keep doing?"

Bobby nodded. "I like working with the crew. They are really first-rate. Couldn't have anyone better to show me the ropes than Henri. The things I've seen so far make me want to see more."

"Is a week's turn-around OK with you?"

"A week," exclaimed Bobby in surprise. "Have you got something going out?"

"Two things. Got some mail and small stuff going to a planter up in the Solomons. You'll drop it in Tulagi, then head southeast to Fiji to pick up a load of copra and bring it to Noumea. That will go to the terminal there, and a freighter will add it to a load it already has." Pete grinned. "If we can keep going like this, we could be rich in a few years, though I ain't counting on it."

"Is it normal to turn around that quickly?"

"No. But it happens once in a while and it's best to grab it now. Come summer, we'll be sitting here playing whist and drinking rum punch. Best to make it while you can."

"How'd you like coming through the reef?"

Bobby rolled his eyes and shook his head. "Not my favorite way to spend time. Do we have to go out the same way?"

"No. When you leave here you steer west out of the bay, through Havanah Pass to Noumea. You'll have to go through the process and paperwork of telling the authorities there you're my partner. It's someplace you'll be spending time so you have to learn the approaches and, once you get there, where to go for what.

"It's where you'll provision and where the government types will want to stick their noses in your business. All you can do is put up with it and eventually they'll give you their blessing and you sail away until the next time.

"Also, you'll need to see the factor whenever you're there, and anything major that needs to be done on the boat will be done at the shipyards there. If need be, they have a cradle that will haul her out of the water. By the time you finally leave, you'll be sick of the whole place but it's a part of this life so you have to put up with it.

"When you leave there you'll head a little south of west through Bolari Pass and then north along the coast outside the reef. Should have the trades on your beam all the way up. Henri knows that route."

Bobby snorted. "What doesn't he know?"

Pete handed Bobby one of his logs. "Read up on the Solomons the next couple of days. Before you leave we'll talk about it. It's different up there. Closer to the Equator. Thick jungle. A few planters but mostly natives, some of them pretty wild. Good place to wear a gun if you got one."

"I brought one with me and a holster."

"Henri tells me you did good. Did you keep a good log for me?"

"Hope so. I've never written so much."

"Any problems with the boat?"

"Just maintenance stuff. Want to keep her looking nice."

"I found out when I write something down, I remember it better," said Pete. "Not always, but it helps. Take it easy tonight and we can get the business out of the way in the morning. I'll read your log tonight and if I have any questions we can get that out of the way too."

He got up using his cane and reached over to squeeze Bobby's shoulder. "Glad you're back."

Bobby watched him walk to the house. His gait seemed steady and he hadn't looked or acted any different than what he remembered. He wondered about the cane. Pete didn't really look like he needed it.

When Marie knocked on his door to say goodnight, he asked her about the cane.

"It's not like he needs it all the time but he has spells when he feels weak and unsteady. Gets dizzy sometimes, too. I guess he feels he'd rather have it with him just in case."

It was his first night in a bed after two months on a boat, and after tossing and turning for a while, he got up and quietly crept out to sit on the veranda. In the light of a full moon, he could see Mirabelle clearly and an occasional light at different places along the shore of the bay opposite. Above him, the stars were dim in the radiance of the moon.

"Well," he thought, "I've seen a little of what life would be like if I stay the course I've begun. Did I like it well enough to continue?" He nodded. "I would say 'yes' to that."

He said it out loud to himself, and after a while, stood and walked back into the house to try to get some sleep.

Mirabelle was moving northward off the west coast of Grande Terre. The wind was steady from the west and the schooner had white water curling from her bow as she reached northward toward Tulagi, a thousand miles away. Bobby and Henri were sitting in the cockpit in one of the companionable silences of men who spend a lot of time together in close quarters.

The last two days had been a trial. The only good thing was that it was all packed into a short time and now it was over for a while. He understood certain necessities, such as food, water, spare parts and gear that needed to be replaced, but the officials who only wanted to exercise whatever authority they possessed and the clerks who seemed to exist to find reasons for delay tried his nerves and frayed his temper.

The fact that Noumea was a nice, even a beautiful little city of maybe 4,000 souls was lost on him amongst all the irritation he felt with a system seemingly designed to make a day as miserable for him as possible. It was his first contact with French bureaucratic mentality that had plagued the island since the 1840s. Henri had guided him through all the things he needed to do and seeing the city sink below the horizon and the mountains grow smaller and smaller as they moved away from land made Bobby feel as though he'd been released from jail.

Henri felt confident running at night in these waters and they sat in the cockpit late into the night, sometimes talking, sometimes just enjoying Mirabelle's rise and fall with the wind on her beam and a quartering sea. They had a run of a thousand miles before them and according to Henri they would seldom alter their course.

"So, tell me of your childhood," said Henri one night. "You grew up in California?"

"Yes. My father was a partner in a horse ranch across the Golden Gate from San Francisco. I practically grew up on a horse. My grandmother lived with a rich widow in the city and my mother and I, and later my sister, spent every other week at her place. We called it 'The Mansion.' One of those big, beautiful places on a hill. Most winters we were in San Diego and I was in a sailboat all winter long. So it was either a horse or a sailboat when I wasn't in school."

"Did you have a sweetheart?"

"No one special. I guess Teressa was the closest thing to one. She and her brother Manny were my best friends growing up." A slow smile spread over his face. "She's what I miss the most. They were adopted by my father's best friend when they were six and four. That's when I met them. She's beautiful and so smart. I think about her, how she'd love Mirabelle and this adventure we're on."

"Are your parents still at home?"

"Oh yeah. He's a Minnesota farm boy, and she's half Sioux Indian. He proposed the second day he saw her."

"Those are the ones that last. Is your father a big man like you?"

"Bigger, at least he was. I think I might still be growing a little. He's six-eight. I'll have to get Marie to measure me when we get home. It will tickle him if I catch up to him."

"Did you say your mother was an Indian?"

"That's an interesting story. My grandmother was living in a frontier settlement in Wisconsin when she was kidnapped by raiding Indians. She became the second wife to a warrior and my mother was born in a Sioux village. He was killed by other Indians, but she escaped, married my grandfather and they joined a wagon train going west. They stopped at a store in the Wyoming wilderness and stayed to help a lady there after her husband died. She died a few weeks later and they ended up with the store.

"Her husband went hunting one day and never came back, so she raised my mother and her brother out in the wilderness by herself. My father showed up one day and proposed to my mother the next. Been happy ever since."

"Did you ever find any gold in California?"

"Never looked. We were ranchers not miners. Some people did. That's why they call it the Golden Gate."

They sat quietly, Henri smoking his pipe and Bobby thinking about home.

"I miss my parents, my sister and my friends." He sighed

deeply. "It will be a long time before I see them again."

"Probably true. I have been to San Francisco a few times over the years. Did you hear whether they were alright after the earthquake?"

"They felt it up in Mill Valley, but no damage. Mama's letter said Teressa was buried in a building that collapsed, but they got her out and she's fine."

He yawned hugely and said, "I'm going to my bunk for a while."

"Good night, Mon Capitan. If the wind holds fair we should see Tulagi tomorrow sometime."

And Mirabelle swooped on through the night with Henri's hand on the wheel and the smoke from his pipe disappearing in the trade winds.

CHAPTER TWELVE

Dr. Annaliese Fry, M.D., was sitting in her office clad in a dressing gown. As she was getting ready for bed, she remembered something she'd left in her office and came downstairs to get it. That was one advantage of having your home upstairs from your office. It was also two floors above The BookSeller of San Diego, which her husband owned as a partner.

The whole house was three stories with attic rooms above and it had been added to so many times at various places it was a city landmark and people sometimes got lost in it. They lived in an apartment on the third floor. To everyone who lived there, it was 'the store'.

She noticed a letter postmarked Boston, Massachusetts, among the mail scattered on her desk, picked it up, and, curious, turned it over and opened it.

October 15, 1906
Boston, Mass.
Dear Dr. Fry,

My name is Colleen Drury. I met your son Manny when I accompanied a friend on a trip to the Naval Academy last month. He took me to a dance at the Academy, and afterward we talked. I told him I'd like to meet his mother, and he replied, "Be careful, she might turn you into a doctor." He then explained that you mentor young girls who want to become doctors to help them prepare for medical school.

I've been thinking about it every day since that night and finally decided to write to you about it. I'm sixteen years old and have always wanted to be a doctor, but everyone has always told me doctors are men.

From what Manny told me, your girls usually begin when they are a little younger than I am, but I would like to ask, if you should consider another such young girl, that you give me the opportunity. I am a good student and a hard worker, and I can pay my way to San Diego.

I enjoyed spending time with Manny. He is the most interesting boy I've ever met.

Yours truly,
Colleen Drury

She finished the letter, looked at it for a moment, then read it again. She was a little amazed that a young girl from all the way across the country would write this letter. Back in her bedroom Johnny was lying on the bed with Little Jinx on his chest. The cat's eyes were closed, and she could hear him purring. She tossed the envelope on the bed, which startled the cat.

"Don't wake him up," said Johnny reproachfully. "He was sleeping good."

"Why not? He wakes me up all the time."

He picked up the envelope, noticed the postmark, and asked, "Who do you know in Boston?"

"Someone, apparently. Read it."

He opened the letter, read it, and handed it back. "Sounds like the boy's doing something right."

She rolled her eyes. "What do you think about it? Liz has been admitted and starts school in San Francisco first of the year but I've been thinking about not having an intern for a while." Johnny carefully moved the cat off his chest and swung his legs off the bed. "Let's go out on the porch. It sounds like you need to talk."

Since a new girl would be part of their life for several years it was something she always considered carefully. She was proud of her 'girls' and what was more important, they were proud to be Annaliese's girls.

Only once in the last fifteen years had she not had at least one and usually two ambitious young girls determined to prove to themselves and the world that women could be trusted to provide care at need as educated and licensed physicians.

She believed having them with her made her a better doctor. Though she only had two hands herself, there were now eight pairs of hands of eight women doctors she had led into the profession scattered around the state. In the process, she had grown to love each of them as she loved her children.

The routine they used was for the girls to share a room in the store and a tutor to keep up with their schoolwork on the days when they weren't working with a doctor. They ate at the table and became part of the family for the roughly three years they spent with her.

"It will be the first time you haven't known one of your girls, won't it?"

"Yes. I won't even get to meet her before I commit to taking her on. The first thing tomorrow, I'll write Manny and see what he can tell me about her. Then, if I decide to accept her, I'll write to her."

"When will she start?"

"Liz will be leaving before Christmas, so I'll invite her to come out by the first of the year. Janet is going to be fifteen in January, so they'll be close in age."

"Sounds like you've already made up your mind."

"There's something about her I like, but we'll see what Manny has to say about her."

"What is it you like?"

Annaliese thought for a moment. "I like that a young girl had the courage to write this letter."

Manny was sitting at his desk reading, which lately seemed like his normal occupation. Usually, the first thing he did when he walked into his room was sit down and open a book. The previous week had been brutal and with exams coming, everyone in their class seemed to have a mild case of nervous anxiety. Academic failure could bring dismissal and the end of a dream.

Yesterday, Sunday morning, he had decided not to pick up a book but instead had sailed a small boat out the Severn River into Chesapeake Bay. Once there, he dropped anchor and took a nap. He smiled when he thought about it. Now he was back hard at work again.

He was deep in a treatise on gearing when Jack came in and tossed a letter on his desk. He looked at it casually and saw the words 'open immediately' written in his mother's hand.

Nov. 1, 1906
Dear Manny,

I got the most surprising letter yesterday. It was from a young girl in Boston you escorted to a dance. She wants to be a doctor. Liz is leaving at Christmas, and I want you to write me immediately about her so I can consider what's next. She seems a little impatient, and I will write her immediately when I receive your letter. I'll write again in a day or two.

Love, Mother

He sat for a moment and slowly a smile spread across his face and became a grin. He had been expecting something like this since he'd received that cryptic letter from Colleen.

Johnny heard his wife suddenly laugh in the next room and stuck his head in the door to see what was so funny.

She held a letter out and said, "From your son."

"So now he's my son," said Johnny as he read the one line written on the page and began to *chuckle*. The line Manny had written was: *She has long red hair.*

"Got to give him credit. That boy has a sense of humor. Doesn't tell you much, though."

Oh yes, it does," she said. "It tells me he thinks she's perfect and exactly what I want as a student."

Colleen carried the letter from San Diego to a path that led to the river and sat down on a fallen tree before she opened it. She didn't want to be around her family when she read it. If Dr. Fry accepted her she would be on a train to a new life in a very short time and she wanted time to figure out the best way to tell them.

She was the middle child with two older brothers, a younger sister, and a youngest brother. She loved her father but his ambitions in life seemed to disappear when his wife died in childbirth ten years before. He was a good father who loved his children and cared for them as best he could, but he loved his beer. Content in the city job his brother had gotten him he was also content to sit in the local pub or hang around the house with a pail of beer and some newspapers or books. He was a well-read, amiable drunk.

She, on the other hand, wanted more from life than marriage to a man of the next generation who also loved his beer. Some of the girls she had grown up with had done just that but not her.

She was just beginning to seek something new when Manny Fry came into her life. Their conversation on the terrace that night had slowly grown into an idea for a new life and the letter she was holding was the key to that life.

She tore open the envelope, unfolded the single sheet, took a deep breath and began to read. Her heart leapt as she read the first sentence. She stopped and closed her eyes, almost dizzy with excitement.

> Nov. 10, 1906
>
> *Dear Colleen,*
>
> *I would be happy to have you work with me and allow me to help you toward becoming a Doctor of Medicine.*
>
> *One of my current students is leaving before Christmas, so any time after that would be fine for you to begin. I will take some time later this week to write to you with more information about what it will be like here with us, but the basics are this. You will spend*

time with me or other doctors and learn by watching, asking questions, and doing. You'll work with us three days a week whenever we work. Other than that, you will go to school and/or study and basically live with the family. There is no pay for these positions, but we provide room and board and the personal things you will need. There is one other student with me at this time, and you will be sharing a room with her. Her name is Janet Gaynor. She's fifteen and has been with me a year. I will let you tell Manny. Give him my love.

Thank you for giving me the opportunity to help you fulfill a dream.

She sat in a daze and stared at the signature, wondering what the woman looked like. She felt dizzy and she could feel her heart racing. The need to plan for the future brought her back to the present. She had to write Manny and tell him. She could picture his face and wondered how he would react to the news. From what she remembered she thought he'd like it.

Molly had asked her to return to the Academy with her for a Christmas dance. Maybe she would leave from there. The idea of a train ride all the way across the country made her stomach swoop. It frightened her a little, but the more she thought about it the more excited she got.

The first thing she needed to do was talk to her Uncle Billy. He was the one who had gotten her father his job. The cousins had all grown up together and he was her godfather as well as her uncle. All the cousins were close but she was the smart one and Billy had told her more than once that if she needed anything for her future just ask. She'd need some money to make this happen but when she became a doctor she would repay him and knew she could count on him.

Now she just had to figure out how to tell the rest of the family.

Manny was standing, arms hanging loosely at his side, looking out at a target about fifty yards distant. His hand movement was almost too quick to follow and the two shots were one rolling sound, with the bullets striking on either side of the bullseye.

CT was standing behind him. "Didn't you say your father was better than you?"

"Yeah, a bit, although I'm pretty close and almost as accurate. A friend of his calls him a magician with a six-gun."

"I'd like to see that."

"He might visit school before I finish. I'll write him and tell him to bring his gun belt."

After study hall the following night two members of the aero club visited Manny in his room. It was unusual for a Firstie and a Junior to visit a Youngster's room but they wanted to talk to him about what he had found in his research on the small gasoline engines used in the airplanes they had seen in magazines and books.

With a bookseller in the family he was invaluable for that sort of thing. They sat and talked for a while then left, leaving Manny content and Jack amazed—content because they were there to talk about flying, amazed because they were there at all.

The club only had seven members at this point but they were all enthusiastic and wanted to learn everything they could about motorized, heavier-than-air machines. The problem was that their study load was so hectic they had only had one meeting. These informal conferences in each other's rooms might replace club meetings until after exams. Manny already felt a camaraderie with these young men, no longer boys, and that boded well for the club's future.

He was examining a schematic of a lubricating system for a steam engine when Jack tossed an envelope on his desk.

"That was with my stuff, and I just noticed it."

There was a noticeable fragrance in the air, and Manny breathed deep and smiled when he smelled it, as did Jack.

November 21, 1906
Dear Manny,

   Your mother has written to say she will take me on as a student. The idea that I will soon take a train ride across the country and begin a new life in another world almost makes me dizzy.

It looks as though I will be coming to the Christmas Hop with Molly, and her sister will be chaperoning us instead of her mother. According to Molly, she has agreed not to take her duties too seriously. That should make for a fun time.

I've thought about this a lot, and it seems like you and I are going to be sort of related for the next few years but at a distance, a great distance. Be that as it may, I refuse to see you as a brother. See you at Christmas.

Colleen

CT was sitting on the porch enjoying a summer evening when Manny rode up. He tied the horse to a post and joined his friend on the porch.

"Do you want to shoot, or would you rather just sit here and talk?"

"Let's talk. Haven't seen you in a while." They talked about the upcoming cruise and CT related events he had heard about on other cruises.

After a while, Manny said, "I moved ahead with the idea about the club. By the way, what should we call it? The Air Club doesn't seem right. Any ideas?"

CT sat and pulled at his chin for a moment. "How about The Club for Naval Air? That tells you what it is and sounds pretty good, too."

"Somehow I bet you already had that answer ready," said Manny with a grin. "Have you been thinking about it?"

"Yes, I have," he admitted. "You said you'd moved ahead; what have you done?"

"The thing with Spruance helped start it. He came to me and asked if I could help tutor some men who might need it. I mentioned the idea and he said he'd spread the word. You know he's the kind of person you'd expect to do whatever he told you he would."

"He's a good one and there are a few others in that class that look like leaders. One thing I've noticed over the years, though, sometimes it's a guy from the middle of the pack that finishes ahead of everyone else."

"The first meeting was good. Seven of us. Tower, Fielder, Ellyson all seem really interested. They came down to our room last night to talk about things I've been looking into. We're so busy right now we have trouble finding time to meet. But they were interested enough to come down to my room to talk."

"Sounds like a beginning."

He looked at Manny intently. "How come you look so happy?"

Manny grinned. "I didn't know it showed."

"Well, it's the first time I've ever seen all your teeth."

"I got a letter from Colleen."

"She's the one in Boston? Jack's cousin."

"She's coming down to the Hop and then climbing on a train to San Diego. My mother has taken her on as a medical student. She's going to live in my house out there. She's going to be almost part of my family for the next three years."

CT looked amazed. "How did this all come about?"

"When she was here before I kidded her about my mother making her a doctor. Next thing I know she's written to her and arranged it all."

"How do you feel about all that? Seems to me it makes you feel pretty good. You've had a silly grin on your face since you walked in. How can your mother make her a doctor?"

"There are eight women doctors practicing medicine right now in California, three of them Mexican, because of her. She calls them her girls. They work with her learning what they need to know and then go on to medical school. She can do it because she's done it many times.

"Remember I told you about Colleen's red hair? My mother has long red hair, and from what I've seen she's a lot like my mother. I'm excited about this whole thing because it will make her part of my life and even at a distance I'd like that."

"She reminds you of your mother?"

CT sat for a minute, obviously thinking about what he had just heard. "Isn't there some kind of a complex or something about that?"

"The Oedipus complex. Yes, I've read about it. I don't know about that, but Colleen looks like my mother's daughter, if she ever had one."

CHAPTER THIRTEEN

Mirabelle was snugged down for the night waiting for the light needed to sail into Tulagi Harbor. The crew were all sitting at the mess table which was something they didn't get to do very often. When they were under sail at least one of them was in the cockpit all the time.

They were far enough from the closest land that the mosquitoes and flies didn't bother them and they were talking about where they were going to sleep. The nice breeze coming off the New Georgia Sound to the north made the idea of sleeping on deck pleasant.

"Have you been in these islands before?" asked Bobby.

"A few times," replied Henri'. "Not my favorite place to sail. Getting too close to the Equator. Hot most of the time, very thick jungle, lots of rain. The reefs here aren't like most you've seen so far. They run close along the coasts of some of these islands, but they don't have lagoons. Too close in. Many times, when you want to go ashore on one of them, you have to anchor and take a boat in at high tide, not that I've ever been on one of them other than Tulagi. Really have no desire to."

He looked at Bobby with an impish smile. "Headhunters and cannibals on some of them and you can never tell which island they're on. They move around. The Brits had a warship here for a while and destroyed some villages to scare them, but they don't stay scared. Even fought a couple of small wars with them and they've only been here since '93. If you hit a reef and go down around these islands you could run into trouble."

Bobby looked at him for a moment. "You're not kidding, are you?"

Henri' shook his head slowly and said, "No, I'm not kidding."

He let Bobby think about that for a minute. "What did Pete tell you about The Solomons?"

"He said it was a good place to carry a gun."

"Do you have one?"

Bobby nodded.

Rudy spoke for the first time. "I've got one, too. Carry it whenever I'm ashore here."

Bobby took a deep breath and ran his hand through his hair. "Maybe I better get it out and oil it."

Tulagi was a small island just offshore from a bigger island. Between the two lay Tulagi Harbor, safe from wind and waves. The island was the administrative center of the Solomon Islands and of British hegemony in the region. The Solomons were a cluster of islands strung out in a line northwest to southeast on the northern edge of the Coral Sea. The New Georgia Sound lay between several islands in the center of the archipelago, and from what Henri said, he'd never sailed in the Sound that he didn't feel hostile eyes on him.

Henri had been here many times and he took care of Mirabelle's needs while Bobby went to find the authorities and deliver the message he was carrying. He was glad the person he was seeking spoke English so communication should be greatly facilitated.

From the time he set foot on shore, Bobby was aware of the pistol on his hip. His father and Johnny had taught him to shoot and while he was not as good at it as Manny, he was pretty good.

The problem was he'd never had to wear it because he felt threatened. Alert for a native uprising even though he wasn't sure what one looked like, he could feel his heart beating against his ribs as he walked across a grassy area toward a house Henri had pointed out to him. Government House was what he called it but it didn't look much different from the structures he passed on the way there.

There was no door, and the interior of the Government House was open to the elements, which mostly meant hot, moist air and bugs. Tulagi was close enough to the Equator that the temperature was pretty much the same all year round, and frequent rains meant thick jungle greenery and heavy air to breathe.

The governor's name was Herbert Abercrombie. He saw Bobby coming and called to him from the shade of a huge tree where a desk, file cabinet and two glasses indicated where he conducted most of his business. There was a tarp stretched across some of the branches to keep off the rain. It was noticeably cooler in the shade under the tree.

Bobby handed him the package. He glanced at the label and gave a grunt of satisfaction.

"Finally here. Herman's been waiting for it. Down here bothering me about it every couple of days for the last two weeks. It's from his sister in Sidney. Usually got two or three bottles of scotch in it. Last time we had to make it last for a couple months."

Abercrombie set it aside and stood to shake hands with Bobby.

"I heard Pete was retiring. You sound like a Yank. Did he meet you when he went to San Francisco to get the new boat?"

"Yep, we're partners now, and Henri' is teaching me the ropes."

"Well, if anyone knows the ropes, it's that Frenchman. He's been around this neck of the woods a long time. Where is he?"

"He's stocking up, and it seems we might have a small load of copra to take with us.

"Where you headed from here?"

"Fiji. We got a cargo waiting there then back to Noumea. Are there any papers to fill out or anything you need me to do?"

"No, I just need to put you on the list. Where are you from?"

"Mill Valley, California. It's a little place just north of San Francisco. How about you? Sounds like you're Australian."

"Bingo. I'm from Sidney. Came out here with Herman years ago but a copra plantation is hard work in this heat and when the last fellow in this office retired I took his place. That load of copra is Herman's, so you'll probably see him. Tell him his package is here. It will make him a happy man."

Bobby stood to leave, and Abercrombie stood too. "I'll walk down with you. I'll say hello to Henri and make sure you're not smuggling anything." He laughed. "Can't imagine what it would be because we sure need damn near everything so I'd probably just look the other way. Unless it's guns, that is. Can't allow that."

He seemed to be one of those men who walked at a leisurely pace all the time. Bobby matched his stride and they talked about the islands. It seemed Henri wasn't exaggerating about the perils of sailing these waters. A planter on one of the islands to the north and his wife had been murdered and the Navy had come in to deal with it. They had just departed.

"They left me a wonderful bottle of brandy. I just finished it last week. Made it last for two months." He laughed. "That's not a record but it was pretty good."

As they were getting ready to cast off the next morning a native runner arrived from the Governor asking Bobby to stop by before they left.

"I wonder what that's about?" said Henri. "You need to hurry. We don't want to miss the tide."

Bobby returned a few minutes later with a locked satchel, and he cast off as he was jumping aboard. "This is for the Governor of the New Hebrides. He said make sure it's the English governor. Apparently there are two down there."

"Did he pay you for it?"

Bobby held up some currency and Henri rolled his eyes. "Pete hates pound notes. He has to take them to Noumea to get francs. I've seen a hundred pounds sitting in a box at his place because he forgets to take them into the bank."

When he looked back on his time in Tulagi, Bobby realized every white man he'd seen had a gun on his hip and no black person spoke to him while he was there.

It had taken him a while but Bobby had finally learned to write when Mirabelle was running with the trade winds on the beam. He was sitting at the mess table writing in the log he kept for Pete to read and his body and mind were so attuned to the movements of the boat beneath him that he could write legibly without thinking about it.

Originally, he had dreaded the idea of keeping the log, but now found he enjoyed it. When he sat down to tell Pete about his daily activities he was reviewing them for himself and these sessions sometimes brought him insights he hadn't seen before. He made sure he recorded them in his own diary when they happened. When he read over something he knew Pete would read, he would occasionally cross out a word or add something in the margin to make sure he said what he wanted to say.

Bobby had begun to notice that sometimes he would begin to write something, suddenly stop and think for a while about what he wanted to write. Knowing Pete would be reading it made Bobby careful about how how he wrote about the things he saw and did which is probably what his friend had in mind in the first place. The life he had dreamed about was not much a part of his everyday life now. But it was a good life. Bobby could see why Henri was content to live it.

"Land ho," called Rudy from forward where he was standing with a glass.

"Where away?" called Henri in answer.

Rudy pointed.

"Right where it ought to be," said Henri. He stuck his head down the hatchway and said, "Good job, mister navigator." Bobby had to work hard to suppress a grin at the words. Of all the things he'd learned since he came on board Mirabelle he was proudest of his navigation skills. Pete had begun lessons on the voyage from San Francisco but he was all about charts and maps, instruments, and records.

Henri taught him other things; the fine points about the weather, the color of the water, green reflected off the underside of a cloud, the direction a bird was flying at a certain time of day, and most important about the stars.

More than just a point on a map with Henri it was a feeling. Certain things he saw and felt gave him impressions and blended with instinct and experience made him part of the ocean around him. He always seemed to know where he was and not with maps and charts. He just knew.

When Bobby asked him about it Henri would shrug and smile. He had grown up on 'The Pebble' as natives called Grande Terre, the main island of New Caledonia. His earliest memories were of time spent in a boat with his father, who made his living on the water, with his friends, white and brown, sailing on the lagoon and occasionally in the Coral Sea. As a child, he ate fish most every day and his life was of the sea and the boats that sailed it.

He had sailed with Pete off and on for twenty years. The people who had taught him about the ocean had no charts and few maps. What they did have was tales told and remembered, lessons learned and passed on, and an awareness of many, but not all, things the wind, the sea, and the stars could tell them.

On nights alone in the cockpit Bobby digested things Henri had taught him and smiled when he came to realize that one day it would be instinct with him too.

The New Hebrides is an island chain of eleven major islands and dozens of smaller ones that lie south and east of the Solomons. Beginning in the 1840s, the New Hebrides was subjected to and colonized by both Britain and France. Since these two nations had enjoyed a few years of peace recently after a century of on-and-off warfare they took a practical approach to governing the islands and 'muddled' through until 1906, when increasing French population forced a decision about administration and they became what they called The New Hebrides Condominium.

The authorities were just beginning to figure out how to put this into practice when Mirabelle dropped anchor there in November of 1906. This was the beginning of summer in these latitudes and the jungle-covered volcanic islands were steaming from the frequent heavy rains. At Port Vila, officials accepted delivery of the satchel from Tulagi and they were quickly back aboard and on their way.

"I lived here for two years when I was a young man." Henri was at the wheel, and Bobby was sitting with his legs stretched across the cockpit, eyes closed, hat tipped over his eyes. He raised the brim and looked at Henri.

"Really?"

"Yes, I lived on a hill outside a village on the north shore. I met a girl who fascinated me and I followed her home. We lived with her family and I worked with her father and brothers. It's where I learned some of the things I taught you about navigation. The men there still sail the way their ancestors did and never get lost.

"Port Vila is on Efate Island and there's a village of Polynesians on the north shore. That's where we lived. It was a nice place and peaceful while I was there. The islands to the north still have some fierce, warlike tribes on them and in years past there have been some problems much like up in the Solomons. Headhunters and such. Good idea to stay away from them."

"So how far are we from home here?"

Henri scratched his chin and looked thoughtful. "From Noumea probably over five hundred kilometers, about three hundred and fifty miles. We should raise Fiji in a couple of days, and you can figure we'll be there a few days and then home, unless we pick up something there."

Fiji was southeast of Efate and on their second day en route, they spotted a schooner off one of the islets of the New Hebrides. The way her course was laid she would pass close to them. The breeze was blowing from them to Mirabelle,and they began to smell something before they closed.

"Blackbirder," muttered Rudy, who was at the wheel. "They all smell the same."

Henri stuck his head out of the hatch and shook it disgustedly. "Looks like he wants to come close," he said. "Don't let them."

He handed Bobby his gun belt. "Might be a good idea to put that on. The more guns they see, the better."

Bobby was settling his gun into place when Henri came on deck carrying a short, double-barrel shotgun.

"Is that a twelve gauge?" Bobby asked.

Henri' nodded, broke it open, inserted two buckshot cartridges into the breach and snapped it shut. He looked at Bobby meaningfully. "Don't give these men any kind of trust. They deserve none. I have no idea why they would accost us, but if they do, be wary."

He looked at the boat for a moment, calculating. "They'll be in hailing distance before long." He turned to Bobby. "I've seen what these men do to an island. They turn up before sunrise, surprise the people there, and before they know what happened, they're on their way to New Guinea to work in the fields for the rest of their lives or down in a mine where they never see the sun from one week to the next. They usually kill one or two just to frighten anyone who tries to resist. They don't know what mercy is."

As the boat came closer, they could see a man standing on the deck with a shotgun at port arms and a man who looked like the captain was standing in the cockpit beside a man at the wheel, a rifle casually cradled on his arm.

Bobby raised his voice. "Shear off. Don't come any closer," he shouted. There was no sign of a change of course and the man with the shotgun raised it as though to fire, though the distance between the boats was too great for effective use of that weapon. "Last warning," shouted Bobby.

The shotgun came up to the man's shoulder but he never pulled the trigger. Bobby's shot took him in the chest and he spun and fell over the side into the ocean. The man in the cockpit seemed to be stunned for a second and before he could recover and bring the rifle into firing position, he was looking down the barrel of a cocked Colt .45.

"Put it down."

The man looked at him for a long moment then slowly lowered the rifle to the deck and turned to face Bobby. The two men stood looking at each other and Bobby could see a look of triumph slowly spread across the man's face.

"Were you planning to take our boat?" asked Henri', his voice a growl. "And do what with us?" He glanced at Bobby, who was standing with the gun steady in his hand.

The shot startled everyone, and they all watched the man fall backward in the cockpit. They had seen the blood on his chest. The man was dead, and Bobby still stood with the now smoking Colt extended, like a finger pointing.

Bobby was writing in Pete's log at the mess table later that day.

Mirabelle was running with the wind on the beam and it was altogether a beautiful day.

Their adventure of the morning had given him plenty to write about, but he was having trouble putting pen to paper. Henri poured himself some coffee and joined him. He sucked his dry pipe while they each sat quietly with their thoughts for a while.

"What were you thinking when you pulled the trigger?"

In the hours since they had left the scene, no one on board had said a word about what Bobby had done.

Bobby looked at his friend and took a deep breath. He sat still, considering the question and finally said, "I've never drawn a gun in anger before today." He shook his head. "I was thinking what he would continue to do if we let him go. How we couldn't take him with us and he would just do the same things again and again if we let him go. I guess I was judge, jury, and executioner. The man was guilty of horrible crimes and there was no one, no law to stop him. So I did." He looked at his friend steadily and said, "What do you think about it?"

"My friend, it is not for me to judge but I hope you don't let it bother you over much. The man and his cohorts were going to take our boat and probably murder us in the bargain. In a way, you were acting in self-defense. But I must admit, you surprised me."

Bobby looked at him in silence for a moment. "Me too. I think I'm a different person now than I was before I pulled the trigger. I didn't expect to commit murder when I got up this morning."

"I know you haven't had a chance to read the log, but something happened on the voyage you should know about." Henri' was sitting in Pete's office, talking to his old friend. He took a deep breath and told the story as he remembered it. Pete didn't interrupt and after Henri finished he sat thinking about what he'd heard.

Henri broke the silence. "Is there anything you want to ask about?"

Pete was looking away from Henri now, looking out the window. He held up his hand. When he finally turned back he shook his head.

"It is impossible to say how this will affect him but it will." He sat quiet again for a while. Finally, he shook his head again and said, "I guess all we can do is be aware of the fact that it will and be alert for it when it does. We have to give him the space to deal with it and the time. He's worth it.

"I say we, but you are the one who will be most affected by these changes. You two are joined at the hip the same way you and I were all those years. The captain and first mate. Of a four-man crew, no less. In a close, almost intimate space. Closer than man and wife or at least some men and their wives." He smiled. "No one will be there for you to talk to but I know you well enough to know you'll probably get through it alright."

CHAPTER FOURTEEN

Thello, the black prince, woke Terresa by licking her ear. She opened her eyes and smiled. The cat had climbed on her chest and was kneading the bedclothes and purring. Among all his other functions this was one of the most important. It meant she usually woke up smiling. Unfortunately, the good mood didn't always last.

She had begun her new job with Jonas two weeks before, and so far it was like unsnarling a knotted ball of twine. When she solved one problem for Jonas, they would often find it caused another one elsewhere. Today would be her first day working in a small shack in one of the city parks where the Army would soon begin watching workmen building hundreds of such shacks to provide livability so people could get out of tents before winter set in.

The shack where she would work today was a place to take, process and organize applications and use the information to compile a list of the people who would move into the shacks as they were completed. Actually, they were being called earthquake houses now.

Working with Jonas and the newly returned Sun Li, she had created an application form that was as simple and functional as possible. Today she would begin the process of translating those applications into a waiting list of potential residents for these new communities.

When Terresa came back from the bathroom, Emily was sitting up in bed petting Thello. "So, today you meet some of the people you're going to try to help."

"Yes, and I'm a little nervous about it. From what I've learned, almost all of them will be women or girls. Most of the men are working around the city so it's their wives and daughters applying for the new housing. Many of them can't read or write. I've gotten a couple of girls from the high school to help them fill out the applications. I hope we can keep them moving through.

"But I hate having to do that. These people are the ones who stayed after the quake because they had nowhere to go or no money. They've lost everything, including family and friends in some cases and I'm supposed to hurry them through the process as fast as I can. No time for empathy, or commiseration. No time to learn anything about them because there are a hundred people in line behind them who tell the same kind of tale."

She crossed the room and began to dress chatting with Emily as she did. As she finished, the nurse came in and began the routine of getting Emily out of bed and dressed. There were days when Emily seemed to be getting stronger and on those days she wanted to join the ladies for breakfast. Today looked like one of those days. Her legs seemed to work better some days than others but at least she was moving toward something. Terresa had no such feeling about her own life.

Because she and Sun Li had agreed to meet at the shack she needed to hurry. She skipped breakfast but passed through the kitchen where she met Geppetto who was going to drive her to work. Jonas or Sun Li would pick her up afterward.

The process of recovery was creating blocked streets, and many wagons loaded with all manner of things were slowly moving in and out of neighborhoods. Among the things in those wagons were the lumber and other materials for building Terresa's houses. That's how she thought about them. When they arrived at the park a long line of wagons was waiting to be unloaded and a soldier was directing traffic.

The shack where they'd be working would be the first one of

them she'd be inside of. To her the whole job was pieces of paper; some went here and others there, some she did this with and some she did that. She'd hated that part of the job at The Crown and this was maddeningly similar.

Jonas and Sun Li were out in the city solving problems, talking to people, getting things done while she sat behind a desk shuffling paper. But today was different. These houses were real, and today she'd begin to see the results of what she'd been working toward.

At first glance the whole idea behind the 'earthquake houses' might seem like the response of a concerned city toward its citizens in need. There was, however, a very practical reason behind it.

Somewhere around 80,000 people had left the city in the weeks after the disaster. The people remaining included many of the workmen necessary if the city was ever to rise from the ashes. Carpenters, plumbers, builders, electricians, and laborers were all needed and to keep them from leaving, the leaders of the city acted.

The houses came in three sizes, 10'x14', 14'x18', and 15'x25' and cost from $100.00 to $150.00 each. They were built of California redwood with fir floors and cedar-shingled roofs. Painted a uniform drab 'park green', they were sited in city parks so close together that, in many cases, a fully grown man would have trouble passing between two of them. They weren't finished inside at all. Just bare plank walls so many would be papered with newspapers, magazines or wallpaper over the years. But all in all, they were a great improvement over life in a tent on a rainy winter day.

Since prospective residents were probably somewhat short of cash they were allowed to 'rent to own' the shacks. For two dollars a month, four if there was a stove, they could buy the shack with the proviso that they had to move it out of the park where it was sited by a predetermined date. At some point, the city would want its parks back. If they fulfilled these requirements, they would own the shack, for many of them the first time they had owned a home.

A lot in certain parts of the city could be bought for $100.00, the great majority of the residents would be able to use them as starter homes in the future. Over the years these beginnings were added to and remodeled and to this day many houses in certain sections of the city have an earthquake house somewhere in their ancestry.

Construction began in September 1906 and within a few days, the first residents were moving in. By November, when the job was completed over five thousand of the tiny homes were occupied by around 16,000 people, the people who had stayed to rebuild the city.

Teressa, with Thello on her shoulder, was waiting on the stoop when Jonas arrived with Sun Li and her two high school helpers. They stood for a while looking at the long line of women stretching for several blocks, all waiting patiently for their chance for a place to live.

Inside, along one of the long walls of the shack, were two small desks, each with a chair behind it and another chair in front for the client. The opposite wall was filled with four standing desks where the girls would assist anyone who needed help with the application. Along the wall opposite the door a low cabinet held forms and supplies they would need to do the job.

The women would begin by sitting at the desks to register with Terresa or Sun Li if she was there. Then, application in hand, they would use one of the standing desks to fill it out and deposit it in a tray on the way out the door. When they finished the application each woman was given a small wooden disc with a number on it. When their new home was ready the number would be posted on a board in front of the shack and they could move in.

To keep down the congestion in the office people were metered in the door as someone left. The idea was to keep the flow of people moving at a steady pace but like all ideas for accomplishing something like this, it was better in conception than in execution.

Some people took longer than others to complete the application so there were people waiting for a place at the standing desks. In this situation Teressa got to talk to some of the people she was assisting and learn a little about their lives and how they came to be standing in line for hours waiting for a new house.

Teressa had been raised in an atmosphere of warmth and trust and reaching out to help people was something she'd watched her parents do all her life. It was as natural to her as breathing.

Now she saw the value of the things she had done to help make this happen. Granted they were boring and tedious at times but sitting and listening to and talking to the people who came through the door hoping for something made her want to help. She was glad she was there.

She was talking to a woman not much older than herself when she noticed a young man in a uniform standing by the desk, waiting patiently for her to finish. When the girl left her desk, she finished writing something on a form and looked up at him.

"May I help you?"

"I just wanted you to know I'll be around all day. My squad is helping on the site. If you should need me, I'll be close."

"And you are?" He was young, blue-eyed, and slightly rosy-cheeked.

"Lieutenant Jonathon Harrison. We're part of the garrison at the Presidio." He touched his cap and squeezed through the crowd at the door.

She saw him off and on the rest of the day, helping a woman with small children, answering questions, picking up things on the floor and watching. He watched the people coming in and out the door and the people working to move them through the system. Most of all he seemed to be watching her. Several times she looked at him only to see him looking back and each time her hand flew to her cheek and she looked away.

She was very aware of the scar and the fact it was still healing and very red. She'd found that things she did to hide it retarded the healing process and, at times, flared into skin issues, so she'd finally decided to leave it to heal in the air. But when he looked at her, looked at her scar, for reasons she didn't understand, she suddenly felt ashamed

They closed the door to new applicants at one o'clock and for a little while helped the people still finishing up their applications. Lieutenant Harrison opened the door for the departing women and stood watching as Teressa and her helpers put things away and straightened up.

"Is someone coming for you?" he asked as he let the last woman out. He was speaking to all of them, and they nodded. "I'll wait with you, if you like.”

“It's not really necessary,” said Teressa.

“It's part of the job.” He smiled at her. “And a part I enjoy.”

“He has a nice smile,” she thought. She looked down at what she was doing and after a few minutes, looked up and asked, “Where are you from? From your accent I'd guess the Midwest.”

“Good guess. I'm from Ohio. A little place just south of Cleveland on Lake Erie.”

When she was ready to go everyone moved to the door. They stood and watched the girls walk down the street then Jonathon turned to her. “I take it you're from San Francisco.”

“No, actually I'm from San Diego. It's a little town down near the Mexican border. I was up here working and a building fell in on me.”

“Yes, that's a pretty common story these days.” He shook his head. “There's a lot of people living in tents. We need to get them under roofs before winter. I hope this idea works.”

They had been standing talking for almost an hour when Teressa began to wonder if Jonas had forgotten her.

“It looks like I may have to walk home,” she said, peering up the street.

“I'll be glad to walk with you.”

“Don't you have somewhere you have to be?”

“No, I'm off duty right now and as long as I turn up for duty tomorrow, I'm free.” He smiled that smile again. “And I can't think of anything I'd enjoy more than walking you home.”

She looked at him for a moment, a slow smile creeping across her face. “It'll probably take an hour to get there.”

His smile became a grin. “Good,” he said, and they both laughed. “Since we'll be walking for a while, tell me about yourself,” she said.

As they walked, he talked to her and she to him and they didn't pay much attention to time passing until a voice called from behind them. “Teressa?”

She turned and saw Sun Li and Jonas in a wagon coming along behind them. “Thank God! We were worried when we got there and you were gone," said Sun Li.

"We decided to walk." She introduced Jonathon to her friends and clambered into the back of the wagon with Thello.

"Sorry about the wagon," said Jason. "That's all we could find."

She waved to Jonathon and turned to speak to Sun Li. When she glanced back he was still standing there watching her. They turned a corner and he was gone but she had the feeling she would be seeing him again.

A noise woke Sarah, and she lay in the dark listening. She looked around, disoriented and tried to remember where she was. Suddenly a shaft of light came into the room and she saw Jonas at the window. He had parted the curtains to check the weather and he hadn't gotten dressed yet.

"Hi," she said.

He turned and grinned at her. "Caught me didn't you?"

She looked at him. The light was behind him so all she saw was his shape but she felt excited to have this man in her bedroom again.

She reached out to him. "Come here," she said. "Come lay down beside me. I want to feel your body next to mine." They lay together in each other's arms and rather than excitement, she felt contentment, a warm happiness.

"I've missed you," she mumbled into his shoulder. "It's so nice to have you lying here beside me again."

They lay like that for a while, listening to each other's breathing, feeling each other's heartbeat.

"Make love to me."

"Again?"

"No, because it was the first time in six years that was fucking, not making love. I remember the first night we were together and how good it was the second time we did it. The one where you took your time and touched and kissed me everywhere just so. Do that for me now." So, he did.

Later she kissed him goodbye at the door and arrived late for breakfast with Madame who was talking to Emily and Teressa. She looked at her friend, sighed, and rolled her eyes, knowing what was coming.

"Well," said Madame. "You look awfully chipper this morning. Care to talk about it?"

It was hard not to grin at her, indeed, she had to keep herself from laughing. "I knew that was coming," she said. "Does that feel better now that you've got it out of your system? And no, I don't want to talk about it."

Emily and Teressa gradually realized what was going on, and the room echoed with laughter.

"Haven't seen that much color in your cheeks for years," said Madame, having to raise her voice to be heard. "When's the last time you slept in that room? Has it been six years?"

Sarah stuck her tongue out at Madame, then smiled, remembering the soaring sensations she'd felt in her chest when she watched him walk briskly across to the car barn where he turned, blew her a kiss, and grinned at her. She knew she wouldn't have to wait six years again.

Teressa glanced down at the watch pinned to her blouse and crossed to the door to open the office for the day. Before she got there, someone knocked and she opened the door to see Jonathon standing there smiling at her.

"Good morning, Miss Fry," he said, nodding his head in a slight bow.

Trying hard not to smile, she replied, "Good morning, Lt. Harrison."

"Please call me Johnny. Everyone else does."

"Oh no," she replied. "I can't do that. That's my Papa's name. That would be too many Johnny's. How about Jonathon?"

It was a good way to begin the day.

For the next couple of weeks her life fell into a routine that was enjoyable and productive. Working six days a week they registered almost 2500 people. Another office was opened on the other side of town and the number of people standing in line gradually diminished. With about seventy new shacks finished a day by the end of September close to 4000 people were living in them and the tent camps were disappearing.

One of the things that made these days nice was Thello. He rode to work with her sitting on the seat beside her. Once at work he spent his time roaming the office and in and out the door. Teressa put a bed for him behind her desk and he was the official greeter much of the time, keeping children occupied while their mothers were busy filling out the applications and generally seeking attention by rubbing against everyone. When petted he purred and everyone who came through the office remembered him.

Teressa's walks with Jonathon were now routine as well. They talked about many things during those walks and soon she was beginning to notice things happening that surprised her. There were times when she would come back to the present with a start because she had been thinking about Jonathon and her mind had been a thousand miles away from what she was supposed to be doing.

"Madame tells me we have a guest for dinner tonight," said Emily. They were still living together even though there were vacant rooms in the house now. The people who had needed it as a haven had metered back into the city and life was returning to a semblance of normal.

"Yes, Jonathon will be staying."

"I haven't asked you about him before but it seems like things might be going somewhere between you and him."

Teressa sat down on her bed and looked thoughtfully at her friend who was sitting up in a chair. After a moment of quiet staring into space, she nodded her head. "Yes, it does seem that way."

"How do you feel about it?"

"I certainly know him as well as I know anyone outside the family. So far, I like what I know." She stood up and began to move about the room while she talked.

"At home I never paid much attention to boys. They were always around, and I knew I was pretty and could have my pick. Maybe I was not interested because of that.

"But it's different now. The world is so different than it was. The life I had planned is gone, never to return and I have no idea where I'm going or what I want from life. Maybe he's stepped into a void, given me a new path if I want to take it."

"Do you think the scar has anything to do with it?"

She stood thinking for a while about that. "Maybe. Everything is so insecure right now and I don't know where I fit. Maybe that's it. Maybe I'm looking for someone to help me fit in somewhere. Maybe the scar on top of the earthquake is what caused me to reach out for the first time in my life."

"Lots of maybes in what you just said but one thing is real right now. It looks like your job with Jonas will be ending soon and you'll have to decide where you go from here. Maybe wanting someone to hold hands with means you're reaching out for help in an uncertain time."

"Is that good enough to build a future on? I like talking to him, and I believe he'd take my hand if I offer it to him, but is he in my future?"

"I guess the question is, is he on the path you want to take? We all have times in our lives when we look back on untaken paths and wonder where they would have led. But whether this will be one of those paths or not is what you must decide."

CHAPTER FIFTEEN

"How do you feel when you think about piloting an airplane for the first time?" Mr. Midshipman John Tower looked around at each of the young men sitting with him on a train to Baltimore one Sunday morning. As one of the two 'Firsties' in the group, he was the unofficial leader. "I mean, what do you feel inside you when you think about it?" He looked at Manny and tilted his head asking for a response.

Manny thought about it for a minute before he answered. "The first thing I do is take a deep breath. I think that's because the idea scares me a little. I think maybe I'm afraid. A little anyway, but I still want to do it."

Ted Ellyson shrugged. "It gets me in the stomach," he said, patting his midsection. "I'd say that's right, but I'm with you," he said, nodding at Manny. "I still want to do it."

They were traveling to the city to meet Glen Curtis at a hotel downtown. Manny had exchanged letters with him and when he learned Curtis was going to be in Baltimore, only 35 miles from the Academy, he arranged the trip. There were seven of them and he was the only 'Youngster.'

"I'd say there's a good chance we might see a plane fly today. That'll be a first for all of us," said Tower. He looked at Manny. "When you take hold things seem to move."

It was Manny's turn to shrug. "When I found out he was going to be in Baltimore, it just seemed like a good idea to try to see him, talk to him."

"Well, I'm glad you wrote the letter," said Tower. "From what you've said this fellow seems to be one of the people working to get the idea of flying off the ground. This is the way new things happen because there are people willing to crawl out on limbs." He laughed. "Of course, sometimes the limb breaks and you fall. In an airplane, you'd fall a long way."

Glenn Curtis was an ordinary looking fellow with a trimmed mustache. Shorter than Manny, he was slender in the same wiry way. He was not only one of the few people in the country who had flown a heavier-than-air machine but he was enough of an engineer that he could design and manufacture the engines that powered many of the planes that were beginning to turn up around the country. He also was savvy enough to design and develop some of the improved controls that made the experience more survivable.

"So, you fellows want to be the first ones in the Navy to fly, do you?" He was grinning when he said it.

The midshipmen all laughed. Yes, there was no question about it. They all wanted that honor.

"Look, I've got to get back to Washington. My plane is being worked on so I won't be able to give you a demonstration, but I did want to tell you a few things that might help you frame your future if you stay in aviation.

"First off, I began as a bicycle mechanic, went to motor cars and now airplanes. As an airman you need to be a mechanic. Every time you go up in an airplane you take your life in your hands." He stopped and stood looking around at them. "You need to understand the machine, understand what it sounds like when it's right and know how to fix it when it's not.

"You need to understand how and why the wings are shaped the way they are and why they can lift you off the ground. You must always know what cable connects to what and why because ultimately, your life depends on it." Again he paused and let the words hang in the air. "There will be people who will work on your machine, change it and repair it, maybe even replace the motor in it. You must know what they are doing and why." He paused again and stood looking at them letting his words sink in.

A bellman hustled up with a telegram. Curtis read it and shook his head. "Alright, I need to get on the road. I'm sorry we can't have more time together, sorry you had to come so far for such a short interview." He stood and shook everyone's hand. As he was leaving, turned and said, "We're the ones who'll make all this work. We're the ones who'll get it off the ground, so to speak. We're airmen now. There aren't many of us yet, you know, but it won't be long and there'll be more. I'm glad to have met all of you and I know I'll see you again in the future." With that he was gone.

On the ride back to Annapolis, the midshipmen sat so that the seven could talk comfortably and naturally, they talked about Curtis and flying.

"What do you think, Manny?" asked Ted. They had been talking about what Curtis had said and how it might affect the way they thought about flying. Manny, as usual, had mostly listened. He recognized his position as the junior officer and as such, usually waited until he was asked for his opinion. It made him feel good that they always asked.

As the originator and organizer of the club he was recognized in a strange way as a leader and they considered his input valuable even though he was only a third year.

"I think what he said is spot on, but somewhere in the back of my mind is the idea that we will be the innovators in this new game we're playing. It could be that the future belongs to those of us who were here when it all began. As far as what he said about us being mechanics, I agree completely."

He paused and looked at Ted and John Tower. "I was thinking about starting a newsletter on topics related to aviation. My father can find us copies of anything printed on the subject and we can share them and talk about what we learn."

Jim Henderson, a Junior, chuckled. "That's just what we need. More things to work on."

John sat quietly with a knotted brow. Finally, he said, "I think that's a great idea. But, like Jim said, who's got time to work on it?"

Manny spoke up. "I'm doing some research on it anyway. Why don't I write some of it up and we can all go over it and see where it leads?"

"You're in the toughest year," someone said. "How are you going to find the time?"

"Well," Manny smiled at them, "I'll do the best I can."

John chuckled. "Manny, when you say that, I expect a thesis."

When he watched Colleen get out of the taxicab, he could feel his pulse quicken, feel a sudden flush in his face. When she stood before him, holding his hand and looking into his eyes, he thought, "This must be what it feels like to be in love."

She kissed him on the cheek and murmured, "I think about you all the time. More later."

When he looked into her dancing eyes it gradually dawned on him what she had said and he smiled, then grinned.

"You're really something, aren't you?"

She leaned forward and whispered in his ear. "Yes, I am. How do you feel about that?"

"It makes me wonder what's happening to me. But I think it's going to be fun finding out."

"Oh, I agree. I agree."

He wandered around in a happy daze for the next couple of days. He and Colleen usually followed Jack and Molly around Annapolis and the Yard, as students called Academy grounds, looking at each other a lot. There were even some furtive kisses, but nothing like on the terrace the previous year.

"There's really not much privacy around here, is there?" she asked. They were sitting on the bank of the Severn and he was pointing out various things they could see in the distance.

"No," he replied. "That's not something that's part of life here. Most of the time, you're with someone."

"I suppose that's the way it is on a ship?"

"That it is. And it's pretty close quarters almost all the time."

It was cold but sunny, and they sat on a bench watching a

sailboat race at the yacht club across the river.

"I know you're excited about the trip and living out there with my family," he said. "Tell me why."

She sat thinking for a moment. "I could just tell you it's a whole new life that will help me realize a dream all of which is true. But you want to know something else. You want to know how I feel about you, is that it?"

When he nodded, she looked away for a moment, out at the sailboats across the river scuttling before the wind.

When she turned back she looked steadily into his eyes. "I'll have a lot of time to think on this trip and the two things I'll think about more than any other are, what it's going to be like out there? and you. Is that what you wanted to hear?"

It was exactly what he wanted to hear.

They had danced with each other and with others, though with others they were constantly glancing at one another and now they were walking onto the terrace again. He'd relived the last time they'd been on the terrace in the dark many times and imagined what it would be like when they were there again. Now she took his hand and led him to the same bench in the same shadows as once before and when they were seated, she reached out and touched his face.

He took her hand and pulled her gently toward him, and then they were kissing, and he could hear the blood pounding in his ears, see fireworks behind his closed eyes.

An urgent whisper came out of the dark. "Cheese it, you two," hissed Jack. "Here comes Kathleen."

Molly's sister, the chaperone, was coming hesitantly out on the darkened terrace. "Molly, Colleen, are you out here?" No answer. "Molly, I know you're out here. You forgot you told me about last year on the terrace."

"I forgot," murmured Molly from a shadow close by. "I didn't know we'd be doing it again." She raised her voice and said, "Give us another minute."

"Half a minute, and I won't tell Mama."

When they reappeared in the light, Colleen whispered to Manny, "Is my face as red as hers?" She glanced at Manny. "Or yours, for that matter."

He nodded with a grin. "Bright red."

She hit him playfully on the arm with her clutch purse but felt like a queen walking with him across the ballroom floor where everyone was watching.

Manny and Jack were waiting in the hotel lobby the next morning and helped carry the luggage to the taxi that would take Molly and her sister to the train. After they exchanged hugs and kisses of farewell in a tearful goodbye, Manny, Colleen and Jack waved goodbye until they were out of sight. Colleen turned to her cousin. "Jack, you know I love you, but Manny and I want to spend the day alone. So this is goodbye for us too."

They hugged, then he said, "You do have a way with words, Colleen dear," and with a wave, he walked away.

She turned to Manny and with an impish look on her face, said, "You do want to spend the day with me, don't you?"

Trying to control a grin, he managed, "Absolutely."

"Good," she said. "I was hoping you'd know a good place for a picnic." She kissed him on the cheek. "And possibly a little privacy."

She stepped back and studied the look on his face. "You look like you think that's a good idea. Do you think that's a good idea?"

Manny came back to himself with a start. Her habit of answering the questions she was asking caught him off balance. "Uh, yeah," he stammered. "Let me think." He stood for a moment with a thoughtful expression on his face. "I know you'll find this hard to believe but I've never been on a picnic around here. It's not part of the curriculum at the Naval Academy."

She burst out laughing and they stood smiling at one another. "For some reason I thought that might be the case so I asked a maid this morning. She gave me explicit directions."

"Jack always says you're the smartest one in the family. He warned me about you."

He followed her into the kitchen, and soon they were walking along a road by the river holding hands while he carried the basket. Considering his acquired Midshipman's appetite, he didn't even care what was in it.

The directions led them to a place where the road turned away from the river and they spotted a path that seemed to lead where they wanted to go. They took it and were soon in a small clearing near a boat dock on an arm of the Severn. The quiet was intense, just the occasional lap of a wandering wave.

They stood looking out at the river and at the foliage around them and gradually got around to looking at each other.

When he reached for her, she held up her hand. "Wait," she said softly, and he watched her open the basket, remove a blanket, and spread it on the ground.

"In case we need a place to sit." She looked at him innocently.

This time she reached for him. In the process of kissing, they gradually sank onto the blanket and for the next little while, the world ceased to exist.

The loud cry of a water bird brought them back to the present and they lay breathing heavily, looking up at the clouds through the trees above them.

"We need to slow down," she breathed.

"As much as I hate to say it, I agree," he said.

"Tell you what. It's getting colder, so let's bundle up and sit here and behave ourselves and talk about what's happening with us."

"Okay, but only if you sit next to me so I can put my arm around you." He paused. "And maybe kiss you once in a while."

When she was settled close to him with his arm around her, she said, "Tell me about your mother, and your father too, for that matter, and the other people I'm going to be living around for the next few years."

So he talked about his mother and how she gave so much to everyone around her, and his father, who had spent his life trying to make his city 'worth the trip.' How he came west, met her, fell in love and decided to do whatever she needed him to do so she could keep on doing what she was so good at. How, with these two at its center, a special family came into being and how, soon she would be a part of that family.

She told him of being one of six who lost their mother with the birth of the last one and who raised the others because their father couldn't; of growing up with Jack and his family and always knowing there was someone to help when things got bad, which at times they did.

"I think we need to always be honest and straightforward with each other. I know that's easier said than done, but it's the way I believe a marriage should be."

"So, you don't believe the man should be lord and master?"

"No, I don't, but there's something I want to tell you. I'm not a virgin."

It was one of those statements that hung in the air while they considered it.

He didn't bat an eye. "Good, then you can teach me but that's a problem we're going to have. Whenever I look at you I want to find a place to lie down. But we can't. I'm committed to following a path that leads to a future as a naval officer and probably a career in the service. It will be another five years before I can consider taking a wife and you are starting a path that has the same kind of distant future." He smiled ruefully. "Not only that, but you're going to be all the way out there and I won't see you again till sometime next summer."

"You're saying a baby could very well destroy both paths we're on." When he nodded, she continued. "I know there are certain ways to keep from getting pregnant but I doubt if you have one in your pocket, so apparently self-control is our only choice at this point."

They lay quietly for a while. "How did it happen?" he asked. She understood what he was asking.

"Will you get jealous if I tell you?" He shook his head, and she continued. "He lived in our neighborhood. He was older, and I fell for him. Didn't take long for me to see he was just like my father and liked his beer too much. The first time he hit me, I picked up a fry pan and tried to brain him with it. One of my brothers chased him out of the house. He never came back."

"Tell me what it's like," he said. "Did you like it?"

She looked at him for a long moment as though she was deciding something. "Let's say it was fun sometimes. I've been dreaming about it with you since last year." She laughed. "Usually, I wake up smiling when I do. Do you dream about me?"

"Sometimes, and I usually wake up with a wet bed when I do."

They laughed together.

"So I take it you didn't get pregnant."

"No, but the problem is I don't know if that's him or me and right now I don't feel like gambling on it." She reached out and touched his lips. "As much as I'd like to."

They rearranged their clothes but her hair was beyond repair without a mirror, so she let it down, and they walked back to the hotel holding hands.

"Is it something worth waiting for?" She had stopped, and he turned to face her.

"Years ago, one of my mother's girls, Este was her name, had the same problem. She was fourteen and fell for a fellow named Roy. You'll meet them. They're part of the family.

"At any rate, they had to wait about five years while she finished studying with Mama and then went to medical school. He was right there with her, waiting the whole time, and they're married now. Have a little girl. I guess if you have a good enough reason."

He shrugged. "Tell you the truth, the way I felt a little while ago I'm kind of glad you'll be way out there and I'll be here. This is the hardest year I'll have to deal with at the Academy. If you were around, I probably wouldn't get much work done."

The next morning at the station, he followed her onto the train and got her settled in a first class carriage well behind the engine.

"Do you worry about men bothering you on the train?"

"Ask Jack about that. We grew up in a rough neighborhood, and I had three brothers and three boy cousins living next door. None of them liked to tangle with me."

He looked at her, at her long red hair, her blue eyes, and the freckles scattered liberally over her face and arms. He wondered where else she had them and smiled when he thought about it.

"You're thinking about where all I have freckles, aren't you?"

His grin broadened.

She looked at him meaningfully. "Well, if you ask, you can see them all."

That gave him something to think about for the next seven months.

CHAPTER SIXTEEN

She was excited and sad in about equal measures, not an unusual reaction for a young woman embarking on a train trip across the country in the winter of 1906 while watching her beloved's face disappear from the window of a train. The reason she was doing it was important, but there was heartache overlaying the excitement about the trip and the future that lay at its end. The word *bittersweet* came to mind.

But she wanted that future. Leaving Manny, being away from him for months at a time was part of the price of it.

And she wasn't just leaving him. She was leaving her life, her family. She doubted she'd ever come back to Boston to see them or lifelong friends again. Those ties, while not severed, could no longer bind her with their needs and she could shape her future as she chose. She wanted to be a doctor. Here was a path to that goal and this was the first step.

Her trip was cold, boring, and most of all long, but by the time the train pulled into San Diego she was heartily glad she had done it.

Her uncle had insisted she buy a first-class ticket and after the first day she blessed him for the choice. While the scenery was interesting at times, there would be long hours of darkness and she could do little in those hours but think about Manny and Dr.

Annaliese Fry. She was glad to have a place to think her thoughts in private without interruption.

After she'd settled in she sat looking out the window. The train was passing through some of the outlying areas of the town, and she could see people walking the streets, maybe shopping or going to visit a friend, ordinary things you did when you grew up and lived in a neighborhood just like hers.

Looking around her at life at home, at the girls and women she grew up with, at the lives they lived, she had come to believe the future they saw for themselves was not what she wanted for her life, and yet she could see the signs she was moving toward that future.

Manny's casual remark on the terrace that night had triggered a cascade of events that led her to this. Ahead was a four- or five-day trip in winter across a wild and dangerous country, some of it so sparsely populated it wouldn't gain statehood for another six years. And at the other end was San Diego, California. All she knew about the place she'd learned from Manny and she wouldn't know a soul.

The compartment she was in was clean, comfortable and even a little luxurious. The first two days she watched as towns and cities, farms and forests came and went in the train's windows, but because of all the thoughts tumbling around in her head, she didn't see as much as she should have.

Early on the morning of the third day she was sitting at the window looking out at the small town of Columbia, Missouri, when she noticed what seemed to be a family of four pushing a cart loaded with all manner of things toward the baggage car. They passed out of sight along the train and after a while reappeared, two girls about the same age and a man and a woman.

She was sitting at a table by herself in the dining car when they came in and looked around for a table. Finding none where they could sit together, they separated, and the woman and one of the girls approached her.

"May we share your table?"

She nodded, and when they were seated, said, "My name is Colleen, and I'm from Boston."

"This is Sam, or Samantha Ann if you're upset with her. My

name is Mary Elizabeth; people call me 'Boo.'"

Colleen's smile grew into a grin. "Why in the world?" she began but the woman anticipated her.

"I've been told as a child I liked to jump out at people and say, 'Boo.' My brother gave it to me. It stuck."

Colleen liked her from then on. Her husband's name was Skip and the girls were Diane and Samantha. They were leaving Columbia but had no real plan to go anywhere. Somewhere in California was close enough.

Skip liked to travel which meant they were usually going somewhere. They'd heard good things about Los Angeles, so that's where they were headed. If they didn't like it they'd go somewhere else.

Later in her berth after she'd turned off the lights, she wondered if her own trip made any more sense to people like Boo and Skip than theirs did to her. The idea that you'd begin a trip without having a destination or a real reason for going somewhere was puzzling. She smiled at that. But how much more did she know about her destination? Just the name of the place. That was about it.

She had shared a bedroom with her sister and various younger brothers until they became too curious and nosey, so the idea of having a roommate wasn't novel, but this would be a total stranger. And the people she'd be working with were strangers. She wouldn't know anything about anyone. Well, she'd jumped into the water so the idea was to swim. To do that she'd have to meet each situation as it arose and do the best she could.

She had no idea what a medical education entailed and never having been to a doctor, had only the sketchiest notion of what they did. She did have faith in her ability to learn, though, and had seen her share of blood growing up back home. Rough and tumble with boy cousins had produced bends and breaks, and occasionally some blood, and she had the scars to prove it.

She believed she could handle the education part of it, but the unknown part, the learning to live around new people and in new situations, she didn't know about. She knew, for example, that the family ate a lot of Mexican food. To her knowledge she'd never tasted any.

She had thought a lot about things Mexican lately. Of course, Manny was Mexican. Raised in an Anglo family or not, he was Mexican. More than that, Manny had told her something of the Mexican or 'Old California' culture of San Diego and she knew many of the people who came to the clinic where she'd be working were Mexican. Living in a city that close to the border she could see a trip to Mexico in her future. Would she have to learn Spanish? Maybe that was part of the education.

She sighed, turned over, fluffed up her pillow, and tried to sleep. But rapidly coming closer to so many unknowns, she didn't sleep very well or very much.

When she woke they were in the middle of the Kansas Plains. Flat country, brown and dusty in the winter sun, it stretched for miles out of sight and then some. Boo and the other daughter joined her again for breakfast and after, Colleen invited them all to join her in her compartment which they did. Skip found it too crowded but Boo and the girls, never having traveled first class, were fascinated by the novelty. Over the next few hours they talked and watched the Kansas plains go by.

"It's almost hypnotizing watching it all go by so fast, isn't it?" They had lapsed into a comfortable silence, the kind of thing rare with a new acquaintance and Colleen felt herself start.

"Yes, it does seem to have that effect," she said. They had been talking about their lives and where they were going. If she understood her new friend correctly, her life was pretty much constantly moving from one place to another.

Skip was a carpenter and could find work anywhere. They'd come to someplace new and it would be exciting and they'd do new things together in new places. And after a while, he'd get a look in his eyes like he was trying to see something in the distance.

"The next thing you know we're moving again." Boo shook her head with a wry smile. "I'd like the girls to have a home, a place to grow up. By the time they have any friends, we're gone."

"I don't understand. What if you said no? I don't want to leave. I want to stay here?"

Boo smiled a strange little smile. "I want him to be happy. I love him." She took a deep breath. "He wouldn't be the man I love if I made him stay. Besides," she grinned, "he always makes it exciting."

A knock on the door and the conductor was there with a warning. A telegraph message told of a winter storm ahead. Heavy snow and cold, and the train's heating system hadn't been working too well.

"We'll be stopping a few miles ahead if you want to get off and lay over till it gets better. They've got a hotel there where you can wait." He looked at Skip, who had come up behind him. "You want to keep going?" Skip looked at his wife. When she nodded he said, "Yes." The conductor continued, "If you've got any blankets and warm clothes in all that gear you loaded into the baggage car I'd say get it up here. Liable to get mighty cold before we get where we're going."

He left Skip standing in the doorway slack-jawed. He looked at his wife and the girls and then at Colleen. "Are you going on?"

When she nodded, he continued. "We can get to the baggage car from here and get the stuff without waiting." He looked at Colleen. "Can they stay in here with you?"

"Of course."

He held up his hand at Boo's protest. "It's going to be easier to stay warm in here but we don't all fit, so I'll find somewhere else. Let's get the things we need right now and get settled in." Boo rolled her eyes at Colleen and leaving the girls, disappeared behind her husband.

"I could help," Samantha said, pouting.

"Best thing to do is help me get things ready in here for when they get back."

It took two trips but by the time they had finished the four of them could burrow into a cocoon of thick warm blankets and quilts to the extent that there was hardly any room to stand. The problem was they had no idea how cold it would get.

The last thing Skip had said before he left to find his own place to weather the storm was, "I've heard stories of forty below in some of the storms out here. Staying under cover and hoping for the best is all we can do."

After he'd gone they were quiet for a while, thinking about what it would feel like at forty below. Finally, Colleen shook her head, looked at her three new friends and said, "It seems this might be a night to remember, one to tell our grandchildren about, as they say."

"I wonder where Skip will be in case we need him." Boo sat holding Diane's hand obviously thinking. "I've noticed the heat in here seems to work sometimes and not sometimes, so if we're ready for the worst, we can hope to make it."

She sighed and looked around the small compartment. "One adventure after another. There's something almost biblical about the idea of having to go through a blizzard to get to all that nice weather they talk about in California."

"Manny told me the last thing he did before he got on the train was buy a pair of long johns. It gets cold in Maryland. Not like San Diego."

"This Manny fellow you talk about seems like more than a friend," said Boo with a smile.

Colleen smiled back, then grinned. "It's the strangest thing." She looked at Boo in silence until her friend said, "Well, are you going to tell me what's the strangest thing?"

So Colleen told her where she was going and how it came to be. By the time she finished, Boo's mouth was hanging open in amazement. "That's the damnedest thing I ever heard. It sounds like you met this fellow one time, then wrote this woman a letter asking her for a job. She said yes and you're going all the way across the country to live with and work for someone you've never met."

Colleen was grinning widely. She nodded. "Yes, that's about right. It's not a job, though. I'll be working with her to learn about being a doctor."

"Where does Manny fit into all this? Is he a friend?"

Colleen, grinning at the woman's directness, decided to respond in kind. "Well, considering the way he kissed me goodbye, I'd say we were more than friends."

"How old are you?"

"Sixteen."

"That's how old I was when I got married. Ten years ago. Do you want to marry him?"

"Well, see, that's a problem. He is a midshipman at the Naval Academy, and he's got four years before he finishes. And on my side, if I want to be a doctor, it will take three years of medical school after I finish my studies with Dr. Fry, and I'll be with her for two to three years. So having children is not a good idea for either of us.

"All this is a problem because when we're together, we're always looking for a place to lie down. It was very hard to leave him." She looked at Boo and was ready to cry.

Boo shook her head. "Well, I'll say that you got a lot of nerve thinking I'm crazy. With us life's always an adventure," she shook her head in amazement. "But nothing like that. Is this like an apprentice thing?"

"No, it's an education thing. She's going to let me follow her around, watch what she does, and eventually learn to do it myself. She practices at a clinic in San Diego, and Manny says she's been doing this kind of thing for years, helping girls become doctors, that is. Manny comes home in August for a month, and then he'll be gone until the next August for a month."

"Wow, that's quite a long distance to carry on a love affair."

Colleen snorted. "Not much like any love affair I ever heard of. But we both seem to think it will end up working. He will become a naval officer and I will become a doctor, probably because we have the whole continent between us most of the time."

She woke up cold. Sam was sleeping on the floor between the seats and had pulled some of the blankets off her. She pulled them back gently and helped the girl cover up again. Then, swathed in blankets and wearing a heavy coat, she sat looking out the window. The weather had cleared, and a full moon on the prairie was beautiful. She marveled at how what had looked so cold and barren all day was now mesmerizing.

The train had stopped, and she assumed it would start again soon when someone knocked on the door.

"Yes?" she said and sat up.

Skip's voice came through the closed door. "Don't open the door. You'll let the heat out. We've stopped on a sidetrack. A train with a plow on the front will pass us and we'll follow it through the passes."

"Are you all right?" Boo asked.

"Yes. We've been working on the vapor heater and it feels like it's getting warmer in here."

"What's a vapor heater?" Diane asked.

"I'll tell you later." He was gone.

Diane laid her head in Boo's lap and was soon asleep. The three of them sat watching night fade away, gradually revealing the flat, formerly gray landscape, they'd become numb to now covered with a trackless white running away to the dark horizon.

The train became warm enough to serve breakfast and as they were eating they saw the snowplow train pass and soon were on their way again. During the night they woke occasionally to look out the window at the snow piled up along the tracks, and morning saw them in Santa Fe where they were able to stretch their legs before heading west once more.

It was here that she first saw the influence of the Mexican heritage that overlay the relatively new Anglo culture of the American southwest. Tan adobe walls, cantinas with guitar music, and shops with bunches of red peppers hanging in the shade of a porch. The men wore sombreros and serapes and the women, colorful dresses with combs in their hair, children, whatever their parents could afford. The occasional Anglo was almost the exception.

Santa Fe was settled before Jamestown and was Spanish and Mexican for three hundred and fifty years. The Treaty of Guadalupe Hidalgo ended the Mexican War in 1848 and the settlement added what became the states of New Mexico, Arizona, California, Nevada, Utah, and part of Colorado to the Union.

Coincidentally, gold was discovered in California in 1848 and when California was admitted to the Union two years later, it was the most ethnically diverse state in a nation of immigrants. People had come there from all over the world drawn by the lure of gold on the American River.

At that time Santa Fe was still in the Arizona Territory. The territory would eventually be carved into two states and enter the Union in 1912 giving the continental United States its final shape. As she watched the town passing in the train window she thought she'd like to come again when she could stay longer.

All day they slowly fell into the desert and by morning, they were in the mountains of California closing in on Los Angeles.

At breakfast on the last morning of the trip, she and her new friends were finally all able to sit at the same table.

"We have a surprise for you," said Boo when they were all seated. When Colleen looked a question at her, she said, "We've decided to go with you to San Diego."

"You mean to visit?"

"No, we're going to stay for a while at least. If it's a new town like you said Skip can probably get as much work as we need to live on. From what you've said it sounds pretty nice."

"Boo, I've never been there. I just know what Manny's told me."

"Well, we've decided, so that's that, but since you don't know anything much about the place, I guess we'll just have to deal with it when we get there."

"That's my plan too. In fact, it's the only one I could come up with."

It was late afternoon when they arrived and she felt her heart racing as the train squealed to a halt in San Diego, her new home. So far, she had been so busy getting things ready to get off the train she hadn't had time to think about it but now she could feel an emotional surge. She took a deep breath and she, Boo, and the girls joined the people queuing up to leave the train.

The first thing she had to do was make sure her luggage was there. Skip had gone back to the baggage car and had already loaded her trunk and bag onto a cart with his family's baggage. She had telegraphed ahead from Los Angeles and hoped there would be someone there to meet her. She looked around and saw a man coming toward her with a look of astonishment on his face.

"Colleen?"

She smiled and nodded at him. "You're Mr. Fry?"

He continued to stare at her, his mouth open. Finally, he shook his head.

"What's the matter?" She grinned at him. "Manny told me he wished he could see your face the first time you saw me."

"Did he tell you why?"

"No, I fussed at him, but he wouldn't tell me. What is it?"

"You look enough like my wife to be her daughter."

CHAPTER SEVENTEEN

Bobby woke up in the growing dawn coming in the entrance to the thatched hut. There was no door. Moving quietly so as not to wake the girl beside him, he quickly dressed and stood looking out at the sun beginning to rise above the mountainous island in the distance.

Of the islands he had seen in this ocean, Nuku Hiva was the one he liked the most. There was the house on the cliff on Grande Terre, he'd always want to return to, but this one was picture-perfect. Towering green cliffs, deep valleys and beautiful waterfalls. A perfect harbor and she was there. The girl in the moonlight. He had seen her once and always remembered and somehow knew when he returned she would be there and she was.

He heard her behind him, turned and smiled at her. She smiled back and stretched, arms framing the cascade of dark hair and beckoned to him. He continued smiling but shook his head.

"I have to meet Father Zacharie this morning."

"Will you be leaving?" Her French sounded strange, the island inflection different from what he was learning with Henri and what he heard at home.

He nodded. "Probably tomorrow."

She looked at him in silence, sadness in her smile. "So soon?"

Mirabelle was shepherding a Catholic priest in visiting his

scattered flock among the French islands of Polynesia. There were several more islands to the south, and then they would turn for Tahiti to take him home. Then Mirabelle would catch the trades and head for home herself, 3,000 miles away. With a stop in American Samoa and Port Villa in the New Hebrides, they should make it in about three weeks.

He nodded. "I'll miss you," he said. "But it's what I do. Someone is waiting at home."

She pouted at that, not realizing he meant Cap'n Pete. He didn't enlighten her but took her in his arms and kissed her.

"When will you return?"

He shook his head. "Don't know. Sometime."

"Will you remember me?"

"Always." He watched her get dressed and holding hands they walked to the dock where the priest was waiting holding a bag with his vestments in it, the tools of his trade, as it were.

He could see her standing on the dock, eyes shaded with her hand while he rowed the skiff out to Mirabelle.

"How old is she?" asked Father Zacharie.

"Tell you the truth, I never asked."

"She looks like a child."

"She's not a child. She knows her way around the bedroom."

"What if she becomes with child?"

"She knows the risks and she came to me. If it happens, she'll raise the child and love it like the people of these islands have been doing with that kind of child for many years."

"I worry for her soul."

"She doesn't, and neither do I."

He stopped rowing and looked at the priest meaningfully. "I thought we agreed you wouldn't try to convert me on this trip."

"It's not you I'm concerned about. She's just a child."

Bobby thought about that while they were boarding and later when they were sitting at the mess table, he said, "These people lived for many years without your God and were happy with the ones they had. I don't know much about Christianity, but isn't it part of your job to make their lives better?"

"Yes, that and to spread the faith."

"Well, you've spread more than faith. From what I've heard, hundreds, maybe thousands of people have died from diseases brought by white people from Christian countries. Sounds like they were better off before your God came along."

Shouts from the deck interrupted them and Bobby was called to maneuver Mirabelle alongside a dock where men waited to help with a small load of copra they would carry to Samoa where it would be transshipped to market.

The Marquesas were in the most remote area of the Pacific. Nuku Hiva was 3,000 miles south of the Hawaiian Islands, 3,000 miles from New Caledonia to the west and over 4,000 miles from the coast of South America. Even Tahiti, the center of French administration in the islands, was almost a thousand miles away. Getting anywhere from here took a long time.

Other than an occasional visit from a warship the islands were ignored by the rest of the world until American whaling ships began hunting in the Pacific in the 1820s. Using the islands for provisioning and repairs these ships brought increased contact with the rest of the world, but the price was high.

The diseases they brought with them almost depopulated some of the islands of the South and Southwest Pacific. Smallpox, typhoid fever, and especially measles raced through populations with no acquired immunity and sometimes as many as ninety percent of the people on an island would be struck down.

Bobby was napping in the cockpit later that day when Henri gradually appeared up the ladder from below decks.

"We are all shipshape and ready to depart. I've told the good Father we set sail on the afternoon tide tomorrow."

"You didn't need to wake me up for that," Bobby grumped.

"Rough night?" Henri grinned.

Bobby thought for a moment. "No, not really. Busy but not rough. Not much sleep. I was having a nice dream just now."

"About your 'moonlight girl'?"

"No. It was about a girl I grew up with. She was my best friend. I think about her a lot. Wonder what she's doing."

"Would this be Teresa?"

Bobby looked at him in astonishment. "It's actually Teressa, but how did you know about her?"

"Her name was on a letter you left on Pete's desk one night."

"Yes, that's who I was thinking about."

They were both quiet for a moment, then Bobby asked, "How long to Samoa?"

Henri stood rubbing his lower lip, thinking. "We should be finished on the islands south of here within four days, then six more to Tahiti, a couple of days there, then another week to ten days if the wind is fair and it usually is. Say three, three and a half weeks."

Bobby shook his head. "How long will it take me to learn what you know about the winds and the waves and this big ocean?"

"You will be an old man by then, my friend. A very old man."

He sucked on his dry pipe for a while. "Over the years I have also learned much about men. I know what to look for and what to listen for. Something tells me you're having doubts about your arrangement with Pete."

Bobby was quiet for a long time, thinking. Finally, he nodded his head slowly. "I'm thinking about home more and more and wondering what my family and friends are doing. Many things have happened to me in the last two years. I'm different. I guess I wonder how life has changed them all, how different they'll be when I see them again. And there's that: I have no idea when, if ever, I'll see them again."

"And Teressa?" Henri asked quietly.

Bobby looked at him in silence for a long moment. "You've seen the girl I was with last night?" When he nodded, Bobby continued. "Teressa is more beautiful. I've never seen anyone like her. She's Mexican. Her mother died, and her father left town, so a friend of my father's in San Diego adopted her and her brother."

Bobby smiled ruefully. "What do you call a man who sleeps with a beautiful young girl one night and dreams about another woman the next day?"

With a straight face, Henri replied slowly and distinctly. "It's the very definition of the word 'cad.'"

While Bobby was climbing the path to the house on the cliff, he usually reviewed all the things he wanted to talk to Pete about. Today, the biggest of those was necessary repairs to the hull. A rogue wave had thrown Mirabelle sideways as she was passing through the reef leaving Port Vila a few days before and as a result, she was leaking from a tear just above the normal water line. Not all the time but when they were beating on the port tack, the tear was below the water line and though the pump took care of the incoming water, the hull would need repairs before they could go out again.

He was thinking about that when he crested the hill and paused to catch his breath. Ahead was something new and he stopped to stare at what appeared to be a tombstone. He was reading the words carved into the stone when Marie came up behind him and put her arm around his waist. 'Cap'n Pete, January 1907,' it read, and below that, in letters carved deeply so they'd last, 'He was happiest looking down on this.'

"I went in to wake him one morning last week, and he was dead. I guess his heart just quit on him."

Bobby turned and saw Mirabelle floating on the clear water looking like a child's toy boat. He stood looking out at the ocean for a while trying to digest what he'd heard. He heard Marie walk away and after a while, return with the glass of tea he always drank when he sat and talked to Pete about the voyage just finished.

He had heard of people being stunned when they heard something unexpected and now he understood the feeling. His mind was blank even though on the edge of it he could sense a host of questions that needed answering before he could move beyond this moment. He needed to take what Marie had said into his mind and soul to somehow accept the reality that his guide and mentor wasn't going to be there to teach him what he needed to know from here on.

Now it would be what he had learned so far and what was in those books lined up on a shelf in the office. He had Henri's strong arm instead of Pete's, a good second-best, but he wasn't Pete. Pete's death would affect the first mate as much as it would Bobby. Twenty years as crewmates on a sixty-eight-foot schooner had made them a part of one another.

They had been so busy teaching him about his new life over the last couple of years they had never talked about what to do if Pete wasn't there. Suddenly his life, which had been moving forward on a plan he and Pete had worked out, was... he didn't know what it was now.

He would need to sit and think. There were many things that needed to be done, about the boat, the house, Cookie and Marie. He would have to go to Noumea, see the factor, and Pete's lawyer. But what about getting Mirabelle's side repaired? He shook his head, but that didn't help clear it at all.

He needed to sit down and think, so he sat in Pete's chair, hoping it would inspire him and help him work things out. The first thing was to get Henri up here. As always, Cookie had been the first off the boat but Rudy and Henri had stayed aboard.

He walked to the edge of the cliff, drew the pistol he always carried now and fired a single shot into the air. He could see Mirabelle clearly and immediately Henri appeared on deck. He looked up to where Bobby was standing, then reached back into the cabin, brought out a long glass and pointed it at the cliff.

When Bobby knew he could be seen he motioned frantically for Henri to join him.

It was an hour before Henri crested the hill, where Marie handed him a drink and pointed to where Bobby was sitting, in sort of a daze, looking out at the Coral Sea. He looked up when Henri stopped to look at the gravestone.

"Well, it's not a surprise, but it's a shock."

He collapsed into a chair and sat with a dazed expression on his face.

After a moment, he said, "Well, now what?"

"I was hoping you could help me with that."

Henri sat up. Gradually the shocked expression disappeared and he looked thoughtful.

Finally, he said, "It looks like Marie has taken care of Pete so I think the first thing is to get Mirabelle to the yard in Noumea and see what it's going to take to fix her hull. I imagine you'll have your hands full dealing with Trudeau. I think that's his name. He was Pete's lawyer for years and Degarde, the factor. Make sure you get all your ducks in a row, and then we can come back here and talk about what we do next."

"We can be ready to sail in an hour so let's get started," said Bobby. "I think I'll feel better if I'm doing something."

Before he and Henri went down the hill, they sat in Pete's office with Cookie and Marie.

"If I remember right, you got a copy of Pete's will?"

Marie nodded.

"Right now things are all up in the air and it will take a while to see how it comes out but this is your home as well as mine from now on, for as long as you live. I don't know what the future will be but I hope when we get back from Noumea, we can sit and make some plans."

They sat for a while talking about Pete. "He seemed like he was fine that night and he didn't call for me," said Marie. "I think he just went to sleep and didn't wake up."

"I'd say that's the best way to go," said Bobby.

Finally, Henri said, "With all we have to do, we should be getting to Noumea."

Bobby paused in his stroke, lay on his oars and looked up at the house on the cliff. He shook his head. "This changes everything, doesn't it?"

"There are questions that need to be answered," said Henri, nodding. "Then we'll know where we stand. First, you need to get ownership of Mirabelle established. Can't do anything until you do that. Then we need to get the repairs done. Once she's seaworthy again and you know she's yours, then we can think about the future. But yes, this does change everything. How and how much will be the next questions to answer once we've taken care of the first two."

It was coming on to dark that evening when they dropped anchor off the boat yard in Noumea. They snugged her down for the night then sat in the cockpit talking about the needed repairs and the need to check the rigging and running gear for wear while she was there.

"She'll be in the yard for a couple of weeks at least," said Henri.

"Could be longer if they're busy."

They were busy. Henri's visit to the yard office the next day gave him the bad news. A storm had caused havoc with some of the boats that worked out of Noumea. All they could do was take her masts down and haul her out of the water. She would sit in a cradle until they could get to her. Could be a month or more.

Bobby's visit to the lawyer and the factor, on the other hand, brought good news. Pete's careful handling of the will and the partnership agreement meant that both men had been expecting him and were ready to deal with all the details. Mirabelle was his. The hole in her side was a problem but they'd be as patient as they had to be. What other choice did they have? Eventually, they would get to her and she would be seaworthy again and he needed to have plans about his next step when she was.

The rest of the day was spent running errands and arranging a way to get back to the house on the cliff. Fortunately, a friend of Henri's had a boat they could hire for the trip and they left the next morning. On the trip Henri and his friend sat in the stern talking leaving Bobby free to sit by himself and think about things.

There were many. The idea of learning from Pete was a big part of his life. Thinking of a future without it was having an impact on him. Did he want to deal with the future he saw before him and remain where he was, or did he want to step away and see how it all looked from Mill Valley?

In truth, he missed his family, his friends, the life he grew up with, surrounded by people he knew and loved. Mostly he missed Teressa. She was the one he'd thought about many nights sailing under the southern stars. He'd wanted to talk to her about the time he'd killed a man, about how it made him feel about himself or about the world around him.

By the time they'd sailed into Prony Bay he'd decided he needed to talk to Henri about all the things on his mind. That night, they sat in what they both thought of as Pete's office and he told his friend what was on his mind.

"Should I go back home and see how things look from there?"

In his measured way, Henri sat and thought about it. "It is a big thing, what you're talking about," he finally said. "This is a cusp for you, a place where the decisions you make, or don't make, will affect the rest of your life. You must think of the life you want from here on."

The next morning, he was packed, and after breakfast, left with Henri's friend for Noumea. And San Francisco.

He would feel Mirabelle's absence every day he was away from her.

CHAPTER EIGHTEEN

She was a little late coming home from work, but when Teressa opened the door to her room, Emily was waiting for her. They usually went down to dinner together, talking about their days as they went.

When they came into the dining room she noticed a stranger sitting and talking with Madame and Sarah, but she was busy getting Emily seated and didn't pay much attention. When she was finally seated she looked across the table and suddenly it dawned on her who it was. She felt short of breath and dizzy and closed her eyes shaking her head.

She opened them to see Bobby grinning at her from across the table. She shook her head again and stammered, "What are you doing here? Where did you come from?" She sat looking at him, her eyes and mouth wide open.

"In answer to your first question, this has been my second home since before I can remember and also," he pointed at Sarah, "she's my grandmother, in case you forgot. As for the second, I got here on a steamer from Honolulu. By the way, Grace said to tell everyone hello."

She sat dumbfounded, searching for things she wanted to ask but suddenly very aware she didn't want anyone else to hear her questions. Or his answers.

Bobby continued. "Actually, I came from New Caledonia. I have a house on a cliff there overlooking Brony Bay, about twenty miles from Noumea, the capital."

Madame, always wise about such things, said, "Why don't you two go somewhere and talk? You obviously need to." Everyone laughed as they took advantage of the opportunity and were soon standing on a porch, holding hands and overlooking the city.

After a few moments, Bobby took a deep breath and said, "Haven't seen so many lights in one place since I left here." He turned to her and she was in his arms, and they embraced for a long time.

"I've missed you. That's the reason I came home. I kept thinking about you and dreaming about you."

"You sure didn't send me many letters, if you missed me so much."

"I didn't know how to tell you what I wanted you to know."

"Bobby, we have a lot to talk about, but first I want to know exactly why you came home."

He led her to a glider and sat holding her hand in his lap with his head hanging so his shoulder-length hair fell around his face.

"I missed you. I thought about you most days and dreamed about you most nights."

"I didn't know you thought about me like that. You've never said anything or let me know."

"Maybe I didn't know it myself until I was away from you for a while."

She punched him playfully on the shoulder. "Sure took you long enough. You know I've loved you since we were kids." She gave him a reproachful look. "What if you're too late? What then?"

"Am I?"

She looked at him for a while, her eyes looking into his as though she was searching for something.

"No. Almost though."

She sat quietly, looking at her hands in her lap. "I've changed, Bobby. When that ceiling came crashing down on me, something happened. I'm not the same person I was when you went away."

"His name is Jonathon. He's in the Army stationed at the Presidio. After the quake, I was working, taking applications for housing and he was assigned to keep an eye on the place. We became friends and he's asked me several times about marriage. So far I've put him off."

"But you're thinking about it?"

"Bobby, since that night I've been different. I'm..." she paused and looked up in the air, "afraid, maybe that's it. I'm nervous and afraid most of the time. But whatever it is, for the first time in my life I felt like I wanted someone to protect me. You were always the one I wanted, but you'd gone away. So, yes, I've been thinking about it."

He leaned forward, elbows on his knees and looked out at the city.

"I'm glad it's only 'almost,'" he said. "I've wanted to talk to you about something but now that I'm here and you're listening, I can't seem to get it out."

"What's it about?"

"It sounds like it's a little like what you just told me. The earthquake changed you. Something happened that changed me, and it's the reason I'm here." He straightened up and took her hand again.

"I killed a man out there."

She looked at him, her mouth open, eyes wide.

"What do you mean, you killed a man?"

"I pulled the trigger of my pistol, the bullet hit him in the chest and killed him."

"Was he threatening you?"

"Yes, he was but he was disarmed and had his hands up."

"And you shot him?"

Bobby nodded.

"You murdered him?"

"That's what I wanted to talk about. It changed me just like the earthquake changed you. I'm not a murderer, but I committed murder. I'm having trouble getting a hold of that."

He stood and pulled her to her feet. He was almost a head taller than she was and his hair fell around her face. She looked at him with a smile. "So they must not have barbers where you've been."

"You like it? Most of the time I wear it pulled back, but today, for some reason, I wanted you to see it. And now I want to kiss you. How do you feel about that?"

"Bobby, you've kissed me before. I think the first time I was ten."

"Well, you're not ten anymore, and I never kissed you when I felt like this."

When the long, thoughtful, and ultimately exciting kiss was over, she looked up at him and said, "It feels like you've been practicing."

He leaned back and said with a straight face, "That was before I knew I loved you."

She thought about that for a while, "I want to hear all about it, but first, kiss me again."

He did, and the whole kiss was exciting that time.

She leaned her head on his chest. "Why did you come back?"

He'd been thinking about that since he left Noumea, so the answer came readily. "Of all the things I left behind me when I left, I missed you the most. When it finally dawned on me that I loved you, I came back because I want you in my life forever."

"We have a lot to talk about so I'm going to make a scandalous suggestion." When she grinned, he said, "My parents are in San Diego and Gray won't mind if we use the house. Let's go up to the ranch for a few days and talk."

She tried to look serious but couldn't keep from smiling. "And the nights? What about the nights?"

"Yes, the nights. Well, we'll have to talk about the nights."

She composed her face into complete innocence and asked, "When do we leave?"

His father, Handy Josephson, with two other fellows, owned the Mill Valley Horse Ranch. It was spread across two low hills atop a plateau overlooking San Francisco Bay and when Bobby thought of home, it was here.

It was dusk when they arrived, and they stood looking around at what they could still see. In the distance, the lights from Gray's cottage were on and they could see horses cropping grass in some of the pastures close in.

He took her in his arms. "Will it bother you when they see us in the morning?"

"No, I don't think so. But let's sit out here and talk for a while. I'm a little nervous."

So they talked. She told him of her adventure that night. Awakened by horrendous noise into a strange, dark, dust-filled world, finding she wasn't alone, yelling, but no one came. Finally, Papa was there, and it was over, but that night had changed her in ways she still didn't understand.

"I was supposed to open in my first play that night. Emily and I had been working on it for months and it was as ready as we could make it. Then the building started to shake. If it hadn't happened, I might have been on my way to becoming a successful actress, which was my dream.

"With Emily and Madame in my corner, I felt good about the future. Then, in less than a minute, it was all gone and here I am working at a job I didn't seek or want but one filling a need at a time when it's important. This year, I helped thousands of people get a home and start getting back on their feet, but all the dreams I had? Gone, burned up in the fire. You know, it burned for four days. You'll see the ruins. There's still much that needs to be done. People like Jonas are leading the effort and I'm his helper. 'Executive Assistant' is what Emily calls me."

She shrugged. "I guess that's what life is. People become what they are because of where they've been and what they've been through."

When she reached that point in her narrative, he kissed her and suddenly they were kissing ardently, bodies pressed together, straining against one another. It was cold and for a moment, he stood with his arms around her, holding her close.

"Are you still nervous?"

"A little, but I might be feeling something else. Kiss me again, and then we can talk about it."

They left the lights off. It was his home, but she had been there many times growing up. She was a little surprised when he led her to his parents' bedroom.

"It's bigger. Mine is a bit small," he said in explanation.

"What will they say?"

"Maybe one day I'll tell them but not today. Come here." He held out his hand.

"Bobby, I need to wash up and so do you."

"That's true. A shower together would likely get out of hand, and there's not much room in there. Let me go first and I'll be quick."

As good as his word, he returned shortly, clad only in his pants. "I left my shirt in there if you want something to wear when you come back."

She took a deep breath. "Bobby, when I come back I won't have your shirt on. Given what we have in mind, what's the point?"

"I was hoping you'd say that."

But a few minutes later, she came out in his mother's bathrobe.

"Did you change your mind?"

"No. But it's cold in here." She turned off the light in the bathroom and gradually they could see each other. A half-moon gave the room an almost magical light, and he watched, mesmerized, as she untied the robe, let it fall to the floor and joined him on the bed. The light played across her body, but her face was in shadow when she laid her dark hair on the pillow and reached out for him. He took her hand and held it, continuing to look at her.

There were so many things he wanted to do, stroke her breasts or explore the darkness between her legs, but first he needed her. He wanted to feel her warm, wetness grasp him, feel her react and hear her pleasure. All the other things they could do later but he needed that first.

If she was still nervous, she didn't show it. He touched her, and suddenly she seemed to want to touch him everywhere, and when he finally entered her she whispered, "I don't know what to do. You'll have to show me."

"Just keep doing what you're doing, and things will be just fine."

And so it was. Actually, more than fine.

For some reason, there was no pain or bleeding, though he was her first, but they didn't even notice that fact until later. Afterwards, he lay beside her, and they held hands and looked at nothing on the ceiling.

After a while, she said, "Remember that time we sneaked down to listen at Mama and Papa's bedroom door?"

Though he thought it was a strange thing to say at a time like this, he grinned at her and nodded. "I remember there were four of us, and we almost trampled Manny when we heard them get out of bed."

"Well, now I know why Mama was making all that noise."

She suddenly twisted, and she was on top of him, almost nose to nose. "You are going to do it again, aren't you?"

He looked up at her with a smile on his face. "And again, and again."

"I was hoping you were going to say that."

In the gray light early the next morning, he built a fire in the stove and they waited naked under blankets on the couch for warmth to seep through the house.

"I'm not used to this cold. Where I come from, people don't wear many clothes."

"Let's talk about that," she said. "Tell me what it's like to live in the South Seas."

So, sitting on the couch, nude and covered with blankets, waiting for the room to heat up on a cold winter morning, he told her about living in the tropics. He took her from his first voyage through Pete's illness to the deal they had made. He told her of Pete and Henri and Rudy and the other people in his life and how his life was tied to Marie and Cookie for as long as they lived. He told her of Mirabelle and the house on the cliff. And finally, he told her of the killing.

When he finished, he sat looking at her, waiting for her to say something.

"Have you ever figured out what you need to do to get past what happened to you that day?"

"No, but just now I realized, since I saw you at the table last night at the mansion, it doesn't seem nearly as important as it was."

They were quiet for a while, then he rose from the couch, pulled her up with him, and enveloped her in his huge arms. After luxuriating in feeling her naked body against his body for a while, he said, "Let's get dressed and take a walk. I haven't seen this place for a while. We can talk about all sorts of things while we look around. Such as what the future holds for us, if we have a future together. Things like that."

She looked up into his eyes. "Bobby, after last night, there's no doubt we have a future together but that's just the first of many questions we'll have to answer."

"You sound like an executive assistant."

"That's another of the questions we'll have to answer. What about Jonas and my job?"

They talked about that and other things while they got dressed, drank coffee and sat on the porch watching the day warm up. While they were sitting there Gray rode into the yard. He was one of his father's partners on the ranch and had watched Bobby grow up.

"Hey, you two," he said as he swung down and tied the horse. "So, are you back to stay? I know they'll be glad to hear it."

"It's probably just a visit. I've got things waiting for me out there. But I want to see them while I'm here, so we might take a train down to San Diego and stay for a few days." His parents like to spend winters there with nice weather and the company of long-time friends.

He turned to Teressa. "Can you get free to go with me? We'd probably be there for a few days."

Gray was smiling as the scene unfolded, and now he asked Teressa, "Will you be going with him?"

She looked a little surprised at the question. Finally, she said, "That's one of the things we need to talk about."

"Well, look, Maxine's going to ask me, so I'll ask you. Are you married?"

It was Teressa who answered. "No. Maybe one day but not yet."

When Gray left, Bobby said, "Now that is something we need to talk about. So I'll start. Will you marry me and come to live with me in the South Seas?"

She laughed. "I hope you're not expecting an answer right this moment."

"No, but that's the first question we need to answer."

"Tell me, what would it be like for you to come home and work with Handy and eventually own the ranch? That sounds like a pretty good life to me."

He sat quiet for a moment. "This is one of those times when I wish I was a poet or a writer." He thought for a minute and then said, "Early one morning I came on deck just about dawn. There was a nice breeze and we were cutting through a blue ocean with white water curling away from the bow."

He stopped and grinned at her. "I remember that phrase coming into my mind at the time. Anyway, it was just about a perfect day and then a green mountainous island began to rise from the ocean in the distance. I knew that island and the waterfall in its green central valley was the most beautiful thing I had ever seen and the next day I'd hike into the valley and stand and look at how beautiful it was. That kind of day has been much in my life the last couple of years.

"The house on the cliff is also something special. And Marie and Cookie take care of it and me very well. But I came home because something was missing. If you come back with me, my picture of paradise will be complete."

She stood up, held out her hand and said, "Let's walk. I think better when I'm walking."

He respected her silence and they walked around the ranch for a while not really seeing that much because of the way their minds were grappling with questions and puzzling out answers. They were leaning against a fence watching some horses being exercised when she finally broke the silence.

"Yes," she said, watching his face, looking for his reaction to her pronouncement. "I'll marry you and go with you. But there are a lot of things to be done and decided. Doing this will affect other people, and we have to deal with those people as part of making it work. It may take a while."

"I'll be here as long as it takes."

"Aren't there people waiting for you to return?"

"They know to expect me when they see me. That's part of the life I live out there."

CHAPTER NINETEEN

Every midshipman who graduates has a period in his second year (Youngster) where he realizes he's going to make it. For two years he's watched the program regularly shed friends and classmates for one reason or another. But when he makes it to the spring of his second year in good standing he realizes he's learned what he needs to know to survive. The Navy has made him what it needs him to be.

On this beautiful spring day Manny was walking down to the boat dock on the river. He was alone, which was unusual at Annapolis and had in his pocket a letter from Colleen. He had decided that the perfect place to read it would be on a sailboat in the middle of Chesapeake Bay. As he sailed out of the river mouth he laid his course south and east and within half an hour, was dropping the sail and the anchor. For a few moments he sat looking at the eastern shore and thinking about the letter.

It was not his first letter from her but it was the first since she had offered to show him her freckles. He grinned whenever he thought about that. She amazed him. When he was with her, she made him laugh sometimes and think sometimes and the questions she asked left him open-mouthed a lot of the time. He was a long way from having her figured out but was definitely going to keep trying.

The idea she might be talking to his mother, having dinner with the family and maybe even sleeping in his bed was a little hard to conceive, but he smiled when he thought about it. Jack had noted and mentioned all the smiling.

He tore open the envelope and unfolded the letter inside. There were four pages and the writing was, as he remembered, a little hard to decipher.

Dear Manny,

I'm the redhead from Boston. Remember me? Hope so anyway. It seems to be best to start from the beginning. Your Papa met me at the train and his face was a study like you said it would be. I've had to get used to everyone looking at me like that. I guess I really do look like her.

When we got home, I was amazed at the house and how it looks. There doesn't seem to be rhyme or reason to it. Lemuel, who I really like, told me it had been expanded when needed, and as long as it worked inside for the people who lived there, no one cared much what it looked like.

I'm going to have fun in the store with all those books and I like my room and my roommate. In just the short time I've been here, I've already realized your mother is something special. She must get tired of answering the same silly questions we ask her. But she's always patient and wants to make sure we understand.

I'm getting to know the other people here and they all seem special too. There are so many who are considered family, I get confused sometimes, but they're all nice and helpful. I enjoy sitting at the dinner table listening to and watching everyone.

Several times a day, it dawns on me that I'm in

the middle of an adventure here and that always excites me. Everything and everyone is new. It's like I've stepped through the looking glass, and it's just been made for me. Thank you. I'm glad I came to Annapolis and I'm looking forward to seeing you in August. Sometimes when I think about the dreams I have, I can feel myself blushing.

Annaliese (that's what I'm going to call her) has suggested I keep a diary. All the girls who've worked here have kept one and found it helpful if they wrote things down before bed. That's when I'm going to write to you. I'll begin a letter each week, write in it every night and mail it on Monday.

I realize your schedule doesn't leave much spare time but write me when you can.

Love, Colleen

P.S. I may get carried away in some of my letters so don't show them to Jack. He'd never let me forget it.

Colleen.

He re-read the letter, tucked it into his pocket and turned to the boat. The clouds had crept across the sky while he was reading and gathering wool. A dragging anchor and the freshening breeze were pushing him toward the eastern shore of the bay but he quickly brought the boat under control and settled down on a course to the mouth of the Severn. Then he relaxed in the cockpit and thought about Colleen.

He thought about her a lot these days, in fact he wondered if she might be the reason his class standing had slipped a little this year. She was constantly popping up in his mind, sometimes in the middle of a class or some activity where he needed to keep his mind on his business. Fortunately, he was able to control it when necessary, as in the middle of an engineering class, but at times, he just let the thought of her take him where it would. Though his studies seemed to have suffered a little, thinking about her made him feel good, so it was a good trade.

That was a good idea she had to write a letter that way and he resolved to begin one that night. The evening study period was over, and he and Jack were getting ready for bed when someone knocked on the door. Jack opened it and was surprised to see Ray Spruance.

"I'd like to talk to Manny if he's here."

"Yes sir," said Jack and called Manny out of the shower.

Manny came out in a dressing gown, toweling his hair but stiffened to attention when he saw Spruance.

Spruance raised his hand and shook his head. "This is just a visit." He looked at Manny. "I'm leaving a day or two after graduation and I wanted to thank you for the work you did in the tutoring program. Those men you helped get through won't forget it. You've made some lifelong friends."

He looked at Jack. "Looks like you boys will have a great team next season. I've enjoyed watching you this year."

As he prepared to leave, he said to Manny, "I hear you flyboys are moving right along."

"We are. Got some new members in the club and we're working on learning all we can about flying."

"Johnny Tower says you're going to be mechanics as well as pilots."

"We met with Glenn Curtiss in Baltimore one time and he told us it would help us to survive if we knew the machines as well as the mechanics know them."

Spruance stuck out his hand. "Manny, do your best to survive. The Navy can't afford to lose men like you."

Almost as soon as the door had closed behind their visitor, there was a knock and Bill, a classmate, stuck his head in.

"What was that about?"

"He just wanted to pat Manny on the back for something," said Jack. "I like Spruance. Not many men would have made the effort."

"He's the kind of officer I'd like to work with one day," said Manny. "He's straight and solid, and when he tells you something you can take it to the bank."

Henry chuckled. "Take it to the bank? Where'd you hear that?"

"A friend of my father's used to say that all the time. It means you can trust what someone says."

Henry nodded in agreement. "That's Ray Spruance to a 'T.'"

Like all of Annaliese's girls before her, Colleen had begun a diary and was writing in it one night before bed when Janet, her roommate, came in.

"More of the family coming tomorrow," said Janet from the closet where she was hanging up her sweater.

Colleen shook her head and rolled her eyes. "I don't think I'll ever get them all straight. It's the darnedest family I've ever seen. So, who is it this time?"

"Annaliese's daughter is one. You met Handy and Rebecca, didn't you?" Colleen nodded. "Their son Bobby is with her."

"I thought he was sailing a boat somewhere in the Pacific."

"Well, he's back."

That evening at dinner she asked Maggie about the 'family'.

Magge smiled and shook her head. "You know, it still amazes me and I'm part of it." She sat thinking for a long moment. "I think it goes back to Madame. Have you met her?"

"Yes, she and Sarah are leaving to go back to San Francisco in a few days."

"Madame is a widow, a very rich widow, who lives in a

big house on a hill up there. She ran a bawdy house during the gold rush, never had any children, married rich and he died leaving her all that money. Living in that big house alone, she surrounded herself with people who helped her over the years when she was down. She remembered them when she was up.

"All the people at the Mansion are loyal to her. She sees them as family and is loyal to them. When Johnny and Annaliese and their friends started a bookstore in San Francisco, it became a gathering place for some people with that kind of loyalty and trust, and those people became family too.

"Eventually, you'll get to meet most of them because they all seem to spend time around Annaliese and Johnny. She and I went to medical school together and one day I showed up on her doorstep. My husband had walked out on me, and I needed a shoulder to cry on. I never left."

She gave Colleen a meaningful look. "You know, you'll be accepted into this family if you wish. It sort of goes with the position." She grinned. "Even if you weren't Manny's girlfriend."

Back in her room she thought about being *Manny's girlfriend*. She liked the sound of it, but she'd have to wait and see. She'd known him for four days in the last year and even though she loved the way he kissed, she wasn't sure a romance across such a distance could remain vital.

Of course, the way she had barged into his life might count for something. She was becoming part of his family and that was good. The nice thing was that she could become a doctor even if things didn't work out with Manny.

She was coming down the stairs when a woman approached her going up. They stopped and looked at each other in silence for a moment, then the woman asked, "Colleen? You're Colleen."

"Ah. I see my reputation precedes me and you are Teressa." They shook hands and Teressa said, "I'm just going up to my room. Would you like to come up and visit?"

"I need to see your Mama about something and then I'd love to. I shouldn't be long."

She found Annaliese in the kitchen, gave her some papers she had been studying and knocked on Teressa's bedroom door shortly after. When she opened the door, Colleen noticed the scar on her face for the first time and remembered that Manny had never seen it. He still knew her as the perfect, dark-haired beauty he'd grown up with.

It was a cozy room. Lemuel had built her a small balcony where they sat and looked out at the city.

"So, tell me about Manny. How is he? I can't imagine him in a uniform."

"He looked great the last I saw of him and he's doing well in the Navy. My cousin Jack is his roommate. He tells me Manny's the smartest in his class. I went with Jack's girlfriend to a dance at Annapolis, they call it a hop and we just hit it off. Fortunately, he likes freckles."

"He did grow up with them." She looked intently at Colleen. "You do look like Mama, but I'll bet you hear that a lot."

"Yes, I do. About Manny, we have this problem of having the whole of the country between us for eleven months of the year for the next three years at least. I sure will be glad to see him when he comes home on leave. You haven't seen him for a while either, have you?"

"And it doesn't look like I'll get to see him then. Bobby's just come back into my life like a whirlwind and asked me to marry him."

"Seeing you smile like that, I'm assuming you said yes."
"Oh yes. We grew up together, and I've always loved him. But it was like another earthquake in my life."

"Manny told me he was off sailing the South Seas, or something like that."

"That's it. He wants me to go with him when he returns there. I may be signing on as a deckhand on a schooner."

"Will you be sailing with him? I understand it's the kind of thing where they sail from one island to another, wherever there's money to be made."

"That's how he described it to me." She smiled. "I know it sounds romantic and all that, but," she shook her head and looked out at the city, "this week I've quit my job, a job I enjoyed and felt useful doing. I also ended a relationship with someone special and said goodbye to a wonderful friend. If I do this with Bobby, I probably won't see Manny again for years, not to mention my parents and the family.

"But I want to do it. It's a totally new beginning. I lost something of myself during that earthquake and what happened after and not just the future I'd dreamed of. Something else. I hope I can find that again by daring this adventure. And besides that, I love him."

Colleen laid her hand on Teressa's and squeezed gently. They already felt comfortable with each other. Teressa was grinning impishly when she asked, "So, what is it you like about my brother?"

It seemed like they were going to talk for a while and since Colleen was off, when Teressa invited her to lunch at The Del, she accepted and off they went.

The Del was a San Diego institution. A sprawling ocean-side hotel, five stories high with over seven hundred rooms, it was on Coronado Island on the west side of the bay, a ferry ride away. It was a first for Colleen and Teressa played the tour guide, pointing out landmarks, telling her about the city and The Del.

They also talked about their men, as young women do. They agreed Manny was very smart and good-looking, but a little shy. Teressa's description of Bobby made Colleen's eyes widen. "He must be something," she said.

"Oh, he is. But he's like his father, never lets it go to his head. He looks like Rebecca but he's big like Handy. He's something, alright."

When the ladies were shown into the dining room, there

was Bobby with his mother and father. Surprise all around. More chairs were brought, and soon five were sitting, talking and eating lunch.

May 1, 1907
Dear Manny,

I'm getting used to wearing trousers. When I started here, Annaliese suggested I wear them because you never know what's going to be on the floor in a sick room. Dragging the hem of a dress around through that all day would be very nasty. I wear them all the time now. It's easier than walking about in a floor-length dress all day.

I had lunch with Teressa at The Del Sunday. When we walked into the dining room, Bobby and his parents were there, so I had a nice time and got to know some of the family better. I'm still getting used to the idea of family the way it's perceived around here. It's much different from any family I've ever heard of, but, because I'm working with Annaliese, it seems I'm a part of it.

I don't think you'll be seeing Teressa when you come home. Bobby has come home to ask her to marry him and return with him to the South Pacific. She's already quit her job and is getting ready to leave. They're getting married this week but don't really know when they'll finally leave. Probably within a month or so. She told me she might have signed on as the deckhand on an island schooner.

I think about you a lot. Sometimes I imagine you counting my freckles and finding them in places I didn't know I had them. Makes me shiver just thinking about it. Teressa asked me what I liked about you, so we had a long talk about your good points and bad. On balance, you came out pretty good.

So what is there about me that you like? Let me know the next time you write.
Love, Colleen.

Manny finished reading the letter just before lights out, so he wouldn't have time to answer it until the next day. He lay in the dark and thought about Colleen and what she'd written.

The idea that Teressa was leaving with Bobby, and he might not see his sister and best friend for years disturbed him. Since he could remember, she had been the most important person in his life. The three of them had been almost inseparable most of their growing up years until he left for the academy, the other two leaving shortly thereafter.

He was glad they were finally together as a couple and grinned when he thought of them. He knew Teressa would write before long and tell him all about it. Bobby, however, was a failure as a letter writer. He'd talk to Manny about it when or if they ever met again.

Besides that, he had a lot on his mind. He had received his assignment for the summer cruise and finals were looming.

The next evening, he was sitting in CT's cabin talking about the cruise and what else was happening in their lives. It was the first time in a while he'd been out. The demanding nature of the curriculum meant that everything came to a head at the end of the second year, and he was busy most days preparing for finals.

He also was a committed attendee at all his roommate's games and this time of year, Jack was a rifle-armed catcher on the Academy Nine. He also stole bases, a skill not usually associated with the position. Whenever he was playing at home, Manny was in attendance.

That evening for a few hours he'd really needed CT's company and it felt wonderful to sit in a comfortable armchair on the porch on a beautiful spring evening talking to his friend.

"Heard anything from Colleen?"

Manny opened his eyes and smiled. "Just got a letter from her. Everything seems to be fine. She writes that my sister and my best friend are getting married and she's going off with him to live on a sailboat in the South Pacific. Actually, they'll be living in New Caledonia, on Grande Terre, near Noumea."

"Sounds like something out of a novel."

"He talked about it for years. She's always loved him, but he never really reciprocated, so it didn't seem to happen. Apparently, he realized it and he came home and asked her."

"Things happen and people change. We call it life."

"Well, I just wish she'd wait until I get home, that's all."

They were quiet for a while, listening to the noises of the evening.

CT finally broke the silence. "I've been thinking about it and I can't quite put a rope on the idea of you two having a romance. I mean, with what you're both doing and where you're doing it, I don't see it working in the long run."

When Manny was a boy, his father told him that when someone says something that needs thinking about, make sure you do it before you answer. He took so long to answer CT wondered if he'd angered his friend.

Finally, Manny took a deep breath and said, "I've been thinking about that myself since she was here and I think maybe you're right." Manny turned to his friend. "But I have to try. I think she's someone special, and if I don't try, I believe I'll always regret it."

CHAPTER TWENTY

"Want to talk about it?"

Over the years and through many friendships, Madame had learned to recognize when a friend or family member was having a problem they didn't want to talk about. In those cases, she usually left them alone, believing they would ask if they wanted her help.

But she and Sarah had been companions and lovers for many years. She knew her friend was troubled by something and thought she knew what it was.

Sarah had been sitting in her usual chair, a newspaper in her lap, staring out at the city and the Bay beyond, seemingly in a trance. It was easy to see her mind was elsewhere.

Now she started and turned to her friend. "I guess I need to." She ran her finger across her lips, smiled a sad smile and shook her head just a little. She took a deep breath and began. "You're a part of me. Have been for years." She reached out and took Madame's hand. "Because of that, I need to talk to you about something that's happening in my life, but I need you to listen to all of it before you say anything."

Madame nodded slowly, smiling.

"Jonas being back has shaken me," said Sarah slowly. "That letter from him on New Year's Eve years ago shattered me, but there was nothing I could do about it, so I learned to live with it."

"I remember," said Madame, still smiling.

Sarah put a finger to her lips. "I love you and have for years. No one could have a more wonderful life than I have with you, but I can't stand the idea of losing him again.

"He's a prominent, eligible widower in a town full of lonely widows and that's like catnip to a cat. I can't let him get away this time."

She was crying when she looked into Madame's eyes. "Well, it's not like I'm surprised," Madame took Sarah's hand and brought it to her lips. "I'll say what I've always said: you're family, come and go as you like."

Sarah looked at her for a long moment. "I have to know exactly what that means. This is too important for a misunderstanding."

"I guessed this was happening," Madame said, "so I've had time to think about it. It's not such a big problem. It means I want you to do what you think will make you happy. I know I'll still be in your life and I love you. If he asks, say yes." She grinned at Sarah. "I'll feel like something is being added to my life. Another member of the family, so to speak."

She stood and pulled Sarah into an embrace, kissed her passionately then said, "Besides, you're more fun when you just had a good fuck."

When the maid came in with more coffee, they were holding each other and still laughing.

Finally, Madame stepped back and said, "See, that wasn't so hard now, was it?"

It was evening and Jonas wasn't home yet. He was spending more and more time out in the city lately. He had taken on the job of planning for the removal of the earthquake houses from the city's parks and the restoration of those parks to what the commissioners thought they should be in the city they envisioned.

The men now holding the reins in City Hall had taken steps to correct some of the building flaws that had led to much of the damage from the quake, and a new city was slowly rising from the ashes.

This progress had to be channeled, and he was one of those who decided how and where. Donations were coming in from all over the nation, indeed the world and they had the money to pay the craftsmen and tradesmen that would give their ideas a shape. Those wages meant some people living in earthquake houses could afford to purchase a lot and move the house into a neighborhood in the city. Though it was almost a year until removal was required some people began the process early.

In addition to his work with the city, he was gradually getting his wagon yard working again, and that was becoming busier. He was working long hours just to keep up, but he was usually home by now. She wandered down to the kitchen and out the back door. The truck he drove at work was parked near the garage and she could see a shape in the front seat, leaning on the steering wheel.

"Jonas?"

She could see him now, dimly and he looked strange. "Are you alright?"

"I guess," he said and she could hear tears in his voice. "Hard to say right now."

She opened the door and slid onto the seat beside him. "Can I help?"

He seemed to think about that for a while. "You know, I think you can. Maybe you're the only one who can," he finally said.

"What happened?" she asked.

"I went by the house today. I've been there a couple of times, but for some reason, today it just did something to me. They were working in the neighborhood, and some have started to rebuild."

He looked at Sarah in silence for a long moment. "They never found the bodies, you know?" he said. "Ashes, probably. The rest of the day I've had this overwhelming feeling of sorrow. Not just for myself, but for everybody who went through this. It's as though the whole thing just fell on me and suddenly, I realized what's been lost. I've been so involved, so damn busy, trying to forget. I lost my only son in that charred pile of rubble and a good woman, a woman I loved."

He took her hand, and they sat quietly for a while. Finally, he said, "I had a good life when I woke up in Sacramento that morning and suddenly it was gone.

"And yet here I am working and healthy and in love." He leaned over and kissed her on the cheek. "I guess maybe I feel guilty. I've been very lucky, and I guess I feel guilty about that. And I think that bothers me too. Never spent much time on guilt. It feels strange."

He pulled her gently into an embrace and whispered, "I'm glad you were here to catch me when I fell."

Later, when she was in bed and he was sleeping beside her, she grinned into the darkness, thinking about what Madame had said. She did feel better afterwards.

When Manny's train left the station westbound early one morning in August 1907, there were eleven of his classmates aboard. There was much conversation among them about what they were going to do with their first leave since they had taken the oath to join the Navy. Manny was one of the leaders of the incoming class of Juniors and looking back on the first two years at The Yard, he felt satisfied about what he had accomplished. He finished the year in the top tier in the class and his quiet, soft-spoken manner and willingness to help classmates with the challenges of the course had made him many friends.

As the train headed west his friends began to drop off one by one at their homes until finally, he was alone. Before they left, they had talked, mostly about what they'd just finished and what they were headed for. Good talks with trusted friends, grousing about the future, hopes and ambitions and the people they would be seeing when they got home.

Now alone, he began to think about home. He would be there tomorrow. He thought about Teressa and Bobby, and Mama and Papa and the rest of the family, but mostly he thought about Colleen. What would they talk about, do together, share?

He could see her face in his mind but didn't really know much about her. Was the idea of a relationship like this across a continent doable? He hoped so because he thought he was in love.

By mid-morning, he began to see familiar landmarks, and when he swung down at the station at noon on the dot, they were waiting, his parents and others of the family. He was glad to see everyone, but as he greeted each, out of the corner of his eye, he saw Colleen watching him, smiling. Finally, he stood before her with his hand outstretched. She took it, pulled him toward her and whispered, "Kiss me."

He looked at her, his mouth open in amazement. She grinned at him and he grinned back. "Really? Right here?" She nodded and he did, and it was just like the last time. When they parted, she leaned her head on his chest and mumbled, "That's what I've been dreaming about."

He held her at arm's length and asked, "Really?" When she nodded, he said, "Me too."

He wondered if he'd get dizzy every time he kissed her. So far that seemed to be the case.

"There's a surprise for you at the store," she said when they were settled in the back seat of the automobile.

"A welcome home party?"

"That too, but something else. Something special."

He cleaned up from travel and when he came down for dinner, the family was waiting for him. He sat down and was talking to Papa when someone put their hands over his eyes.

"Teressa!" he said, grinning, and he was out of his chair and embracing his sister.

That night at the table, Colleen sat with her roommate as usual and he sat with the family talking, but their eyes were constantly meeting. Of course, everyone noticed and smiled about it. They would have their time together but tonight was for family. That night she slept in her bed, and he slept in his. But they had plans. A note, passed when he bid her good night, led to a nice early breakfast in the kitchen and a hasty escape to a one-horse shay for use on a beautiful day.

Even in the short time she had lived there, Colleen had her special places, but she let him drive and trusted him to go someplace special to him. He did. The cabin sat in a small clearing, and it made a perfect picture of what a home should be like.

When he pulled in and stopped at the hitch rail, she was surprised.

"Do you know who lives here?"

"Sure, the couple who live here are two of Papa's oldest friends." He held out his hand to help her out of the shay and looked at her curiously. "You've met Wash and Woman, haven't you?"

"I've seen them, but we were never introduced. They're family, right?"

"Oh yeah. Wash is an old fellow now. He came west with Papa back in the 1880s. He was a slave who joined the Union Army when he was freed. He was a 'buffalo soldier' for a while, then he just left and came west. Roamed around the Rockies for years and met Papa and Handy in Wyoming, and they just seemed to be comfortable together. Been together ever since.

"She was Madame's bodyguard who became her friend. She carries a Bowie knife in her back belt and if tales be true, she's used it a time or two. Papa told me when I was growing up that they were scarred and because of that, they don't like to be around people." They stopped walking and he looked at her meaningfully. "When Johnny Fry needs to talk about something, he wants to see Wash."

"That's something to remember. So where are they?" She looked around, taking in the small, neat cottage, the well-kept yard, and the creek she could hear as it ran by the house on the way to the beach. "Where are we going?"

"To somewhere we can be alone," he said, grinning at her conspiratorially.

"Where did you say they were?"

They had arrived at a small clearing with a large flat stone in the back part of it and he stopped.

"I imagine they're at work. They manage the nursery for Kate. I think they're part owners, actually. She's on the council and it leaves her free to do what she wants which she usually does with Lemuel.

"Lemuel is Papa's partner in The BookSeller. They came west with them to San Francisco. All of the people we've been talking about are family, in case you were wondering." She stopped his flow of words with a kiss and they embraced. It became an all-encompassing thing and the world ceased to exist for a moment that seemed at once forever yet not quite long enough.

When they came back to this world they sat holding one another until she finally said, "We need to have a talk. What do we do about this?" She shook her head, searching for a word to describe what she'd been feeling. "This thing which seems to happen whenever we're together?" she finally finished. She sat looking at him keenly. When he didn't respond, she continued. "You need to ask your mother about ways to keep from getting pregnant."

He looked at her in silence for a long moment. "You want me to talk to my mother about how to keep from getting a girl pregnant?" he said in a tone of disbelief.

She closed her eyes, tried to keep from laughing at the look on his face, but failed. She burst out laughing and eventually, he joined her and eventually, they ended up kissing and just looking at one another. Time passed, and he finally stood up and said, "This is getting painful."

"I noticed," she said. Standing, she took his hand. "Let's walk. By the way, why are you wearing your pistol?"

"I thought since we were coming out here, I might go down on the beach and shoot a little."

"Jack told me you're really good with that thing."

"Papa's better. He's been shooting since he was a kid and he started teaching me when I was about seven. When we're home, we practice together regularly."

He was leading her along a path while they were talking and eventually helped her down a cliff to the beach where a small bay opened up to the ocean.

They found a piece of driftwood and sat holding hands while he pointed here and there at things, sharing what he knew of the place with her. Finally, he stood up and asked, "Would you like to try?"

She shook her head. "Maybe later. For now, I'll just watch."

For the next half hour he worked with the Colt, reducing several pieces of driftwood to splinters. He always enjoyed handling the gun. On rainy days he and Papa would sometimes sit in the stable and clean the weapons and work on drill, just drawing and cocking the pistols with no ammunition involved. For the last two years, his sessions with CT had reminded him of home, of his father, and of this secluded little beach. It was one of the reasons he enjoyed the man's company. They usually talked about home.

He stood looking down at her loading the Colt. "I like doing things with you. Of course, when there's kissing involved it's better, but just talking to you is nice. It's going to be hard to leave when the time comes."

"Yes, and we need to talk about that. It seems to me we have feelings for each other. The question is, can these feelings survive seeing each other one month a year for the next however many years?" They sat looking at each other pondering the question. Finally, he sighed deeply. "I sure hope so. I like feeling like this and I would like to have it be a part of my life." He leaned forward and kissed her and when it was through, she whispered, "For the rest of my life."

Every once in a while there's a kiss you'll always remember.

They were in the shay on the way back to town when she said, "About that other thing. I guess it would be easier for me to ask Maggie about it. I like her. She's easy to work with and I learn a lot from her."

"It won't take them long to figure it out anyway and I'll have to ask Mama about sleeping together, assuming that was what you wanted."

"I'll have to think about it. Annaliese has given me three days off since you're here, but I'm here to learn and we'll have to work around that."

The next day when she saw Annaliese she decided to talk to her after all. It was a serious question and they would not be able to keep it a secret if they found a way to mitigate the possibility of pregnancy and began to sleep together while he was here.

Annaliese looked up and smiled at her when she came in and seated herself in a chair beside the desk. "It's nice to have him home. And I'm glad you two seem to have hit it off."

"That's what I need to talk to you about. It's getting difficult for us to spend time together. It's not easy to talk to you about it, but I can't think of any way around it. I need to talk to you about how to make love without getting pregnant."

Annaliese grinned in spite of herself. "It's not like that's a surprise. It was easy to see it coming." She thought for a moment then said, "We had a girl here a few years back that had a similar problem. They worked it out and I was pretty much a part of the solution, so I know what's possible. What I need to do is to see what's new in that area. Then we can make a plan. Can you two behave for a couple of days?"

"We'll make it. It's really a problem though. We both have futures we're working toward and a child could end it all."

"I understand. I'm glad you felt you could come to me. Makes me feel good. I understand your impatience. I've seen articles in some of the journals we get so it shouldn't take too long."

They were sitting on a terrace at the Del waiting to have dinner with Maggie and her friend. Of the people she'd met since her arrival, Maggie was her favorite.

"Our relationship, such as it is," said Manny, "has some strange contrasts in it." They sat side by side in rocking chairs, his hand resting on hers.

"What do you mean?"

"One moment it's the stuff of daydreams and fantasies, the next we're wrestling with the realities of it." He took off his hat and ran a hand over his short hair. "I know it wasn't fun for you to talk to Mama about that, but the realities of our situation have to be considered. The idea of seeing your hair spread out on a pillow is exciting, but how much is it worth?"

"You can see my hair on a pillow anytime you like. We just have to keep our clothes on."

"No, I'll wait. Mama will let us know as soon as she can. She's good about things like that, and she knows how important it is to us.

"When I see your hair like that, I want to see the rest of you too. All your freckles."

She grinned at him. "How long do you think it would take to count them all?"

When he lay in bed that night, it was all he could think about.

CHAPTER TWENTY-ONE

It was early and Teressa came out on deck wrapped in a shawl. Even though it was August, the breeze was chilly. She stood near the stern where she could see the wake and looked toward home. There was nothing but the gray line along the horizon. It was gone. All she could see was water, dark water. She wondered when she'd see home again, if ever.

Behind her, Bobby put his arms around her and buried his face in her hair. "I love to smell your hair."

They stood like that for a while. Finally, she turned and asked, "What else do you love about me?"

"Everything." He kissed her and when they parted said, "But you knew that already. You just like to hear me say it, don't you?"

She leaned against his chest and smiled when he wrapped his arms around her. "Yes. Every day for at least the first year. Then we'll see."

They stood like that for a while, the wind whipping around them. "Let's take a walk," he said.

The ship was not really very long and there were places where things were tied down under tarps on the deck but they were able to navigate along the rail to the bow where the breeze was even stronger. Now she was looking into tomorrow.

For a while they stood there letting the wind buffet them, arms around each other, braced against the rail to the heave and pitch of the small steamer. They were in the lee of the bridge before he spoke again.

"You're awfully quiet."

"Just thinking. I'm glad we waited for Manny to come home before we left."

"I'm not in a hurry to get back. I wanted to see him too. You know, I think he might have his hands full with Colleen. She seems to be a live one."

"That's a good description of her. She's not shy, that's for sure. I'm glad Manny's found someone like her although I'm not sure it will happen. There are a lot of things working against it. But I'll say this, he'll really look forward to coming home. He's become a man in two short years."

"Mama likes her, says she's quick and works hard. She seems to be settling in really well."

"She sure does look like your mother."

"I'll be willing to bet Mama was a lot like that when she was that age. She started working with the Doctor when she was about ten, and by the time she was sixteen, she was pretty much his nurse and ran the hospital when he wasn't around. I can just see Colleen doing something like that. Did Mama show you the letter she wrote?"

"No, she told me about it."

"It took a lot of courage for her to do this thing with the clinic. She's a long way from home if something goes wrong."

"I'll bet she's got courage to spare. Like you. You're going halfway around the world with a strange man to a place you've never been."

Suddenly he picked her up and stood holding her in his arms. "I just realized. I never carried you over the threshold."

"Bobby," she squealed, "you can't carry me down the steps to that tiny cabin. You'll break your neck, mine too probably."

"Hmm," he said. "You're probably right. You won't decide to leave me over it, will you?"

When she shook her head, he lowered her to the deck. "You know that cabin's so small the only thing we'll be able to do in there is lie down.”

She tried to suppress a grin. “I think you’re right. Well, if we have to, we have to.”

Of course, on a trip across the largest ocean in the world that takes more than three weeks, small room or not, you can’t spend the whole time lying down, even if you’re just sleeping. So they talked.

They had one advantage over the average young married couple. They had grown up together and knew each other pretty well. The two of them, plus Manny, had spent a lot of time together growing up despite living almost five hundred miles apart.

His parents usually spent winters in San Diego and there were visits and longer between the families regularly. She knew her way around the ranch because she had spent many summers there, and he had sailed San Diego Bay almost as much as San Francisco Bay.

Besides all that, they could talk about the future. She had a million questions and he usually had the answers. She learned about the new people in their life, the places they would go, where and how they would live.

She also learned about her chief rival for his affections, the graceful, beautiful schooner, *Mirabelle*. She saw the look in his eyes when he talked about her and smiled to herself. Maybe she’d come to love the boat herself before much time had passed. That was the best way to handle a rival.

They arrived in Honolulu in the evening, spent a last night aboard and were at Grace’s office at nine the next morning, totally surprising her. They arranged to meet for lunch, dropped their luggage at her house, and took a walk along the beach the rest of the morning.

Teressa had picked up the habit of wearing trousers when working in the recovery effort and found them so convenient and comfortable she continued it. She got some strange looks at times but ignored them and soon saw an amazing variety of dress and language in this, her first contact with the culture of the South Seas. She and Bobby had decided that pants made sense on a boat, male or female and didn’t care what anyone else thought.

They sat over lunch for several hours and talked. Grace had been

Annaliese's first intern and was there when Teressa joined the family. Teressa remembered sitting, watching her and Este, another intern, talk together at dinner and had always looked up to her. She remembered how sad she'd felt when Grace departed for medical school.

Bobby left to check on their berths for the rest of the trip while the ladies continued to sit and talk.

"Don't you have to get back to the office?"

"No. Emily knows where I am if they need me. I'm never very busy. There's a lot of cultural resistance to the idea of a woman doctor here. Not the natives, but many of the Orientals still go to quack apothecaries or use folk medicine."

"That was my best friend's name in San Francisco, Emily. We lived together in a nice little apartment. I had to give her my cat. No cats allowed on board. He saved my life one time, during the earthquake. I miss him."

"Was he black?"

"Yes He looked like Jinx, but a little bigger."

"I heard about you getting trapped in the building. You were working on becoming an actress, weren't you?"

When Teressa nodded she continued. "But now you're going off to the South Sea to live your life."

Teressa smiled ruefully. "Yes. You never know, but if the quake hadn't happened, I don't think I'd even be married, much less going halfway around the world to live on a sailboat. When I went to bed that night I expected to open for the first time at the Crown Theater the next night. I was going to be an actress." She paused, shook her head and shrugged. "Suddenly the world changed and I had to change with it."

"You know we have something in common."

When Teressa looked at her, a question on her face, she continued. "Annaliese Fry. We were lucky when we hooked up with that family."

"Yes, we were. Manny's home on leave, so at least I got to see him. We've been saying goodbyes for the last three months to the rest of the family. And now we're on our way."

"It sounds like you and Colleen have a lot in common."

She thought about that for a moment. "I think so too. We're both walking away from a life we don't want and into an unknown. I'm sorry I'll miss getting to know her better."

"There are always letters."

"That's true. I guess I'll have a lot of time to write, living the life Bobby has described."

"How do you feel about that life?" She held up her hand. "If you don't want to answer that, I understand, but I sit around a lot here and I've taken to writing while I wait for patients that never show up. I'm looking for ideas."

"I don't have problems with talking about it. Bobby has told me a lot and it sounds like it will be lovely, challenging at times, but lovely."

"I thought you wanted to be an actress?"

Teressa touched the scar on her cheek and looked at Grace meaningfully. She sat quiet for a while, thinking. "I guess I felt while I was on stage everyone would be looking at this," she tapped her cheek again, "instead of listening to what I was saying or watching what I was doing.

"I feel different since the quake. I almost said yes to a young soldier in San Francisco during the recovery but Bobby showed up, so I married him instead. I guess I feel I need someone to protect me, to keep me from being hurt. At home, Papa was always there and Mama and everyone else in the family. While I was trapped in that building for two days it dawned on me that I was on my own. I was a big girl and the world wasn't quite as safe as I'd always believed."

She shrugged. "I've loved Bobby since I can remember and I'm glad we're married, but a friend of mine told me once that I didn't have to hitch myself to someone else's wagon." She smiled at Grace, a rueful smile. "But that's exactly what I've done. And yet I'm excited and looking forward to what we've planned. But this was his dream. I had no idea about living halfway around the world on the edge of civilization."

She sighed and shook her head. "It's his wagon."

They sat in silence for a while, then Teressa gave her a meaningful look. "I hope I can count on you not mentioning this conversation to Bobby."

Grace was having trouble keeping from smiling.

"As of a minute ago, you're my patient. My lips are sealed. You know I'm family, don't you?"

"I hadn't thought about it. I just trusted you."

They were at sea again, this time on a working steamer with a stop in Noumea sometime in the future. It was not designed for passengers but carried a few from time to time. It was crude but livable, and since they were going to be aboard for a month, they added what they could to make it more comfortable.

On the third day out, Teressa woke up nauseous and before she could control it, vomited into a container by the bed. After several mornings like this it dawned on her that she was pregnant, not seasick. Considering she and Bobby were young lovers, she shouldn't have been surprised, but she was.

She lay on the small bed in the small cabin, stomach growling, the smell of vomit in the air and wondered if her sometimes oblivious husband realized it. Like always, he'd been up with the sun and when she'd finally gotten washed, dressed, and staggered onto deck, she saw him sitting in a deck chair near the stern.

He looked up at her. "Still feeling bad?" he asked.

She nodded and took a lungful of the ocean air. "I think I'm pregnant."

He looked at her with his mouth open while the words hung in the air. "Pregnant?" She nodded. "Are you sure?"

She nodded again. "No one else is getting sick from the food and I've never been seasick in my life, so yes, I'm pretty sure."

She sat in a chair next to him and they both stared at the ocean.

After a while, she continued. "Over the years I've learned enough from Mama to know all this vomiting is making me dehydrated. That's bad. I need to drink water or maybe tea. Not coffee."

"On a voyage this long that could be a problem," he said. "We'll likely be at sea for another two weeks and all the freshwater we have is what we carry. I'll talk to the captain and the purser. You know we don't have a doctor on board."

"I remember. Is there a chance we can get there a little quicker?"

"I don't know. I'll talk to the captain about that too, but first let me sit here and try to understand it."

"I think I need to do the same thing. I never thought about children before we got married. I was going to be an actress." She took another lungful of ocean air and leaned back with her eyes closed. "Tell me about the house on the cliff again."

For the next few days, whenever she felt like it, they sat on the deck in the shade and he told her of the house on the cliff, about Cookie and Marie, how Pete's will had bound him to allow them to continue with him as they had with Pete. He told her about standing on the cliff and looking down at Mirabelle floating on brilliant blue water and how every morning the birdsong was so loud it was impossible to get up in a bad mood.

"This thing with Cookie and Marie. Is it like they're slaves? Do you own them?"

"Of course not. If either of them wants to leave at any time, they can. I'm the one who's bound. It was a part of the contract we signed when Pete first brought me in with him. They've been with him since they were children."

"You've talked to them about it since he died?"

"Oh yes. They're in the will and heard it read after Pete died. They want to stay with me." He paused and smiled at her. "With us, that is."

"What about Henri? Was he in the will?"

"No. If he wants it he can have Pete's half. But we've talked about it. He's not interested in owning Mirabelle, or any boat for that matter. He's a first mate and that's all he wants to be."

"Tell me about Noumea."

"Not much to tell. It's a decent-sized town. Got a couple of boat yards because a lot of people on the island make their living on the water. Lots of government offices." He rolled his eyes. "Not my favorite places to spend time."

"How far is it from home?"

"Probably about twenty miles as the crow flies. There's only one road and it gets washed out a lot. We'll get Mirabelle in the water and do some things to get her ready. Probably be in town three, maybe four days, then we'll sail her home. If we leave on the morning tide, we'll be there in the afternoon." He reached out and took her hand. "I'll be happy the first time you see her under sail."

She sat quiet for a while and drifted off to sleep thinking about different things in this new life of hers.

New Caledonia came into contact with the western world rather late. Captain Cook, the English explorer, discovered it in 1774 and named it after the Roman word for his native Scotland. For the next fifty years it was left pretty much alone until the 1820s, when American whalers began hunting in those waters.

The largest island in the archipelago, Grande Terre, is two hundred and fifty miles long and oriented almost north to south so that the northern end of the island is tropical, and the southern a more moderate clime. A line of formidable peaks runs from one end of the island to the other and is high enough to force clouds to rise and empty most of their rain on the eastern slopes. As a result, the eastern side of the island is lush greenery with many creeks and rivers while the west is somewhat like the high plains of North America, not a lot of rain and a whole lot of grass.

The coming of the American military in the war against Japan brought the archipelago into the modern world with startling suddenness in the early 1940s, but in 1907 the island Bobby and Teressa were sailing to was still primitive and wild in many ways. Being aware of the possibilities that entailed was part of life on Grande Terre.

The French under Napoleon III claimed the island in 1853 and in the intervening fifty years the capital of Noumea became the only city of any size on the island. It still is.

Teressa was standing at the rail watching the small steamer anchor in the harbor of Noumea and looking out at the capital. It was smaller than her native San Diego by a lot, but was spread out over a beautiful site and she was still letting her eyes wander when Bobby came up behind her and, like he usually did, buried his face in her hair.

"Oh Bobby, don't do that. I haven't been able to wash it for a week. It smells awful."

He took her by the shoulders and asked, "Are you still feeling bad?"

"I still get nauseous almost every day."

"Looking at you, I'd guess you've lost weight since we left Honolulu. Maybe five pounds, maybe more."

"Three weeks of throwing up and not eating much will do that to you."

He pulled her into an embrace. The breeze felt good and they were glad the trip was at an end. He leaned on the top rail and looked out over the city.

"First thing we have to do is check at the yard and see if Mirabelle is ready to go back in the water. Henri' and Rudy will sleep aboard while she's in harbor. We can stay at the hotel and maybe you can get fed up a little. Are you still having trouble keeping things down?"

"Yes and you're right. I can feel the difference in my clothes since we got on this thing. Do you think she's ready?"

" If she's not, she will be as soon as I get hold of Henri."

She was in the water by that afternoon and Teressa did fetch and carry for the three men in getting her ready for sea. When Bobby showed her their cabin, she looked at him curiously. "Why are we staying at the hotel tonight?"

"I thought maybe you'd feel better to be off the water and would want to."

She looked around the cabin. "No, let's sleep here tonight. What time will we leave?"

"On the morning tide, probably about 7:30."

"So, this is the first night of my new life. Let's sleep here. It'll be a good start."

The next morning she had the coffee ready when the men came yawning into the galley and was beside Bobby at the wheel while they motored out of the harbor among the others on the morning tide.

Bobby was watching her when Mirabelle's sails billowed out to fill and she began to glide through the water of the lagoon. He heard the deep breath of excitement, saw the open-mouthed wonder the beauty of the scene painted on her face. He raised his arm and she nestled against him.

"Welcome to my world," he whispered.

CHAPTER TWENTY-TWO

"Are you busy?" Colleen looked up from what she was reading and shook her head.

"What's up?"

"Let's take a ride," said Annaliese. "It's windy out. Might want to take a scarf."

Annaliese was just learning how to drive an automobile and still wasn't comfortable by herself, so together they hitched up a small carriage and were soon on the road south out of the city.

"Are we going somewhere in particular?" asked Colleen.

"Have you been to the cabin yet?"

"Wash and Woman's cabin?" Annaliese nodded and she continued. "Yes, Manny took me out there the other day. We sat on a rock and talked."

Annaliese looked thoughtful and then smiled. "I know that rock. Over the years I've had some good talks sitting on that rock."

They stopped under a tree, tied the horse on a long lead so she could crop some grass and were soon sitting on the rock listening to the ocean sounds in the distance.

After a long silence Colleen said, "Did you want to talk to me about something?"

"Yes, I did." Annaliese took a deep breath and exhaled through her mouth. "We have an unusual situation here." When Colleen just looked at her she went on. "And the question is, do I approach the situation as a professional, apply my education and my inclination as a doctor to help someone solve a health problem, or do I approach it as a mother and future mother-in-law and bring my emotions and hopes and dreams for my son's future happiness into the calculation?"

Annaliese looked at her future daughter-in-law. "So, what do you think?"

Colleen looked back at her for a moment, trying to keep a straight face. "I wish you could have seen his face when I suggested he ask you about it." The laughter sort of bubbled out of her and soon Annaliese was laughing too.

"I'll bet," said Annaliese when she caught her breath. "That's got to be one to remember. So, tell me how you feel about the whole thing. No, wait. Let me tell you how I see it.

"You two seem to have a love-at-first-sight thing. Now you're finding out it can get complicated from here on. Fortunately or unfortunately, you have both decided to do things that point you toward a future and now suddenly this comes into the middle of it.

"I remember what it was like to have trouble keeping my hands off Johnny, so I can understand that part of it, but don't forget your attempt to guard against pregnancy could fail. Make sure you keep that in mind. The consequences of that failure would change your life."

They sat looking at each other in silence for a long moment.

"What you're telling me is to keep my pants on, is that right?"

"Not at all. I'm telling you to consider what you would do if it did fail. Have you and Manny talked about it?"

Colleen shook her head. "No, maybe we should have, but we haven't."

"Is Manny the man you want to spend the rest of your life with?"

Colleen slowly nodded her head. "Yes, he is."

"You know, one of the things that made being a doctor and staying married to Johnny all these years possible was that he let me put being a doctor first. If Manny stays in the Navy that can never happen for you. Your being a doctor will always be second to what the Navy demands of him. Are you ready for that?"

Colleen stood and held out her hand. "Let's walk down to the beach."

Wash or someone had carved some steps into the low cliff leading to the beach, but exposure to the ocean elements had worn them so that in places they had to take long steps and in some places slid a little before they got to the sand.

Once down they waded the creek, shoes and socks in hand, found a big piece of driftwood and sat watching the long Pacific rollers crash onto the rocks offshore.

"Manny brought me down here to watch him practice with his pistol."

"That boy sure knows how to entertain a young lady." They laughed. "He and Johnny have been shooting down here since he was little."

"What happens if I have a baby? I'm a long way from my family. Would I get to finish working with you?"

"The child would be Manny's son or daughter and my grandchild. You'd be part of the family."

"What does that really mean? I've heard it a lot since I got here."

"It means someone will always be there to help when you need it. It means when you need someone you can trust, they'll be there and you can trust the people around you. Always with anything."

"You know Manny can't marry until after he goes to sea for two years. Then he'll be an ensign and we'll be married under crossed swords sometime in the future. But what about medical school? If we time it right we'll be able to get married sometime in this decade. What you're saying is a baby will change all that."

"Married or not, you'd still be the mother of his child and my grandchild. Oh, by the way, I got a letter from Teressa. She's pregnant."

"So they made it OK?"

"She's recovering from the voyage but says she's feeling better."

Colleen was silent on the climb up. When she was seated on the rock again, she asked, "What would you do?"

"I knew that was coming." Annaliese closed her eyes and sucked on her lower lip for a moment. "OK. When I was your age, I'd probably have taken my pants off too. I remember when I was seventeen and in love, but I also knew what I could do was not necessarily what I should do.

"The only advice I'll give you is to talk to Manny about it. You both have to live with whatever you decide, so talk about it."

Manny and Colleen took a walk somewhere in the city most evenings. Holding hands the whole way, kissing when they could sneak it in, it was a good time to talk.

"We talked about getting pregnant and how if we have sex and I get pregnant, even when we're trying not to, it will change our lives. She thinks we should talk about it."

"She's right about that. We need to think about the possibilities before we jump into bed. This love thing is getting complicated."

"Tell me what it is you like about the Navy," she said. They had moved to a bench overlooking the city.

"You already know all that. Why do you want to hear it again?"

"My talk with Annaliese today made me think about it a little differently."

"What did she say?"

"She told me about the arrangement with Johnny. How he agreed he would make his life fit hers instead of the usual way. She pointed out with you in the Navy we couldn't do it that way. So put on your Navy hat and tell me what life we could have if I'm a doctor and you're an officer on a battleship halfway around the world. How's that going to work?"

He sat quiet for a while staring at nothing. Finally, he took a deep breath and said, "At this point, I don't know and to tell you the truth, I'm not sure I ever will." He took her hand, kissed it and then her lips lightly. "Not long ago CT and I were talking and this relationship came up and he said he couldn't see it working in the long run. I said I couldn't either, but I was determined to keep trying because you were so special. I know I'd never find anyone else quite like you."

She leaned against him, and he put his arm around her and squeezed. "That's how I feel," she said, pulling away and turning to face him. "So what are we going to do?"

"I'd like to say let it happen and deal with it, but I've a lot invested in this future I'm working on and so do you. We need to make a plan we agree on and try to make it work."

"You sound like an engineer."

"I am an engineer, or at least I'm halfway there. I guess I want us to agree on what to do so we won't be able to blame it on anything if it doesn't work. You know, it might just be a bigger bite than we can chew and swallow."

He paused and took her in his arms. "But I want to try because if we don't try, we won't do. I think we have to try. We'll have something special if we can make it work. So let's try."

The next day, Colleen spent the day working with Maggie at the clinic and Manny and Annaliese went for a ride. His time was getting short and they hadn't spent much time together. As much as he loved and respected Johnny, his mother was his lodestar. When he first came to her he was a quiet child, happy to read and play by himself. In those early days she was always there to put her arm around him and make him feel special. Now she was usually far away but at times he still needed her arm around him to make him feel special sometimes more than ever.

They had stopped at a place where they could sit and see the ocean stretching away to the horizon.

"Colleen and I had a talk yesterday."

"She told me. So tell me how you feel about the whole thing."

"I don't know what to think." He shook his head. "Every time I try to think about it, try to come up with some answers, I end up thinking about something else." He paused, looked at her. "You know what I mean."

She smiled. "Yes, I know."

"She's got the most amazing way of looking at things. She doesn't really care about what the rules are, what people think. She only cares about solving the problem in front of her. Because this problem is so different, maybe it needs that kind of thinking, so I'm going to let her lead me on this. She might have an answer I wouldn't even think about."

"How do you feel about going back to Annapolis?"

"It's the darndest thing. I don't want to leave here, leave you and Colleen and Papa and all the family, but at the same time, I'm looking forward to getting back to the Yard." He chuckled and shook his head. "They set out to make me a sailor, to make me aware of what they expect of me and they're succeeding. That's how I view myself now, and it colors all my thinking. I'm an officer in the United States Navy and that's how I think about myself."

"Johnny tells me you're interested in flying."

"Yes, it's the future and those of us who get into it now will be important later."

"If you survive."

He smiled ruefully. "That's always in the back of your mind."

"Have you flown yet?"

"No, not yet. The club is putting forth the idea of the Navy adopting flight into the curriculum at the Academy. We met Glen Curtis in Baltimore a few weeks ago and I've been exchanging letters with him. We're going to try to get him to bring a machine to the Yard so we can go up. Five of the graduates this year were members of the club, and I believe they'll keep their ideas about flying and want to take them further. Ultimately, I think the club will be important to the future of naval aviation—if there is a future. I'm betting there will be and I want to be right in the middle of it."

"What does Colleen say about it?"

"We've talked about it. She hasn't really objected. I understand it could be a problem, especially if we have children. I imagine you might look at life and taking risks a little differently when they're in the picture."

"It sounds to me like you have your life pretty much in hand. Of course, it would be so much simpler if she lived next door."

They spent the next couple of days doing things with other people, she working and he with family. She was learning and helping others, and he was enjoying San Diego in the summertime, usually in a sailboat on San Diego Bay. But no matter where or what, sex was there in the backs of their minds, ready to push to the surface if they let it. One another and the future were what they thought about mostly.

On this day, he was eating lunch with Lemuel and Kate and answering questions about life at the Naval Academy.

"I understand they had you shoveling coal and mopping floors when you were on board ships," said Lemuel. "That bother you?"

"No. It made sense. How are you going to make a ship run if you don't know how it works? How can you supervise men to do something you don't know how to do yourself?"

He grinned. "It's a subtle thing but very obvious when you think about it. What the navy needs is for its ships to go where they need to go and their guns to go boom. They need men who can learn what it takes to make them do that and then make sure it's done right. To get these men, they've created a system for young men to learn what they need to know to make the whole thing work. That system is the Naval Academy."

"Sounds like you're in the right place for you," said Kate. "People thrive in different environments. Personally, I couldn't stand the regimentation and discipline, but it looks like you're just where you belong. When do you leave to go back?"

"I leave Wednesday."

"Are you excited about it?"

He didn't even have to think about this answer because he'd given it so many times in the last three weeks. "Yes," he said. "I like what it's pointing me to, and I want to get on with it."

Maggie came into the room where Colleen was cleaning up after the treatment of a patient. "When does Manny go back?" she asked.

"He leaves Wednesday morning."

"And you won't see each other until next year?"

Colleen dried her hands and looked glum. "Next August when he comes home on leave again."

"I know there were things you wanted to work out while he was here. Did you get them out of the way?"

"Most of them, but there's one that's still unsettled."

"Is that the one I'm thinking about?"

"Probably, but I think I've decided how to deal with that one."

"And that is?"

Colleen looked at her with a mischievous smile. "Now you don't think I'm going to tell you before I tell him, do you?"

Maggie laughed. "I can see your point. Let me know how you worked it out."

"I think you'll be able to tell just by looking at me."

It was Tuesday, and they were at the cabin again, sitting in the carriage, doing things lovers do.

She sighed. "No matter how frustrating this is, I want to keep doing it. Kiss me again."

"Whatever you say, dear."

After a while, he handed her out of the carriage and they stood for a moment holding one another, her head on his shoulder. Then she led him onto the porch, and they sat in rockers side by side, his hand over hers.

"So, thanks to your mother, we have what we need to keep from getting pregnant and we're here. But like your Mama said, we need to talk." She was looking out at the view instead of at him. "Tell me, what ideas do you have about what we do if it fails?"

He sat quiet for a while pondering the situation. They were young, alone, there was a bed nearby, and she wanted to talk. He shook his head.

"You amaze me," he said. "I have no ideas, but you always seem to have one so I'm going to leave it to you. Tell me how you feel about it."

She looked at him, incredulously. "You're dumping it in my lap?"

He grinned at her indignation. "Look, I can't come up with a plan where we don't end up where we don't want to be. The way you think may be better, who knows? I know it's definitely different. The only thing important is that we find a way, right?

She looked at him and her face gradually relaxed. "All right," she said the idea is to make a relationship that survives the future we plan. Do you agree?" She could see he was thinking, and when he finally nodded, she continued. "First thing is you and Annapolis. You don't have much room to maneuver there. You have to fit your life into what they require, so it's a given that most of the bending will have to be on my end." He nodded again.

"Your mother has let me know that any child we have will be your son or daughter and her grandchild. Whether we're married or not, I'll be family. I know what that means.

"That being said, the idea of using that thing with all the creams and preparations and everything," she shook her head and made a face. "I'm sorry, but I want today to be something special, something I'll remember all my life. A Dutch cap with spermicide has no place in a romantic memory."

He looked at her for a moment, fascinated. "So, what do you propose?"

She closed her eyes, took another deep breath and said, "I want you to wash me all over, then take me into the bedroom and see what happens. If I have our child, I'll deal with it while you finish up at the Naval Academy."

Now it was his turn to look incredulous. While he sat open-mouthed, she continued. "The way I see it, this solves all our problems. You get to finish at school and you're still in the navy. Your mother has assured me I will continue as her student and the baby will be loved and cared for if there is one. So, baby or no, I can still learn how to be a doctor." She smiled at him. "So you don't have to worry about me getting pregnant. If I do, I'll handle it."

He looked at her in silence for a while, starting to smile, fighting it, and then began to chuckle. "I knew it. I knew you'd come up with a solution. It's one of the reasons I love you." He held out his hand. "Let's go count your freckles."

Wash had plumbed the cabin, but there was no hot water, so they heated water on the stove and sat in an old clawfoot bathtub and slowly washed each other. Suddenly she had a new toy to play with and using it she guided him to the bedroom.

He stood looking at her in the afternoon light coming in through the curtained window by the foot of the bed, looking at her curves and the red hair down there and her freckles. She lay on the bed while he looked. It excited her.

"See," she said, "I have them everywhere, even here." She spread her legs to show him and he came to her.

"Teach me," he whispered. She held out her arms and began the lessons.

"Slowly and gently at first, time for other things later."

Afterward, they lay in bed looking at nothing on the ceiling, catching their breath. After a while, he turned to her and, leaning on his elbow, asked, "How many times did you do it with him?"

"Two. Then for some reason, he thought he owned me. That's when I went after him with the frying pan."

"Two? You learned all that in just two times?"

"No, I didn't learn all that with him. All of a sudden, I had something new to think about, to wonder about." She touched her breast. "When I discovered this felt good when I touched it, I wondered how it would feel somewhere else." She pulled him to her, and they kissed slowly searching each other with their tongues. "I have an active imagination, you know and using my fingers just made sense."

He shook his head in wonder. "I love the way you think. I, on the other hand, am in the navy. There are certain boundaries. If I thought the way you do, I don't think I'd last very long."

"You never did answer that question I asked you about the doctor and the officer on a battleship."

"You know, that's not something they teach at the Academy. None of the 'Middies' are married. It's against the rules, so I have no one to ask about it. I think every other assignment is usually a shore billet, so sometimes wives can follow their husbands. Also, ships have home ports. If my ship had San Francisco as a home port, for instance, we'd live there and you'd be waiting for me when I was in port."

She looked at him for a long moment, a smile playing around her lips. "You know, I'm getting a lot of practice waiting. Maybe I'll get used to it. Annaliese told me one of her girls had the same problem with a man. Maybe she'll have some ideas about it."

"That's Este and Roy. They waited five years. They're married now, and I think they have a little girl."

Manny was back in the 'Yard' near the end of September sitting at his desk woolgathering when Jack came in with the mail. He sniffed an envelope, then handed it to Manny. "She still smells about the same."

Manny tore open the letter. It was a short note.

Dear Manny,
    Well, I'm not pregnant. Don't know if that's me or you or chance, but I guess we can try again next year.
              Love you, Colleen.

When Jack looked up, Manny was staring off into space with a grin on his face.

CHAPTER TWENTY-THREE

Teressa woke up looking at an unfamiliar ceiling. She lay for a moment trying to orient herself by recalling the last thing she remembered. She was climbing the path to the house on the cliff, and suddenly it was a blank. She had a dim memory of someone carrying her but had no memory of who or where. She closed her eyes,and when she opened them a black woman was standing by the bed, smiling down at her.

"Glad to see you awake. How do you feel?"

Teressa looked at her rather blankly for a moment, seeming to think about the question.

"Hungry," she finally said.

The woman's smile grew into a grin. "We can do something about that right away." Her English sounded strange, but Teressa couldn't place it.

"What," she began, but the woman held up her hand. "You have many questions. I have the answers. I will tell them while you eat."

Teressa closed her eyes, and when she opened them again, the woman was carrying a short-legged tray into the room with a nice breakfast on it. She positioned it on Teressa's lap, left and returned immediately with a tall glass of liquid.

"Drink this while you eat."

She took a drink and a bite before she looked up and asked,

"You're Marie, aren't you?" The woman nodded. "I am Marie, and with my brother Cookie, we live here and work with Bobby. We take care of him when he's home."

Teressa ate in silence for a while, then asked, "What is this drink?"

"I make it with ginger root for morning sickness."

Teressa looked thoughtful. "You know, I just noticed. This is the first time since I got on that boat in Honolulu I've been able to eat without feeling sick." She looked at Marie. "It works."

Marie nodded. "It works," she agreed with a smile.

With the tray gone, she leaned back and stretched luxuriously. "How long have I been here?"

"This is the third day. Bobby carried you in and I cared for you."

"Where is Bobby?"

"On the boat, where else? He'll be home before dark. I think he has a present for you."

She lay back on the pillow and let her eyes stray around the room. She could hear the chug-chug of a generator and noticed a slowly revolving fan in the center of the ceiling. Though it was daytime she switched on the light, turned it off again and craned her neck to see out the window at the green lawn that ran away to what looked like a patio.

"I'd like to try to get up. Is that alright?"

In answer, Marie held out her hand and let Teressa gently pull herself to a sitting position on the side of the bed. She sat for a moment, then, with an effort, she stood and let Marie support her until the dizziness passed. One step, then another and she made it to a veranda, where she sat in the shade for a moment. She needed Marie's strong arm over the uneven ground but made it to the patio, where she sat with her eyes closed, catching her breath.

After a moment, she opened them and caught her breath again, not from weakness but from the beauty of the scene before her. On the bay below her, Mirabelle floated on the most beautiful clear blue water she had ever seen. Gradually, she looked away to the horizon. "Is that the Coral Sea I've heard so much about?"

Marie nodded, took a whistle from a nail where it hung and

startled Teressa by blowing a shrill blast on it. After a moment, she saw Bobby in the cockpit of the boat looking up at her. He reached into the cabin, brought out a pair of binoculars and focused them on the cliff. Marie waved and pointed to Teressa, who also waved.

They sat feeling the breeze while Teressa took in the view, and Marie told her what she was seeing. After a while, they could see Bobby and another man get into the dinghy and row it out of sight below them.

"They'll be up here in half an hour if you'd like to wash up a little. You've been in bed a while."

She closed her eyes, stood in the cold shower and sponged herself, coming out with a glowing feeling and was sitting on the veranda in a summer dress Marie had given her when Bobby crested the path with Henri and Rudy.

Bobby had a small black kitten on his shoulder. She carefully lifted it off, cradled it and looked up at him with a smile. "Thank you, dear. Can we call him Jinx?"

"Call him anything you like. He's yours."

"Jinx it is, then," she said, looking into those big green eyes and falling in love.

For the next two days, she rested, got to know the people she'd be living with and played with Jinx. He was at the 'bouncing around ball of fur' stage, curious and into everything. She spent a lot of time laughing at his antics and realized it felt good to laugh. The entire time on the steamer from Honolulu, she had been miserable. Now she was beginning to look around, see what was here and look forward to tomorrow.

Over the next few days, she found out the native people of New Caledonia are the Kanak tribe and that Marie was a medicine woman among them; that the always-smiling Cookie was a miracle worker in the kitchen and always willing to lend a hand; and that her husband really loved Mirabelle and wanted her to learn to feel the same way.

All these were facts in this new adventure she was on. Around her were people, things, and places that would become as familiar to her here as the people, things, and places of her home had been.

Sitting, thinking about it and where it would lead her, she nodded her head and smiled. She touched the scar on her cheek and thought about the cusp it represented. When that building crumpled around her, it brought down her world with its hopes and dreams. For months after, she had drifted along in a sort of daze, no ideas, no plans for the future, just existence.

Then Bobby reached out to her, and now she had a new life with plans and ideas and she was excited about it. She stood up, took a deep breath and threw her arms wide to the ocean in the distance.

Bobby had been walking across the lawn and saw her. The image was so beautiful, so poetic, he stopped to take it in. After watching her for a minute in silence, he came up behind her and whispered in her ear.

"Do you feel good enough to celebrate our honeymoon tonight?"

For an answer, she turned and they melted into a long, passionate kiss. He lifted her gently in his powerful arms and began his lovemaking on the way to the house.

One of the more unexpected aspects of their life now was Jinx. Wherever they were, he was and they found out that night that the best of amorous intentions are doomed to fail with an unfettered, rambunctious kitten around. The first night it was hilarious and they almost fell out of bed laughing at him and his antics but after that it was a little aggravating. He was loving and playful but also curious, constantly turning up in places he wasn't supposed to be and at times attacking anything that moved, including moving toes under a sheet in the middle of the night.

"He's a kitten," said Teressa. "He'll grow out of it."

"I hope so," said Bobby. "I was thinking about throwing him off the cliff."

On the voyage from Hawaii, they had talked about her role on Mirabelle and she knew enough of sailing to envision it. Now it became a reality.

She would be a member of the crew, responsible for certain duties, not just along for the ride. Cookie was going to sail with them, and she would help him in the galley and learn, so that if need be, she could keep the crew fed and happy. Bobby also wanted her to learn the ropes and how to sail Mirabelle so, need be, she could bring her home. She knew it would take a while. When she asked Bobby how long, he shrugged. "As long as it takes. That's what Pete said to me when I asked him that question.

"There's a lot to learn, but you'll be living the life and I know you can learn anything. For a lot of years, you'll probably have the same shipmates. Need be, they'll help."

She looked at him wide-eyed, said, "When do we leave, Captain?" and threw him a salute.

"Could be right soon. Maybe later this week."

"Really? That soon?"

"That boat that was here yesterday brought a message from the factor. Remember him? Degarde. You met him in Noumea."

"Did I? I don't remember."

"He's got several jobs for me in hand and he got a notice on another in Tahiti. We can button up here and be on our way in a couple days. Day or two there, and we'll be headed north to Tulagi."

"Where's Tulagi?"

"In the Solomons, about a thousand miles north of here."

"How long will it take to get there?"

He grinned at her.

"What are you grinning about?"

"I asked Pete the same questions on my first trip to The Solomons." He scratched his chin, looked thoughtful. "Five, maybe six days. Depends on the weather. It's due north, so we'll have the trade winds on our beam most of the way."

"What will it be like?"

"I'm not going to tell you. I want you to read what Pete had to say about it. Read his logs and then I'll answer any questions you have. While you're at it, read what he has to say about 'black-birding.'"

"You said something about that."

"He says a lot more. Read it and then we'll talk. Probably be good to have Henri sit with us when we talk about it. He was with Pete for a lot of years."

He stopped at the door leading to the veranda and turned.

"Remember, you can ask Henri about things. He knows a lot about these islands and this life. I can navigate using charts and equipment. He just knows where we are. With him, it's instinct. If I hang around with him long enough I hope to learn how he does it."

Later, at the table at dinner, she asked, "What do we do with Jinx?"

"Take him with us."

"Take him with us?"

"Teressa, cats have been on boats for centuries. Never heard of one falling overboard. That's why they have claws. When the weather gets bad, he'll be below."

Henri' and Rudy had spent most of the time while Teressa was recovering sleeping on the boat, recognizing that Bobby might want to be alone with his new wife. Now she began to learn about these people who were going to be her crewmates.

A sixty-eight-foot schooner with a twenty-foot beam is a tight fit for a crew of five and a kitten. Everyone has a small personal space that can't be allowed to get cluttered. Things out of place can be dangerous, cause falls, or worse. Ropes and other running gear must be coiled or stored properly so, in an emergency, they're ready for use when needed. No one has many possessions because there's no place to put them. Jinx was in everyone's personal space at one time or another, but that was expected. He was a kitten. He'd grow out of it.

She'd be working with Cookie in the beginning and knew him a little from her time at the house on the cliff. She knew he was amiable, slow-moving and helpful, though a little hard to understand. From him she'd learn to manage the galley, what stock was necessary to begin a voyage, how to cook it with the equipment and utensils on hand and how to cook and serve meals in whatever weather the ocean would throw at them. Jinx was the assistant to the assistant cook and would likely take advantage of the fact.

Rudi, the mate/deckhand, was a taciturn man who never seemed to smile but would always patiently demonstrate anything she needed to know. Fortunately, she had spent many hours sailing with Bobby and Manny on the bays near their homes. Though the boats there were much smaller, the principles were the same; it was just a matter of degree. She knew she would adapt quickly.

Henri' was special. He was polite and gallant, usually smiling and considerate. If she asked him something, he answered carefully whether the question was important or not. He seemed to be a part of the boat, like a spar or a mast and according to Bobby, moved easily with confidence no matter how the boat was behaving or whatever the weather. He was the kind of man you felt was important even if you hardly knew him, not for anything he said or did but just because of what he was.

When they had climbed the path and settled on the veranda to enjoy the cool evening breeze, Bobby announced, "Afternoon tide tomorrow, we'll raise anchor. Should be in Noumea before dark. Are you excited?"

She looked at him for a moment, then nodded. "Nervous," she shrugged. "I'm a little anxious, Yeah, maybe excited."

"Have you read anything in Pete's logs yet?"

She nodded and pointed at a stack of five of the logbooks waiting to go down the hill. "I'm taking those with me. Pete was a good writer. They're easy to read."

"Any questions?"

"No, not yet. I'm sure there will be and we'll have plenty of time on the voyage for answers. I don't remember much about the trip from Noumea, so this will be my first time on her under sail. I kind of relate being on a boat to being sick, so I'm a little worried about that."

"When we get outside the reef and headed north on the trades, it's a regular motion mostly. Like you said on the steamer. You've never been seasick in your life."

The next morning, she was up early and was packed and ready when she came out for breakfast on the patio.

Marie had things set up for the crew's breakfast, and she poured Teressa a cup of the ginger root tea.

"This should help you today. Maybe your tummy is a bit," she wagged her hand. "I don't think it will take you long to be OK."

"When was the last time you sailed with Pete?"

Marie sat down with a cup of tea and pushed a plate of pastries toward her. "Fifteen years ago. My daughter's fourteen years old, and she's the reason I stay home that time. Didn't go out for a while after that because they didn't need me and it got to be a habit, I guess. Pete liked me staying here and taking care of the place."

"Where does your daughter live?"

"She lives with her grandmother most of the time. When Mirabelle is gone, she comes to visit me. Also my son."

"Are they the only two you have?"

Marie nodded and smiled. "They were never here when Pete was here. This place is far away from everything. They need to be with the tribe. This would be a," she paused, searching for a word, "an artificial life. Once I am gone, they must know the old ways. That way, they can choose which life to live. If they want to go to the city, that's fine, but the tribe is always there when they need to come home."

"Do you miss them?"

"Yes, I do, but it's best for them. That's what a mother is. Someone who does what's best for the children. They come to visit and stay while I'm alone, but when Mirabelle comes home, they go back where they belong."

"Where is their father?"

"Pete was their father."

Teressa's mouth dropped open in amazement. "Does Bobby know that?"

Marie shrugged. "I never told him. Maybe Pete did."

Bobby leaned over Teressa's shoulder and kissed her ear, then took down a pair of binoculars and began his morning scan of everything he could see, which was considerable.

"Looks like we'll have good weather for it." Finally, he turned, seated himself, and poured hot water over some tea leaves. "High tide will be early afternoon, so we should begin to go aboard by noon. That way we can get settled in and be ready when it turns. We should be in Noumea by early evening."

She felt a little uneasy about leaving Marie. The woman had been a constant, strong presence since she awoke to this new world.

She felt a sinking feeling when she thought about the uncertainty of that day and the ones following and thinking of Marie was like a balm on that uncertainty.

The things she had learned about Marie fascinated her. The woman was a mother, a leader in her clan and a healer among them. Tribal members came and went when they needed her or she needed them. The part of the house where she lived had a rich, warm fragrance and this is where she met members of the tribe. It was part of the house and yet separate, hers alone.

She had come to understand that Marie was protected by the tribe and though quite alone at times, she never felt lonely and was never afraid. It was as though she had a shield around her, and she knew she was safe. The tribe was always there.

"What I'd give for that kind of certainty in my life," she thought. She felt that leaving Marie, she was leaving the strength she'd need to make it, to be a good partner for Bobby, a good member of the crew and to wake up with a smile.

"I'll just have to find that strength in me," she thought as she watched Bobby take the oars and begin the trip out to Mirabelle. About halfway there he came out of the loom of the point and stopped rowing so she could look up at the patio, at Marie shading her eyes, waving and beyond, the house on the cliff.

Settling in amounted to each of them doing a certain thing until everything was done and the anchor hoisted. One of the additions at the shipyard had been a glass-enclosed case that held a rack of rifles and shotguns. She wondered about that but thought she'd ask Bobby about it later.

Their passage to Noumea was in the lagoon. It was an unknown wonder of the world at the time, though explorers and scientists had begun to realize the majesty of the longest continuous barrier reef in the world and the special nature of the enormous, beautiful lagoon it contained. For everyone else, it was just a beautiful place to sail, what most people envisioned when they thought of the South Seas.

To the north and east, green hills came down to white sand beaches, and behind them, impressive mountains rose and marched away north into the distance. In places, she could see the red soil that indicated the presence of the mineral wealth that had led the rest of the world to finally come calling at this, one of the most remote places on the planet.

West and south motus or islands were scattered here and there and she could see a larger one away to the south. When she asked, Bobby told her it was the Isle of Pines and it was the largest penal colony in the world, a place where France sent political prisoners, transported after the Paris Commune in the early 1870s.

"I've never been there. It's a good way from here and it's surrounded by the same reef we have here. It's said to be beautiful, but the authorities discourage visitors. Supposed to be three or four thousand prisoners still there, and they're all looking for a way to get off the place. Might lose the boat down there."

She remembered little of being in Noumea before but now was struck by the large and beautiful harbor and how the city was spread out on the hills surrounding it. The boatyard was on one of the large islands in the harbor and they tied up there and began their list of chores.

First, she went with Cookie to resupply the galley and later with Bobby as he made his rounds of the officials and businesses necessary at the beginning of a voyage. "All this is part of the job. We have to go through all of it to get ready to leave."

"What happens if you just leave?"

"They get you when you come back. They don't have a lot to do, these colonial officials. I think they keep track of this stuff as sort of a hobby." He shrugged. "Whatever the reason, we have to abide or there's a price. Pete believed you keep things simple and problems with these people complicate things. Best to let them think they're important. Keeps 'em happy."

That night after dinner, Bobby cleared the mess table and spread some charts across it. "Here's where we are, and," he ran his finger across the map, "here's where we're going. Tulagi. It's one of the smaller islands in the Solomons but it's in a very protected spot. The British use it as the administrative center and capital of the islands."

Henri' was sucking on his dry pipe. "As many times as I've been up there," he said, "the only islands I've been on are Tulagi and

Guadalcanal across the sound. The rest of them are not nice places to vacation."

"I read about them in Pete's book," said Teressa. "They sound pretty bad."

"I've heard tales of cannibals and headhunters," said Bobby. "Doesn't surprise me. Not much game on these islands. I guess they just get tired of fish."

He gestured toward the gun belts hanging on the bulkhead. "I carry a gun when I'm ashore there. We all do."

The next morning, they motored out of the harbor on the morning tide, sailed through a pass in the reef and turned north to begin a voyage of a thousand miles.

CHAPTER TWENTY-FOUR

As the train crossed the state of Missouri on the way to the Mississippi River Manny realized he'd thought of nothing but Colleen since he left San Diego. Soon he would be in the east, and the east was Annapolis, the Yard, Bancroft Hall, and the Brigade.

He had finished the first two years, the hardest by all accounts and now he must learn how to apply the basics he had learned so that, as an ensign standing watch on a United States Navy warship, his part in what was required for it to accomplish its mission. If he was thinking about the redhead back home and not the tasks at hand he might fail, as had so many before him.

He'd never been in love before so the emotions were new and a bit disorienting, but here in the east he was a naval cadet, and thoughts of a naked Colleen lying in bed in the half-light of a summer afternoon were somewhat distracting.

For one reason or another, four of ten of the men he had begun the Academy with were gone. To continue to excel and move toward graduation would require focus. He could think about her on his own time, but not on the navy's while he was learning his profession.

He wondered if he had the discipline to accomplish this and finally decided he'd have to learn. After all, discipline underlay all he had learned since he arrived at the Academy. He'd just have to figure out how to exercise it in the right direction. As much as he missed her he was glad she wasn't around. She would be hard on his class standing.

For her part, Colleen was having similar thoughts, but the freedom of her situation allowed her to handle them with a smile. She had a place to sleep, food to eat and a feeling of belonging that wasn't love yet, but she thought it would be, someday.

She hadn't realized how much the uncertainty about that wonderful afternoon had affected her until she began her period. Relief washed through her in a wave and led to a deep breath with closed eyes. But the question "what if" would be somewhere in her mind until Manny came home and they could talk about it.

As it was, she plunged back into her studies and worked hard, studied hard, but at times each day she'd stop and smile at a memory flitting across her mind.

Manny looked up from a letter when Jack came into the room. "Glen Curtiss is going to be in Baltimore next week," he said. "He's found a place at a farm in the area and is planning to put down here for a while so we can talk to him, look at the plane and if the weather's right, maybe some of us can go up."

The weather wasn't right. The rudimentary technology and fragile structure of the airplanes beginning to appear around the country made flying in any but near-perfect weather problematic. So seven naval cadets sat on the floor or whatever they could find in Glen Curtiss's hotel room and talked for three hours during an afternoon thunderstorm. It was a conversation none of them ever forgot.

They had many questions to ask and here was a man with the answers. They talked about the basics: lift, thrust, control, wing shapes and wing warping, the latter a maneuver whereby twisting the wing made the machine turn in flight. They talked about problems with stability, altitude gain and landing on different surfaces. And they talked about engines.

Curtis designed and manufactured engines and was his own test pilot. He also developed mechanisms to improve maneuverability and power and was constantly testing and refining equipment.

The reason he had taken the opportunity to spend time with them was an extension of his budding cooperation with the Navy on aspects of flight that could be used to advance naval doctrine. He wanted to have contact with people in the Navy who were interested in the future of flight, and he had found some at Annapolis.

The important question was saved for last.

"You've been sitting there listening without saying much, Manny," said Ted Ellyson. "What's on your mind?"

Manny shrugged. "I'm surprised no one has asked about it. Are you ever afraid? From what I've read, you've crash-landed a few times."

Curtis chuckled. "More times than I'd like to remember." He looked at Manny in silence for a moment. "I agree with you. I'm surprised no one's asked about it.

"The answer is yes, I've been afraid many times. When your machine is falling and you don't know why, you're afraid. When your engine fails and you're a hundred feet off the ground, you're afraid. People are beginning to die in airplane crashes and you're a fool and a liar if you say that doesn't bother you, give you pause. I have a wife and a child. So yes I've been afraid."

He smiled at them, looking at the serious faces around him. "I have to take that into account every time I fly. But I still fly. You fellows are fortunate. You've learned discipline. That's an important thing in a pilot. With judgment, it can get you through a crash. But don't forget there's always a chance it won't."

Manny went to bed that night more determined than ever to fly. The direction CT had pointed out had become the focus of his career. Now if he only survived.

And then there was Colleen. He had no illusions about their future. If they continued to believe in a future, it might happen, but for the life of him, he couldn't see how. Thinking about her made him feel good, so he did. Hopeless or not, it was something he was usually thinking about when he turned out the lights.

December 1, 1908
Dear Manny,
> *It felt strange when I found out I wasn't pregnant. It*

was a great relief, of course, but it has made me think about it and I think I'd like to have our child someday.

Your mother made me feel better when we had our talk, and I think we used our heads about the whole thing. The day we had was something we'll always have. That's what cherish means.

I love it here. Janet and I really work well together and we both realize that when we help each other we both come out ahead. Your mother is special. I feel I can take any question to her, and she's let me know she's happy with me and my work. Whether you and I have a future together or not, I'm part of the family now and I know what that means.

There are a group of us that go sailing together. I have to be careful of the sun, but I enjoy it. It's funny, at home I was never on a sailboat even though there was plenty of water around. Never occurred to me until I came here.

I've met Lemuel's twins and we've gone out in their boat several times. The weather here is so nice. You've no idea what Boston's like in the winter. It's nice to be able to wear what you want without having to worry about the north wind.

I wish you were here, but I don't wish to be there. I'll wait because my future's here. Yours is there. Be that as it may, I can't wait for August to come. I love it that you get dizzy when we kiss. Me too.

Love, Colleen

It would be springtime before Manny flew for the first time. After a blustery March, early April was nice and they had a break from school. The problem was finding an airplane. It's a good bet man has wanted to fly since he first looked up and saw a bird in the sky. It took him a long time.

Colleen's letter to Manny was dated less than five years after the Wright brothers left the ground in the first mechanically powered controlled flight. At the time there were others who had the same vision and were working toward that end, which is why the brothers were so obsessed with secrecy, both before and after the momentous event.

The word got out though and gradually heavier-than-air flying machines began to appear here and there around the country and the world. And of course these flyers needed places to land and to service and maintain their machines. In the beginning, airfields were scarcely more than pastures, but soon became more specialized and more noticeable.

The development of float planes and flying boats in this era was fueled by the fact that airplanes had to have a place to land. Since the average farm field had crops in it, small airports dedicated to providing the needed services were beginning to spring up around the country. In the area between Baltimore and Annapolis in 1908, there happened to be one on a railway just three-quarters of an hour from the Yard.

One Sunday morning, four naval cadets and budding pilots stepped down from the train at the little town of Arnold and began the four-mile walk to the new airfield on the outskirts of town. Actually, it was three budding pilots. Jack was just curious. It was easy to guess what they talked about on the walk out to the field. At first glance, it looked like any other fenced pasture, but in the distance, they could see what looked like airplanes parked near a barn and some outbuildings with gasoline pumps outside.

As the four of them stood by the fence and looked at these, Ted Ellyson asked, "So who's nervous?" Manny and Marc Mitchner raised their hands. They looked at Jack.

"I'm just here to see what you guys have been talking about for the last year."

As they let themselves in through the gate a tall bald-headed man came out of what looked to be an office and walked across the grass in front of them toward an airplane parked beside the barn.

The other three continued on toward the field where another plane was sitting with the engine running and a man was in the cockpit wearing a helmet and gloves. Manny had watched the man cross the yard and when he altered his course and entered the barn, he followed. In the gloomy interior of the building he thought he could see wings and a frame. He stopped and looked back at his friends, now standing and watching as the airplane began to move onto the field prior to taking off.

When he looked back at the barn someone had opened the back doors and in the new light, he could clearly see the shape of the machine inside. Wings and a frame, but where was the engine? Was it a glider? Then he saw two engines in cradles sitting to one side where they were being worked on.

The tall, bald man looked up, saw him, and came over to greet him. "How can I help you?"

"This is my first time out here. I'm just looking around."

The man held out his hand. "I'm Cyrus Walker. This is my place, such as it is. Any questions you have we'll try to find answers for. Are you from around here?"

"Manny Fry. I'm at the Academy. We have a club for naval air, and we've been reading about it and talking about it, so we finally decided to come out and see it for ourselves."

"Is this for the Navy or just for you?"

"Both. It's our interest right now, but we're hoping we can get the Navy interested and we can stay with it. It has to be something they'll be interested in. It's too important not to be."

Walker chewed on his bottom lip, thinking apparently. "Why don't we go inside and talk for a spell?" he said. When they walked back across the yard, Manny could see the others out on the field looking at a plane. Jack saw him and waved.

"Where are you from, Manny?" asked Walker, ushering Manny into his 'office'. "Oh, by the way, call me Cy." Manny sat in an old, overstuffed chair in an office area that was delineated by some filing cabinets, a room divider, and a couple of hat racks, all in the corner of the barn. This was very clearly a 'seat of the pants' operation.

"I'm from San Diego. It's in California, just north of the Mexican border."

"What year are you?"

"A junior."

"From what I hear, you're over the hump. I hear those first two years are tough."

"We still stay pretty busy. Now that the weather's nice, we decided to make the trip out here and see what we could find out about flying."

Cy looked disgusted. "Well, right now we're not doing much flying ourselves. We got those motors down and then couldn't get the parts. We just got some of what we need today, but it's been down for two months."

"I'd like to watch them work on it, but it's tough to get away from school except on Sunday."

"Hmm," said Cy, pulling on his lower lip again. "We almost always have some or another machine in here every week. If you just come out when you can get away, we'll see if we can teach you a thing or two but tell me something. Most young fellows who come out here can't wait to get in the air. It seems like you're a little different."

Manny thought about that for a moment, then said, "Mr. Walker, Cy that is, we met with Glen Curtiss when he was in Baltimore and he told us that knowing your machine as well as your mechanic does would help you survive. I want to fly, but I'd like to live to tell about it. Those planes out there will be there tomorrow or next Sunday. When I'm a hundred feet off the ground, I'd like to feel I know the machine I'm flying."

It became important to him. Every Sunday his studies allowed, and usually with another middie or two, he caught the earliest train to Abbott Junction. While his companions spent time on the field watching the planes and talking to the pilots, Manny spent hours immersed in the wonders of small engine mechanics.

He also learned about steering gear and pulleys and wires and struts. He learned how the shape and pitch of a propeller affect its performance, and how the shape of a wing is an essential part of the final product. In fact, he learned something about all the mechanisms it took to free a machine from the bonds of gravity.

And oh, by the way, he flew occasionally. Manny was different from most of his fellow club members. He was excited but not passionate about flying. He enjoyed it, the rush of air across his face and the thrill of being suspended between the earth and the sky, but there was always this small nagging fear in the back of his mind or the pit of his stomach that came with every flight.

He became a pilot, a competent flier, but he never loved flying the way some of his friends did. Much of flying was in the 'touch' you developed, and like most endeavors in life, it was there in some men and not in others.

Instead, he was fascinated by the things man had done to make flight happen, and he spent time whenever he could with a wrench in his hand and grease on his nose. Cy was a natural teacher, the kind of person who loved to watch a boy become a man while learning a trade, finding a way to make his mark in the world.

He looked forward to Manny's visits as much as Manny looked forward to coming and always had something for him to do that would teach him, a little at a time, the way Cy had learned things himself.

Besides being in the Navy and the family, he thought of himself more and more as an aeronautical engineer. Considering that the Navy was making him into a marine engineer, it didn't seem to be much of a stretch.

He also spent enough time in the air to feel comfortable and competent in some of the planes occasionally available, and before long felt he was accepted by Cy and the fellows at the field as one of them in every way.

He was becoming an airman.

Colleen was writing in her journal when the buzzer beside her desk sounded. Within a minute she and Janet hurried into the treatment room and began the routine tasks necessary when an emergency patient was coming in the door.

Annaliese and Maggie were already standing by the table in the middle of the room with a body on the table between them, examining it.

"He's still breathing, although I don't see how," said Maggie.

Annaliese grunted in reply and bent to examine a horrible bruise on the patient's right side at least six inches square. There were also numerous gashes that were bleeding and the blood had run down to stain the sheet on the bed.

"What happened to him?" asked Janet.

"They said he fell from a roof about twenty feet to the ground and landed on his side on the top of a cinderblock wall," said Annaliese. "With all that bruising he has to have internal bleeding and likely broken ribs, too." She put her stethoscope on his chest, moved it around and said, "He's moving some air but not much."

She looked at Maggie. "I don't think there's anything we can do for him. Is his family here?"

"No. It happened on a jobsite, and they brought him right here," said Anna, the receptionist. "I think they're going to send someone to his house to let his family know."

Part of Colleen's training required her to help clean and arrange a body for the undertaker and she and Janet were doing that when she gasped. "I know him," she said. She screwed up her face in concentration trying to remember where she'd seen him before and suddenly remembered. "Skip, that's Skip, Boo's husband. I met them on the train out here from Boston. They've got twin girls." She sat down and looked at Maggie who was completing some paperwork about the deceased.

"Can I go to their house and be with her tonight? This is going to flatten her."

Maggie nodded. "Go ahead, I'll tell Annaliese.

Someone opened the front door just as she raised her hand to knock. She stepped back and could tell by the man's face that Boo had heard.

"You are?" he asked abruptly.

"I'm from the clinic. She's a friend. I thought I should be here."

"Thank you, come in." he stepped back and she slipped inside.

"Thank you," she said.

He turned to leave. "First time I've had to do this. It was hard."

"Yes it is," she said, squeezing his arm. "It never gets easy."

Boo was sitting at a table in the small room. She looked up at Colleen and smiled tremulously. "Now what do I do? What'll I do when the girls come home? How am I going to tell them?"

Colleen realized she didn't expect an answer, so she just sat, held her hand and listened. Sometimes silence is the best medicine.

"It has been going well since we got here. He's been working. We talked about staying here. I stay busy and the girls love it. And suddenly it's over and now what?

"They'll be here in a little while, probably arguing when they come in, smiling when they see me. And then I have to tell them and watch their faces when they realize what it means." Tears were running down her cheeks and Colleen's too.

She shook her head and smiled sadly. "We haven't saved anything."

She shrugged and looked up at the ceiling, looked at Colleen as though totally bewildered. "What'll I do?"

Colleen stood and pulled her to her feet and into a long, long hug, the kind that makes you feel much better when you need it. "We won't let you starve, if that's what you're worried about."

CHAPTER TWENTY-FIVE

The best time was in the early evening. Everything that needed to be done was done and they could sit in the cockpit, a hand on the wheel, talk, and watch the sun go down. This evening he was standing at the wheel and she was playing with Jinx, a sometimes painful pastime since he was still learning to use his claws.

Henri came halfway up the ladder and said to Bobby, "So what do you think?"

"Day after tomorrow. Should be in the morning."

Henri grinned at him and nodded. "OK," he said. He came on deck and worked his way to the bow where he lit his pipe and let the wind blow the smoke away.

She looked at Bobby. "What was that about?"

"What was what about?"

"The two of you understand what you just said, but I don't."

He looked puzzled then grinned. "It's something we do when we're getting close to a landfall. I use the charts, my instruments, and dead reckoning to figure our position. He's just telling me I'm right."

"So he's checking you."

"I'm still learning this stuff, sweetheart. This is the biggest ocean in the world. If you don't know where you are, you're in trouble."

He sat for a while looking up at the sails and checking the

heading on the compass.

"When he was a young man, Henri lived with some Polynesians. They had migrated from their kinsmen a long time ago and were living in their own little colony on the north shore of Espiritu Santo in the New Hebrides.

"These people remembered some traditional methods of navigation that had been forgotten elsewhere. He learned these things from them. He always seems to know where he is. It's observation and experience more than anything. I'm learning these things from him a little at a time. I'll teach them to you the same way.

"The way to understand how isolated and separated from the rest of the world we are out here is to remember three numbers. Tahiti is three thousand miles from Noumea. It's almost three thousand miles from Honolulu and five thousand miles from the coast of South America. Almost all of that distance is covered by water.

"When I went to work for Pete, part of our deal was that he would teach me to navigate using the stars. I needed him for a while longer. But Henri has taken his place.

"I realize I couldn't do this without him. Not yet and it will be a few years before I'll feel I can. That's why anytime he wants half of Mirabelle, he can have it.

"I like having him around."

He pointed, and she stood and saw a small green mound on the horizon.

"Is that it?"

"That's it. You're seeing the top of Mount Orohena. It's big so we won't be there until tomorrow morning sometime. Pete's book says it's almost 5000 feet high. High enough to catch a lot of rain clouds. I haven't spent much time here but there are a lot of streams running off that mountain. Did you read about it?"

She nodded, staring out at the mountain top.

"We pick our passenger up in Papeete. That's the capital and it's the only place I've been on the island. Usually, we come in to get something or unload something and don't stay long."

He took a note from his pocket and unfolded it. "Doctor Fernau is his name. We'll check in at Government House. They'll know how to reach him."

"How long will we be here?"

"That's up to him. He's been waiting a while, so it's likely he'll be ready to go."

The next morning, they were up before light and she sat, mesmerized, by what was revealed by the dawn. The green mountain rose into the only cloud in the sky and she only gradually became aware of the houses and buildings of Papeete. There were deep valleys reaching up to the mountain and the lush green told of lots of rain and many streams.

"This is a place where I'm glad I've got the engine," said Bobby. "Getting into the harbor here is tricky. You just sort of slide into it through a small break in the reef. If the tide's not right, it can be a problem under sail. At a place like this we use the engine to maneuver at close quarters and it's a lifesaver."

Bobby started the engine, then dropped the sails and motored into a surprisingly small lagoon where he dropped anchor. She sat in the stern of the dinghy, sightseeing and watched while Bobby and Henri rowed them to a rickety-looking wharf jutting into the harbor.

Government House was impressive-looking; three stories, each with a sitting porch that ran along the front of the building, and all looked out at the harbor. They were shown into an office and after a short wait, a small, slender woman dressed in khaki trousers and a shirt entered with an officer dressed in white.

"Hello. You must be Captain Josephson. I'm Dr. Fernau. Is this your wife?"

Bobby stood, taken aback and stared for a moment before he said, "Yes, yes, it is." Bobby was stumbling over his words, so Teressa stood and extended her hand. "I'm Teressa Josephson." She gestured at Bobby. "."He's not usually tongue-tied like that, you took him by surprise

The woman smiled. "I get that a lot. I take it he hasn't seen too many women doctors?"

Actually, my mother is a doctor and he's known her all his life. It's just he was expecting a man."

"My apologies Dr. Fernau," said Bobby. "She's right. I grew up around women doctors."

"Why don't we go down to my room, and we can talk while I get my things together."

They followed her down a long hall to a nice room and sat and talked while she put things in a suitcase and an old-fashioned carpet bag.

"So, do you have a plan, Captain?"

"Bobby is fine," he said. "Sort of, but you're the boss. Tell me where you want to go and if I can get there, we'll go."

She picked up a sheaf of papers, looked at them for a moment then said, "They pretty much leave it to my discretion, but I'd like to visit all or at least most of the islands. In some cases, it will be for an hour or two. Some more than that."

"You do know there are 108 islands in French Polynesia?" asked Bobby.

"I know, and some of them have only a few people on them. Maybe the best way is to go to the farthest ones out and work our way back."

"That's fine. They paid me in advance for three months, and I can bill them if it takes longer."

"So we'll take as long as it takes," she said, smiling. "I have several cases of medication and medical equipment at a warehouse on the waterfront. Other than that I'm ready. Oh, by the way, my name is Anne. That's better than Dr. Fernau."

Thus began an idyllic period in their lives, one they could look back on and marvel at how much they had learned. Anne's job was to make a yearly visit to the islands of French Polynesia and she was young and dedicated, so the Josephsons enjoyed a long honeymoon at someone else's expense and got paid for it.

They tried to arrange the work so they could sit together and watch the dawn every morning when under sail. This was the life he had seen in his dreams of the future. He hadn't imagined Teressa in that future until she wasn't. Now she was here and she loved him and he had the trade winds on his beam.

Anne's job was to go from island to island, examine as many

people as possible and compile certain statistics and observations about each island. The last thing she brought aboard was a typewriter with several reams of paper. Most evenings she sat in the galley after dinner and 'wrote in her diary,' as she put it.

One evening, they were sitting in the galley, Anne typing, Bobby playing with Jinx, and Teressa reading when Anne stopped typing and said, "Could I ask a favor of you? Either one of you, actually." Bobby and Teressa both nodded.

"I wonder if you'd proofread what I'm writing. Look for mistakes, that kind of thing. If you want, we can discuss what you read." They looked at each other, heads nodding.

"I think that's a great idea. I'd love it," said Bobby. "You know, you should read Pete's Logs. We've got a few of them with us if you'd like to look at them."

"Well, that's great. Which one of you?"

They looked at each other. "Both," they said.

There were times when she would be typing, seemingly oblivious, while Cookie was cooking and the rest of the crew was passing through the galley, admittedly close quarters. Now there was usually someone, or more than one, sitting with her, reading.

Jinx seemed to adapt to the new environment seamlessly. He was Teressa's constant companion, was involved in most conversations, and was usually attentive to any food in the offing. She soon lost any fear they'd lose him overboard.

Anne's father had been in the American Foreign Service, met and married her mother in England, where she grew up. She had been educated at medical school in France and during her studies, crossed paths with a cultural anthropologist with a passion for the islands and islanders of the South Pacific. Soon she adopted that passion for herself.

This assignment was for the French Health Service and she also had a commission to write a book about her experiences for an organization that would, in turn, present it to the British Museum for publication.

Before they came ashore on a new island, all three would have read both Pete's Logs and also everything Anne had about the island and its people. They had specific questions that would get them the background Anne was looking for. Language difficulties or not, they learned volumes.

Usually, Bobby would go off to deal with the authorities while Anne and Teressa began talking to the islanders, more often the women than the men. In the evening, after dinner they would share information and discuss what they had learned.

Early on, Anne had decided to spend at least a full day and one night on even the smallest, populated island. On the larger ones, she was sometimes there for several days and at several different places on the island. On those days, Teressa and Bobby were able to hike into the mountains or swim in the lagoon if there was one. They visited with the islanders and learned what was beautiful or interesting in the neighborhood. They ate many pleasant and fascinating meals with smiling people and their happy children.

Following Anne's decision Bobby had laid a course for the Marquesas, an archipelago almost a thousand miles north and east of Tahiti and the first large island they visited was Nuku Hiva.
Unlike most of the rest of French Polynesia, the Marquesas are not guarded against the ocean by barrier reefs. As a result, there are no lagoons and people don't tend to settle on the coast, but instead in the deep, almost fjord-like, valleys the ocean has carved into the volcanic rock of the island. They also don't have the same rainfall as the Society Islands and Tahiti, a thousand miles to the south and west. Indeed, occasional drought is a problem and some of the islands are only inhabited during the wet season.

Since this was Anne's first stop on her first trip, she began to find out what her position entailed and it turned into a weeks-long odyssey for Teressa and Bobby. Usually daytime would find them hiking into the central valley or to small villages in the interior. They ate with the islanders in different places and tasted new foods, especially different kinds of fish, cooked in many different ways.

One of these evenings, they were at table with their host on a nice veranda when a beautiful young woman came out of the bungalow next door, stopped suddenly and stood on the porch looking at them. No, she wasn't looking, she was staring. At Bobby. And suddenly Teressa knew.

This was the girl. The girl he had told her about. He had slept with her, then dreamed of Teressa, realized what she meant to him and began the trip to San Francisco to find her. She turned to look at Bobby and it was clear that he recognized the girl.

He turned and with a hopeful smile, reached out and drew Teressa into a warm embrace. At first, she didn't respond, but then her arms went around him. She closed her eyes and laid her head on his shoulder.

"He's asking me to understand," she thought and squeezed harder, telling him she did.

That night back on the boat lovemaking was intense and exciting and afterward, they talked.

"Did you think about her?"

He was quiet for a moment. This was a dangerous question.

"I remembered her, but at the end, it was you," he finally said and took her in his arms. "Only you."

She lay quiet for a while. "It's strange," she said. "The thought of you doing to her what you were doing to me was exciting." She turned on her side. "It made me want you more." She kissed him. "And I already want you a lot."

He kissed her, and what began as a peck gradually became savoring, then searching, and finally passionate.

Anne was looking thoughtful at breakfast one morning, the fifteenth day of their stay on the island. "I think if we don't go soon, I'll never get out of here. So let's leave on the morning tide. Is that OK?" she asked, looking at Bobby.

He looked at Henri, who said, "Probably about ten o'clock."

Later that afternoon, Teressa and Bobby were in Taioha'e getting supplies when she said, "I want to see her again before we leave."

Bobby looked at her, surprised, then thoughtful. Then nodded. "Do you want me there?"

She thought for a moment. "Yes. I think so."

"She doesn't speak English, you know."

"I don't want to talk to her."

"What are you going to do?"

She just smiled at him. She left him standing in the yard and climbed the steps to the porch. Someone heard her and a small boy came to the door. He turned to speak to someone inside and the girl came to the door.

They looked at each other in silence for a moment, then Teressa smiled, took her hand, and kissed it, all the while looking into her eyes.

They stood like that, holding hands and looking at one another for a long moment, then Teressa turned and left. When she got to where he was standing, he held out his hand. She took it, looked back at the girl, and smiled at her again.

They were back on the boat before either spoke again. "Do you want to talk about it?"

"No. I want to think about it for a while. We'll have the rest of our lives to talk about it."

She was up early and in the galley working before Cookie came in. When breakfast was over, they all did their parts and Mirabelle weighed anchor and left on the morning tide. She was sitting at the mess table when Henri came down the ladder, got a cup of coffee and sat across from her.

"Bobby tells me you saw Marie yesterday."

When she nodded, he said, "Can I tell you a story about her?"

She looked at him for a moment, then slowly nodded.

"One night, when we left here, there was a beautiful full moon. He and I were rowing out and he saw her on the dock waving. After that we called her the girl in the moonlight." He smiled. "He took a nap on deck one afternoon after he'd been with her and he dreamed about you."

Teressa grinned. "Why would he tell you about that?"

"Maybe because he thought it was important. After all, it was a dream that changed his life," he paused, "and yours too."

Late that afternoon, they dropped anchor in a small bay at Ua Huka, the next island and so on. They became proficient in getting the anchor up and down because they did it so much over the next month.

And they learned. About the people, their lives, and what was important to them. How many there were and how many years were the oldest and the youngest. What they ate and drank. They watched dances and celebrations, people working, and children playing.

When any of them looked back on this time, they'd remember those nights in the galley when they wrote and talked with Anne and shared what they had learned that day.

CHAPTER TWENTY-SIX

Privacy was rare at the Yard. Every minute of every day, Manny was surrounded by the members of his company, one hundred and thirty strong. They rose at reveille together, donned their uniforms and marched in formation to meals and classes together, carried out a myriad of activities during the day together, and every night they turned out the lights at the same time. Two things you could count on in the Yard: you were in uniform and you were surrounded by men.

And they were men now. Not the boys they had been when they arrived. They had lived together, grown together and learned together, and soon they would leave and board a ship together and be even more crowded and cramped than they were at Bancroft Hall.

Which is why Manny felt strange on a Sunday morning when he took the train to Arnold and the airfield by himself. Usually there were one or more members of the club with him, but on this beautiful April morning in the spring of 1909, everyone had something else to do. Not Manny.

He did have things to think about, though. This was his spring as a 'firstie'. He had made it through the Academy, had survived to stand in the top ten of his class and risen to command a battalion of men with four stripes on his arm. Next he would take his final cruise then home to Colleen for August and finally, he would begin his career.

To Manny the important things in his life were his family, Colleen, the U.S. Navy, and flying. The problem now seemed to be that flying was pushing the Navy for his attention.

He wanted to fly, to be an airman, but in less than two months, he'd be boarding a battleship as a graduated Ensign to serve a two-year tour before he could get a commission as an officer.

He saw no place for flying in that future. His approach to the whole idea of flying had been different than most and his time spent in the repair shop at Cy's place much more than his time in the air, had moved him into the ranks of the few who knew the structure and nomenclature of a flying machine and understood the theory behind it.

He could see a future for himself in bringing flying to the Navy but knew enough about the Navy's makeup to realize the futility of someone in his position trying to have an impact on the decision-makers in the service.

He loved the Navy but felt he could serve it better by being one of the few who knew his way around this exciting new field of human endeavor than by being one of a hundred and fourteen in his graduating class who would spend two years at sea on a warship.

On the other hand, what were his options? He could allow himself to be swept along with the rest of them into the same future. Airplanes and new technology would still be here when he got back from sea. He could also keep an eye out for opportunities to continue learning and hope that sometime in the future, the chance might come for him to fly for the Navy.

He could also resign from the Brigade. He knew several in the class had left voluntarily in the past for one reason or another. He knew Glen Curtiss would hire him in a minute and there were others. He could find a place in the field of aviation, but he shrank from that possibility, not really able to look resigning in the face.

Cy immediately noticed his preoccupation and since he was not really needed at the shop that day, suggested a ride in his new automobile.

"We could go somewhere to sit and talk, since you obviously

need to."

"You noticed," said Manny sheepishly.

Cy parked along a creek, and they got out and sat on a log someone had placed as a bench.

"So, what's bothering you?"

Manny laid the problem out for him and when he finished, he looked at his friend in silence. Cy looked back thoughtfully and after a while, said, "You know Glen Curtiss would hire you in a second, don't you?" Curtiss had flown in several weeks before, and in their talk, Cy had mentioned Manny to him. "He remembers you. Said he talked to you a couple of times last year."

When Manny remained quiet, Cy continued. "You don't want to leave the Navy. That's the nub of it, isn't it? You've tied a lot into this future the last four years and don't want to give it up. That's understandable."

He swept his arm around the field and said, "You're young and impatient. This will all be here when you get back and knowing you, you'll read everything you can get your hands on about flying and keep up with what's going on. By that time, the Navy might wake up and you can be a flier for them."

He ran his hand over his bald head. "You've got a lot invested in the Navy. I think you should go on the cruise. But," he put his hand on Manny's knee, "if you ever need a job, come see me. I'm going to miss having you around."

"I graduate in about six weeks and as much as I hate to say it, I probably won't be able to come out and work with you again. The closer we get to graduation the more I'll have to do."

In the automobile on the way back to the field, Manny said, "My family will be coming for commencement. I would like to bring them out to see the place and meet you."

"I'd be honored."

April 20, 1909
Dear Manny,
    I've been accepted to the University of California Medical School in the class beginning in January of next

year. I can't believe all the things going through my mind since I found out about it.

Of course, I thought about you first and what you'd think about it. I'm excited about coming to your graduation with Annaliese and Johnny. I hope we can find a place to be alone and talk about all the things I feel since I got the letter. I feel proud and afraid and happy and weak in the knees whenever I think about it. Come to think about it, it's the same way I feel when I think about you.

She told me yesterday we'd be there a week before and stay for a week after. I hope we can sneak away and be together alone sometime.

Boo and I took the twins and went sailing with Lem and Mary last week. The twins are going on twelve and it's fun to do things with them. Boo is finally coming back to herself and we spend a lot of time together. She and Janet and I went to a play at the high school and enjoyed it.

Janet and I are both in the incoming class at school in January and Annaliese told me she was going to take a vacation and not have any girls for a while. Then she can look at the pluses and minuses of having interns and decide if she wants to have another one.

I got a letter from Teressa. Little Vanessa is going on two and the apple of her father's eye. She hopes we can get to know each other with letters. She seems to be content with her new life and apparently has plenty of time to write. She also writes to Sarah.

That's something else. Madame's here and Sarah's not. I haven't heard why.

If I wrote all that's in my mind I'd never stop but I have to be up early so one more thing and then I'll say good night.

With all this time and all these miles between us are you still excited by the idea of counting all my freckles?

Love you, Colleen

Manny was grinning the rest of the day.

Manny's chair hit the floor with a thump. He had been leaning in the chair with his back against the wall, sorting his mail.

Jack looked up, startled. "What's the matter?"

Manny didn't answer. He tore open the envelope and read, 'Midshipman Manuel Fry will report to the Office of the Superintendent at 1000 hours tomorrow morning, May 6, 1909.'

Slack-jawed with amazement, he handed the order to Jack, who read it and looked back at him the same way.

"What's that about?" asked Jack.

After a moment of thought, Manny shook his head. "I have absolutely no idea."

"Save that one for your scrapbook," said Jack, indicating the order. "You'll never see another one like it."

The next morning at 0950, he took a seat in the 'Badger's' office with his heart beating a little fast. In the language of the Academy, that was the Superintendent's name. Charles W. Badger was at the end of his two-year tour. He was an alumnus, as were all Superintendents and had enjoyed his time back at the Yard. He also had fond memories of his time in the Brigade and a certain amount of empathy with the young men under his command.

The office was official-looking with various photographs and memorabilia around the room and windows overlooking the Yard and Bancroft Hall. When Manny stopped at the desk and saluted, Captain Badger looked up from something he was reading, returned the salute and smiled at him.

"At ease, Mr. Fry. Take a seat." He finished what he was reading, looked up and said, "I'll bet you've been wondering why you're here, haven't you?"

Manny tried to keep a straight face. "Well, I didn't sleep much last night, if that's what you mean."

The Captain laughed and leaned back in his chair. "I have an old friend who's just been given a new job by the Navy. They want him to create an operations plan for developing an air corps." He watched Manny's face when he said this and had to smile at the reaction he saw.

An expression of open-mouthed shock gradually gave way to a wide smile and then a grin.

"He asked me to find some of my middies who were interested in flying and everywhere I turn I hear your name. Why is that?"

So Manny told him. How the germ of an idea planted by a friend had focused him on flying and led to the founding of the club. How he now spent all the time and energy he could spare from schoolwork on learning what he could about how flying worked and thinking how it could apply to the Navy.

"Sounds like I've found the perfect man to work with Irving to set this thing up, but I want you to think about something. If you decide to try this, it means that the usual regime for your career will probably go out the window."

"What do you mean?"

"I mean you probably won't go to a ship and serve at sea the way all the other graduated midshipmen do. You'll likely report to Captain Chambers right away and go from there. The Navy wants this done quickly and it's the young that are part of it. Most of us in the Navy are old dogs. This is a thing for young dogs.

"Because it's a new field and the Navy is a hidebound outfit, I have no idea how it will affect your career or your chances for promotion. It's the kind of thing you need some time to decide. I want you to get back with me by next week on it."

"Where would I be stationed?"

"For now, probably San Diego. If I remember right, that's your hometown, isn't it?" said the Captain with a grin.

For the second time in the interview, Manny's mouth dropped open.

"I don't think they've decided where the headquarters will be just yet. Some say Pensacola."

"In Florida?"

"Yes. I understand there's a place down there they can expand and develop. But for now, it's San Diego. North Island, from what Irving says.

"I've hunted rabbits on North Island," said Manny, still grinning.

"If you decide you want to try it, I'll contact Captain Chambers and get some more information so you'll have some idea of what you'll be doing. He mentioned some recent graduates he's talked to and some of them are already on board. You know John Tower and Ted Ellyson, don't you?"

"Yes, sir. They were both in the club. They've both flown and are as hot about the idea as I am. Marc Mitcher in my class is another one who's flown and wants to stay with it."

"That's another name I've heard. When you make up your mind, stop by here and tell my chief yeoman you need to see me. He'll be looking for you. If you see Mitcher, talk to him about it."

Manny and Colleen had enjoyed the excitement of meeting for the first time in a long time a few times and learned to do it a certain way. Usually, these happy greetings would be in the presence of family and she would stand aside and smile and watch the affectionate greetings from everyone. He would glance at her during these greetings and everyone would notice this with a smile and he'd be hugged and kissed and handled by all. Eventually, she'd be the last, and then the rest of them would cease to exist.

And yes, it still made him dizzy.

The week before, he had gone to their place by the river and found it wasn't lonely anymore, so he found another place. They took a picnic basket again and forgot all about it again because they were doing other things instead of eating.

Eventually, they lay in each other's arms on a blanket in a clearing by the river, eyes closed, each breathing in the essence of the other.

"It seems as though we still think this whole thing is a good idea," he mumbled, his face in her hair.

She was grinning up at the clouds when she replied, "Yes, it does seem that absence makes the heart grow fonder, after all."

They walked back to the Yard holding hands occasionally looking at one another. They continued holding hands and looking at one another while he showed Annaliese and Johnny and Lemuel and Kate around and explained his life to them.

Sunday morning they were all on the train to Arnold, where a wagon took them to the airfield to see what Manny was so fascinated about. Over time, Cy had added an office overlooking the repair shop where they sat and talked for a while. He had also installed a large window overlooking the field and while they talked, they watched several airplanes take off and land.

"I'm going to miss having Manny around here every Sunday," said Cy, leaning back in his new swivel chair. "He's been a big help, and I think he's learned a bunch."

With everyone seated and looking out the window, Manny stood and began talking about his problem, hoping they would help him decide where his future lay.

"I know all of you know me well enough that I don't have to talk about wanting to be a sailor. It's all I've ever wanted to be since I was a boy. But that was before I'd flown. There is a possibility the Navy will eventually decide to get into the air. A good possibility. So on one hand I want to be a part of that, on the other, I want to go to sea and do what it takes to make me a seagoing officer.

"Up until yesterday, the idea of continuing to fly seemed to be out the window, at least for a while, but then this happened." He read them the note from the Superintendent and told them about the meeting and the opportunity it represented, and also about what he was risking if he left the track the Navy had laid before him.

"What would you be doing if you did it?" asked his mother. "I mean, what kind of job would it be? And where?"

Manny shook his head. "Couldn't tell you. All I know is the Navy's looking for ideas and a certain understanding of airplanes. Someone has told them I can help them, but it's my choice."

Johnny stood at the window looking out at the field. "Manny, I've watched you grow up and for many years you've dreamed that one day you'd finish here and go on to become a sailor." He turned and looked at Manny. "If this is such a thing as to make you want to do something other than that, it must be important to you." He shook his head. "It's a tough decision. No matter your choice, you'll always wonder about the other path. This is one you have to decide for yourself. That way there's no one to blame if it doesn't work out like you planned."

"What does Colleen say about it?" asked Kate.

"I'd like to hear that myself," said Annaliese.

"We've talked about it a lot the last couple of years. I guess I want him to do what he believes will take him where he wants to go. It frightens me when I think about it, so I don't, well, not much anyway. If and when we have children, that may change, but I want him to be happy. I guess that's the important thing, and I believe he wants the same thing for me."

Lemuel laughed. He looked at Manny and said, "So let me get this straight. You've been seeing each other one month a year for three years, and now you're coming home and in a couple of months she's moving to San Francisco for three years, and you're going god knows where." When Manny nodded slowly, he shook his head. "Good luck with that," he said, grinning and looking amazed.

When Manny kissed Colleen good night, she looked at him with a wry smile.

"Have you decided what you're going to do?"

"No, but it seems to be a choice between the U.S. Navy and flying. I just have to figure out which comes first."

CHAPTER TWENTY-SEVEN

The next evening, CT was sitting on the porch of his little cabin at the pistol range when Manny and his father rode up and dismounted. He stood and extended his hand to Johnny in greeting and raised the other one to Manny, who was pulling saddlebags off the horse.

When they were seated, CT said, "I think you're the only one who still comes out here on a horse. Everyone else is in an automobile or a truck these days."

They talked about the trip from San Diego and a little about the city before CT said, "Manny's told me you went out there from Kansas. In '84 or '85 was it?"

"Actually both. I left Junction City in the spring of '84, spent the winter in Salt Lake City, and got to Sacramento in June the next year." He shook his head. "Hard to believe we got here in three and a half days on the train."

CT swept his arm around the room. "I spend most of my time here. This leg they gave me never did fit right, so I don't get around too much. Over the years I've become friends with many students and fortunately they come back or write once in a while, and that's how I see the world, through their eyes. I know about Manny, so tell me a little about yourself. Manny tells me you're a 'magician with a six-gun."

"A friend of mine called me that years ago," Johnny said, smiling. He nodded slowly, thoughtfully. "My Pa was a gunsmith, among other things. After Ma died, he never remarried, and we spent most of our time together.

"Every Sunday we'd go out along the river to a shooting range he used to test-fire the guns he worked on and he'd teach me to shoot. The first time I was maybe six years old." He smiled. "Had to hold the gun with both hands. After a while it became a contest. I seemed to have a knack for it, and by the time I was fourteen, I could beat him and hit my target firing from the waist."

"Over the years I've continued to work on it because I enjoyed it and when Manny got old enough, we spent a lot of time shooting down on the beach."

"Manny tells me you've had to fight with it."

Johnny shrugged. "The West was still wild in those days. Everyone wore a gun and used it if they felt it was necessary. There were a few times when I felt it was necessary."

"So, what do you think about your son graduating from the Academy?"

"Oh, we're all excited about it, but something's come up and I think he wants to talk to you about it." Johnny looked at his son. "Isn't that right?"

Manny nodded and told CT about his conversation with 'the Badger.' After he finished, they sat in silence for a while, thinking.

"Have you decided what you're going to tell him?"

"I wanted to talk to you first. What do you think about it?"

CT's smile gradually turned into a grin. "Since I'm the one who brought up the idea of flying to you in the first place, I think you know how I feel about it. I believe it's going to become important and not just to the Navy." He smiled at the father and son sitting on the settee. He nodded at Manny. "I believe you could become important with it too."

"What about what he said about promotions and such?"

"That might be true. It would be like the Navy. The ones in power want to keep things the way they are. Don't rock the boat, as it were. It could be they'll try to put you in the bottom of the locker, but I believe it's too important to stay there. Might make you some enemies, but I think there'll come a time when they'll be glad you're around.

"On the other hand, how important is that to what you see in your future? Do you want to fly or be Captain of a ship?"

Manny looked at him for a long moment, then at his father. "I want to fly," he said. He sat quiet for a while looking out the window at nothing. Finally, he said, "But it's not just flying. This is all new. There's so much to learn, to conceive, to design, to build. I'll talk to the Badger tomorrow," he said, looking at his father. "It will be nice if he can give me a little more information about it before I have to make up my mind."

"You'll likely get some of that tomorrow," said CT. "For an outfit that seems stuck in the mud at times, the Navy can move pretty fast when it really wants something done. Sounds like this is one of those times."

They spent some time shooting, talking while they did and when they finally said goodbye, CT held Manny's hand for a long time. "Write me when you get a chance." He turned to Johnny, took his hand and said, "Manny wasn't kidding about you and a gun, but with Manny, that doesn't surprise me. You can always take him at his word."

On the way back to the Yard they paused to let the horses drink at a stream that ran beside the path. "I learned a lot of important things from that man. Sometimes I'd come out and we'd sit and talk for hours about everything under the sun. He's the reason I got interested in flying. I'm going to miss him."

"Speaking of flying, you've made up your mind, haven't you?"

"I think so. What do you think about it?"

Johnny shook his head. "I can't help you with this one, Manny. You've been away from home for four years and have had all sorts of experiences I know nothing about. How can I advise you? You have to live with this decision the rest of your life and I'm sure you'll do just fine, but it's got to be your decision. Over the years I've come to believe you find those kinds of decisions easier to live with."

They were almost back in the Yard before Manny spoke.

"This is the future, Papa. I know these airplanes are crude and flimsy, but several times I've talked to a man who's right at the front of this new idea. No, that's not right. It's not a new idea." He shook his head. "Man's wanted to fly since he looked up and saw birds, but after thousands of years, we've finally done it. We can fly and live through it, control it. Men like Cy and Glen Curtiss and the Wrights are the pioneers in this field, and they want to teach me about it.

"The Navy has taken four years to teach me to be a marine engineer. What I'd like to do is take what they've taught me and become an aeronautical engineer instead. With what I've learned here, what I can learn from Curtiss and his friends and what I can learn from experience, I might just be the first one." He shrugged. "Or maybe the third or fourth," he said with a grin.

"Sounds like you've put some thought into it." He squeezed his son's shoulder. "Try to live through it, will you? I'd like to have grandchildren to tell stories to."

"When I told Papa what I'd decided, he said something about grandchildren. Is there something I should know?" Manny looked at Colleen meaningfully. They were sitting on a bench in a somewhat secluded alcove one evening, doing things young lovers do.

She tried to keep a straight face, failed, and looked at him thoughtfully.

"How would you feel about that?" she asked, an impish smile on her face.

He looked at her for a moment, turned to gaze across the river in silence, and finally said, "I guess it would make our life interesting. Probably some good, some bad. Like most lives."

He turned to face her. "But I'd like it because I'd be with you. I like the way you look at life. It makes my life more fun. I love you."

She leaned forward two kissed him on the nose. "You always say the right thing." She kissed him on the mouth. "Well, I'm not, but it would be nice if we could practice more. The motto of this place should be 'never alone.'"

"It's worse on a ship."

"But you're not going to be on a ship, are you?"

Silence. Finally, he took a deep breath and shook his head. "I'll probably take my First-Class cruise, come home for a month and then report to Capt. Chambers."

"So, you're decided to take the position?" When he nodded, she continued. "Where would you be stationed?"

"I don't know. Originally it was San Diego, but that will be temporary. I'll know more when I talk to the Badger."

"And when will that be?"

"It will have to be tomorrow sometime. Too many things going on this weekend."

"So tonight, you'll make your decision about your future. About our future."

He nodded and they sat looking at one another. "I feel like I'm crawling out on a limb here. If it breaks, I could fall a long way. In the past this was always something in the future, so we sort of pushed it aside to be considered when we had time or when we needed to.

"Well, it's time. We need to. When I walk out of his office tomorrow, I'll have chosen and that choice will affect both our lives. Tell me what you think about it now that the choice is here? Are you sure you want to tie your life to the U.S. Navy?"

He was asking her if she wanted to join him on this path or take one of her own. It was something that needed thinking about, but tomorrow it would be happening. It wouldn't wait, so she needed to tell him now whether or not she'd be with him going forward.

When he entered the Badger's office the next morning, there was another naval captain sitting, talking to the Superintendent. Manny stopped at the desk and saluted. Captain Badger returned his salute.

"At ease, Mr. Fry. Congratulations on graduating tomorrow. Since we talked, I've learned a few things about you. This fellow here," he gestured at the other man, "is Captain Chambers. He's the one I told you about that's going to be looking into the idea of flying and how it might apply to the Navy. Why don't you sit down and we'll talk about it?"

Captain Chambers looked at him thoughtfully out of bright blue eyes. "Your boss here has been telling me a little about you. What I need is an aide, preferably one that will work cheap." When Manny looked puzzled, the captain laughed, then shook his head and sighed.

"Over the last year, I've been bothering the Navy about flying. Everyone thinks I'm crazy about the idea and I think they gave me this job to shut me up. But there's a fellow in personnel who feels the same way I do about it and he wrangled me a spot for an ensign as an aide if I find one that fits.

"It would probably be the kind of thing where we'd be spending a lot of time together. You'd be expected to help me find answers to questions and figure ways to make my superiors realize that flying should be an important part of the Navy.

"I really don't know much about what the job entails, but it looks like we'll have to make it up as we go along in the beginning and follow where it leads us. From what Badger tells me, you'll have to go on your First-Class cruise before we can even get you assigned. To tell you the truth I don't really have any plans at this point, just ideas. But I tell you what, go on your cruise and I'll have some orders for you when you get back." He looked at Manny with a grin. "That is, assuming, of course, you're interested."

"Yes, sir! I'm interested and just so I understand, I'm to go on my cruise, take a month at home and then report to you?"

Chambers nodded. "I'm headed to the west coast where it looks like we'll be spending a lot of time, at least at first," he said. "You know Glen Curtiss, don't you?" Manny nodded, and he continued. "I saw him in Washington the other day and we talked. When I told him I was looking for someone as an aide, he suggested I look at some of the new graduates here. He mentioned your name."

"Yes sir, I know him. He flew into the airfield where I was working one Sunday."

"He told me you're a mechanic as well as a theoretician of sorts."

"That's true. For the last three months, I've gone out to an airfield at Arnold, just north of here, to work in the shop and fly whenever I got a chance. Cy, the owner out there, has taught me a lot about theory and the mechanics of flying and has let me fly whenever there's an opportunity."

"Badger here has told me a little about you. I understand you're top of your class in engineering and very good at understanding and using schematic diagrams." Manny nodded. "He also tells me you're 'hell on wheels' with a pistol."

Manny grinned. "My father taught me to shoot when I was a boy and we've spent a lot of time working together at it. I still practice whenever I get a chance."

"Well, that's about all I can tell you about the job. It will take you out of the Navy, off and on, for a while. We'll be working with Curtiss on some of his ideas and with some of his people at the start. The Navy might forget about you for a while and I have no idea how it will affect your career." He looked at Manny quizzically for a moment. "So, what do you think? Want to give it a try?"

Manny had decided before he came in the door. He nodded. "Yes, sir," he said. "It sounds like it's just what I've been thinking about."

"Well then," Chambers stood and held out his hand. "Welcome aboard. It ought to be interesting if nothing else."

"You two haven't had much time together since we've been here, have you?" Annaliese and Colleen were sitting on the porch of the inn where they were staying.

Colleen looked glum and shook her head. "Manny tells me privacy isn't on the curriculum at the Academy." They both laughed.

"Remembering what it was like when I was your age, I made some arrangements so you and Manny can use our room tonight."

Colleen looked amazed. "Where are you going to sleep?"

"Lemuel and Kate have an extra bed in their room. They don't mind."

"Thank you," she said. "It sounds romantic, on a blanket in the woods, but it gets old in a hurry." She took Annaliese's hand. "I don't know what to call you. You've become the mother I lost years ago. Thank you."

Annaliese stood and pulled her into an embrace. When they parted, she grinned at Colleen. "I'd love to see the look on Manny's face when you tell him." They both laughed again.

It was just getting dark when they turned out the lights. The only light was under the door from the hallway outside. After getting the bath ready, they undressed each other and he stood and looked at her in the dim, romantic light, reaching out to touch her here and there, gently, smoothly.

There was a candle in the bathroom. They washed each other slowly, completely, patted each other dry, then she led him to the bed.

"It's going to be hard to count them in this light," he murmured. "I'll have to get really close."

She lay down on the bed and put her finger just above the line of her triangle of pubic hair.

"Start counting right here." He didn't even make it past ten.

Afterward, she lay on her side and ran her hand over his chest, drawing figures with her finger lightly.

"You sound like a cat," he murmured.

"Do I? It doesn't surprise me that I'm purring. It's a mark of contentment."

They lay like that for a while, in silence, minds drifting here and there. Later, when he came back from the bathroom, she was sitting cross-legged on the bed.

She patted the sheets. "Let's talk." She pulled back the coverlet. "You can lie down if you promise not to go to sleep."

"No, I'll sit with you."

When he was seated, she kissed him and began. "It seems the life we're headed for needs a lot of planning and coordination, so let's do this. I'll tell you how I see the next year in our lives, and you tell me what you think about it." He nodded and she went on. "When we leave next week, I will go back to San Diego, and you will come home when you finish here. Then we will have thirty days together before you report to your captain somewhere, you don't know where just yet.

"I will be finishing up, studying, working and getting ready for my new life. I've met Este and she and Roy have a room, Janet and I can stay in while we go to school. I'll be in school for three years with summers off.

"While I'm there, you will be fulfilling your obligation to the Navy but have no idea where. When I graduate we'll have to make further plans, but I want you to know I will do all I can to make it work. I also believe we have something special and eventually we'll settle down together and have a normal life." She smiled thoughtfully. "Probably not too normal. Until then, we should just enjoy the times we can spend together." She kissed him on the nose. "So, what do you think?"

"Sounds about right."

"OK, now. We decided when we had sex for the first time how we would handle things if I got pregnant. With these changes in our life, we need to think about that too."

"I think about it every time we're together," he said. "But there's so much uncertainty in our lives, we can't make any plans except to say, we'll decide everything together. I see lots of letter writing in our future, but I want you to remember. If you get pregnant, we'll deal with it together."

"I am a naval officer and they've taught me to think about things from a naval point of view. In the life we're headed toward, that kind of thinking won't work. This whole thing is a puzzle. How do we maintain a relationship when we're never together?

"To solve this puzzle, we need your kind of thinking. It's not on the curriculum at the Academy." He kissed her and smiled at her thoughtful expression. "I love you and trust your instincts," he said, and kissed her again, and again, and again. She had a lot of freckles.

One thing Manny had noticed about Jack over the years was that most of the time his writing was confined to study hours. To see him with pen and ink on a Saturday was almost unheard of.

"I'll bet you're writing a letter, aren't you?"

Jack looked up with a smile. "No, actually, I remembered that thing you wrote at the end of our first year, Franklin's ledger?"

"Oh yeah. Good and bad things on a ledger." He chuckled. "It would be a long ledger."

"Not so much," replied Jack. "Not if you keep it to big things." He looked down at what he had written. "Friendship was the first thing on my list back then and that's the first thing I wrote today. I guess I think it's the most important."

"What else?"

"Camaraderie, loyalty, trust."

"I'd think they'd all be part of friendship."

"Maybe so." He continued. "Discipline, honor, commitment to something bigger than yourself."

"Willingness to submit to authority," said Manny ruefully. "What about the bad side?"

"I haven't gotten to that yet." He looked thoughtful. "School work!" He rolled his eyes and made a wry face.

"I know it was hard for you, but you made it through."

"Not without a lot of help."

"You had to put in the work. I made a lot of friends among people I tutored. Spruance was right about that. When you help someone make it through, you've got a friend for life."

"How about your list?"

"On the bad side?" Manny looked thoughtful, shook his head. "Bad usually has to do with people. Hazing at first and some pettiness. I can still feel it with some people, but long before I came here I learned to deal with that kind of thing.

"Another bad thing was the constant anxiety, wondering if you were good enough to make the cut and constantly having to prove it."

"Do you have any more information from Chambers about where you're going?"

"My orders are to report to him at the Hooper House Hotel in San Diego." He smiled. "That's about three miles from the store."

"Do you know what you'll be doing?"

"In the letter that came with my orders, he says we'll be working with Glen Curtiss and his people. He says Curtiss has some ideas we need to try out."

Jack shook his head. "That sure doesn't sound anything like what I'll be doing." He had been assigned to a battleship as a graduated ensign. There was a rumor the captain was a football fan and had pulled some strings.

He sat quiet for a moment then shook his head again. "For most of the time I've known you, I would never have believed anything could make you change directions like this. All your life you've wanted to be a sailor and suddenly you want to be something else."

Manny nodded. "Papa said the same thing, but he put it a little differently. He said it must be important, or I wouldn't do it. Well, I believe it is important. It's the future. Since time began, man has wanted to fly. The fragile machines we use to get off the ground now are the beginnings of something important, something momentous.

"I have an opportunity to learn from far-seeing men who have ideas they want to share with me, ideas that will change the Navy and the world for that matter. It's a new dimension. From now on the Navy will need to take the capabilities of flight into their strategic and tactical deliberations.

"The Navy has taught me to think as an engineer. I want to apply that thinking to flight. I'm being given the chance to design and create the machines of the future with men who have vision and the influence to make it happen.

"This is a cusp for me. It's a place where my life will take a sudden and radical turn, and I can't wait to get started."

This was not an age when men embraced, but the handshake they shared at parting had the same emotion and warmth.

BOOK TWO

CHAPTER TWENTY-EIGHT

1914

Mirabelle was running with the trade winds three days into a voyage to Samoa. There they would load a cargo of copra and whatever else needed to go somewhere. In the meantime, the breeze was fresh, the sky blue and the sun low in the sky when Teressa came on deck carrying a cup of tea. She stopped in the cockpit and nodded to Henri, then worked her way forward, sat on a hatch and watched her daughter read a story to Jinx, Teressa's cat and Rudy, one of the hands. Rudy was Vanessa's slave and Jinx, her best friend.

Despite her best efforts to discourage it, everyone called her six-year-old daughter Van and Teressa finally gave up the fight when she found she was doing it herself. Jinx spent a lot of time with the girl and whenever she saw them together, she smiled.

Raising the cat on a boat had been good practice for raising a child on a boat. The main thing was making sure they were safe. Van was everyone's pet and there was always someone keeping an eye on her. She and Jinx spent bad weather below, a. Marie had fashioned a jacket for her to wear on deck, and she was always tethered to a stanchion or a cleat.

Once she had gotten over her initial anxiety about the cat, she found him a big part of life on the boat. He seemed to have slept on every flat surface aboard at one time or another. She was never surprised when she came across him taking a nap in some of the darndest positions, anywhere on the boat. It never failed to make her smile.

Cookie's forced retirement with arthritis meant that Marie was cooking and a part of the crew, the crew that had become a large part of Teressa's life. Van was lucky to have Marie with them. It was as though the girl had two mothers and one or the other was constantly with her, usually just watching, but always there.

Teressa felt the same kind of love for Marie she remembered having for Annaliese. Just having her around made life better. She smiled and closed her eyes, feeling the breeze, listening to the sounds of the schooner rushing across the ocean.

Whenever she looked at her life, she liked what she saw, though it took her a while to feel comfortable on days when there was nothing to do. Just Mirabelle and the great blue ocean under an endless blue sky.

She was not only Bobby's wife, she was also a member of the crew. She could keep them fed and haul a halyard and if necessary, climb the mast, as she had twice, to clear a fouled pulley. She was learning what it took to keep Mirabelle sailing and while not as good as the men, good enough if she had to be and she was learning every day.

She was an important part of Mirabelle's business, too. She did the books, kept all records and helped Bobby with building a library of logbooks similar to Pete's. But her most important contribution was in dealing with the myriad of officials, different languages and customs of the islands and the ever-present paperwork.

Bobby had trouble with these people and saw every situation as a trial. She simply charmed them. She'd found out early that a smile and a laugh got more done than exasperated sighs. She was fun for the men to be around while she enjoyed their admiration and took advantage of it to accomplish something that needed doing.

But over and above the business of being a mother and a woman, above what she had learned about caring for Mirabelle, there was the ocean and the islands, and she never got tired of seeing a beautiful coral atoll or a huge, green mountain rise from the blue

Pacific.

Many of her days ended sitting in the cockpit with Bobby and Van, talking to Henri or Marie, watching the sun slowly disappear and catch the ocean on fire all along the horizon. She loved the nights when the moon was full, was awestruck by the night sky and how large and bright the southern stars were before the moon rose.

Being mother of an infant becoming a toddler and at this point, an inquisitive chatterbox on board a 68-ft schooner, was in turn satisfying, puzzling and frightening. But whenever she looked at her daughter, she marveled at the perfection she saw. So far, so good.

At home, at the house on the cliff, it was different. You didn't have the constant breeze or the sound of water as it curled away from the bow. At home, there was quiet. It was restful to spend several weeks without the responsibilities of a voyage. The house on the cliff was special to the crew, to each of them for a different reason, but special to them all.

When they were home, Bobby would spend his days working on the boat while Teressa, Marie, and Van were free to do what they wanted or needed to do, usually in wonderful weather. Everyone in the house played with the little girl and helped her with the lessons Teressa had devised to help her learn her sums and ABCs. She loved to listen to stories and was constantly asking questions of everyone around.

Marie called them for dinner and Henri lashed the wheel and joined them at the table, questioning Rudy closely on what he had learned from Van's teaching.

Henri's son, Andre, had joined the crew on the previous voyage and this time, Pete and Marie's son, Pete was new in the small fo'castle. Pete had grown up in Marie's home village and usually sat quietly at the table, watching and listening, his eyes alertly focused on whoever spoke. Both boys had grown up on a boat, sailing, fishing, and swimming and now wanted to join the crew and learn the trade.

Jinx was served first, as usual. He then climbed on a cushion to watch and make sure nothing landing on the floor would go to waste. Tonight they had two guests, so they divided into two messes. Henri,

Andre, Pete, and Rudy ate first with Marie, then Bobby, Teressa, and Van with the passengers.

Beni and Claude were from Maupiti, a small atoll in the Society Islands, about three hundred miles north and west of Tahiti. They lived in the village of Vai'ea on the small island in the center of the lagoon. Six months a year, they worked at the shipyard in Noumea, then returned home and spent the rest of the year on Maupiti with their families.

Mirabelle had taken them home once before and Bobby and Teressa had spent some time there with Anne on her tour of the islands. They had come to know some of the people there and were planning to spend a few days while the two men helped Bobby do some repairs to the rudder and wheel.

The atoll was unusual because, in addition to its volcanic origin, gradually, over eons of time, a reef had grown up until a protected lagoon had formed, with several sand and coral islands around the lagoon and inside the reef.

On the center island, a dormant cinder cone dominated and rose to twelve hundred feet above the lagoon. The only flat, usable land was a strip around its base and on this strip, the villages of the island were built, most houses within a stone's throw of the lagoon. Because there was nowhere to build inland, the village of Vai'ea stretched for almost a mile along the lagoon.

Their two passengers were brothers. Beni, the older, was somewhere in his forties and Claude about fifteen years younger. They were typical in the way some men on the islands supported their families working away for half a year and bringing cash and needed supplies when they returned. The largest village on the atoll, Vai'ea, had fewer than two hundred inhabitants; indeed, the whole island had fewer than a thousand.

When they beached the dinghy, everyone in town came out to greet them and helped the brothers carry their dunnage to their house within sight of the lagoon. Bobby and Teressa were invited to stay with Beni's family and accepted. Over the years, they had become accustomed to the open, relaxed household of most islanders, where everyone slept on mats in rooms open to the air unless it was raining.

Rudy and Andre remained on Mirabelle at anchor watch, and the rest of the crew joined a happy return feast to welcome the two wanderers home.

The feast was fish, fruit, and vegetables cooked and served in the fashion of islanders and eaten with the fingers. It was delicious, though a little strange, and they talked and listened and learned as they did whenever they spent time in an islander's home. Sitting and chatting in the relaxed, comfortable time after a meal seemed to be universal and Teressa loved these times and found she learned something new almost every time.

"How did you come by the boat?" asked Claude. The younger of the two brothers, he seemed to be the more outgoing and brought up the thing most on their mind.

Bobby laughed and shook his head. "A once in a lifetime thing that came to me out of a clear blue sky. In essence, Pete gave it to me. Why do you ask?"

"We have been talking," he nodded his head at his older brother, "and we don't like working at the boatyard anymore. We'd like to find something else to work at. It is a problem since many men from the islands go away to work and there aren't enough jobs."

"We'd like to get a boat," he shrugged. "We don't know many of the things we would need for such a thing, but it would be good to work for ourselves."

He gestured around the room and smiled, and they knew what it meant. "We would all own it. And all would want to make it work."

"I'd have to think about it, talk to Henri. We'll be here for a few days, so he, Teressa, and I will talk about it and see what we come up with."

Later, they walked on the beach and talked about it.

"The biggest problem is, where are they going to get the boat? I was purely lucky to get Mirabelle, but the money it would take to get one right now," he shook his head. They stood on the tide line, let the water wet their toes and looked out at Mirabelle. Henri had gone back on board, but as they looked, Henri and Andre climbed into the dinghy and began to pull for shore.

Bobby raised his hand, called out and they altered course and grounded in front of them.

Henri hopped out of the boat. He turned to his son. "Stay there, we might be going right back."

He faced them, a little winded and said, "Blackbirder."

Bobby looked around, saw nothing. "What? How do you know?"

"I smelled them."

"You smelled them?" said Teressa, doubt in every word. But Bobby nodded and looked at her. "If you ever smelled a blackbirder, you'd remember."

"Any idea where he is?" he asked Henri.

"If he's close enough to smell, I'd say he might be just inside the pass, to one side or another."

The reef encircling the atoll had only one pass. It was small, and the best time to make a passage was when the tide was making, as it had been for the last hour. There was no moon, but the stars gave enough light to create shadows. They could see no light anywhere around the lagoon.

"We've got to think about this," said Bobby. "No sense in going off half-cocked. Their method seems to be attacking at dawn. They rush in making a tumult and even shooting a couple to terrorize the rest. If that's the case, we have a few hours to decide what to do."

"You can't count on that. We need to alert the village now, and something else, you've got a wife and child to think of. Are you sure you want to get in the middle of something like this? If we just warn some of the men and then go about our business, there is no blame."

Bobby looked at Teressa, who met his eyes. She shook her head. "No. We've got to live with ourselves and I don't think I would like myself very much if we left."

"We've got the firepower to stop them," said Henri. "I think their way is to round up a bunch of young men and women and get out as fast as they can. To them it's like harvesting. This is how they eat."

Bobby had been looking out at the lagoon. Now he turned to his mate and said, "Go back aboard and bring my shotgun and the Henry; hell, bring it all. Choose some of the crew to defend her, whoever you think's best and leave them the weapons they'll need.

Tell them, 'Shoot to kill.'"

While Henri returned to Mirabelle, Bobby and Teressa roused the house and before long, men, women and children began to congregate in the yard. All of the men had clubs or spears. "First thing is to get people watching the lagoon for any sign. They probably move closer toward shore in the early light. If we've got good eyes looking, that could give us time to get ready."

"These people don't want a fight. They want to grab young men and women and be gone before anything can be done." Bobby was talking to the leaders of the town. "If we can be ready and waiting when they come ashore we can make them pay."

Claude spoke up. "We must destroy these people. They are worse than murderers."

Everyone looked at Bobby, who shrugged. "We have enough guns and ammo to destroy them if that's what you want to do. Is it?"

For less than a minute, they talked among themselves, and then Beni said, "Yes, it is what we want. If we let them go from here they will do it elsewhere. Destroy them. We will help."

Over the next two hours they put everyone in place and made sure they understood their part in the events that would unfold with the dawn. Marie and Van followed several island women a good distance up the coast to wait until it was over.

The odds were, not one of the islanders, men and women who waited weapons in hand, had ever killed anyone. Very few of them had even been off the island more than once or twice, yet tonight they stood ready to ambush and strike down the invaders, men who threatened to steal away their friends and lovers into a life of slavery if they survived.

"You're awfully quiet tonight," said Teressa. They were sitting on a fallen tree trunk, weapons at hand, waiting for the news of the invaders and when the attack was coming. Bobby had an express shotgun he'd recently bought and a pocket full of shells. He liked its size and short double barrels.

Teressa was holding the seventeen-shot Henry rifle Bobby had been given by his father. It was like one she had fired many times down on the beach with Johnny and Manny. She'd never fired it at a human being before.

"Are you afraid?" she asked. She closed her eyes and continued, "My mouth is dry and all I can think about is Van."

"That's because you're a mother. She'll be alright with Marie. They've moved back out of the area where we'll be fighting."

"You didn't answer my question."

After a moment he replied. "Yes, I'm scared. We're pretty safe in this situation. They don't know we're here. By the time they find out, quite a few of them may already be dead. But when bullets are flying around, you never know if someone unintended will stop one. And, of course, there's always the possibility the other guy is smarter than you give him credit for and ambushes you." He leaned over and kissed her. "Keep your head down, OK? Van needs her mother to help her grow up."

"You know the ones we knock down in the beginning will be the lucky ones," he continued. "Did you see the size of some of those clubs? Some of those men are big and they know how to handle those things."

"How many do you think there'll be?"

"Henri said probably about 20-25 in the crew. They have to leave some on board, so I'd say twenty, and they'll all be armed." There were three times that many men concealed in the trees along the beach.

"Does it bother you we're going to open fire and shoot these men down, giving them no chance to surrender?"

Bobby was quiet for a time, clearly thinking about how to answer this question. Finally, he said, "Teressa, when's the last time you saw a policeman out here?" He looked at her, eyebrows raised. "Never, that's when. There aren't any or any kind of law for that matter. Tahiti's three hundred miles from here. If we confront them and they surrender, then what? What do we do with them?

"These men are outlaws. They come out of the dawn to kill and enslave young men and women. If they succeed here they'll do it again and again. If we stop them we not only help save these people but all the lives these monsters would have destroyed in the future."

She was quiet too then, thinking. Finally, she said, "This is like the one you shot before, isn't it? That's the same reason you killed him?"

"Yes, it's the same reason. If we don't stop them, who will and they must be stopped."

Light was just stealing across the lagoon when they came quietly with muffled oars, because surprise meant success. When the boats were beached, they heard no voices as the men scrambled out and formed into two groups, one moving straight inland and one swinging out to the right as flankers.

It was still dark under the palms bordering the beach when they began to move inland. Suddenly lit torches flew out of the trees and landed in front of and behind them, lighting the clearing with startling suddenness.

Bobby's shotgun was the signal for the others to open fire. He fired both barrels, one after another. Teressa triggered the Henry three times, and the hail of projectiles from them and the rest of the crew wreaked havoc among the invaders.

They ceased fire quickly. The plan was for the islanders to charge after the first volley. Forty or fifty men came screaming into the clearing and there was enough light to see the fear and horror on the invaders' faces. The last thing Teressa saw was a huge war club crashing through a man's upraised arms and smashing his head like a rotten pumpkin.

Later that day Bobby and Henri stood on the beach with Claude and Beni looking out at the blackbirds' boat. Several canoes full of island men had attacked and overpowered the crew that had remained aboard when they heard the fighting on shore. It was amazing how quickly any signs of the battle disappeared. The bodies were carried out beyond the reef and dumped in the ocean.

"Well, it looks like you've got yourself a boat," said Bobby. "It will take some work to clean it up and make it what you want it to be. Make it bright and pretty so people won't mistake you for a bad guy," he said, slapping Claude on the shoulder.

"What if someone claims it?"

Bobby scratched his nose and smiled. "I know some fellows in Tahiti who'll do anything for Teressa. I'll talk to her and when we get to Government House, I'll bet she can work it out."

CHAPTER TWENTY-NINE

In the years he had worked as Captain Chamber's aide, Manny had been to several American cities and he had sailed from New York City, but he was still amazed and befuddled by the crowd of people that swirled around him at the King's Cross Railway Station in London. It was a beautiful summer day, yet he saw no smiles, heard no sounds of laughter, no excited children playing. Everyone seemed to be going somewhere but not very happy about it.

A train connection took him to Vauxhall Station where he quickly realized that getting a taxi wasn't likely, so carrying his luggage and asking directions along the way, he walked toward the American Embassy ten blocks away. Working with Captain Chambers had taught him to travel light so the few blocks wasn't a problem.

He was surprised when he encountered a line of people that apparently ran to the front gate of the Embassy several blocks away. A young fellow passing by noticed his uniform, introduced himself as aide to the military attaché and led him to a gate for embassy personnel.

"They told us you'd likely be here in a day or two, so we've been looking out for you." He was an Army captain named Craig Etka. "It looks like you'll be rooming with us. The other guy in the room is also a captain, George Carmichael. I say room but it's really a nice flat." He paused. "So, you're a second lieutenant? That's the same as a first lieutenant in the Army, right?" When Manny nodded he continued. "You'll have your own room and we share the rest of the place. You won't see George much. He works somewhere else in the city."

They stopped before a door. "This is Captain Henry's office." He held out his hand. "Welcome aboard. I'll stop by on the way out and if you're still here, we can walk over together. I'm in Colonel Marlowe's office, just down the hall, if you need anything."

Commander Grover Henry, USN returned Manny's salute and looked at him steadily for a moment, his face expressionless. "Irv Chambers was a classmate of mine at the academy. I was just reading what he has to say about you. Pretty nice."

"Thank you, sir. Captain Badger got us together at the Academy."

"So, tell me where are we with flying? Irv seems to have put all his eggs in this basket, so he must think it's going to be big."

"Yes sir. He believes it's going to be an essential part of the Navy going forward."

"What does he want from you?"

"I'm to visit as many British and French naval installations that could be used for float planes as I can and write reports about each. Looking over the installations will be helpful in case we have to make our own one day. What he really wants is an assessment of what they have and how it flies, plus any ideas on tactics and strategy I pick up in the process."

Commander Henry looked at him with a slight smile. "And I suppose you already know what we have and how it flies." When Manny nodded, he sat in silence for a long moment, staring out the window. Finally he said, "I'll look forward to reading your reports before you send them to Captain Chambers. The yeoman will get you settled in. Dismissed."

Manny's hand was on the doorknob when the Commander said, "By the way, what class were you at the Academy?"

"1910, sir."

"How old are you?"

"Twenty-four, sir."

"And you're already a second lieutenant." This last he said as much to himself as to Manny.

July 10, 1914
Dear Colleen,

Well, I'm here. I walked about ten blocks from the station to the embassy and took a walk after I met with Capt. Henry. It was like walking through a seventeenth century painting. It's definitely a well-to-do kind of neighborhood.

I've volunteered to help the staff at work tomorrow. All the war talk has created a rush of Americans to the embassy for any one of a thousand reasons. I'll be helping people fill out and process passport applications. Lots of strange jobs in the Navy.

The building I'm rooming in seems to be a sort of dormitory for the embassy. I have a room to myself in a flat with two Army captains and there are about ten small flats in the building. I'll have to find out where to go to get groceries, but it looks like it will be a hike. Corner greengrocers aren't very likely around here. I'll need to find out from the embassy about pay and such. With all the traveling, I'll be broke in a hurry.

I don't know how much time I'll be spending at the embassy. I'm supposed to report to Chambers on what I learn. I think I'll be traveling around the coasts but have no idea how to make arrangements. Chambers gave me a name at the admiralty to contact. I'm going to need someone to show me how to get around the country so I can see what I need to see. Someone who knows the geography and how the trains work.

With all the uncertainty about how I'm going to do it, I've got to keep in mind the reason I'm here. I think the information and ideas I send him will be important, especially in war, and more and more it looks like we'll get in. When and if we get involved is up to others. I still have to do my job.

I've become a resource for Chambers. He spends his time talking to people, dealing with budget problems, trying to get people's attention and traveling all over. I spend time getting my hands dirty. I'm in the middle of everything he and Glen are doing. I work on engines and know almost everything about how an airplane works and, more importantly, why it works. He does the hand shaking and talking and I give him the information he needs so he'll have something to talk about.

Enough of that. I miss you. Of course that's not unusual. You'll notice I haven't said I love you yet. I guess that's because you already know I do. As much as I'd like to have had you with me on that walk today, I think you should think very carefully about coming over here right now.

Everywhere you turn, preparations or actions are driven by the idea that, more likely than not, the country's going to war. You could be endangered on the way here and you might be stuck here with no way to get back home.

Of course, this seems to be the way our lives are going to be lived, so we might as well enjoy them. Intense, beautiful times when we're together and aching loneliness and wonderful memories when we're not.

Speaking of wonderful memories, we could really make some around here, if you decide to come, but it might not be what you expect. There is no question the danger exists. Believe it or not, wars and soldiers don't respect beautiful, freckle faced women with hot knickers. Sorry about that but it's what I keep thinking about.

Also, I have no idea how much I'll be around or how

much free time I'll have when I am, but I can't hedge on these reports. I have to put my heart into them. Chambers will read them and Glen and probably many others, so it's important to get them right. I'm not boasting when I say there aren't too many people in the country that know as much about aviation and airplanes as I do.

Well, over the next few months I'm going to learn more, and not just about flying. About new people and places, about new ideas and new challenges. War is the kind of thing that defines lives. No one's immune to that. If we're in the middle of it, we could end up in strange places doing things we could never have imagined.

I love you but if you decide not to come, I trust your judgment.

Manny.

She was on her way.

Boo and the girls had decided to come with her as far as St. Louis. They hadn't seen Boo's folks since Skip was killed. As for Colleen, this was her fourth train trip across the country and the novelty had long since worn off, so she enjoyed their company.

Boo had gone to work at the bookstore during the year after Skip's death and was now managing it. Johnny and Lemuel were stepping in to handle the store while she was in St. Louis.

"What's it going to be like getting on a great big ship like that?" asked Diane. The twins were sixteen now and were in and out of the bookstore constantly. They didn't live in the house above, but they and their mother were part of the family now.

"I'll write to you from the boat when I find out. How about that?"

For the last four years Colleen had lived in Oakland with Roy and Este and attended medical school, first as a medical student and then for some classwork related to her specialty field. For the last nine months, she had been interning with a surgeon who practiced at hospitals in San Francisco.

Now, after a month in San Diego and feeling good about herself and her life, she was returning home to Boston, a place she hadn't thought much about since she left it seven years before. There hadn't been many letters either. When she left Boston, she left behind friends and family, people she'd grown up with and cared for, but the new life she'd entered had been so exciting, so challenging the past was easily forgotten.

Sometimes, when thinking about her life back then, she remembered what it was and where it was going and felt a sense of relief that made her close her eyes and take a deep breath. Nowadays, when she thought of home, she thought of San Diego and The BookSeller.

Now she was traveling to join her husband. She would have to cross the continent and then an ocean to reach him in England where war was looming like a dark cloud on the horizon.

When she thought of Manny, which was pretty regular, she felt a pleasant warmth flow through her and into the pit of her tummy, which was the reason she was not only willing, but eager, to follow him halfway round the world at a time like this.

The voyage was so much more pleasant than the train ride. The cabin she had was cozy and comfortable. She could spend time writing letters in the salon and walking the deck thinking about the future for hours at a time. One of her cousins in Boston had advised her not to eat too much the first few day and when it was rough, clear soups and tea were best until she got used to the motion.

On the third day out the weather was brisk to the point where she retreated to the salon to write in her diary. The diary was important to her. All the young girls that came to work with Annaliese were advised to keep a diary. Colleen made a tentative start on one and though not enthusiastic about it in the beginning, soon came to enjoy writing her day down, reliving and remembering things that had happened to her; in essence, digesting what she had learned.

This was her seventh volume and she carried them in her luggage, kept them in her room. On this day the ocean was making it extremely hard to write. It got to the point where she lifted her hands in frustration and when she did, the diary slid rapidly off the table and was headed for a wet place on the deck when a young woman caught it and handed it back to her.

She grasped the book to her chest and let out a relieved sigh. "Thank you."

The woman smiled at her. "From the look on your face, it must be something special."

"Oh yes. It's my diary. I've kept one for seven years."

The woman laughed. "I've started more than one and never get past the first week. How did you do it?"

"Actually, it's been part of my education. For the last seven years, I've been studying to be a doctor. The first woman I worked with suggested it and I found I liked it. Sometimes I won't write in it for a week, but I always come back."

"Is this your first trip to England? By the way, my name's Lynn." She held out her hand.

"I'm Colleen Fry. Yes, my husband is in the Navy and he's stationed at the embassy."

"He's in the British Navy?"

"No, the US Navy."

For the next three days, weather permitting, they walked and talked and exchanged stories. Lynn and her father lived in London, not far from the American embassy. Her mother had died when she was young and her father believed that traveling and reading good books was the best way to get a young lady educated and at the same time see a lot of his daughter. Over the years they'd done a lot of that.

This was her first time traveling alone. Her father had stayed in New York for business and she wanted to go home. She had a first-class cabin and invited Colleen to move in for the duration which she did. She was two years younger and full of questions about medical school and Manny and life in San Diego.

She and Colleen were the same height, but that was all they had in common. Blonde, blue-eyed and beautiful, Lynn was also fun to spend time with and they made each other laugh a lot.

Another way they were alike. Lynn was liable to say anything about anything, at any time, usually with a straight face. She seemed to love to say unexpected things and was very direct. Some of her questions about Manny made even the doctor roll her eyes and blush. Colleen loved to do the same thing to Manny. She really did remind Colleen of herself.

Their embrace at the gangway was long and heartfelt. Colleen felt they had spent an almost magical time together and thought Lynn felt the same way.

Colleen had come to feel that the dizzying sweetness of seeing Manny again was almost worth their time apart; almost. Watching him work his way carefully and respectfully through the crowd to greet her at the bottom of the gangway she saw the man she'd come halfway round the world to see and she was happy.

After the first embrace, a first kiss, a joyous greeting that became something more, and then a sudden realization of where she was and that she didn't care where she was or what she was doing. She just wanted to keep doing it.

When it dawned on her that Lynn was probably standing there watching them with a big grin on her face, she began to grin herself, and the moment was broken. When she turned to face her friend, she saw she'd been right.

Colleen introduced Lynn to her husband, and she joined them on the train to London.

When they were settled in a carriage, Colleen asked, "What's been happening in the world while we've been at sea?"

Manny, who was looking a bit dazed, shook his head, as if to clear it. "It looks like there's a war going on in Europe. Austria declared war on Serbia, Russia declared war on Austria." He shook his head again. "Most people I talk to believe the Brits will be dragged in the way things are going."

"How will that affect us?" asked Colleen.

Manny shrugged. "I don't know, but I'm in the Navy. I'm sure they'll let me know."

They sat in silence, contemplating how this new thing suddenly thrown into the middle of their lives might affect them.

"Well, the first thing we have to decide is where are we going to put you? This war scare the last couple weeks has made any kind of lodgings out of reach for our pocketbook, even if you can find anything."

Lynn raised a finger. "I can help with that, temporarily at least. I have some extra rooms we're not using and you can stay as long as you're not too noisy." This last she said with a mischievous grin.

Colleen, who had expected something like this, burst out laughing while Manny's eyes widened and his mouth fell open.

"Just ignore her," said Colleen, rolling her eyes.

"Whatever you say, dear," Manny said.

Lynn's home was a comfortable villa in a nice West End neighborhood and she was greeted by several servants who cared for the place in her and her father's absence. He had sold an inherited business in order to be able to spend time with his only child after her mother's death and they were able to live comfortably and travel frequently.

At table shortly after they arrived Lynn announced, "If you're interested, I might have an answer to your housing problem. It seems our caretaker has rejoined his old regiment, so his cottage is available. His wife is my maid and it will be easier for her if she moves in the house."

Colleen and Manny looked at one another. When she nodded, he said, "All right, but only if you let me apply for a housing stipend. The Navy can pay you for it."

Lynn looked at Colleen and shrugged. "OK," she said. "We can look at it after dinner if you like, or tomorrow if you'd rather. I realize you might be busy tonight."

After the first time, they lay on the bed looking at nothing and touching one another. Rays from the afternoon sun through heavy drapes allowed them to see and he turned on his side, reached out and ran his hands over her body. "I could look at you all day. Course, there'd be times I'd stop for something else." He kissed her nipple and tasted it, sucked on it.

"Where did you learn to do that?" he asked after a minute of counting her freckles.

"Learn what?" she replied. She opened her eyes and realized what he was asking and closed them again.

"You know how much of an imagination I have. Well, sometimes at night I think about you. I think about what we do that feels good and I get excited and I pleasure myself. Sometimes I wonder if something new might feel good and want to try it."

"Like what? What new things?"

"Things like this," and while he watched she let her hand drop to her tummy and spread her legs. "See what I taste like," she whispered huskily.

He looked at her for a moment and then moved slowly down the bed, all the while looking into her eyes.

Annapolis had taught Manny that dawn was the proper time to be out of bed and long before Colleen was stirring, he was sitting in the kitchen talking to the cook and drinking his first cup of tea. It was a warm, pleasant place to be, sitting and thinking 'all's right with the world.'

The maid brought in a newspaper and laid it beside his plate. When he glanced at it, his mouth fell open, and he stopped breathing in shock.

Headlines blared out the words: **War With Germany**. His eyes raced across the page. No surprises there. It had been in the air since he'd stepped off the boat and once Austria jumped the rest of it was probably inevitable, but the question was where did this put him? And Colleen?

He knew what he had to do. Get to the embassy. Report to Captain Henry and stand by for orders. But what about her? She just got here. I'm the reason she's here and God knows where the Navy will send me.

A bell jangled and a moment later Lynn came into the kitchen. She smiled at him and sat down with her own cuppa. When she looked at him, saw the expression on his face, she blurted, "Are you alright? What's the matter?"

Mutely, he handed her the newspaper. He sat looking at her but not seeing her, and she could almost hear his mind racing.

"I've got to tell Colleen."

"Tell me what?"

She entered the kitchen in a bathrobe, looking drowsy-eyed and smiling. She kissed him good morning and he handed her the newspaper and sat in silence while she read.

When she put it down, she looked up at him with a question on her face. "What does this mean? For us? For me? I mean, you've got someone to tell you what you've got to do, but what do I do? Knowing the Navy, you're probably not going to be around much, but God knows where I'll end up."

He shook his head and took a deep breath. "I think this doesn't change what we need to do today. We need to find you a place to live. So let's go look at the cottage. We need to get you settled in, and then I need to get to the embassy. This could become very complicated, and we need to spend some time thinking about how to make it work."

"She's got a place to stay, so don't worry about that," said Lynn. "And if you need to go, go. She and I can do what we need to do around here, and who knows, maybe we'll come up with answers to some of your problems."

CHAPTER THIRTY

It was early twilight when Mirabelle limped through the pass into the lagoon at Maupiti and dropped anchor. A usual three- or four-day run from Papeete had turned into an ordeal when, on the third evening, a freak burst of wind almost laid her over on her side and a following wave caused them to ship water below. This out of a clear blue sky, so they weren't prepared.

Though she righted herself, Mirabelle was a mess for a while. Water had cascaded down the hatch into the galley, and when they finally got her pumped out, the mess revealed was amazing.

Now at anchor in the calm, beautiful lagoon, Teressa closed her eyes and hoped it had all been a nightmare. When she opened them she found it hadn't; the mess was still there. The only casualty was Van, who had broken her forearm. Fortunately, the bone hadn't come through the skin, and they had been able to set the arm and splint it, crudely but effectively. She was sleeping now.

Bobby's arms went around her. Actually, she always thought of them as enveloping her. She had grown up thinking Handy Josephson was the biggest man in the world and now she was sure his son was. Bobby had filled out with muscle on his young giant's frame as he aged and his arms were impressive.

"I'll help you. We'll all help," he said in her ear. "And we can have help from the village. She'll be ship-shape in no time, though

I'll grant you there'll be some work involved."

She sat in the stern of the dinghy beside Van and closed her eyes on the trip to the beach. When the dinghy grounded, she opened them to see probably the whole village standing in a large, quiet semicircle around where the boat had landed.

Beni stepped forward and pointed at a large schooner moored in the lagoon. "Welcome. That is Maupiti, our boat. It is owned by the people of the village and we thank you for helping us have it."

"Thanks, Beni," said Bobby. "But we've got some damage aboard. We need a place to get settled on shore till we get her shipshape again."

"Of course, follow me and we'll help you all we can." He and Bobby talked about the damage and what help they might need while he led them down the beach a hundred yards or so. He stopped before an obviously new house built in the island fashion.

The entire crowd had followed and watched as Beni led them onto the porch. He turned, raised his hand toward the people looking up at him and said to Bobby and Teressa, "This is yours. When you are here, this is your home. It is from the people of the village. We thank you for our Maupiti and for our future."

He turned to the people watching. "They need to rest, so we will leave. Tomorrow we will help with the boat. Workmen, meet here in the morning and we can talk. Bring your tools."

"We didn't have a chance to thank them," said Teressa, standing open-mouthed and staring at the throng rapidly melting away. She felt dazed and had to lean against Bobby to steady herself.

"We'll be here for a while, so you'll have plenty of time for that."

Teressa had noticed she always had trouble sleeping the first night off the boat, but tonight she was so exhausted that within five minutes of kissing Van and Bobby goodnight she passed out on the new sleeping couch.

When she awoke the next morning, she lay for a while staring up at the unfamiliar roof above. She heard Bobby's voice outside talking to someone and it dawned on her where she was. The first thing that came into her mind was Van, and she got out of bed, put on a dressing gown, and stood for a moment watching her daughter sleep in the next room.

The girl had been in pain from the break, but as always, Marie had something to help with it and after one restless night, Van seemed to be sleeping peacefully.

She wandered through what was now her home, at least for a while and ended up on the front porch where Bobby and Henri were sitting on the steps talking to Claude and Beni and several other men.

"How did you get it out of the water?" asked Bobby. "From the looks of it when I saw it last, there was probably a lot hanging on the hull for the ride; barnacles and such." He looked up at Teressa, held out his hand and she moved to stand behind him.

"When we worked at the shipyard, Claude worked with the dry dock and he took a lot of boats out of the water. We found a place a little way up the river and built our own."

"Hey," said Bobby with a big grin on his face. "I'd like to see that."

"Come, we will show you. But first we show you Maupiti."

Everyone stood, and Bobby asked Teressa, "You coming?"

"No, I want to be here when Van wakes up. You can tell me about it."

Marie joined her and they stood looking out at the lagoon and at the motu in the distance with its white sand beaches. A motu is a sand islet created where a reef exists. They usually form a circle and with the reef, protect the lagoon from the ocean's power.

"It's so pretty here," said Teressa. "Bobby said we would be here for a while." She smiled and shrugged at Marie. "It could be worse."

Bobby, Claude, and several of the islanders boarded a boat at the village pier and rowed out to Maupiti. Several men were at work on the big schooner and all were proud to show it off. It was easy for Bobby to see how everyone he saw seemed to be proud of the boat. Why not? After all, it was theirs.

It was spick and span and ready for the wind and the sea, but Bobby noticed a strangeness in some small details, an unusual pulley or line, for instance and the paint looked mismatched. When he mentioned this to Beni, the man grinned.

"When we worked at the boatyard, there were many things that were thrown away. We set aside things we thought we might have use for and brought them home. In many cases, it was paint that was left over after a job was done, so the boat has many different paints on it. We repaired some of the things we brought home and used them on Maupiti. That's why she looks different."

"It looks like it just came out of the Noumea boatyard. And the bottom's clean?" When Claude nodded again, "And you did all this here on the island?"

Claude nodded proudly. "Come and we will show you."

They took another boat into a small river that entered the lagoon just outside the village.

Claude had selected the place to begin, and the islanders responded. Large coconut logs were sunk into the riverbank and gates were set so that they formed a barrier to the tide when closed. Claude laid out a line for a space behind the gate and they began to dig.

That was the longest and most laborious part of what they eventually created, moving the earth. Not having a machine for the job meant that manpower had to be used. Fortunately, they had plenty of that.

As the pit was dug, it was lined with mats to retard erosion and fitted with a set of rails so that a boat could be floated into the dock on the high tide, left sitting dry on a cradle when the tide was out, and pulled up a set of wooden rails to sit above the water and expose the bottom for cleaning and repair.

"So does it work?" asked Bobby.

"Some things needed to be changed to make it work, but it did."

"How many times have you used it?"

"Once on the big boat, but four times on smaller ones. We tried smaller boats first so we could see what needed to be done to make it work."

Bobby was looking at the 'drydock' and thinking about Mirabelle. She was fifteen feet shorter than Maupiti, and narrower. He looked at Henri', who was doing the same thing.

"What do you think?"

"I'd say yes. She'll definitely fit and she needs it."

"So it looks like we can get Mirabelle out of the water to clean her bottom and do all the other things we need to do." Bobby was sitting on the porch watching Van and Claude's daughter, Moana, help Teressa clean some fish her mother had sent for their dinner.

"That's good. You know you could help us do this if you wanted to." Teressa stood, hands on her hips, knife in her hand, glowering at him.

"I could, but it's so much more fun watching you do it. You look so much better than you did when I left," he said, coming down the steps and taking the knife from her.

"A shower and a nap plus clean clothes will do that for you. So, what did you see? It must have been something, you were gone most of the day."

"We looked over their boat, Maupiti and then at the drydock apparatus they built. We think it will work for Mirabelle, so we're planning to try it tomorrow. It will be a lot easier for us to do what has to be done to her than if she's still in the water."

"How long will we be here?"

He looked thoughtful before he answered her. "I'd say three, maybe four weeks. Once she's out of the water, Marie and Henri will stay with us, and Rudy and the boys with Beni or Claude." He was quiet for a moment, then said, "When we got here, I was all on fire to do everything in a hurry and get back home. Now I think maybe it would be nice to stay here for a while. We could relax and get to know these people better."

She put her arms around his neck and he lifted her for a kiss. "I'm glad. It's a nice place with nice people. Good place for a holiday."

The next afternoon, Mirabelle was pulled out of the water, and they found the islanders' drydock worked beautifully. Once she was out of the water, Bobby and Henri joined Claude and a crew of islanders and made a run to Tahiti in their schooner to get some of the supplies they'd need to get Mirabelle repaired and back in the water.

While they were gone, Teressa and Marie, with several of the island women and children helping, completely emptied the schooner. The islanders were used to working together and knew each other. They were an enormous help and by the end of the day, Mirabelle was an empty shell. The next day, they sorted, washed, and hung out to the wind the things they could salvage and set aside the things they couldn't.

At the same time, Beni and another of his brothers pulled up the floorboards, dried and inspected the bilges. When Claude and Bobby returned they would coat the inside of the hull, replace the floorboards and then the inside could be reorganized.

Which is when Teressa and Marie came back into the picture. They had kind of a gang of young island women who worked with them. They worked well together and seemed to enjoy the novelty of the situation. Instead of taking care of their young children, like they did every day, they were working at something new with their friends and family. The gang formed a relay line from the boatyard to a clearing where Teressa and Marie were deciding what to put where.

The below deck of a small schooner like Mirabelle has no extra space. Now that she and Marie could rebuild the galley to be theirs, they found that Cookie had a pretty good system worked out over the years and put things pretty much back to the way they'd been.

Henri had been living in a small space just off the galley off and on for twenty-five years, so they left that for him to do as he wished and Marie, the same in hers. But Teressa brought Bobby in to help her rearrange their cabin to get it the way she wanted it.

Bobby had read in Pete's log that years ago he was hit by the same kind of weather phenomena they had encountered. He was sailing in perfectly clear weather and suddenly 'boom.' A 'williwaw' is what he called it and the memories of what had happened made Teressa more aware of the need to have some things in a secure place, safe from the ocean's reach as best as they could figure.

Into this place would go important papers and cash. They also devised a place in the galley to store the books and things they worked on and made it a requirement that, unless someone was working on them, everything be kept in this safe place.

The main cabin was much like the galley in that what had worked over the years was kept. Overall, they made few changes below deck in the schooner after all.

The women were finished with their work by the third day, but the men would take more time. The bottom was gone over closely and scraped clean of parasites and assorted worms and things, then repainted, and all the woodwork and brass fittings were cleaned and repaired.

Ropes were replaced or rewoven, all rigging inspected, and the sails were replaced with a suit brought from Papeete. It was fully two weeks before Bobby was satisfied and they carefully went through the process of floating her again.

Only when he stood on her deck and watched as the hands took control, so they would work her out to her anchorage, did he realize what a relief it was to feel the deck moving beneath his feet again. He'd learned something this time about the feelings of the captain of a boat that's out of the water.

It was early dark when the dinghy slid onto the beach in front of the house where Teressa and Marie sat watching some children play under a large banyan tree.

Teressa led the children, running and screaming around her, and stopped behind him, so when he pulled the boat up the beach, he stumbled over her, and they fell in a heap with children piling on top. After much laughter and screaming, they disentangled and walked through the sand to the steps where he picked her up and carried her up and into the house.

"I should have done that on the boat," he said and, followed by a gaggle of children, he carried her in and deposited her carefully on the mat that served as a bed in their new home.

That night after lovemaking, they talked, the best talk there is between two people who love each other.

"I'd say another two days and she'll be ready."

"Two days?!"

"Why? Do you want to stay longer?"

She was quiet for a moment, then said, "Yes, I do."

"How much longer?"

She sat up in bed. "Bobby, would it be a problem if we stayed a couple more weeks? Van has some friends her own age here, and that's something she's never had before. I'd like to talk to her before we leave, to get her ready for the idea of going."

"Sure, that's no problem. Besides, we need to talk about something that happened today."

When she looked a question at him, he continued. "Claude and Beni want to talk to us and would like us to come to dinner at Beni's house tomorrow evening. Afterward, we can talk."

"What about?"

"They didn't give any details. I got the feeling they wanted to talk together a bit more before tomorrow. Of course, it has to be about the schooner. They probably want some advice."

The next evening, with Van splashing in the lagoon and running along the beach ahead of them, they strolled along the beach to Beni's house. Much larger than most they had seen on the island, three brothers had joined together to build it in the beginning and as the families had grown, so had the house.

After the meal, Claude motioned to Bobby to follow and led them to a circle of seats around a fire pit under a banyan tree behind the house. Bobby, Teressa, Marie, and Henri sat on one side of the fire pit, and Claude, Beni, and several other men sat around the other.

"So, what's on your mind?" asked Bobby, and Beni answered.

"Because of how you helped us when the blackbirders came, we have Maupiti and we have worked and feel it is ready to bring good things to the island. But we know little of business and trade. Can you help us to learn these things?"

Bobby was nodding his head as Beni spoke. "So you're ready to put her to work but you don't know how. Is that what you're saying?"

When Beni nodded, Bobby looked at him in silence for a moment, then at his crew. Finally, he said, "I thought maybe this was what you wanted to talk about, but this is the kind of thing that needs time to consider."

He looked at his crew, waiting for him to speak. They all sat in silence because he was clearly thinking. Finally, he stood and said, "Beni, you've given us something important to think about. We'll be here for two more weeks. Let us get together," he motioned at his crew, "and talk about it and when we have some ideas, we'll talk with you and decide how to deal with this in a way that works for us all."

CHAPTER THIRTY-ONE

Captain Henry's yeoman looked up and smiled at him. "Go on in. He's expecting you."

Captain Henry returned Manny's salute and motioned to a chair.

"So, let's talk. Tell me about your travels." For two weeks Manny had ridden trains along the eastern coast of England to major naval bases to see and assess what each was and what facilities were available for pressing future use. He also saw estuaries and coastal areas that might be used to fit their needs in the future. They discussed these things and others and the captain made some notes.

"You'll have my report by tomorrow, Sir," said Manny. Henry looked at him for a long moment and finally said, "We are in an unusual position, as I'm sure you've noticed. I'm going to need you to stay in touch with me and stay closer to home for a while. No more long trips."

He continued to look at Manny in silence. "If you want to comment on what I'm going to say, raise a finger, Ok? You're not only learning about the coasts and rivers, you're also meeting people, usually young people, who, if they live, are going to be the ones flying and fighting in this war.

"It's alright, in fact, it's expected that you might come to feel sympathy and loyalty to the British in this fight." He paused and looked meaningfully at Manny. "Don't forget you work for the

United States Navy and need to remember what that means. Your job is to observe and learn and consider how what you learn applies to the Navy.

"Intelligence! What you're learning about these people is intelligence. How they deal with what they're going through is intelligence. Remember that. It's every bit as important as harbors and rivers. His face lightened and he smiled. "I understand that you already know all this. I just wanted you to realize that I know it too."

Manny smiled for the first time since he sat down. "There's something I need to talk to you about. I'm going to be around people who fly and they're going to want to see what I'm made of, so I'm going to be flying. There's a certain danger in that, plus I heard yesterday about a chap who fired a pistol and a rifle at a German plane. How far am I supposed to pursue this quest for information? What does the Navy allow?"

Henry sat back in his chair, rolled his eyes and gradually a reluctant smile stole over his face.

"How the hell am I supposed to know?" He chuckled. "Try not to get killed or upset the locals, I guess. Look, Lieutenant, I've only known you a short time, but Irv Chambers trusts your judgment so I guess I will too.

"Try not to make fools of us, will you?"

Playing the tourist around London, Colleen had noticed the strangest thing about the people she saw in the first few days after the war began. There seemed to be a feeling of pride and a certain camaraderie, even with perfect strangers, as though they were all watching a sporting event. This feeling gradually disappeared as the casualty lists from the front began to chronicle the trickle of blood in the first few days.

That trickle quickly swelled to a flood as Europe began to feel the consequences of the new weapons of war developed in the industrial boom in Europe in the late nineteenth and early twentieth centuries.

The massed frontal assaults with the bayonet common in the wars of the early Nineteenth Century were still there, but the musket and saber had been replaced with the machine gun, long-range artillery, airplanes, tanks, poison gas, and barbed wire. Napoleonic military doctrine was offensive in nature, but the changing technologies and realities of the battlefield in this new century demonstrated the power of the defense.

The use of brass-jacketed, rifled projectiles made of lead that were accurate at much longer distances meant attacking troops had to undergo fire for a much longer time. These weapons and the recently developed machine guns could kill or maim men in groups and at much longer distances. This indicated the need for a change in infantry tactics. Unfortunately, the generals of this generation stubbornly refused to accept this reality.

A truism in military history is that generals of this war fight it with the tactics of the last. The massed attacks of the early days of the war were reminiscent of many of the early battles of the American Civil War of fifty years before. Losses at the Battle of Shiloh in western Tennessee in the spring of 1862 were 24,000 killed and wounded over a two-day battle.

In the Battle of the Frontiers, the first major battle of the Great War, the French alone lost 330,000 killed and wounded and the total casualties of all combatants were well over a half a million.

The people who lived through it called it the Great War or just 'the war'. It was greater than any war in history up to that point and when it was over they didn't understand many of the changes it had wrought in their everyday lives.

Over twenty nations participated in it and it was fought over the entire globe. At the center of it were the great industrial nations of the world at the time and the weapons and munitions they produced resulted in the deaths of over seventeen million people, seven million of them civilians. The crippled and maimed were seen in the nations of the world for many years after.

Four years at the academy meant that Manny was usually up with the sun. The embassy had a nice canteen in the basement and he'd developed the habit of beginning his day there with a cup of tea, a pastry, and a London newspaper.

"Mind if I join you?" Manny looked up and sprang to his feet.

"At ease, Lieutenant," said Captain Henry, who seated himself. "Were you coming up to my office when you finish here?"

"Yes, sir, I wanted to give you my report on the Norfolk Coast."

"Good, when we finish here we can go up. I enjoy beating the yeomen to work."

He smiled. "I like the way you write. I can see why Irv is impressed with you and with flying. Have you been doing anything dangerous?"

They chatted until they were seated in his office and suddenly he was all business.

"So, tell me about the Norfolk Coast."

"I went as far as Hunstanton and worked my way south. Saw what I could. Got about halfway. It's a flat and fenny coastline. Lots of tidal rivers. It would take a complete survey by a team to get it all. But I saw enough to give me a general picture."

For the next twenty minutes, they talked about flying related to the east coast England geography and how it was relevant to the US Navy.

"I also wrote about my meetings with some people I think might be significant in aviation over here. You'll be hearing about some of them." Suddenly he smiled ruefully and shook his head.

"What?" asked the captain, puzzled.

"It's just you have to qualify that remark if you're talking about aviators. If they survive. Many don't. I met a fellow the other day. Just saw in the paper that he was killed in a crash." He looked at Henry with a grimace and shook his head and shrugged. "But we still fly."

"Have you flown lately?"

"Haven't had any opportunities. Not many planes around just yet."

"The weather's a big factor in flying, isn't it?"

"Yes, sir, that and places to land. That's why I'm here. Most of the planes up to now have been a bit fragile. The idea was they had to be light to get them off the ground. As engines have gotten more powerful and designers learned more, they began to experiment with heavier material for increasing the structural integrity and carrying capacity.”

"Are the English keeping up?”

"I'd say so. We've got the Wrights and Glen Curtiss, but they've got some good ones too. John Cyril Porte is one. He was working with Curtis on a seaplane that could fly across the Atlantic via the Azores before the war. He got recalled by the British Navy, so the war messed that up.

"He's back in the Navy here and he's still working on the same design. Trying to make it heavier and stouter. He's at Felixstowe. The North Sea over there gets pretty rowdy at times and the machines have to be able to deal with that.”

"Rowdy's the word for it. I got a letter from Captain Chambers. He said Curtiss is coming over here. Bringing a couple of his planes over and several motors.”

"I'll bet he's headed to Felixstowe too. Good, Glen always knows what's new in the air. The Wrights were always secretive, but Glenn believes in everyone working together and sharing what they learn. He's got a lot of people sharing things with him. Will he come to the embassy?”

"Most Americans do. We were thinking you could meet him at the pier in Southampton and bring him out here.”

"I'd be glad to.”

"I'll look forward to meeting him.”

"He's a strange fellow. All he talks about is flying. If that's your interest, he's a gold mine. Other than that, he's a rather quiet person. Doesn't talk much.”

As he was packing up his briefcase to leave, Manny said, “I believe Curtiss is coming over here to work on a flying boat for the British. I think it's probably something we might want to get involved in for our Navy. Until we get more airfields built, flying boats make sense.”

He stopped and let his superior think about that for a moment. "The British are thinking about using seaplanes as bombers and observation planes. They also have been useful in tracking submarines that are submerged. These are things our Navy should be interested in, but my job is to survey and gather intelligence.” He paused. "I think getting involved in what they're doing is important, but does it fall within my orders? Can I focus on it if the opportunity arises?"

Henry sat with his chin on his fist for a while before he answered. "Manny, I want you to realize we're both crawling out on a limb here. It's difficult to get a decision this far from things, especially on a sensitive topic. I agree with you. This is something the Navy needs to know, but if we run it through the system, by the time we get an answer, the moment will have passed and it could be an important moment.

"On the other hand, if we make the wrong choice, we could get our tails in a crack. This seems to be one of those times when you have to use judgment and initiative. So I will say, explore the opportunity if it arises, and I'll contact Captain Chambers for further orders."

Colleen knocked tentatively on an office door, heard "come in," and opened it. This was her first time at the embassy without Manny and she was a little nervous.

"May I help you?" The man was seated in an armchair reading a newspaper. He put the paper down and stood up, looking at her with a question on his face.

"I'd like to talk to a doctor, if one's available."

"I'm Doctor Blackmore. How may I help you?"

He seated himself behind a desk and indicated the chair for her.

"I'm American. I came over here to be with my husband, and suddenly there's a war. He's so busy all he can do is sleep and work. He works here. He's a naval aide. I've just graduated from medical school and would like to do something besides sightsee and wait for him to come home."

"You're a doctor?"

She nodded, and they looked at each other in silence while he digested what she'd said.

"Again, how can I help you?"

"I'm a doctor. People are wounded and dying and I'm not doing anything about it. What I need from you is the name of someone in the British medical service I can contact if I want to help. I'm a surgeon, by the way."

That was stretching things a little. Yes, she had spent a year after school working with surgeons in San Francisco, had seen many surgeries and performed several under their supervision, but to call herself a surgeon was, ah, premature, to say the least.

On the other hand, being Colleen she believed she could learn the rest on the job. She remembered a story Annaliese had told that her father really learned how to be a doctor during the war. It sounded like that was where she felt she should be.

She was sitting on the porch when Manny came walking briskly up the walk. He was smiling strangely, as though thinking about something interesting.

"Hello," he said, suddenly looking up and seeing her. He came up the steps, stopped, held out his hand and pulled her to her feet and into a warm embrace.

"It feels so good coming home, knowing you're here," he murmured into her hair.

She leaned against him, listening to his heart. "I did something today I need to talk about, but you look like you've had a good day. Tell me about it."

"Glen is coming over. I'm to meet him at the pier in Southampton the day after tomorrow and bring him back to the embassy." She could feel his excitement. They sat looking at each other in silence.

"Tell me why that's so important to you?"

He looked at her slack-jawed.

"I want to make sure I understand why you're so excited."

"I've thought about that myself. I think he's my pathway to the future and that excites me. You see I believe in aviation and when I'm around him I'm learning. The nice thing about Glen is he's a natural teacher. Also, Johnny Tower is coming to the embassy. He's going to be Captain Henry's naval aide."

Her mouth fell open. "I thought you were his aide."

He shook his head. "No, he's the way I connect to Captain Chambers. I write my reports for him and he sends them to

Chambers. Chambers is still my boss."

He looked around. "Where's Lynn?"

"She's upstairs packing. That's part of what I wanted to talk to you about." It was early evening, but she could still see his face clearly as he gradually began to understand the meaning of her words.

"I was at the embassy today. I talked to Doctor Blackmore in the medical office. He said he'd never met you. I asked him to help me contact someone in the British medical service who could help me find a way to be useful. I have an appointment with him tomorrow."

He looked at her in silence for a while in the growing darkness.

Finally, he said, "This must be important to you. Tell me where you're going with this and how. Help me understand."

"I can't tell you what I don't know. I'm going to see a man tomorrow who will answer some questions that are relevant to my future, to our future. But I'm looking for information. We make decisions about the future together like we always have."

He was quiet again looking at her thoughtfully, "So we've discussed my day and yours. What shall we do now? I have an idea. Let's go to our little cottage and make love. I've been thinking about two particular freckles that need some attention."

She looked at him in astonishment. "That's it? That's the reaction I've been dreading all day? You want a tumble in the hay?" It was fully dark now and he was a shadow. She reached out, touched his face and could feel his broad smile.

"I've been deprived for a long time." He shrugged. "I've got to catch up."

"Come here, you poor deprived boy," she said. They embraced and after a long kiss, remained in the embrace, a long warm hug. Finally, she broke away and led him through the house, out the back door and to their little cottage in the backyard. In a surprisingly short time, they were naked and touching each other in nice places.

Afterwards, they lay and talked. "I don't understand you. How can you hear about that appointment tomorrow and the first thing out of your mouth is 'let's go screw'?"

Years ago he'd learned that at certain times you need to think before you speak. This was one of those times. He lay quiet for so long she wondered if he'd drifted off to sleep.

Finally, he said, "We're different, you and I. In our world, when people marry, they're bound by fences that keep them inside what's right and proper. We don't have those fences. We do things our way. I'm in the Navy. If I want to stay in the Navy I have to obey orders. You're a doctor. You want to do what doctors do. Apparently, life's leading us in different directions right now.

"Since we've known each other we've been living our lives and snatching time together whenever we could. So far that's been enough, but will it stand a war? Hope so. Because it's times like this that make it worth it." He turned and pulled the blanket off her, leaned to kiss her breast.

"But it's not just that." He reached out and ran his hand across her stomach. "Having you in my life is exciting. I love the way you think. You bring ideas into my life that I would have never come up with. I believe if we keep trying, one day we'll settle down into a 'normal life'. Until then, let's do what we have to do. In the Navy, they call that duty."

They lay quiet for a while, then he said, "You never did tell me why Lynn is packing."

"Oh, she's leaving tomorrow. She's joined up to be a volunteer aid and she'll be going to school for a while to learn what she needs to know."

"And that's what got you thinking about going to work as a doctor?"

She nodded. "As much as I love learning about London, there's only so much sightseeing I can stand. I'm a doctor and there are people out there who need me."

He took her hand and squeezed it and she knew he understood.

CHAPTER THIRTY-TWO

A hurricane, a typhoon and a tropical cyclone are the same weather phenomena, just happening in different parts of the ocean. In New Caledonia, it was a tropical cyclone, a large circular storm fed by heat energy in warm water that includes winds in excess of 160 kilometers an hour, heavy rain that sometimes lasts for hours and a storm surge which lifts the ocean onto land anywhere the storm comes ashore.

This juggernaut of disasters varies in size from 150 to sometimes as much as 600 miles across and unbelievably, usually moves only about 25 kilometers an hour over the surface of the deep. Fortunately for some of the smaller islands in this part of the ocean, the coral reefs that surround them provide some protection from the power of the ocean in such a storm, or many would eventually disappear.

Grande Terre is a large, mountainous island surrounded by a huge reef and lagoon, all of which help defend it against the storm. But when a full-fledged tropical cyclone comes ashore anywhere in the world, it's a catastrophic event.

A knock on the bedroom door awoke them. Bobby, Teressa, Van, and the cat were staying with a friend in Noumea. From the light coming through the French doors, he could see it was early and couldn't imagine who or why someone was knocking on the door. He opened it to find George, their host and Henri, the latter in a dressing gown and slippers.

"Sorry to bother you so early my friend, but there is something George thinks we should see," said Henri.

George led the way to a southwest-facing second-floor porch where he pointed toward the horizon. "If that's what I think it is, we're in for some bad weather."

Henri stood still, gazing intently at the band of dark clouds seemingly rising out of the horizon as they watched. "Yes, I think that's what it is." He turned to Bobby. "I don't think you've any experience with this type of storm, but you must not underestimate it. It is dangerous and will not forgive your mistake."

Bobby looked at him open-mouthed in shocked silence. Henri' turned back to George. "What's the strongest room in the house?"

George answered immediately. "There's a place my father built for the family years ago. We went through several of those storms when I was a child. We'd sit in there and play games and tell stories until the storm was over."

"Let's go look at it," said Henri. To Bobby, he said, "Go and get them dressed and pack up anything you want to save."

"It's going to be that bad?"

"The last storm like this destroyed Mirabelle and roughed up Noumea pretty badly too. It took years for them to get over it." He chuckled dryly. "Took Pete quite a while too."

When he opened the bedroom door, Van was up and dressed, sitting on the bed holding Jinx and Teressa was at a dressing table brushing her hair. She looked at him in the mirror and seemed to sense there was a problem because she had a question on her face.

"It seems there's a storm coming, a bad storm," he said. "Might be a cyclone. Apparently, this has happened several times before and the house has a shelter. We have to pack up and be ready when Henri gets back."

Over the years, they'd learned to keep things to a minimum when they were ashore, and they were ready when Henri and George returned.

"The place is big, but we should make sure there is space for food, water, and blankets so we can't carry too much in. These storms can last for a day and night." He pointed. "It's about fifty meters from the house."

"How long before it gets here?" asked Bobby. "Do we have time to check Mirabelle?"

Henri' shook his head. "No, I don't think so. We'd have to find someone to take us over and no one wants to be caught in the harbor with this coming." Mirabelle was out of the water at the boatyard on one of the larger islands in the harbor. They had taken down her masts and rigging and put her in a cradle the day before. Bobby was already fidgety, as he always was whenever she was out of the water.

"I suppose there's no way to let Marie and Cookie know it's coming," said Teressa.

Henri chuckled. "Don't worry about them. They'll know. They probably knew yesterday. They'll be ready. The house on the cliff is in a protected spot. They won't take the full brunt of it."

The shelter was built into the side of a hill away from the ocean. It wasn't comfortable by any means, but they helped the servants clean off the accumulated dirt and dust and it was habitable and large enough for all the people in the house. There were enough chairs and mattresses for everyone.

Some of them had possessions, but Bobby and Teressa had only what they had brought for a stay of several days. Everything else was still on Mirabelle, totally out of reach.

The site had been chosen to provide protection against this kind of thing, so it was built to face away from the ocean. It had several ventilation shafts and a small wood stove for heat and cooking.

When they were all settled in, Teressa stood at the door with Van and looked out on what seemed like a beautiful late summer day, if a little warm and muggy, but there was something about the way the air felt, almost as though it were electric. When they walked around to the ocean side of the hill they could see the dark, threatening storm clouds in the distance. They seemed to grow closer while they stood watching.

Lightning flared and flickered across a black wall of clouds so high she had to tilt her head back to see the tops of them. The wind was gusting now and there were scattered drops of rain on it. They stood still for a while looking at the storm, mesmerized by how dangerous it looked. 'The wrath of God,' Teressa thought, standing frozen in fascination and awe. She'd read about cyclones, she'd heard them called typhoons and could see why they were feared.

Bobby and Henri came out to stand beside them. "No way to get to the yard before it gets here," said Bobby. "At least she's out of the water." Bobby usually hauled Mirabelle out on Maupiti, but an examination of the hull revealed something that needed to be done here, so they'd hauled her out at the boatyard in Noumea two days before.

The people of Noumea were getting ready. They'd been through storms like this and knew what had to be done. Stay safe and clean up after; that was the best way to get through it in one piece, but they still closed their shutters and tied everything down.

"I've been through a few of these," said Henri. "At sea, I've been on the edge of one, and Pete and I went through a couple here. We were right in the middle of it both times. The last one put Mirabelle on the rocks." He paused and shook his head. "I don't think he ever got over that."

"I read about it in his journal," said Teressa. "You could feel the emotion when he wrote about it." She put her arm around Van and squeezed. "Looks like this might be one we tell the grandkids about, little girl," she said, looking out at the approaching clouds. From where they were standing, they could see a thick, dark curtain of rain in the distance.

"It's not just the wind," said Henri, "though that can be bad enough, but it rains like a waterfall and sometimes it rains for hours. It's good we're up high here. All that water runs down the hill and some things down there will probably wash away."

Van picked up Jinx and led the way back to the shelter. The room was large and everyone had found a place where they settled to wait for what came. They had two kerosene lanterns for light, but reading was not really an option, so they sat and waited with Jinx providing a little comic relief by investigating the place and causing some nervous laughter.

Large coconut logs had been set as a palisade, forming a wall enclosing the mouth of the cave and creating a room that was dry and dusty and had obviously not been used in a while. The room was an enlarged natural cave carved into the red rock hillside.

There was a heavy door in the wall with a small door at eye level for observation so they wouldn't have to open the door to look out.

The door looked stout and strong, but what if it wasn't strong enough? That thought was in Teressa's mind when the noise of the storm, the rising wind and the pounding of rain gradually became louder and as it did, the room became quieter.

"It's really strange," said Henri after a while. He had to raise his voice to be heard over the wind. "Once before I was in this kind of storm, all wind and rain, and suddenly it all stopped. The wind just died away and there was no rain. There was a strange gray light outside, and we went out and just stood there looking around. I guess we were in a daze of some kind.

"Pete brought us back to reality when he said it wasn't over. He said he didn't understand it, but he'd seen it in the West Indies, in a hurricane, he called it. That was the eye of the storm, a calm place in the middle. He said it will begin again in a little while, and it will be as bad as ever, maybe worse on the other side.

"So I'd suggest that if the same thing happens today, don't go far from the shelter. I have no idea how long the calm will last, but you don't want to be out when the wind comes back. Oh! And Pete said the wind changed directions, completely turned around, when it began blowing again."

"If that's so we'll hear and feel the wind more," said George. "It might be blowing toward us more directly."

The wind was getting stronger and over its shriek was an occasional crash of something that it had carried away. They never felt the calm Henri' had talked about, but a change in the wind took place as night fell. It was louder and stronger than before. The door began to shake, and water began seeping under it.

Van was lying on an old mattress with Teressa's arm around her. "Mama, are you afraid?"

She came out of a daze with a start. "I didn't realize it until you asked me. I think I am. This storm is enough to frighten anyone."

"Are you, Papa?"

Bobby thought for a moment. "I don't think so, Button, but if fear makes you cautious, sometimes that's a good thing. That door makes me a little nervous, watching it rattle like that. We need something to prop against it. A couple of two-by-fours would do it." He got up and motioned to George, and they began to rummage in the back of the cave.

Since Van had mentioned it, Teressa realized she'd been frightened for hours, sort of curled up inside herself, wishing it would stop. The noise was loud and constant and the tension in the room was palpable. She realized that Van's question was the first words spoken for a long while.

She remembered years before when she'd been trapped under a collapsed house, how the utter helplessness was so terrible. That's what she felt now. They could do nothing but crouch in terror, like some small, frightened animal who hears the growl of a predator digging. That's why she was afraid, because she could do nothing but wait until it was over.

Bobby had found several long pieces of lumber, and he and Henri used them to reinforce the door, but other than that, they waited. The sound, loud as it was, was such a constant that it became almost mesmerizing and she fell into a doze, starting up whenever the violence grew. Each time she would reach out and touch her daughter, just to make sure she was there, then close her eyes and retreat into herself again.

Eventually, the long night passed and with the dawn, the wind was a mere fresh breeze. The rain still fell, but not in the torrents of before.

Bobby and Henri were the first ones out of the cave that morning and they were still gaping with amazement at the devastation they saw before them when Teressa and Van joined them. While it was still standing, George's house was almost a shell, and they had to work hard to recognize any of the usual landmarks they'd seen for years.

Bobby's first impulse was to get to the yard and see how Mirabelle was and within half an hour, they were all on their way.

Getting there, however, took most of the day.

Early on they had to abandon the car and go on foot. All that rain meant that normally placid streams became raging torrents that swept everything away. Off and on during the day, they were waist-deep in standing water, and a road that wasn't washed out was the exception. When they got to the harbor, they discovered finding a boat fit to take them to the yard was close to impossible.

At the harbor they found that part of the city that hadn't been blown away. It was floating in the harbor. The tremendous rainfall had created tremendous torrents that swept down the mountains behind the city and washed the lower town into the harbor. They stared at the flotsam of the city

Noumea was spared some of the storm's fury by the lagoon and by the mountain behind it, but wind and the rainfall in the mountains and hills turned into water running downhill and had left most of the buildings in the lower part of the city floating in the lagoon.

George, Teressa and Van went back to the house, such as it was and late in the day, a friend of Henri's ferried them to the island where the yard was busy getting things cleaned up. The first sight of Mirabelle made Bobby close his eyes and shake his head. He stood looking at her, open-mouthed, like a man trying to understand the impossible.

Teressa's arms around him brought him out of the trance. The schooner was still secured to the cradle, but the whole thing had been blown over and broken apart, and the schooner was lying on her side with her keel parallel to the ground.

The owner of the yard was there, and they began to talk of what was necessary to get her in the water and more importantly, when. The yard was a hive of activity with workers moving in all directions, but they had much to do before they could begin work on a boat, and there were jobs of much more importance than Mirabelle. Could be a year. Could cost a lot.

For two days, Bobby was quiet, staring out at the lagoon and the ocean beyond, thinking about what to do. Did he want to try to bring her back for the right reasons? Pete had faced this same choice, and he had decided to find a new boat. On the second day, he had begun to talk, and he talked for an hour.

He loved Mirabelle, but she was gone and they were faced with many choices, not the least of which was whether or not to get another schooner. Did they want to stay in the South Seas, to continue to live as they had for the last ten years?

Or did they want to go back to life on a ranch in California? Or try something completely new, a new adventure?

But that would mean giving up Marie and Henri' and their friends on Maupiti and the other things that made their life special, like starry nights under the southern skies and sunrises and sunsets at sea, and ultimately, the house on the cliff.

Did they want to give up all these things they loved to begin a new life? Van joined them and was included in the conversation and encouraged to ask questions.

How would her life be different if they chose a new life? She would live on a ranch and do the things her mother and father had done when they were growing up; her face had glowed at the thought. But then she thought about Marie and Cookie and Henri and all her friends on Maupiti.

And what about Maupiti? The people of the island and the time they spent there were important to them and the business they had built with Claude and Benni was beneficial to them all. These were people they loved and trusted, local allies in any trial life would hand them. It was likely they would never see these people again.

On the other side of the coin, these people in their life would be replaced by family and people they had known all their lives before they came here, people they loved and trusted. Van's life would have so many opportunities instead of knowing only the life her parents had raised her into, and she could touch base with all the things that shaped them growing up.

A week after the storm, they were able to get passage on a freighter enroute to the nickel mine across the bay from home. One evening when they'd been back a few days Bobby was sitting on the patio on the cliff, looking at the clear blue water where Mirabelle had floated so many times for so many years.

"So, have you made up your mind yet about where we're headed from here?" She had come up behind him and put her arms around his neck.

"I think so," he replied. "Before I talk about it, I want to hear what you think about it."

"Oh no," she replied, grinning at him. "No. Years ago I told someone I was hitching myself to your wagon. Tell me what you think, and then we can talk about it."

He smiled at her and began. "I have given up on the idea of repairing Mirabelle. As far as deciding what to do about our future, let's go home to Mill Valley for a while and decide then. It's time for a visit anyway, and we can talk to some people we trust about what a good next step would be."

"That sounds like a good plan. How long before we leave, and how long will we stay?"

"I've got things to do about Mirabelle, and we have to let them know at home we're coming, so say a month? As far as how long? What about a year? That will give us time to decide what we want to do and then make it happen."

She stood and pulled him into an embrace. "That's a good plan. It makes sense not to rush the decision, especially on something this important." She reached up to kiss him. "How'd you get so smart?"

"I'm sure you had something to do with it, dear," he said in the sweetest possible voice.

Later that day she suddenly realized she felt different. Since the storm drove them into the cave there had been uncertainty in their life. None of them really knew what tomorrow would bring. Now, with this choice, they had a future again, one she was excited about.

CHAPTER THIRTY-THREE

Winston Churchill once said the English people had many reasons to be thankful the English Channel was such a disagreeable body of water. The same could be said of the North Sea. Manny stood looking out at a curtain of rain racing across a horizon of gray and white water. He shook his head and turned away from the window just as a man in uniform came into the cavernous seaplane hangar, shaking water from his uniform hat.

Manny rarely saw a uniform at Felixstowe. Between the work and the weather, you were going to get dirty or wet, probably both, and the laundry bill would have been prohibitive. Most people wore some form of protective clothing, but uniforms they weren't.

"Glad to see you, sir," said Manny, grinning and taking John Tower's hand. The 'sir' was something he'd thought about a bit. Technically, they were equals, both second lieutenants, but John had been two years ahead of him at the Academy and the courtesy cost him nothing.

"You look out of place," said Manny. Behind him, Glen Curtiss, hand extended in welcome, said, "Glad to have you back." For Curtiss, that was the equivalent of a welcome home speech. He didn't talk much. Stoic was the word that came to mind. Of course, when he did say something, you needed to make sure you were listening. You'd probably learn something.

"I'll change in the room. Just wanted to stop by and see what you're up to."

"Precious little thanks to the weather," said Cyril Porte, head of design and experimentation at the Seaplane Experimental Station at Felixstowe, England, and Manny's boss. Well, technically, Manny's boss was still Captain Chambers back in San Diego, but whenever he was at the station, Cyril was the boss.

"Welcome, John," Cyril said. "We're glad to have you back. Any idea for how long?"

"Until the telephone rings. When Captain Henry needs me, he'll call. Until then I'm here." They were glad to have him.

John Tower had his faults, but he was a team player, and though he could be disagreeable at times, when a decision was made, he came on board and worked hard to make it happen.

He was part of a team that was trying to develop an airplane to specified needs and he and Manny were among the test pilots. The British wanted a large, stable aircraft to fly patrols over the North Sea for anti-submarine patrol and for reconnaissance of shipping along its east coast. If it could be armed for defense and carry bombs, that would be a plus. Ultimately, it was decided a flying boat made sense and that's where Manny came in. He had expertise and experience with that kind of airplane. Within twenty-four hours of landing in Southampton, he and Glen Curtiss were at Felixstowe.

Glen Curtiss and John Cyril Porte had been working on just such a craft as the British Navy wanted in the United States before the war and when Porte was handed the job of creating their hypothetical warplane, he contacted his American friend, and Curtiss agreed to join him, bringing some equipment, three flying machines and most importantly, ideas.

They chose Felixstowe because it was at the joint estuary of two large tidal rivers, the Stour and the Orwell and about fifty miles north of the mouth of the Thames River. It had a sizable navy presence with some heavy equipment and dock facilities available.

Because Felixstowe was a small village, they had rooms in Ipswich, twenty miles up the River Orwell, and every morning the entire crew would sprawl sleepily about a train car for the ride to the yard.

They had taken over a larger metal structure that was built over a tidal basin of cement deep enough to have planes moored out of the weather and accessible to be worked on. They also had a crane on a track that could lift a plane out of the water and onto a cradle if necessary.

In the rear was an upstairs room with windows that looked out over the hangar. It was in that room they spent a lot of time when the weather was bad, which it was a lot of the time.

Being from San Diego, Manny was constantly amazed by how many stormy, rainy days there were. There was still plenty to do in the hangar, but what they really wanted was to be outside testing ideas about how to achieve what the navy wanted them to do.

One nice thing about stormy days was when three or four of them would sit in the office with Glen and Cyril and talk about solving problems with new ideas or maybe adapting something they had into something else that would solve a problem.

Usually on those days, he thought back to a stormy Sunday afternoon in Baltimore when seven Annapolis cadets sat around a hotel room listening to Glen Curtiss talk about flying.

He'd met Glen at the foot of the gangway when he arrived at Southampton and since then, they had been almost constant companions. At the embassy Manny introduced him to Capt. Henry and after a few minutes, they were on their way to Felixstowe.

It was amazing how much his life revolved around Felixstowe now. Usually, he spent six days a week there and one day to meet with Captain Henry and put his report in the diplomatic pouch.

Since Colleen had joined the Royal Medical Service, he didn't get to see her very much, but one night a week, if she wasn't there, he slept in their bed and usually felt better the next day.

Felixstowe was a small village on the North Sea whose people kept a history of all the times they'd tried and failed to pull survivors from the angry water. It was a brown and gray kind of place and given its location, probably destined to stay that way. Not too many of the residents worked at the hangar, so the navy, enlisted and officers alike, and civilian workmen, slept, ate, and drank in

Ipswich, twenty miles up the Orwell. Anything to get away from that stormy, angry sea. And yet, there were days when it was magnificent, sunshine and brisk breezes, but on those days they were usually busy and didn't notice.

Much of Manny's time on those nice days was spent with boats of one kind or another, including flying boats and float planes. They were at Felixstowe because the estuary was large and protected from the sea. They could take off and land a flying boat or float plane safely. With that and having the facilities they needed, it was perfect, if a little rustic.

An undertaking such as they had been tasked with naturally proceeds from solving one problem to solving another and so on. Manny was usually in the middle of any discussion of any note, and these were the times he loved. As a group, they were using intellect and skill to overcome what was known to be a law of nature.

From time immemorial, man has said, "If man was meant to fly, he'd have wings." Well, what do you know, we can fly. So it wasn't a law of nature after all.

Over the months since he arrived, Manny had become the person Glen talked to, the one who helped him work out the problem, one problem after another and in the process, he learned much.

His friend knew every nut and bolt in these machines, every wire and strut, what it did and why it was important. Manny knew that half his conversations with Glen were just his friend talking to himself, musing out loud, but that didn't keep him from listening and learning.

He'd found early in life that he learned more by listening than by talking and listening to Glen Curtiss talk about airplanes and flying was like mining gold as far as he was concerned.

The problem they were working on now was about a modification of a machine Glen had brought with him from his factory in upstate New York. They quickly found it needed more power and when the bigger engines were installed, they were turned around so that instead of pushing the airplane, which was normal in the early models, they were pulling it.

These were times when Manny was seldom out of coveralls or a life vest. He loved to work with his hands and to see the inside of an engine, to understand how it worked, to watch it lift a plane into the sky.

But power didn't seem to be the answer they were looking for. The aircraft now had a dangerous tendency to nose into the water during a take-off attempt, which had resulted in several near mishaps. Manny and John had each been in one of those mishaps and had a vested interest in solving the problem.

It was amazing how often one of their problems was solved by a group of four or five of them standing around a drafting table, looking down at something either Glen or Cyril had drawn. This time it was Cyril. He had drawn a hull that was notched down its length and he believed it would allow the airplane to break free of the surface tension that was keeping it from getting airborne. That's why they were all pacing the floor, cursing the weather. They believed they had the solution, if only the weather would cooperate.

Colleen was headed to France. It was a spring day of uncertain weather, but she was excited and didn't mind the wind or spray. She spent most of the trip standing at the railing, looking back at the English shore and thinking about Manny.

When she had first contacted the British Medical Service, she had set in motion a chain of events that led her to this steamer crossing the English Channel into the middle of a war. Again, they were living their lives apart instead of together. She sometimes wondered if they'd ever learn.

Though the British needed doctors, it seemed like there was much confusion about how to go about getting her into the system. She was told to go home and wait for them to figure it out. Lynn was gone, working as a volunteer nurse and Manny wasn't due for a couple of days. In the last letter, Lynn had spoken of France in a field hospital, but she'd heard nothing from her friend for a while.

Manny came home every week for a day and a night to check in at the embassy, but when he left each week, the silence in the cottage was deafening. Even when he was home, he was restless to return to Felixstowe and the challenges there.

Early in November, she finally received a letter asking her to come to a government office for an interview. Eventually, she was assigned to a treatment center at a requisitioned estate outside London and there, for the first time, she ran into the war.

She worked with enlisted men recovering from wounds they'd suffered or illnesses they'd contracted on the battlefield. The new weapons of war created ghastly injuries and she was thrust into the middle of something she hadn't imagined and had to learn to deal with.

From early morning till late at night, she was washing and dressing wounds, examining and treating men and helping soldiers learn to deal with a somewhat different view of what their life would be from then on. She was the kind of doctor who helped care for the patients, not just treat them. The staff lived on site and she was on call several times a week.

But when she had a chance to stop and catch her breath and think, she realized how far these men were from the battlefield. How many people, men and women, had helped them get this far? What had been done to them and for them and by whom? The more she thought about it, the more she came to believe she wanted, indeed needed, to meet some of those people.

Over the next year, as she gradually moved through the system, she met and worked with many of them. Now she found herself traveling to a field hospital in France and disembarking into a nation at war.

She had learned to carry most of what she needed in two large carpet bags that never left her side. Now she carried these across the wharf to where a man in uniform was talking to several young women. Boulogne-Sur-Mer (Boulogne by the Sea) is a small trading city on the French side of the English Channel. It was not unusual in those days for several young women to land there enroute to one medical facility or another in the French countryside.

Doing some detective work, she'd found out where Lynn was working, and when she saw that CCS number on her choice list, she grabbed it. A Casualty Clearing Station was as close to the front as the military would allow a woman to get and 29CCS was her destination.

It was quiet on the bus ride from the dock to the hospital, probably because everyone was thinking about what they were riding into.

She was last off the bus and was puzzled that all the girls were standing still, looking at the horizon. Then she heard it—a rumbling thunder that could only be artillery. She had no real idea where she was or how far from the front, but she could surely tell what direction it was in.

A loud voice behind them got their attention, and they turned to see a sergeant with a list in his hand. The man began to take names with an attitude that said he had more important things to do.

When he finally turned to her, he asked, "Name?"

"Colleen Fry."

"Over there with the others," he said, writing her name on his list and gesturing at the girls.

"I'm not a volunteer," she said in a quiet, even tone. "I'm a doctor. I'm your new surgeon."

It was hard not to smile at his reaction. His mouth fell open, he straightened in shock, stuttered at first and finally asked, "You're a doctor?"

"I have my certificates and my orders if you'd like to look at them."

"No, ma'am," he said, recovering quickly. "No ma'am. Let me take your grips." He turned to the girls and said, "I'll be back in a few." When he turned back to her, he said, "We've never had a woman doctor here before."

"Really? Fancy that."

By evening, she was settled into her quarters and after asking around, found Lynn in the dining room eating dinner at a long table with several other women. Colleen stood and looked openmouthed at her friend, shocked at how different she looked. She had cut her hair and it looked like she'd lost weight. She was listening to someone at the table and she looked tired, her face emotionless.

When she looked up, her face suddenly changed, and she was Lynn again, with the same mischievous grin. They embraced and stood holding hands, grinning at each other. Colleen was introduced around the table, didn't catch any names, then followed Lynn to a bench outside the dining room where they sat and talked into a darkening night. Whenever they weren't looking at each other, they were looking at flashes that regularly lit the horizon.

"Until I saw you standing there, I'd forgotten about everything back home." She gestured at the station's tents. "This is my whole world now and for some strange reason, I can't remember much of my life before I got here." She smiled wistfully. "Papa came to see me once. He wanted to take me home as soon as he saw me."

"I was thinking the same thing when I saw you."

Lynn smiled again. "You know, I've been here longer than anyone I came with. They're all gone, but for some reason, I stayed."

"Any idea why?"

Lynn appeared to ponder the question for a moment. Finally, she said, "I think so. This place changes you. Maybe it's because, for the first time in my life, I felt I made a difference in someone else's life. Of course, it helps that Papa sends me money every once in a while."

They sat quietly in the dark for a few moments before Colleen broke the silence. "So, tell me a little about this place."

This place was a CCS in the rural countryside near the ocean in coastal France. Their patients usually came from the trenches on the British line, which ran from the channel to the end of the French line, a distance of about 90 miles.

At present, the front was quiet, but even so, there was always a steady, though not usually overpowering, stream of wounded or those suffering from one illness or another.

When the army was fighting, there were days and nights of little rest and much discouragement. Their task was to take the hasty repairs done at the dressing stations and provide hospital care leading to return to duty or transport to a field hospital for further treatment.

The 'ticket to Blighty' was what the men prayed for. It meant they were sent home for rehabilitation or further treatment. Yet, when they got their ticket, they usually wished they hadn't. The wounds in this war were more horrific than in wars past.

When an artillery shell explodes, it throws out a thick shower of shrapnel and these jagged pieces of metal do terrible things to human flesh. Death on an operating table was not unusual with shrapnel wounds.

She presented for duty the next morning and was taken to the office of the superintendent and told to wait. She didn't have to wait long. Lt. Colonel Powell was a short, balding man who looked to be in his thirties. He stood to greet her with a look of surprise and gestured to a chair.

"You're my new surgeon?"

When she nodded, he said, "They didn't mention you were a woman." He looked at her in silence for a while, then smiled and said, "Tell me a little about yourself."

When she started to answer, he held up his hand. He was looking at the paper on his desk, apparently reading something. He looked up at her, suddenly more alert. "You're an American, aren't you and you're not in the army? Is that right?"

She nodded, "Yes, that's right."

"What in hell are you doing here?"

CHAPTER THIRTY-FOUR

Manny settled into the pilot's seat on the flying boat and adjusted his parachute so he was comfortable. Not many pilots used 'chutes,' but he'd meant what he said to Cy years before. He wanted to survive the experience of flying, and the chute was a rational measure to tilt the odds in his favor. Early in the war, many young pilots felt carrying a chute was somehow unmanly, as though it demonstrated a lack of courage or elan, so they wouldn't wear one.

Manny also installed a seat harness in the planes they tested. On an early test, a sudden, unexpected nosedive before lifting off had nearly thrown him from the plane. Within a week, a harness was in whatever plane Manny was in, pilot or observer. Glen and Cyril seemed to be all in favor of any devices that would help keep their pilots alive.

As pioneers in aviation, the men around Manny had one thing in common: They believed their ideas would work. When they sometimes didn't work, they wanted to know why and how to fix things so they did.

Someone had to find out whether these ideas worked, which is where Manny, John, and the other test pilots came in. They had to see if the ideas would fly and bring the pilot home alive. So far they had, though they had been forced down a time or two.

Fortunately, they could land on water, which was a

tremendous advantage in an era when airfields were still few and far between. The east coast of England and the west coast of the continent opposite were similarly indented with many protected estuaries and bays where they could land safely in an emergency and they had to take advantage of some of them a time or two. Manny had been amazed at how far they'd been able to taxi to get home when they were occasionally forced down by problems or the weather.

Today, they were flying an adaptation of one of the machines Glen had brought with him, a Curtiss 2H with tractor engines. At Felixstowe, they had strengthened the hull, reinforced the frame, and tried several new, more powerful engines.

This was the initial flight test for Cyril's new design of the hull, already known among them as 'the notch,' and they were all excited to see how it worked.

With John in the observer's seat in the nose, Manny started the engines. He always got a sense of satisfaction at watching the two large, shiny, maple propellers slowly begin to spin into almost invisible motion. It gave him a sense and feeling of power. The idea that these engines could lift the plane into flight never ceased to amaze him.

He never flew one of those big boats without feeling a thrill at the long, smooth takeoff, with the three or four little bounces just before it was airborne. This time, however, it was different.

It took them half the time to get airborne, and there were no bounces, just a smooth lift from the surface. It worked! Cyril had been right. This was how they could break free of the surface tension holding them on the water and get airborne. He couldn't stop smiling.

Once it was up, the plane was stable, but by no means maneuverable. It was designed to do a certain job. A stable, long-range airplane for reconnaissance and bombing was what the navy wanted. The first required photography; the second, getting the bombs to hit something.

The bombs themselves were loaded by passing them, one at a time, through the cockpit windows. The pilot then passed them to the bombardier, who stacked them by a portal through which he would throw them when the time came. The plane had to be stable so as not to affect his aim. Every time Manny read that in the specifications for the plane, he had to laugh.

Though John was the observer, it was also Manny's job to observe. They had found that observing the same thing from different places sometimes meant different conclusions. Did the modification affect turning or climbing? What do you think, John? Manny? Was there enough instrumentation? What about landing? Did the new, notched hull cause any problems?

"Manny!" John raised his voice so Manny could hear him over the roar of the engines. "There's a sub down there, to starboard. It's headed south, toward the channel. Can we get another look at it?"

"I think so. It'll take a while." At that point, they were flying in a straight, level line toward home. Manny put the plane into a slow, wide turn and they gradually came back to the sub's line. They had fallen behind, but at full throttle, the H-2 could reach ninety KPH, so it didn't take long to catch up.

"Got it," roared John over the engines after he had confirmed the submarine's location and direction. "Let's go home!"

Landing a flying boat is like skipping a stone over a pond. Bring it in low and smooth, with the nose up a little, and let it bounce across the water. Each time contact with the water took a little speed off until it settled down and floated, rocking gently on the surface. The new hull seemed to settle down in less distance than it had taken in the past.

The first thing they did was report the sub sighting.

"There's a good chance he didn't see us."

"Probably not," said Cyril. "How high were you?"

John looked at Manny. "A hundred feet, you reckon?"

Manny nodded. "Maybe a little more."

"What did you see?" asked Glen.

"A long, thin shadow. Couldn't see it very clearly, but you could surely tell what it was."

"Tell us about the plane," said Glen.

While Cyril reported the sighting, they answered questions and talked about their observations, impressions, and intuitions during the flight. Finally, Cyril said, "All right. Sum it up. John, you first."

"I'd like to fly it myself before I talk about that. All in all, I think it's something we can build on but not the finished product by any means."

"Manny, the question is, are we ready to show it to the navy for use?"

"I think we need to work on a bomb release," said Manny. "Also, we need to get someone to help us develop a bombsight. If we're going to drop the bombs, we should try to drop them where we want them to go."

"You didn't answer the question. Would it be useful the way it is until we develop the next ideas for the plane?" He looked at John and then at Manny. "What do you think?"

"I'd say yes," said John. "It's fine for reconnaissance the way it is. The bombing aspect is problematic right now, but they can work around that until we get it to where we want it."

Cyril looked at Manny for an answer.

"I agree. We have to let them know its limits and then work to correct them. In the meantime, let's put the boys in the shop on the bomb release question while we work out the other problems."

"Such as?"

"It's still underpowered. We need those new engines we were talking about, and we also need to improve the way it taxis. It would be nice if we could make it nimbler up there and we need to put the guns in place to see how that affects the trim and performance before we turn it loose. With it unable to maneuver any better than it does I'd say three guns would allow it to survive an attack by scouting planes."

"So we're talking about a four-man crew and the additional weight from the machine guns and ammunition."

Manny nodded. "That should do until we can get them something better."

Cyril looked at Glen. "How long should it take to get three of them ready for service?"

Glen was quiet for a moment, calculating. "I'd say three, maybe four weeks."

"Can you handle it before you leave?"

The US Navy wanted Glen back in the states to help them develop their own ideas for a flying boat. He was scheduled to leave in less than a week.

"I can get them started on it and they can deliver whether I'm here or not."

Cyril nodded and picked up the telephone. "I'll talk to the navy and let them know the timetable. You get the process of production started. I'll let you know what they say."

"What in hell are you doing here?"

When she first heard the Colonel ask that question, she had no idea how many times she would ask herself that same question in the days ahead. She was sitting on the porch of the wooden building where she shared a room with Lynn and two of the nurses, too tired to move. A convoy of wounded had come in early that morning and she had been on her feet practicing medicine for sixteen hours.

She closed her eyes, leaned back, and asked herself, "What am I doing here?" As tired as she was, it was probably not a good time to think about that, but she knew the answer. She was a doctor and as such, she had an obligation, indeed had sworn an oath, to help people who were sick or injured and at CCS29 there were plenty of both. The fact that this place was more than she bargained for was beside the point.

Besides that, she had come here to learn to be a doctor, and she couldn't think of a place where she could learn more. The problem was that sometimes it came all at once.

Her first day at the 29th Casualty Clearing Station at Gezaincourt, France, Colonel Powell gave her a cook's tour of the place, then introduced her to Captain Torkelson, who was the chief surgeon of surgical team three. He would be her mentor and guide while she learned what she needed to know. He was very tall, had a bushy blonde mustache and large blue eyes. He reminded her of Handy Josephson, though not quite as big.

He led her to a place where they could sit and talk. "So, you're a volunteer and you're an American?" When she nodded, he said, "I'd say that makes you unique around here. On top of that, you're a woman and a surgeon."

He sat looking at her for a while. "You are a doctor?" When she nodded, he asked, "Where did you study?" For the next few minutes, she shared her background and her service in England.

"Doctor Torkelson, Colonel Powell asked me what I was doing here. I didn't tell him, but I'll tell you. I'm here because I once heard a man say he really learned to be a doctor during a war. I'm here to learn, and as I learn, to help you help people who need it."

Again, he looked at her in thoughtful silence for a while and finally said, "Call me Swede. Everyone else does. We have a routine here we usually use to get a new hand used to our ways. What you'll do is follow me for a day or two, then I'll follow you for a while. That way, I can learn what you know and how I can help you. We'll do this whenever we can, and when I think you're ready, you'll begin working in the OR as part of the rotation. All of this is contingent, of course, upon the war. If our end of the line gets into a fight, you may be pressed into service before you're ready."

He looked at her with his eyebrows raised. "Are you going to be able to deal with that?"

"I'll give you the best I have," she replied.

He nodded. "When there's a fight going on, we can get snowed under quickly, but we stay pretty busy most of the time anyway. We can handle about a thousand patients a day in a pinch, but that doesn't happen unless there's a battle going on."

He introduced her to the other doctors and to some of the matrons. "The rest of the staff you'll have to learn on your own. It's a pretty big place, and we have a lot of volunteers, plus the supporting military people. It's like a small town, really." He laughed. "Of course, it gets a little loud and crowded at times."

"We use the triage system when patients are admitted. We sort them into one of three categories: critical, for immediate surgery admittance; medical, for eventual treatment and surgery; and ambulatory, walk in and walk out. The last is for returning to duty as soon as possible. When there's a battle on, we put aside the patients that are hopeless, make them as comfortable as possible and leave them to die peacefully."

"I've read about triage, but I didn't know about the last category," she said.

"It's a necessity when we're overwhelmed with wounded. There simply aren't enough resources available and we have to prioritize. You'll work in triage starting tomorrow and then every third or fourth day until you're ready for surgery."

As usual, the next day she saw 'the look' from the staff, especially the nurses, but she'd learned to ignore it and after a while, it went away. Her partner was an older doctor, and he guided her around the triage tent, showing her the supply closet and equipment storage and letting her observe how he dealt with the first few soldiers who came in.

It wasn't hard to grasp the idea. Triage means sorting. It was up to her to use her judgment to put a patient in one of the three categories Swede had told her about. Each stretcher case came with a card describing the problem and what had already been done. The walking wounded were examined, treated, and sent on their way, usually back to the front.

Much of her time that first morning was spent with soap and water. The wounded coming in were almost universally covered with mud and blood, so the first task was to assess their condition and then clean them up as best they could, especially those destined for surgery.

That afternoon she watched her first surgery. The soldier had been injured when an artillery shell exploded over his trench and showered him with shrapnel. The surgery was to remove the jagged, irregular pieces of metal from a half dozen places on his head and shoulders. A local anesthetic deadened the first area, the shrapnel was removed, and another area was deadened, and so forth until it was all gone and the wounds could be dressed.

One of the great problems in the area of France where they were fighting was that for centuries manure had been plowed into the soil. As a result, the bacterial count was very high, and dirt in wounds led to an abnormally high incidence of infection which, in the era before penicillin, many times meant amputation as the only option to save the patient's life. Many died anyway.

Bullets and shrapnel carried dirt and dirty bits of cloth into most wounds, so one of the surgeon's jobs was to examine any wound carefully and remove what foreign material he could find. Given the poor lighting they had to work in, most times it was challenging and time-consuming, but necessary for the patient's recovery and even survival.

Within a week, she began working in surgery under Swede's watchful eye. One thing she learned right away was that the techniques in aseptic surgery and sterile procedure she'd learned in school were only practiced as well as conditions allowed. They did the best they could under the conditions war imposed on them.

But she wasn't just a surgeon. Disease and illness were a part of life in the trenches and each week she worked with things like typhoid, dysentery, trench fever, trench foot, rat bites and lice infestations, not to mention colds and the flu. Every man with a wound of any kind got a tetanus shot because of the bacteria-laden mud he was covered with.

In surgery, she was amazed by the variety of wounds and the damage inflicted by high-velocity bullets from rifles and machine guns. But shrapnel wounds did the most damage. She spent a lot of time removing shards of jagged metal from all sorts of places in soldiers' bodies, placing drains, binding up wounds and hoping she'd gotten everything out before she closed. Shrapnel didn't kill as often as bullets, but it maimed, tearing great chunks of flesh from the body. In some cases, all she could do was leave the wound open and dress it lightly to protect it until they reached a place where it might be treated and healed.

She had promised herself to view it objectively and not let her emotions intrude, but some nights she would fall into bed exhausted and yet find every time she closed her eyes she saw images of wounded and bleeding men on an operating table, and she would sit up on the porch dozing in a chair the rest of the night. Many nights she went to bed resolved to tell Swede she had to go, she couldn't handle it anymore, but she always reported to work the next day.

The original purpose of the CCS was to repair and treat to save lives   and once the patients were stable, they went to the field hospital for further treatment and recovery. As the CCS staff became more experienced, their work became more professional and many times patients were able to be passed up the line more quickly.

This experience and expertise rippled up through the system so that by the middle of 1916, the British had worked most of the problems out of the system of evacuation for the wounded.

The necessities of war had forced them to look for solutions to medical problems that had never before existed. In doing so, they found that many of those solutions benefited mankind when there was peace again.

Surgical team three was outside on a beautiful spring day in the middle of June. They had been released for lunch and a rest period before they went back in the tent, back to the table. Several of the surgeons were sitting on a small rise that looked over the whole camp, talking and smoking.

Swede was looking at Colleen speculatively. Finally, he stood and motioned to her. "Let's take a walk."

He was quiet while they walked along the ridge overlooking the village. "You're married, aren't you?" He was looking out toward the smoke on the horizon.

"Yes. My husband is in England. He's in the Navy and works at the American Embassy in London."

"If I gave you ten days to go home and see him, would you promise to come back?"

She looked at him in astonishment. "How would I get there?"

"There are hospital steamers leaving Boulogne most days taking wounded home. We can get you on one of them."

"Why me? I've just been here for three months."

"I know. You're the new kid on the block, but I like the way you've taken hold." He paused for a moment, then lowered his voice. "This is just for your ears. Beginning next Sunday, we're going to begin shelling the Boche. It will go on all day and night for the whole week. I doubt if anyone here will get much sleep. Supposedly we're going to fire a million shells at them. When we stop shooting, we attack. You're turning into a good surgeon and we'll need you when the wounded start coming."

He gave her a searching look. "You will come back, won't you? I'll need you no later than the end of June."

"I promise."

"OK, then. You can catch a ride to Boulogne in the morning. I'll give you a pass and they should have you on a boat before lunch."

CHAPTER THIRTY-FIVE

"Mail call!" John Tower tossed several envelopes on Manny's drawing table. He was working intently on a design for a new bomb rack, but he stopped at the sight of his wife's handwriting on a postcard.

Dear Manny, I'm in England on a ten-day pass. Hurry.
Love, Colleen.

It was dated the day before.

"Manny boy, you're supposed to open the official mail first."

"Oh, that's right. Sorry, I saw the card from Colleen. I didn't even look at anything else."

John walked away chuckling, and Manny carefully opened the one from the US Navy. There were times when he thought they had forgotten about him, but as long as he got paid he didn't worry much about it.

He unfolded what he recognized immediately as orders. He read the letter through and as was his habit, reread it more carefully. The basic fact jumped out at him very quickly. He was being ordered to a destroyer stationed in Norfolk, Virginia as a deck officer.

He stared blankly out the window for a while, pondering just what this bland sheet of paper meant to his life, his future. When he finally looked down he saw another envelope and recognized Irving Chambers' handwriting.

> *Dear Manny, I tried to keep this from happening, but they went over my head. They want you in the system, back on the standard career path. I tried to explain how you were doing something important, but it was no good.*
>
> *I'm sorry to be losing you. They tell me John and Marc are all I need and that makes you the odd man out. Good Luck and let me know if I can ever help. Irv.*

Within an hour, he'd caught a ride to his rooms in Ipswich and shortly thereafter boarded a train for Waterloo Station. Not having seen Colleen for five months, he was surprised he wasn't thinking about her and what they'd be doing ten minutes after he walked in the door. No, he couldn't get the orders off his mind.

A destroyer, the greyhound of the ocean. It was the kind of posting he'd once have loved. That was the kind of Navy he'd dreamed of. But he'd moved past that point in his life and saw the future differently than he had before he came to England. His career had moved in a new and unexpected direction, one he loved and didn't want to walk away from. So what should he do?

He knew he could resign his commission and stay right where he was, right in the middle of something important, but he shied away from that idea and looked for ways to avoid such a step.

Suddenly he decided to change the subject and called up an image of Colleen in his mind's eye, how she would look and what she would do when she saw him. He smiled to himself and felt better.

She was waiting when he came in the door. Without a word, she reached for his hand and the robe she was wearing fell open. She was naked and what he saw in the afternoon light made him weak at the knees.

They embraced and he mumbled into her hair. "I still get dizzy when I see you like that."

She smiled and led him to the bedroom where she discarded the robe and sat on the bed, watching him undress. When he was naked, she held out her hand and they embraced, standing with their bodies pressed together, realizing how much each of them needed this, or the promise of it, in their lives. In bed, they touched and caressed and tasted and kissed each other and for a little while at least, the war and the rest of the world ceased to exist.

Unfortunately, even as they lay in bed afterward, the rest of the world had a way of intruding.

"How long have we got? I'm home for ten days – well, nine more and then I'll be traveling one day, so eight days. What about you?"

"I didn't ask. I'm here as long as you are."

"That's good." She was quiet for a moment, thinking. "I get the impression you've got something on your mind."

He reached over, cupped her breast, and kissed it. "You mean besides that?"

"Yes, besides that," she said firmly. But she didn't push his hand away.

After a moment, he said, "Yeah, I do," and he told her about the orders and the dilemma he was facing because of them.

"Let me make sure I understand what's going on here," she said. "You're saying the Navy has assigned you to a ship across the ocean and you've got thirty days to decide if you want to carry out the assignment or resign from the Navy?"

He looked at her glumly. "That's it. I may have to choose between what I want to do and what they want me to do."

"Isn't there another choice? Does it have to be one or the other?"

"That's what I've been trying to come up with, but so far I haven't found anything." He shook his head. "When I have this kind of problem, I like to talk to Papa. He never tells me what to do, but he's good at helping me find answers. Since he's halfway around the world, I'd say this is one I have to solve myself. That's why I'm telling you. I'm looking for ideas. Got any?"

She thought for a minute, holding up a finger when he started to speak.

"I remember you had a system, something of Ben Franklin's,

where you listed things in columns of good and bad, or say plus and minus. Why not do that here?"

"I've thought of that, but I think I'm afraid of the answer I'll get." She didn't reply, knowing he needed to talk.

"I need to make sure I know what the question is. Where do I want to be in ten years? The skipper of a destroyer? I'm one of the best in the world at this new science of aviation. I've had the opportunity to be around the founding genesis and have learned much. I can't let the Navy throw that away just to put me back on the standard career path.

"I see my future in flying, not as a pilot, but as an engineer who conceives and builds airplanes, makes them better and safer. I think flying will become important and I want to be there when it does.

"I'll talk to Captain Henry about it, and Cyril, and maybe write to Captain Chambers and see what he thinks. I'll keep looking for an answer that will keep me in the Navy, but I'm not expecting to find one."

He shook his head and chuckled. "Listen to me doing all the talking. Tell me about your life."

She had been focused on what he'd been saying, and it took her a moment to gather her thoughts. Finally, she said, "It's like nothing I ever even conceived. And it's not the blood and gore, but it's as though you're a machine. You never get to know the person on the table; you just look at the damage and do your best to repair it.

"I like the days when I work triage because at least I can talk to the men. It makes them seem a little more human." She was quiet for a moment, staring at nothing on the ceiling. "Swede told me that during a battle, you have to decide which men are hopeless and they're moved to a tent and made comfortable until they die. I haven't had to do that yet.

"I'm jabbering," she said, fixing him with a measured glance. "You're not a German spy, are you?"

"What? No," he said, raising his hand, "On my honor, I am not."

"Don't tell anyone, but the day before yesterday, the British began an artillery barrage that will continue all week. Night and day. They're going to fire over a million shells at the Germans. On the day after I return, they stop shooting and send our boys to attack.

"Swede made me promise I'd come back." She smiled at the memory. "The problem is that I know a little of what it's like. Dirt and time are enemies of the wounded. When we're overrun during a battle, men have to wait and they die because they're dirty and bleeding, and we can't get to them.

"When I started there, Colonel Powell told me we do the best work we can, given the conditions we have to work in. It took me a while to accept that, but it's a reality. All you can do is the best you can do, even when you want to do more.

"But I'm learning. That's the saving grace of that place and what I'm going through. I'm learning things I'd never ever learn anywhere else. No one criticizes my mistakes because they make plenty of their own. But I learn from those mistakes, be sure of that and before it's over, I'm going to be a damn good surgeon and this is going to have been a very important time in my life." With a dry chuckle, she added, "If I survive it."

"I thought aviators were the only ones who said that," said Manny, reaching out for her once more.

Manny's meeting with Capt. Henry at the embassy the next day was difficult. He followed the yeoman in the front door and found Henry was already at his desk.

"So, no report today?" He had noticed the lack of a briefcase.

"No, sir. But I have something I'd like to talk to you about."

He explained the situation and the decision he saw before him. Henry's face became more serious as Manny talked, and when he finished, Henry said, "You're saying you're going to resign your commission?"

"That's what it looks like. It's not something I want to do, but these new orders put me in a difficult position. That may be my only option."

"Fry, I think that would be a bad decision, both for you and for the Navy."

"These orders take me out of a valuable project that has great potential for the Navy's future and put me on the deck of a destroyer in the Caribbean. There are a thousand men who could do that. There's not many who know anything about what I'm doing. It's a waste and I'm not sure I can allow it, sir."

"I'm not at all sure you can do anything about it, Lieutenant."

"What I can do is resign, though if you have a reasonable alternative, I need to hear it. I'm all out of ideas."

"I'd really hate for the Navy to lose you, Manny. The time we've spent together has shown me you have the potential to be a fine officer. Is there no other way?"

"If there is, I haven't found it. I'm not sure there is one."

Manny would remember the warmth of that handshake for many years.

For the rest of the time he was home, he was distracted and restless. They went on long walks and he told her of the turmoil inside him over this decision and what he saw as the future if he stayed in aviation.

Because of the war this was a time of innovation and progress. They were making giant strides in the development of new aircraft, and he needed to be a part of that. They also talked about the agony and pain of loss he felt at forgoing a lifelong dream, now seemingly a part of his past.

And since she couldn't bring herself to talk about all that was penned up inside her, she just listened.

Right now, he needed to confront the consequences of his actions and begin to move toward finding out what sort of future he had now that he didn't have the Navy as a guide. She recognized his need and released him early so he could begin learning about his new life.

She stayed by herself in the cottage one more night, spending much of the time rocking on the front porch, thinking about her life, and Manny, and what she was going to face when she returned to France, and Manny, and how she'd like to talk to Annaliese right now, and Manny. She didn't sleep very much. The next morning, she was on her way back to France, a day earlier than she expected.

The way the British general had figured it, the Germans should be shell-shocked or dead from the weeklong barrage, so this should be a walkover. Don't run. Stay organized. Keep in touch with your officers. The officer of one outfit brought a football for the troops to kick as they walked over no man's land.

On the other side, the Germans had dug deep holes. They sat in those deep holes during the barrage, and when the British troops arrived, they were sitting behind barbed wire and machine guns.

In every sense of the word, it was an epic slaughter. It is the bloodiest battle in the long and storied history of the British Army. Fifty-seven thousand four hundred men were killed, wounded, or missing from the ranks of the army in that one day. The French and the German losses combined amounted to less than 11,000, less than one-fifth of the British loss.

And yet, for all the staggering cost in lives and treasure, it achieved its strategic objective, which was to force the Germans to move troops away from Verdun to bolster the line against the British thrust. It succeeded. The French were able to break the German encirclement and with help from the newly arrived Americans, eventually drove them back to the armistice line of 1918.

Before dawn on the morning after Colleen returned, she and Lynn walked down to the dining hall and immediately noticed that the thunder-like rumble of artillery and the flashes on the horizon to the north and east had ceased. The silence was eerie after the constant noise for the last week.

As usual, the dining hall was crowded, but there was not much conversation. People ate hurriedly and left. By now, most of these people were professionals at this business of trying to repair the folly of their fellow man, and they felt they were ready for whatever came. They had no idea.

There were thirteen casualty clearing stations on the one hundred- and seven-mile-long British end of the line, each serving one of the divisions in the trenches. Each one of them was charged with stabilizing their patients and sending them on in the system. At a maximum, each could complete this mission for about a thousand patients a day.

On that early summer day, from dawn to dusk, about forty thousand wounded men were poured into this system, the majority wounded with high-velocity machine gun bullets that did massive internal damage and always carried the risk of disease.

The prepared professionals had no idea of the red wave that was about to descend on them.

Strangely, one thing she remembered about that day was eating: standing with other staff in a tent where a table was spread with meat and cheese and bread and hot tea and eating standing up, because if you sat, you wouldn't want to get up. Five minutes was usually what you had, and then back to the table.

Back to more arms and legs to cut off, back to more time spent trying to pick all the pieces of a man's dirty overcoat out of a wound in his leg, knowing if you miss some of it he could die, back to having a man or a boy put on the table who's already dead and having to watch as he's carried away and someone is put in his place; back to having a man die on the table and feeling a loss when you washed his blood off your hands.

It was the longest day of her life and one she'd never forget. Except for grabbing a bite twice during the day and taking an occasional pee, they were at the tables for the entire day and night of July 1st, 1916, just as everyone in the entire CCS was up all night doing what they needed to do for their patients to live, or sometimes die.

One day, at Colleen's request, Lynn showed her where they disposed of the body parts that were cut off in various amputations. She stood looking at the little oven for a long time, thinking about some of the amputations she'd had to perform.

The Battle of the Somme lasted till the middle of November 1916. The British lost some 400,000 men killed, wounded, or captured, and the Germans over 420,000. When the French contribution was added, the total was well over a million. The total British gain was a sausage-shaped portion of Belgium, six miles deep and twenty miles long. Whether or not it was a British tactical victory would depend on who you ask, but it did weaken the Germans significantly and taught the British lessons they used effectively in the battles of the next two years. The problem with those lessons was what they cost.

As the battle settled into a costly draw, CCS 29 stayed busy, though not at the pace of the first day. One evening, Colleen was sitting on a hillside that faced the railroad tracks that serviced the camp with her boss, discussing a surgical procedure she'd performed for the first time. They were watching hospital staff loading patients on a train for transport to the field hospital in Boulogne.

"Does it ever bother you that we'll never know anything about these men whose lives we saved today?" she asked. "We wouldn't recognize them if we saw them on the street."

"Does it bother me? No, but I've thought about it a time or two. What it boils down to is we're at war. We must do what's necessary, not what's just or courageous or compassionate. Our duty is to get these men on a train to a hospital as soon as possible." He shrugged. "We're at war. That covers a multitude of sins."

When she thought about it later, she realized he was right. But she also thought about the ones who'd passed under her hands and gone on to life. She'd given them their futures, and she didn't even know their names. There were tears on her cheeks when she thought about that.

CHAPTER THIRTY-SIX

All the grandparents were at the pier in San Francisco when Teressa and Van came down the gangway. Bobby came down behind them and Johnny clapped his hands and burst into laughter at seeing the black cat on his shoulder. They had given in to Van's pleading and included Jinx on the trip. His curiosity and antics made the stateroom more fun and they were all glad he was with them. So was Johnny, apparently.

Shortly after they arrived at the Mansion, they sat down to lunch, and at the head of the table, Madame tapped her water glass and said to the visitors, "I'm glad to welcome you home to San Francisco. You're family, come and go as you like." Everyone talked to everyone for several hours. When she looked around the table, Teressa could see nothing but welcoming faces, and she smiled to herself at the joy of seeing so many she loved and hadn't seen for a long time. It was nice to be home.

And yet it felt strange. Because she'd never thought about it, she hadn't realized the difference in time between here and the house on the cliff. This was a world that was beginning to move on schedules. In the last few decades of the nineteenth century, Thomas Edison came along and banished the dark. New sources of power meant that hands on a clock became important. People had places to be at a certain time, to catch a train, get to work, get their teeth cleaned, or meet a sweetheart for tea and conversation.

Years before, Pete had hauled a big old clock up the hill because it reminded him of home in England. She looked at it as a piece of furniture, but rarely to find out what time it was because it didn't matter. The only one who wound it was Marie, who had done it for Pete and still did it.

She remembered once when she had asked Bobby how long it would take for her to learn how to handle the boat. He'd shrugged and said, "As long as it takes." Truly, time was different in that part of the world.

Meeting the family after being away for ten years felt a little awkward at first. Nothing makes you as aware of the passage of time as seeing someone you haven't seen for a long time. When she was finally in their room that first night preparing for bed, she sat in front of a mirror and looked for the changes in her face she'd seen in her mother, her father, and others.

She found them. The scar on her cheek that had changed her life had faded under sun and wind and sea and she rarely even noticed it anymore. Those same elements had given her lines around her eyes and mouth, but with her long, silky black hair, warm brown eyes, and creamy brown complexion, she was still beautiful.

"Are you happy to be home?" asked Bobby. He was lying on the bed, covered by a sheet to the waist.

"Oh yes," she said, smiling broadly. "I'm glad we're staying a year, so I'll have time to catch up with everyone. It was all too much to take in today." She looked at him thoughtfully. "That's why we're here, isn't it? To decide where home is?"

"Yes. It's not the only reason, but yes, that's something we have to decide. We need to talk to Van about it. She's old enough to be in on our decisions."

"You know everyone's going to try to talk us into staying, don't you?"

"I'm going to tell Sarah about it, about how we want to deal with it ourselves, as a family."

Suddenly she was suspicious. "What have you got on under that sheet?"

His smile was a leer as much as anything. "There's one way to find out."

It was what she thought.

The next morning, she was sitting on the bed watching him get dressed.

"Do you remember the first time we made love in this bed?"

"Yes. I was thinking about it last night. It was the night we got married."

She shook her head. "When I think back on the time right after the earthquake, it's amazing how little I remember. Amazing when you realize how much I thought about it at the time. Our lives are so different now, but at the time, that was my whole life; trying to put everything back together after it happened."

She stood and embraced him. "Thank you for taking me away from all that, dear, even if you were just looking for another deckhand."

He grinned down at her. "You did turn out to be a pretty good hand after all." He kissed her. "And there are some benefits." He tried to kiss her again, but she shook her head. "We've got too many things to do and people to see today and probably for the next week, for that matter. Let's go see what our daughter is up to."

Van, it turned out, was having breakfast with her grandmother, her great-grandmother, and Madame in Madame's sitting room. She was sitting enthralled, gazing out at the city spread out below her.

"Mama, Papa, come look."

"We've seen it before, Button. It's really something, isn't it?"

When they were seated, Sarah asked, "So, what's the plan while you're here? It's for a year, right?"

"That's what we planned," replied Bobby. "We were thinking we'd stay up here for a few months, go to San Diego for a few months, then back up here for a while before we leave."

"So you're definitely going back?" asked his mother. "We were wondering, since you lost the boat, if you might decide to come back here to the ranch."

"Mama, we haven't decided one way or another," replied Bobby. "We're going to think about it and talk about it and enjoy ourselves, and sometime before this time next year, we'll make up our minds."

"I'll bet when you say 'talk about it', you mean among yourselves, don't you?" remarked Madame, grinning at him.

Bobby and Teressa looked at one another, then he nodded at her.

"We talked about it," said Bobby. "While we're here, we'll see all the good things about living here again, but no one here knows anything about our lives out there. It's something the three of us need to decide together over the next year because we're the only ones that know both sides of the question." He paused and looked around the circle at them with a grin. "We'll be sure to let you know when we do."

"So you're saying don't bother you about it, is that it?" said Madame.

Teressa interjected. "I wouldn't put it like that, but yes. We don't need to be sold on California."

"I can understand it," said Sarah. "Everyone in the family will be giving you all the reasons to stay." She thought about it for a moment. "I'll pass the word. They won't bother you about it."

For the next three months, they spent their time between the mansion in San Francisco and the ranch in Mill Valley.

"Van, come out here," called her grandfather from the front porch. "I've got something for you."

It was her first morning at the ranch and she had just finished breakfast. When she pushed open the screen door, Handy was standing at the hitch rail beside a horse.

She stared at it, eyes wide, mouth open.

"Come here," he said, holding out his hand. When she was standing beside him, he handed her the reins and said, "She's yours. She's a buckskin filly, about two and a half years old. She's just about old enough for you to ride." The filly was cream-colored with a dark mane and tail.

Van just stood and looked at the horse in wonder, her mouth open, a little breathless. After a moment, she asked, "What's her name?"

"She doesn't have one. We've been calling her Van's Girl since we heard you were coming.”

Rebecca squatted beside her and said, “Take a little time to think about it and come up with a good one. You can tell us tomorrow.” She gave Van a hug. “We’re so glad you’re here.”

After a night of reflection, she announced the name at breakfast. “Ghost.”

“Why Ghost?”

“That’s what I thought when I first saw her. She looks like a ghost, like she’s not there.”

“Well,” said Handy, “I guess ‘Ghost’ it is then.”

For the next few days, a number of different people were teaching Van how to ride and care for a horse. Jinx had watched the whole thing with interest and was friendly and curious about the new friend.

Within a week, she and Jinx were both at home in the saddle and were there most days, all day, until she was called in for meals and darkness. When they packed up to go to the Mansion for two weeks, Teressa was surprised when Van showed enthusiasm for the trip.

“She’ll be here when I get back and I know they’ll take care of her.”

The first thing Teressa saw when she came down for dinner at the mansion was Emily sitting at the window talking to Madame and Sarah. She stood watching them for a minute, remembering things about a time when Emily had been at the center of her life, indeed the pathway to her hopes and dreams.

Madame looked up and saw her. “Come join us, Teressa.” Emily stood, and they embraced warmly for a long time.

“It’s so good to see you,” said Emily, her hand on Teressa’s shoulder.

“I’m glad to be back home for a while. How are you doing?”

Emily picked up the cane leaning against her chair. “This is my constant companion now, but I get where I want to go. It just takes me longer than it used to.”

“Amen to that,” said Madame. “On the other hand, I don’t mind it as much as I used to. If you feel like it, Teressa, we have some tickets to the theater tonight. Emily is the co-producer of the play, so we get a special box."

Teressa looked at her friend and said quietly. "So you stayed and put it all back together. That makes me so happy. Instead of staying, I got married and ran away to the South Seas and honestly, I couldn't be happier. But," she shrugged, "sometimes, I wonder what my life would have been if that building hadn't collapsed on me?"

"So what about it? Do you want to go see *Midnight Rendezvous*?" asked Madame. "Because if so, we need to go soon to make the curtain."

It was the beginning of an amazing two weeks. With Emily as a guide, Teressa and Van attended the theater every night when they could find a production and afterward sat over something hot at a cafe Emily knew about and talked about actors and acting. Usually, Madame and sometimes Sarah and Rebecca tagged along, and a few times the men had joined them, but regardless, the three of them went to a show.

Some of their talks brought to mind her hopes and dreams from that past and she enjoyed talks with Van and Emily about what might have been. She thought she might have seen stars in her daughter's eyes. If so, that was fine, just try to avoid earthquakes.

The first two nights back at the ranch, Van slept in the stable with Ghost and Jinx. She was a natural on a horse, at home with a saddle or without, though Jinx needed the saddle to hold on to. The two of them spent most of the daylight hours in the saddle or helping around the ranch.

Teressa had suggested Van look around the ranch and ask questions about living there. If they ever decided to live here, she would know what it was like.

"Are we going to come back here to live, Mama?"

"I don't know, Van. We've only been here a month. We've got a long time to make up our minds. We're going to think about it and talk about it, and we're going to enjoy the time we're here. You have to let me know what you think about it too. Don't make me guess. You'll have a say when we make our choice. This is important because it's about what we'll be doing and where we'll be doing it for the rest of our lives.

"Here's a couple of things to think about. First, if we leave here next year, we probably won't come back for a long time, maybe never. Second, if we decide to live here, we probably won't see Gran Terre or Maupiti for a long time, maybe never. It's not an easy choice, so think about it and talk to Papa and me about it. We've got a year to make up our mind, so let's not rush it."

They spent another three months in the north, two weeks at the mansion and two weeks at the ranch turnabout. When they boarded the train to San Diego, Teressa was excited about coming home and was grinning when she walked in the front door of the store. She had spent many hours reading and dreaming in her own little corner of the back room where she had her 'study,' and was amazed how small it was when she showed it to Van.

For the first couple of weeks, that's what she and Bobby did—show Van the people and places that had been in their lives before she arrived on the scene. After the second time, he left them to it. After all, it was her hometown, not his, and she had a sneaking feeling he was looking at boats. From one place to another, they held hands and talked, sat in the grass and talked, and stood on a beach looking out to sea and talked.

The best day was when they went out to the rock.

"So tell me what you're thinking." Van was sitting on the rock, brushing her mother's hair. They both knew what she was talking about.

"I was thinking we've been here six months," said Van. "Have you made up your mind yet?"

"You first."

"I think about it a lot. I love it here. I love Ghost and the ranch and the mansion and especially the people, but…" she paused.

"But it's not home?" Her mother finished her thought for her.

"That's right. It's not home. Are we going back home?"

"Well, since your Papa's probably looking at boats today, I'd say there's a good chance. We talk about it now and then and I think I can see a look in his eye."

"How do you feel about it?"

"It's home to me too. We'll be here another month, then back to the ranch. Let's not tell anyone. Let Papa tell everyone at dinner one night."

Bobby and Johnny were riding a nice breeze across San Diego Bay in Manny's old sailboat.

"This is as nice as I remembered," said Bobby, relaxed and holding the tiller.

"You and Manny spent a lot of time out here over the years," said Johnny. After a pause, he continued, "So, have you decided yet?" He held up his hand. "I'm not nagging you about living here, but I just wondered if you'd made up your mind."

"The three of us seem to feel the same way. We love it here and we'll miss the people, but Grande Terre is home."

"Well, I understand. Are you going to stay the whole year?"

"Yes. A few days before we left the mansion, I went down to the boatyard in San Francisco where Pete got Mirabelle. He's got another one he's refitting."

"Schooner?" Bobby nodded. "How big?"

"Seventy-three. It should be ready just about the time we're getting ready to leave."

"How much does he want?"

"Forty thousand, rigged and ready. I know his work."

"Can you swing it?"

"I think so. It'll be a bit of a stretch, but we'll be alright. Your daughter is much better at keeping the books and running a business than I am. We're OK."

Later, they were walking back to the auto when Johnny asked, "If you buy it here and sail it home, won't you need a crew?"

"Oh yeah. It's too big for the two of us, even with Van to help. Usually there are people hanging around the harbor looking for a berth. I shouldn't have any trouble."

They were quiet on the ride home, but as they were going in the front door of the store, Johnny said, "Madame has a thing she does when she sees a new business she feels is good for the city. She offers to help by purchasing a share to give them some needed capital. She did it so Gray would have the money for his share of the ranch and with us when we expanded into the house next door. It's strictly a money-in, nose-out kind of thing."

"I'd heard that about her."

"I wondered if you wanted to have the same kind of arrangement with the new boat. I could put up some money to buy a piece of the business and if you ever wanted to buy me out, you could, anytime."

"I'd have to talk to Teressa about it, but I don't see that it would be a problem."

"One thing though, you'd have to take me on as a hand."

"What? What do you mean?"

"I want to be part of your crew when you leave."

"You'd come back home on a steamer?"

"Eventually, not right away. I'd like to see what you love about that place so much. Probably be there a couple of months anyway."

After dinner that evening, Bobby led his wife and daughter onto one of the many porches at the store and when they were seated, told them of his conversation with Johnny.

"He seems to think Papa will want to come along too, so that means just one more for the crew and we'll be set."

"So you decided on the boat?" asked Teressa.

Bobby nodded. "I think so. It's all we'll need to get back in business again. With Johnny's money, we can do it easily. The yard said they'll have it ready by October and that's when we'll be ready to go home."

CHAPTER THIRTY-SEVEN

Handy Josephson and Johnny Fry were talking one night after an interesting day. They were settling into their places as members of the crew of *Wind Song*. Tonight was Johnny's turn at the wheel and Handy was sitting, looking up at the stars and keeping him company.

Handy shook his head. "Don't think I've ever seen 'em so bright. Not even in Utah on a winter night." He stood up and looked out toward a horizon dimly lit by the stars. "No lights anywhere." He sat back down, was quiet for a moment, then said with awe in his voice, "We are in the middle of the biggest ocean in the world. One thing about hanging around with you, Fry, it's always interesting."

They both laughed. "I guess that's true," said Johnny. "We have had some interesting adventures together over the years." He looked up at the mainsail, at its shape, trying to remember what he'd learned about it. He had been learning a lot in their new lives and found he wanted more.

Bobby was teaching Johnny the basic ideas behind celestial navigation. When they crossed the Equator, he would have to learn the different stars of the southern hemisphere and he was looking forward to it. Though he would probably never use it in his life, it still was something new and he wanted to learn it.

"I was thinking about that fight we had with the Apaches and wondered if you ever remembered anything about it?"

"No, never have." Handy reached up and touched the scar on his hairline. He had been wounded by a ricochet in a fight with some Indians, and the only thing he remembered was a soreness in his shoulder. When Johnny told him he fired a ten-gauge shotgun and cut an Indian in half, it explained the soreness, but he'd never had any memories of those two days in his life. "Once in a while it hurts but, no memories."

They were quiet again for a while.

"I miss Wash," said Johnny. "He's usually with us when we do something like this." Their friend and traveling companion had settled into a domestic life far different from his life as a former slave and mountain man who roamed the wilderness savoring his freedom. He had refused Johnny's invitation to join them.

"When you come back, we can sit on the porch and you can tell me about it," he'd said.

Handy had jumped at the chance but had to approach his wife gingerly with the proposition. Several times in the past, adventures with Johnny had led to injuries and bullet wounds of one kind or another. This one did seem safer and she understood him, knew this was the kind of thing he needed to do every once in a while.

When the time came to leave, Bobby hadn't had to look along the docks for a hand. He found one in a young student at Berkeley. His name was Homer Jensen and he was a friend of Roy and Este. When he heard them talking about the voyage one night, he jumped at the opportunity. He was from Michigan and had sailed Lakes Michigan and Huron as a boy.

"School will be here when I get back," he said. "But I might never get another chance like this."

So Bobby had a crew for the trip to Grande Terre. When they got home and went to work again, they would probably add a couple of boys to help them, but for now, it was enough to get them home. Of course, there'd also be Henri. That's the first thing Bobby would do in Noumea, send a message to Henri. He wasn't really comfortable if his first mate wasn't aboard.

Saying goodbye to friends and family was a weeks-long process, but eventually, they put *Wind Song* in the water and spent a few days sailing her around the Bay. They had chosen the name from among three that had been proposed, it being Teressa's choice. One day in late October, they finally put her before the wind, passed through the Golden Gate and plotted a course to the South Pacific and home.

A day short of three weeks after they left San Francisco, they dropped anchor in Honolulu Harbor and surprised Grace Spreckels at her office. She was glad to see them but busy and invited them to dinner that evening at her home.

After the meal, Bobby and Grace's husband, Grady Harrison, left Teressa and the others talking and sat on the porch smoking cigars.

"Since you're going to New Caledonia," said Grady, "I'd advise you to cross the Equator somewhat to the east of your normal route. I've had some news about the Japanese in the area west of here.

"They became allies with France in the war going on in Europe and the first thing they did was grab off German-controlled islands north of the Equator in the Central Pacific. That's the Marshalls, the Carolines, and the Marianas. From what I've heard, they are beginning to fortify some of them and they're occupied by troops." Grady managed the Spreckels Sugar Company and was involved in routing steamers through the Western Pacific.

"The British negotiated an agreement with them to stay north of the Equator. That doesn't necessarily mean they won't push the line a little. I'd say be wary of any contact with them."

Bobby sat quiet and thought about what he had just heard. "Have you had any problems with them?"

"No, but we've taken precautions. Route changes have pretty much kept us out of that area. Now, if we route a ship into those islands, it would have to be for a good reason, a damn good reason."

When he told the others what Grady had said, Bobby suggested they change their plans and sail to Maupiti, spend a few days, then go home from there. That would keep them comfortably south of the Equator. That meant they would sail due south and cross the Equator far east of the problem.

Besides, Maupiti was special to them. They naturally wanted to share it with the family. He grinned at their reaction to the news that it was 2,600 miles to Papeete and another 3,000 to Noumea.

"It's the biggest ocean in the world, Papa, and there isn't much land out here. It's almost 8,000 miles from Santiago, Chile to Noumea, and it's almost all water. That's why I like to have Henri around. He always knows where he is."

They dropped anchor in the lagoon in the late afternoon. The surprised islanders fell on them in celebration and led them to their house, where they had the good manners to leave and let Teressa show off her home.

One of the nice things about Maupiti was the mountain. It was tall enough to catch the rain clouds, and there were several year-round water courses that ran into the lagoon. It also took up most of the land, so it forced the people on the island to live along the skirts of the mountain. This meant everyone was close to the only road and to the lagoon and the bounty it provided. Like living next door to a fish market.

Van and Jinx disappeared with some friends and the crew relaxed from the trip. Maupiti is just far enough from the Equator that it's not too hot or cold. The weather, the lagoon and the people made it a wonderful place to spend time, a true paradise. Though the lagoon was literally in their front yard, they rarely fished.

Almost every morning, there was fresh seafood when Teressa came into the kitchen. The islanders saw the people in their midst as benefactors. The people of the island jointly owned the schooner *Maupiti* and for the last four years, the two boats had worked under one flag, so to speak. Bobby had treated Beni and Claude the way Pete had treated him and the islanders were grateful for the results. Whenever they were on the island, they were treated as valued guests.

One evening later that week, the crew was sitting on the front porch looking out at the lagoon when Johnny shook his head and said, "I can't imagine why you'd leave this place."

"We love the time we spend here, but the house on the cliff is home," said Teressa.

"The way you talk about that place, it must be something

special," said Handy.

"I don't know about anything special," she said. "It's just a small cottage that's been added to over the years. Other than the nickel mine across the bay, there's not much around for twenty miles. To get to it, you have to climb up a pretty good hill and on a hot summer day, that's not fun.

"But it's where it all began. Pete's buried there and Marie and Cookie are there. It's where Pete gave Bobby *Mirabelle*, the beginnings of his life down here." She paused, then continued thoughtfully. "I think it's like a wellspring for him. He needs it once in a while to touch base." She shrugged. "It's home."

Leaving Maupiti, they reached northward into the trades and came into Noumea Harbor at the southern tip of Grande Terre in the Archipelago of New Caledonia on the afternoon tide three weeks later. They introduced their new crewmates to Noumea and left them to explore it while they took care of the paperwork, provisioning, and a few minor repairs on *Wind Song*.

Teressa handled the paperwork required to register a new boat with the locals, while Bobby sent a message to Henri and visited his factor and his lawyer and let them know he was back in business. They were able to give him information about how Beni and Claude were faring with their schooner, and news from the house on the cliff that Cookie and Marie were alive and well and anxious for their return.

Several years before, Bobby had arranged a message service with the nickel mine across the bay. When a message for them came in, the company would raise a blue flag that could be seen from a point several hundred meters from the house. Marie or Cookie checked it daily and would cross the bay when the flag was flying to get the message.

The crew met for lunch at a small waterfront café, and afterward, Bobby tied the schooner up to the pier and loaded provisions for the next month or so at home.

The next morning, not having heard from Henri, Bobby hiked out to where he lived with his wife's family when he was in port. He could see some children playing in the front yard, and one of them disappeared at his approach. He saw a woman come to the doorway.

Instead of calling Henri', as he expected, she waited for him and when he stepped onto the porch, she said, "He's inside. He's very sick." She turned and led him to a room where Henri was lying on a low cot propped up with some pillows.

Bobby stared at his friend, totally taken aback at what he was seeing. He felt a little breathless and closed his eyes for a moment to get his bearings.

When he opened them, Henri was smiling a sad smile. "Well, old friend, it seems like I have a problem."

"What is it? What's the matter?"

"The doctor tells me I have cancer in my lungs."

"What does that mean?" asked Bobby.

"It means there's a tumor growing in my lungs, and it's getting worse."

Bobby sat down on a low stool by the cot and tried to comprehend what he had just heard.

"Can they do anything to stop it?"

Henri shook his head. Since Bobby had last seen him, he was noticeably thinner and his skin had an unhealthy pallor. When he moved to get off the cot and stand, Bobby held out his hand. "Should you be up?"

With an effort and an assist from Bobby, he stood and reached for a cane hanging on the bed. "I get around alright with this thing. Let's sit on the porch and talk." He led the way, and when they were seated, he asked, "Did you get a new boat?"

"Yes. A 73-foot topsail schooner. She's named *Wind Song*."

"Ah, that's a nice name. I'll bet she's beautiful. Bobby, my friend, I have a request for you. Will you take me to Maupiti?"

"Sure, probably take a few days to get ready, but we'll take you. Why?"

"I'm in the way here and with all the kids from the neighborhood playing out front, it's too noisy. I make her and her mother's lives harder by being here. I want to get away somewhere and die in peace. I've got my little place there and they'll look after me."

"Did the doctor say how long?"

Henri shrugged and spread his hands. "Could be weeks, could be months. I'll let you know when I get there."

"Are you hurting?"

"It comes and goes. Not bad so far. I've got something for it."

"How about a week? We need to see Marie and Cookie before we can go."

"I'd love to see the house again, but I don't think I could make it up the hill."

It took a day to get him installed on *Wind Song*. He could still move around with help, but needed to catch his breath after any exertion. Bobby put him into the cabin closest to the hatchway and someone was always standing behind him whenever he slowly climbed the steps to sit in the cockpit, propped up on pillows, dozing off and on.

During the three-week voyage, Henri' seemed to improve a little and he spent many hours talking to Bobby and the rest of the crew.

When Henri wasn't with him, Bobby was quiet and thoughtful. Unable to sleep at times, he sat alone in the cockpit or on a hatch cover and looked at the ocean for hours.

He remembered his father's friend, Lemuel, saying once, "Nothing's real until it happens." He clung to this idea. Henri was alive and looked like he was getting better. Maybe the doctor was wrong and he won't die after all.

But when he looked at his friend, he knew it was no good. His prominent cheekbones, increasingly gaunt frame and unnatural pallor told Bobby to stop kidding himself.

Of course, accepting it as inevitable meant he had to imagine life without his first mate and he wasn't ready to accept that, even though it seemed he had no choice.

Johnny, Handy, and Homer had become a seasoned crew by this time and all stood a night watch. Tonight, it was Johnny's trick at the wheel and it happened that Bobby was ready to talk, so he and Teressa joined Johnny in the cockpit and they talked.

Actually, Bobby talked. They listened. He told them of the thoughts that had been tumbling around in his mind, things he'd thought were important but now not so much.

"I've been thinking about this for a couple of days. All the things I've been thinking come down to the idea that I've never been without Henri. He's always been by my side since I first met him at the house on the cliff. Eleven years now. Can I do this thing without him? He's my last link to Pete. I've leaned on him all these years and he's always been there when I needed him."

Teressa put her arm around him. "You've still got him just like you still have Pete. Those books he wrote, and the ones you and I have written, have Henri between their covers. You also have all the things he taught you over the years and all of the memories. By the way, Henri wasn't your last link to Pete. Marie is at home with Cookie."

Johnny had been listening and finally he asked Bobby, "Are you thinking you're afraid to be without him? Is that what it is?" Bobby looked at him but didn't answer. "You know that feeling you get in your stomach when you think about Henri's loss? That can be many things besides fear, but even if it is, there's only one way to deal with it. Live your life.

There'll come a time somewhere in the future when you have to use your judgment about something and you will because he won't be there to help. And you'll do alright. You can't be afraid of tomorrow. When the time comes, you'll do fine, but don't make it a problem before it gets here."

Later, when Bobby checked on Henri before he went to bed, his friend's voice came from the shadowed bunk. "I heard the conversation just now." Neither of them spoke for a moment, then Henri broke the silence. "I need one more favor from you."

"Anything."

"When I'm ashore in my little hut, I want you to leave. Go back to work. Make your living. An island schooner can't sit idle. No money to be made like that. Say goodbye and go."

"If that's what you want, of course," said Bobby. "You know, if we leave, we could be gone for a month."

Henri chuckled. "Who knows that better than I?" he said.

"So you want to die alone?"

"I want you to live your life. Besides, I won't be alone. They'll take care of me. It will make me happy to think of you sailing your beautiful Wind Song."

It was actually five weeks before they returned. Claude's wife saw them drop anchor and met them at the landing.

"He is gone," she said in answer to his look.

"When did he die?" asked Teressa.

"I do not know," she answered. "Two men who cared for him at the last, when he could no longer walk, carried him to a small boat, laid him in it and took him out through the reef. The ocean took him. It was what he wished."

Over the years, Teressa had learned a lot about her man and knew there were times when he was silent, when something in life had roiled the waters of a normally smooth lake and needed thinking about. She knew enough to leave him alone. He'd talk when he was ready.

Later that night in bed, Bobby finally broke his silence. She was lying next to him and his arm was around her. Jinx, who usually slept with Van, was curled up on his pillow in the corner.

"It doesn't surprise me that he did it that way. I always thought he was a poet of sorts."

CHAPTER THIRTY-EIGHT

In the Spring of 1918, the German high command came to realize that Germany was losing the war. At that point, the one advantage they had over the allies was manpower. The Russian surrender in the east had released fifty divisions of battle tested troops they could deploy against the allies on the western front.

With the declaration of war by the United States in April 1917, the Germans, realizing the potential power the Americans could throw into the conflict, decided to use their temporary manpower advantage in an attack to overpower the British and drive them from the field, forcing the French to seek an armistice.

The German people at home were starving and on the verge of revolt and mutiny and German industry was falling behind in supplying the army with what it needed to continue to fight.

The British naval blockade had cut off needed food and other imports necessary to continue the war and feed the populace, so General Eric Luddendorf, in command of the German army, devised a plan designed to break the deadlock before the U.S. Army arrived to bolster the allied line. This plan was known to history as the Kaiserschlacht, or Kaiser's Battle.

April 10, 1918
Manny dear, I'm so sorry I didn't write to you last

week. The following will tell you why, but right now I want you to know that the only thing that's kept me sane the last two years has been the few times we spent together. I'll be so glad when this war is over and we can be with each other all the time, and I mean all the time. To this point in our lives, we have spent a lot of time apart. Let's not do that anymore. I realize for now we each need to be where we are. That doesn't make it any easier.

About five in the morning of March 23, the German guns began firing over us. I thought nothing could ever sound like the artillery barrage fired by the British before the Somme, but this was worse. And it didn't stop. For about an hour the shells screamed overhead. Trying to get anything done in the middle of that sounds impossible, but we did it anyway. When you're in the middle of taking a man's leg off, it doesn't matter what's happening around you; you have to pay attention to what you're doing.

At first, it went over our heads. Then suddenly it changed, and we began to hear it from the opposite direction, toward the front.

Some of the patients told us this meant the Boche infantry was coming. The artillery was being targeted ahead of the advancing troops. A creeping barrage was what one fellow called it. The idea was the artillery was targeted a couple hundred yards ahead of the men and it kept that distance as they moved forward.

We were already beginning to admit casualties from the fighting, and with them came rumors that the German attack was very strong and pushing the British and French back. It seemed they were coming in our direction.

We got orders to begin to pack non-essential equipment, and we were doing that when an artillery shell exploded nearby. The blast blew down several patients' tents, and patients and staff were trapped under them.

We spent an hour just getting everyone out from under those tents. Those things are heavy canvas, and getting them out was hard, exhausting work. We were fortunate there was no fire, but even so, we lost nine patients, a volunteer nurse, and a sister.

Sorting the situation out while continuing to pack was hard enough, but with the sounds of artillery coming closer, it was nerve-wracking. I was naturally afraid for the patients, but for the first time in the war, I was afraid for myself.

I won't go into the details, but in addition to the station's problems, over a hundred stretchers were laid out in rows, exposed to the weather, in a field near the surgeries. There were also dozens of horse-drawn wagons and motor lorries queued along both roads leading into camp.

At that moment, we got orders to pack up and move. It was chaos.

Col. Powell had been through this before and he was marvelous. He organized the tasks that needed doing and the staff did them. For the rest of the night and into the next day, we worked without stopping. Across the railroad tracks, there was another CCS, and we were ordered to transfer our patients and supplies to them, pack our equipment, and leave. ASAP.

Thinking about the next two days makes me tired all over again. The staff of the station and its support unit were responding to orders, so it had to be done. It was that or surrender to the oncoming enemy. We all worked until we were ready to drop and must have gotten it done because I'm not in a German prison.

During this time, we moved with most of our equipment to the small town of Grevillers, about fifteen miles from the front. The sound of artillery was still constant but much farther away. We set up the station beside a rail line and began to take in wounded. On the other side of the tracks, 3CCS was set up, and we worked together to cope with the overload of patients.

For the next day and a little more, I worked triage, spent eight hours in surgery, helped to set up the station, and rarely had time to sit down.

That day, the two CCS's had admitted over 3,600 patients and discharged almost 3,000 onto ambulance trains. I lost track of the number of arms and legs I amputated, how much shrapnel I picked out of wounds, how many bullet wounds I cleaned and dressed. In many cases, I never saw the face of my patient, and the ones I did see, I don't remember. There were just too many of them.

I came here to learn and help people and I've done a lot of both. I've seen and done things over the last two years that I never believed possible, and there are few parts of the inside of the human body I haven't seen, usually in the worst of circumstances.

By the morning of the third day, things had begun to settle down when we got orders to evacuate again, and not only that, but we were to transfer all our equipment to CCS3. The idea that the things we carted around for two days were to be given away caused some grumbling, but it sure made life easier for a while. After three days of little rest and constant work, we woke up the next day with nothing to do. It felt strange.

Of course, it didn't last. By that night, we moved again and finally came to rest at a railroad junction near Amiens, along with four other CCS units that had also been forced to move around. When all the units were up and running, the whole place covered two square miles on either side of a double railroad track. For the next ten days, there was always a train on one of the tracks, and we kept them filled.

Because much equipment had been lost in all the moving around, the commanders got together and pooled resources. They set up rotations for the medical staff and we were finally able to get some rest.

Things are almost back to normal, but we hear there

might be a big offensive in the next month. I've noticed there doesn't seem to be much difference between advancing wounds and retreating wounds.

We've also been getting a lot of admissions with respiratory problems in the last few days, and it seems a flu is going through the area. We have to be careful. It's one that spreads easily.

That question Colonel Powell asked me the first day I got here still runs across my mind once in a while, and I saw something the other night that answers it. After three days of almost constant activity, the Colonel, Swede, and I, and several others, were stranded with about forty patients and without transport to a place five miles away.

In a decision I know he didn't want to make, the Colonel gave orders to separate the patients into two groups: those who could make a five-mile walk in the dark and those who couldn't. With volunteers to care for them, the second group was to be left to surrender to the oncoming Germans as prisoners of war.

The patients refused to separate. The ones who could, carried and supported the ones who couldn't, and we walked five miles in the dark.

I'll always remember what one young man said to the Colonel. He said, "It's alright, Sir, we'll look after 'em. No need to leave anyone behind, Sir." That's what I'm doing here. Taking care of men like that who need me.

I think this is the longest letter I've ever written to you, but there was a lot to tell. Write and tell me how it feels not to be in the Navy. I don't know when I can be home again, but I dream about it. Love, Colleen.

P.S. We have a new woman doctor working with us. Her name is Anne Frenau. The other day I mentioned I had gotten a letter from New Caledonia, and she told me she knew someone who lived there. Turns out it's Bobby and Teressa.

She works for the RMC and is charged with visiting

CCSs on the front and sending reports back to London on their operation. Making sure we're behaving ourselves, I guess.

Anyway, she worked for the French government before the war, and her job was to visit some of the islands in the South Pacific. Bobby and Teressa were hired to take her to them. She was with them for several months.

Like us, she was in London when the war began and joined the RMC.

Manny was tapping the folded letter against his knee, deep in thought, when John Tower's voice brought him back to the present.

"Cyril tells me you're going out on a bombing mission tomorrow morning." When Manny nodded, he continued, "How'd you swing that?"

"I want to see how it performs on a mission. See if it needs any adjustments or modifications."

"Where are you going?"

"I couldn't tell you if I knew, which I don't. Somewhere on the Belgian coast, as a guess. They'll tell me in a briefing before we take off."

"What are you flying, do you know?"

"An F3."

"The one with the new bombsight?"

"Yeah. I'm the bombardier on the mission," he said with a grin. "And the observer and the forward machine gunner as well."

He tucked the letter into his shirt pocket.

"That from Colleen?"

"Yeah. Boy, she's right in the middle of that German offensive. Her whole medical unit had to pack up and run ahead of the Germans. She's OK, but they're working her to death with all the casualties from that fight."

"Where is she?"

"It sounds like Amiens. That's where the Brits held and began to push back a little. Are you heading out?" John was picking up an overnight bag.

"The Embassy calls, and I have to jump." He rolled his eyes. "How do you like being out of the Navy?"

"We'll talk about that the next time I see you. It'll take a while to tell you about it."

The F3 flying boat was the latest evolution in their efforts to build what the British Navy wanted in a reconnaissance and long-range bomber. Even as a new model was put into production, the team at Felixstowe was working on improvements and modifications for the next model.

Manny had flown it many times, but this time an RNAS pilot would be at the controls, and Manny would be observing the flying boat and how it performed under service conditions. He knew the machine inside and out. Since leaving the Navy, he had become Cyril's chief assistant and sounding board for ideas to improve the F-series planes. No one was more qualified to critique its performance.

He missed the Navy, but Cyril kept him busy. The pain and feeling of loss had receded and life moved on. Things were a little different now. He no longer went to London regularly but lived in Ipswich and was beginning to feel comfortable there. He only went to the cottage when he knew Colleen would be there. As he became more involved in the development of the F-series, he was convinced he had made the right choice.

He missed Colleen too and the memories of the time they spent together never failed to make him smile. He agreed with her about being together after the war, but he had no idea what they'd be doing or where they'd be doing it.

For some reason, planning for the future wasn't high on their list of priorities when they were together. In Europe in 1918, the war was the future for everyone. 'When the war was over,' was a phrase used regularly by people all over the world.

He didn't sleep well that night. His mind was alive with the mission, and he was very aware of the danger it posed. He wondered if somewhere inside him, he needed to feel he was doing something daring. After all, his wife was in the middle of this whole war. He was doing something he loved, while she risked her life to save men fighting for their country. Be that as it may, this was the final check on whether this model could go into production, so like it or not, it was part of his job.

They would be flying in a formation with two F2a's, and this was the model he loved most and was looking forward to seeing in the air. He was a little biased, but he felt the F2a was the most beautiful airplane he'd ever seen and he loved flying it.

Dawn was just coming when they taxied into position to take off. Manny was in the observer's place in the nose. It was a recently enlarged but still small, egg-shaped nest, open to the air, that he shared with the bombsight and release mechanism, a .303 caliber Lewis double machine gun, a rack of extra ammunition wheels, and a pair of binoculars.

Even though it was spring, there was still a chill in the air, especially at two thousand feet and he was clothed in a heavy fleece-lined jacket and leather helmet with ear flaps and heavy gloves. There were four other men in the crew, but he only knew one, Ian Gordon, the top wing gunner. That didn't surprise him. The station was so big now that he didn't know half the people anymore.

He watched the other two members of the squadron take off and then came the long, smooth run over the water, a couple small jumps and they were airborne. From his position in the nose of the plane, he could see the other two above them, already turning toward the destination and smiling at how beautiful they were.

Their mission was to further damage and obstruct the entrance to the canal leading from the North Sea at Dunkirk to the interior of northern France. The Germans had controlled the area since 1914. The raid was an attempt to further tighten the British blockade by choking off interior supply lines.

An earlier raid had sunk a ship in the canal, but the Germans had created a way around the obstruction, so they were tasked with further occluding the mouth of the canal.

They could expect resistance in the form of anti-aircraft fire and pursuit planes flying from fields placed in the area to prevent just such a thing as they planned to achieve.

When the F3 was conceived, the Navy wanted it to have a bigger bomb load and longer legs (greater range), so it was larger than its predecessors and had larger, more powerful engines. Attached below the lower wings on each side were 460-pound bombs, released from the bombardier's position. These were twice the size of the bombs carried by the F2a, and the six-hour range gave the 'big boy' a comfortable margin on a mission such as this.

This increase in size and weight contributed to the stability and range of the plane, but in return, there was a noticeable lack of maneuverability and agility that made it vulnerable to pursuit and scout planes. In addition to the mission, Manny was there to gauge its performance under attack.

The flight time to the target was a little over two hours, and halfway along, they were joined by a squadron of three DH4 light bombers and three DH2 pursuit planes, the latter to keep German fighters from interfering when they came and they would come. The light bombers were to add their smaller bomb loads dropped from lower altitudes to increase the chances the mission would be successful.

Manny had been instrumental in the development of the bomb sight and had used it many times during development and testing, but this was the first time he'd tried to hit something in earnest. They were striking at the enemy where he was most vulnerable.

It was a clear, sunny day, so they could see the enemy planes climbing to meet them. Almost before he knew it, Manny was in the midst of a serious, dangerous dogfight with planes and bullet tracers filling the sky around him. He had two Lewis machine guns available, but he couldn't fire them because they were approaching the target and he had to ignore the whole thing and concentrate on hitting something with the bombs.

The three bombers had plenty of firepower. Each had four .303 caliber Lewis machine guns, two in the waist, one in a pit atop the top wing, and the one in Manny's compartment, and they did succeed in knocking down one of the Fokker D7s, but the others were on them in a swarm.

Even with all the guns on board, the F-series planes were not meant to tangle with the nimble and agile D7s. These new German fighters were developed late in the war to contest with the French Spad and the British Sopwith Camel, which had given the Allies air superiority through 1917 and into the spring of 1918. Thousands of these new weapons were flung into battle in the German spring offensive in an attempt to gain local control of the air. They were more than a match for Allied airmen they met.

Manny had heard about the D7's ability to hang in the air beneath an adversary and fire upward into its underbelly. Now he saw it when he watched one of the DH4s shot down this way. It was the first time he'd seen a plane shot down in flames and as he watched it fall in a spin and saw one wing come off, he wondered if the pilot was still alive.

Suddenly they were surrounded by bursts of anti-aircraft fire and the port engine caught fire from the blast of a near miss. At the same time, the plane took raking fire from a plane on that side and he heard the pilot cry out.

"I'm hit." He was still holding the wheel and the plane was still under control. "Got me in the back," then weaker, "I think it's pretty bad, a lot of blood." Then nothing.

The sound of the engine drowned the rest of anything else he said, but the nose of the plane began to sink. Ahead and several hundred feet below them was a large expanse of water. Manny knew nothing about it, but safe or not, it looked like that was where they were headed.

At present, the descent was too steep and too fast for a safe landing. The radio operator, who was trying to push the pilot aside, wasn't having much luck and the plane continued to nose down. Manny had no idea whether the burning engine would collapse the wing before they got down, but all he could do was watch.

Another burst of fire from a plane on their tail, and the radio operator at the wheel was hit and the dive steepened but suddenly began to level out as he regained control. The plane was about fifty feet above the water when the man suddenly slumped against the steering yoke. Manny felt the nose of the plane tilt forward, and they struck the water.

CHAPTER THIRTY-NINE

Teressa heard Van laugh and looked up to where her daughter was sitting with Marie, doing schoolwork. Marie taught her French and some Kanak, her native language, and how to cook. Teressa taught her English, math, and histories from around the world, and her father and Henri, when he was alive, taught her how to sail and care for the schooner.

"Let's clean all this up and get ready for dinner," she said. The long table where they were working was also the dining room table, and together they quickly cleared it off and laid eight places.

Tomorrow they would weigh anchor to begin a voyage and they had a tradition of a farewell dinner the night before departing. Things had been slow for a while and they had waited two months to get this job. Fortunately, it was a good one.

In the mid-nineteenth century the Catholic Church had scattered missionaries through French Polynesia like grains of wheat. When these seeds took root and sprouted, certain rites became necessary for the faithful, so annually the church sent a priest, usually a young volunteer to minister to their needs.

Since there were over a hundred islands under the French flag in the South Pacific, it was a long-term charter, probably four to five months, and would help them turn a decent profit for the year after all.

At dinner, there was laughter, good food, and conversation and when the plates were cleared, Bobby tapped his water glass.

"Since everyone here is family we have no secrets, so let's talk business." He nodded at Teressa and she gave them the numbers for the year.

"With this job, since we've been back, it looks like we've made enough to save about half of what we paid for Wind Song. As for the company, it seems to have been a good investment. Claude and Benni learn fast and the idea of taking vacation charters has been profitable and we get a share of their profits. Of course, they get a share of ours too."

"Any questions? No?" She nodded at Bobby, who looked at his father.

"Are you planning to stay with us the whole voyage? I can let you guys off at Papeete, and you can get a steamer home."

"Won't you need us as crew?"

Bobby shook his head. "We can usually find someone hanging around looking for a berth in a place like Papeete. Don't get me wrong. We'd love to have you stay aboard, but we understand if you think it's time to go home."

Johnny looked at Handy. "What do you think?"

"Why don't we sleep on it?" replied Handy after a moment.

The next morning, after saying goodbye to Cookie, they weighed anchor and motored the schooner into the lagoon for the trip to Noumea, where they'd do a few chores, leave the books for Claude and leave on the morning tide the next day. Bobby loved to begin a voyage thus, ghosting across the lagoon under a light breeze in the morning sun. From the house on the cliff to Noumea was one of his favorite places to sail.

The next morning, they left Noumea on the tide, cleared the reef through Boleri Pass on the south end of Grande Terre, turned east and set sail for Tahiti, almost three thousand miles away. (That's almost the distance from London to New York.)

A schooner on a long reach requires little attention. If the sails are drawing and the compass is steady and points to your destination, it pretty much sails itself. This gives the crew who aren't at the wheel time to do whatever they can find to do, given the limited space on a seventy-three-foot schooner with a twenty-one-foot beam.

This is one reason why, on sailing ships in years past, old sailors would find a place on the deck, arrange their tools around them, and, sitting in the same place, work for hours on things small and intricate, like scrimshaw and macrame. These are crafts that don't take much space.

They had left Handy on the dock in Papeete with a yen to see his wife and daughter and a steamship ticket in his pocket. Johnny had spent most of his time with his friend since they joined Wind Song and suddenly he was alone. It took him a few days to adjust to Handy's absence.

Handy's replacement was two people instead of one. Jared and Amanda Green were a couple crewing their way around the South Pacific, he as a deckhand and she as an extra hand who helped in the galley. They were pleasant people in their twenties, well-educated and well-read, as well as being the experienced hands Wind Song needed. They slung their hammocks in the forecastle with Rudy, apparently having no problems with the lack of privacy or space.

Father Renne Lefebvre, their passenger, was a young man who didn't look much like a priest. He was young and new on the job. The only mark of his office was a clerical collar around his neck when on board, though he was suitably attired when performing rites ashore as a priest.

He did have enough sense to lean heavily on Bobby and Teressa in laying out the plan for the voyage. Wind Song was to sail to the Marquesas and work their way westward from Nuku Hiva, calling on whichever islands had any acolytes. He wasn't a missionary; rather he came to provide the rites of the Church to its adherents. He wouldn't turn away converts, but he wasn't seeking any.

Over the years, they had done this sort of thing twice for the French government and both times it had been like an extended vacation they were getting paid for. This promised to be much the same. Father Rene (it felt strange to call someone Father who was noticeably younger than they were) would give them an estimated time of departure for when he'd be ready to leave. Other than being available, they had no other responsibilities.

The crew took turns being responsible for the boat when they were at anchor, which gave everyone a chance to see things ashore. Johnny had brought many of the Logbooks from home, and this became his craft, to sit in the galley for hours reading them and talking to his daughter and son-in-law, who had written half of them.

Since this was his first contact with the people of his 'flock', Father Rene also took advantage of the Logbooks, learning things about the people and places of his 'parish'. And since two of the authors of the books were at dinner with him, every evening meal ended with a discussion, Rene and Johnny asking questions and Teressa, Bobby, and Van answering them. The volumes they had with them were the ones written on their voyage with Anne back when Teressa had just arrived.

The idea of using the word parish to describe thousands of square miles of ocean is a little ridiculous, but that's what it was. On each island, he would call people together, give them the rites of the Church and bless them when he left. All told, there were over a hundred islands under the French flag, not all inhabited. Each stop took a few days.

Johnny took advantage of these opportunities to learn about the people and the places of a whole different culture. Whenever he had the opportunity to see or experience something new, he usually did, though he did manage to keep his pants on, even though he had an occasional temptation.

He did, however, come close one time. He was walking through a village on the lagoon of an island one evening when he saw a young girl standing in a doorway. He stopped, and she stepped out into the moonlight. Her beauty almost took his breath away. He had no idea how old she was, but there was a look of invitation on her face such as he'd never seen before.

She held out her hand to him. He took it and stood looking at her for a long moment. Finally, he smiled, shook his head a little, and turned away.

He continued his slow walk to the edge of the lagoon where he took off his sandals, put them in his back pockets, then plunged into the water and swam, fully dressed, out to where Wind Song was at anchor.

Needless to say, Jared and Amanda were surprised he arrived sans boat, dripping wet, in the cockpit, but had enough sense to ask no questions.

The next morning he was on watch and sitting in the cockpit with a cup of coffee when he saw her again. She was walking along the beach in ankle-deep water, kicking water ahead of her like a child. She looked toward the schooner, met his eyes, raised her hand and waved tentatively.

She continued along the beach, looking down at the water she was kicking up, but every few steps, she'd look up, see him watching and smile. After a while, she turned away and disappeared into the village, turning to wave before passing out of sight.

For the rest of the morning, he thought of nothing but her, how beautiful she was, how she'd look on a bed inviting him, how she'd look with her face contorted in passion or relaxed in satisfaction.

Years before, when he was leaving to travel in the desert for a while, his wife had told him, "If you find some senorita to play with, don't tell me, just make sure you come home." This was the first and only time he'd ever been tempted to use that license or even considered it.

He knew it could happen if he made it. She'd invited him, and no one would know. He pictured her and thought about the excitement of making love to an exotic creature like that. How it would feel to touch her, kiss her, caress her. And how would it feel to have her touch him, kiss him, caress him? What new things could he learn from her?

Even as these visions passed through his mind, another thought kept vying for his attention. When it formed fully, he rolled his eyes and looked exasperated. What would Teressa say if she found out? What would he tell her? He could imagine her face when she asked if it was true and he nodded. Nothing like a vision of your daughter's face to put an end to an adolescent sexual fantasy. Be that as it may, he'd remember that girl for the rest of his life.

Nuku Hiva was the largest and most populated of the islands in the northern group of the Marquesas. The islands are volcanic, and no reefs have formed to protect them from the power of the mighty Pacific Ocean that batters the islands from the east. Because of this, there is no lagoon. Almost all the people on Nuku Hiva live on the leeward side of the island, where the ocean is more amiable.

The capital, where they first landed, was at the bottom of an almost completely circular bay that had formed when a volcano collapsed eons before. Getting an anchor down on the rocky bottom was problematic at times so at least two crewmen were aboard Wind Song while she was at anchor there.

It was here that Bobby had seen the 'girl in the moonlight' as a young man and later spent the night with her. Odds were, both Teressa and Bobby were thinking about her while they walked down a path to a dinner invitation one night in a village near the bay where Wind Song was anchored.

They had seen the girl years before at another dinner at this house and though he believed it wasn't a problem with his wife, he realized he was nervous about the possibility of seeing her again. If his wife was nervous it didn't show.

They came to an open area in the village where a group of boys were playing a game of football and they stopped to watch. Teressa's eyes immediately went to a dark-haired boy who was at least a head taller than his companions. Where the others were stocky, he was tall and almost lanky.

When they walked on, her mind stayed behind. She was trying to make sense of something and when she finally did, her mouth fell open in astonished realization. For the rest of the evening, it was on her mind. When she saw the boy enter the house where they had seen his mother years before, she couldn't help herself and knocked on the door.

The woman who answered was clearly not the girl and told Teressa the person she asked about had died the year before.

"Was that tall boy her son?" Even as she said it, she wasn't sure she wanted to hear the answer. When the woman nodded, Teressa's mouth fell open in astonishment.

She stood for a moment, staring at nothing, fingers across her lips. Finally, with a start, she thanked the woman and returned to the gathering. Bobby hadn't missed her and she decided not to bring it up until she'd thought about how to handle her suspicions.

Later that night, when they were lying in bed, he asked, "Did you see her?"

She was a little startled by the question. "No, she died last year."

"Is he my son?"

He couldn't see her nodding in the dark, so she said, "I'd put money on it."

He was quiet for a long time and finally she realized he'd fallen asleep. In spite of herself, she smiled and shook her head in disbelief. Only Bobby Josephson could fall asleep after news like that.

The next morning, there was no question he'd been thinking about it, and he brought Van into their stateroom after breakfast.

He was clearly nervous. The two of them were sitting on the bed holding hands when he took a deep breath and began.

"Years ago, before I married your Mama, I slept with a girl here on the island. Last night we found out that there is a good possibility that she had a son. One who looks a lot like me. His mother died last year.

"So, I have several questions I need to ask you before I decide what to do in this situation. First off, how would you feel if he became part of the family? It's something that needs thinking about. I mean that question for both of you. It would be asking both of you to alter our lives and futures.

"The second question is, do I need to do anything? What if he's happy here and doesn't want to leave? He's a year older than Van, so he should have that choice.

"And then there's the most important question. Do you really understand what we're taking on if we do this? If he's going to become a part of the family, we have certain responsibilities about his welfare and his education. There's a lot of things he'll need to learn to feel at home among us instead of among the people he's known all his life."

He paused and looked at them meaningfully.

"I think you need to bring Marie into this conversation. It's going to affect her life too," said Teressa. "Can we have some time to talk about it and ask questions?"

"Yes, but we're scheduled to leave here the day after tomorrow. If we're going to do it, it will take time, probably not a lot, but some. I might have to ask Father Rene to lay over for a few days."

The next day, in the stateroom again, they talked for a while about the boy.

"Of course, the first question we have to deal with is, do we want to do this? It's a big commitment, so make sure you understand that. If we do this, we must do it right. Either he's part of the family and my son, or he's not. None of that stepson nonsense. What do you think?" he asked, looking at Teressa.

"That's the way I feel, and I'm ready to do my part to welcome him as a full member of the family," she responded.

"Me too," said Van. "And I understand that it's going to be the sort of thing that lasts a long time. He'll be a part of the family for many years."

"So," Bobby said, "it seems we're in agreement that we should do it. The next step should be going to their house and finding out what he wants to do. Once we know that we can begin to make arrangements to bring him on board."

That evening Bobby and Teressa knocked on the door and the woman greeted them with a smile, gestured a welcome, and served them some tea.

"I think you know why we are here."

The woman nodded and said something to a girl standing nearby, who darted out the door.

"You are here to talk about Enoah." It was a statement, not a question.

Bobby nodded.

"He is your son," she continued, "and we must talk about his future."

"We must talk about all our futures," Teressa answered. "Because this will affect us all."

CHAPTER FORTY

When the nose of the airplane crashed into the water, Manny's hand went to the harness release, pulled it and he began to rise to the surface. When his head cleared the water, he saw the burning engine had been doused in a cloud of smoke, and only the wing and a part of the fuselage were above water and as he watched, they slowly disappeared.

He tried to struggle out of his jacket and found that his wrist hurt badly. He turned away from the sinking plane, searching for his crewmates but saw no one. Then, suddenly, someone cleared the surface nearby long enough to take a breath before disappearing again. Manny reached out to the man, caught his hand and pulled, which made his arm and wrist shriek with pain.

Attempting to tread water while holding someone up and trying to get out of the jacket was beyond him, but fortunately, the man, gasping and blowing, was able to help himself by then. They both turned toward the several boats pulling toward them.

There were four of them, each with several men in it, and before long, Manny and Ian Gordon, the top wing gunner, were pulled from the water and lying, covered in blankets, in the bottom of a boat.

One of the men asked, "British?"

"Yes," replied Ian.

"American," said Manny. "I work for the British Navy."

"You're not in the army?"

"No, I was in the plane as an observer. Are we in France?"

"No, this is Belgium, just across the border."

It didn't matter which country they were in, they were German prisoners of war.

Two days later, his wrist in a cast and arm in a sling, Manny was aboard a train headed somewhere; he didn't know where. "To a camp," was all they were told.

His right wrist had been broken in the crash and he had a gash and large knot on his forehead with no memory of how or when it happened. He spent his first night as a POW sitting on a hard bench waiting for a German doctor to have the time to stitch the gash on his head and put a cast on his arm.

The next morning he joined Ian and five other POWs for a day and a night in a dank, dark cellar and in the predawn hours the following morning, they were herded into a cattle car and told their destination was a camp. None of them had any idea where they were or where they were going and the guards told them nothing.

But they were alive. Three of their crewmates weren't, at least as far as they knew. No one would answer any questions, but German soldiers were everywhere they looked. All in all, they were treated decently, but there was no question they were prisoners.

Since Ian had a badly sprained knee, they helped each other and got through the next few days together. He was from Yorkshire, and his father worked as a mechanic in the garage of the local lord, so he grew up around machinery.

He joined the navy early in the war where his penchant for tinkering with gadgets eventually landed him in the cockpit of a flying boat as a gunner. He'd worked with Manny enough at the base that they were friendly. That would become important to both of them in the coming days. Having a friend at that place and time was an important part of surviving.

Since the German people were starving, it was a pretty good bet they weren't going to be eating well as prisoners, so having someone at your back you could count on to help rustle grub was important.

From time to time over the next few days the train would halt and remain motionless for a while. Fortunately, these were cattle cars and their walls were more like fences with gaps between the boards, so they had some idea of their immediate surroundings and the direction of their travel.

Many times at these stops the doors were thrown open and they would be allowed out for a short time. When they returned, there were always new prisoners in the car.

It never really got crowded. There was enough light in the daytime to move around safely and they could see who they were talking to. Though it was springtime, it was damp and cold at night and since none of the prisoners had any belongings, they huddled together for warmth and slept fitfully during the night, occasionally coming awake to the strange noise of the train in bewildering absolute darkness.

At other stops, kettles of soup and loaves of bread were handed in and parceled out among the men. By the time they got to eat, the soup was cold and there was never enough. Over it all hung their uncertain future.

Since most were of one rank or another in the military, the idea of organization was natural and quickly evolved. Men with wounds or injuries were assisted and rations and water were shared. They were in the cattle car for the better part of three days and nights and as dreary as the camp was, they were relieved to finally get there.

On the third night, the train stopped on a siding and unloaded them directly into the camp. It was several rows of long barracks with tar paper walls and tin roofs. Each had a stovepipe jutting through the roof.

The camp was surrounded by a high fence topped with barbed wire and inside the compound, a warning wire ran around the compound five feet from the fence. This wire was pointed out and it was emphasized that crossing this wire would cause the guards to fire, and they were all excellent marksmen.

There were various other structures scattered haphazardly around the compound and watchtowers and lights at intervals along the fence with a clear area on the other side. Apparently, the lights swept the cleared area as well as the compound itself on a random schedule, which would make it difficult to remain unseen if the guards were at all attentive.

Outside the compound were a half dozen buildings for the guards and the administration. In front of one of them, the officers in charge stood and watched the POWs fall into a formation reflexively and answer to their names on a roll call. The new men were then separated, added to existing groups to make up squads of ten, then followed the man in front of them into their new home.

It was a routine they became familiar with, since roll calls were held at least twice a day and once a week at random times in the middle of the night, and whenever new prisoners arrived. That first night, Manny and Ian were fortunate enough to be chosen for the same squad and ended the night in lower bunks beside each other. Talking in low tones, their messmates let them know what was expected of them. They would likely be up for a work detail before dawn, regardless of their injuries.

"They'll find something for you to do," said Phillipe, who slept above Ian. "If not here, then on a detail going out to work some of the farms in the area. They don't believe anyone here's not fit to work, no matter what injury or illness you have."

The prediction was accurate. Injured wrist or not, Manny spent the day with a bucket carrying water for the prisoners who were working on a farm in the neighborhood. In conversations with others at the farm, they learned they were near the French/German border, south of Luxembourg, a long way from the sea and freedom.

Actually, they were fairly close to the French border, probably less than ten miles, but between them and the freedom it represented was the German Army and no man's land. Escape in that direction was impossible. In the other direction, the coast of Europe was a hundred miles away at the closest and neither of them spoke the language. They had no clothes, no food, and inadequate footwear.

By 1918, the Germans had over two million prisoners in compounds of one kind or another scattered around Germany and the occupied areas. In a nation on the verge of national starvation, POWs might end up fighting for scraps.

That was one of many reasons for a prisoner's chief

preoccupation, thinking about escape, dreaming about one, planning one, or taking part in one. Since Manny and Ian were injured, they couldn't take part in one, but they could listen, learn and help with one all the same.

The prisoner in command of the POWs was a British army Major named Murphy, and he and the escape committee had organized potential escapees into groups of five. Each group had a week to carry out their plan. Then, successful or not, the next five would have a week and so on.

The thing Manny found right away was how boredom was a major part of life as a POW. During the day, they performed mindless work of one kind or another. According to the Hague Convention, they could not work at any task that was at all military in nature.

What they could do was work on roads and bridges, for local farmers or businesses in nearby towns. There were not enough guards to go around, so many times they were unguarded. After four years of war, the locals were accustomed to using them for labor and returning them to the compound at night.

Manny's biggest problem was he was used to using his mind, solving problems and making things work. Suddenly, he was mucking out stables, digging ditches, and weeding between rows of crops. With all their young men at war, the two million prisoners did things for the German people that had to be done when there was no one else to do them.

At night the lights went out early and he had to lie in his bunk, in the dark, thinking until he fell asleep. He thought about Colleen a lot and wondered if he'd ever see her again. There were men in the camp who were captured in the first year of the war. It was easy to tell an old-timer when you saw one. They were slowly starving and were skin and bones.

He also thought about his family. When he thought about Teressa and Bobby sailing the South Seas, he always smiled. He thought about Mama and Papa and the family and the things he did as a kid. He missed the family, that group of people who always had someone around they could trust.

And, like every prisoner everywhere, he thought about escape. He talked to Ian about it regularly and half the conversations in the barracks after lights out were about it, but successful escapes were rare. If they were closer to the North Sea, maybe, or Switzerland, maybe, but they were halfway between the two. The odds against it were high, and the risks were great.

It was early summer and he'd been there about six weeks when one morning at roll call, the guard began by calling Manny, Ian, and five others out and sending them to the office with a guard.

"You are all airmen, and we have a special camp for you. You will take the train tomorrow."

"Where are we going?" asked Ian.

The man smiled and shook his head but didn't answer.

The next morning, in special tunics that identified them as prisoners, they once again boarded a train with no idea where they were going.

Colleen was sitting on the porch of her barracks, thinking about Manny, when Swede walked up and dropped into a chair beside her. They sat for a while in silence, both looking out at the station spread out below them.

"I hear you're leaving."

She nodded but didn't speak.

"Day after tomorrow?"

"I'll spend tomorrow night in Boulogne and catch a ship home in the morning."

"How long have you been here?"

"Two years this month." She reached out and took his hand. "Thanks for the times you let me go home for a week. I don't think I'd have made it without them."

"Have you heard anything about Manny?"

She nodded and handed him a sheet of paper she'd been reading.

He glanced at it. "He's alive and a prisoner of war?"

She closed her eyes and nodded, crying silently.

"You just got this, so it couldn't be the reason you're leaving."

"No, I told Jim the other day that I'd reached the end of my rope.

I can't do this anymore. I needed to go home and try to get used to the idea that he might be dead. Now that I found out he's alive I need some time to solve my own problems." She chuckled. "Leaving's a lot easier when you're a civilian. I just told him I was going."

"You'll be missed. You were the one I counted on. I'll have to find a new Colleen. Where will you go?"

"We've been using the caretaker's cottage at Lynn's place. I think she'll be glad to see me."

Lynn had left with her father the month before after almost four years at the station.

"First thing is to find out as much as I can about where Manny is and whether he was injured when the plane went down. What I do after that will depend on what I learn."

When he stood to leave, they embraced. She watched him walk down the hill and before he disappeared into a tent, he looked up and raised his hand.

One amazing thing about the station was how quickly you could go from the frantic necessities and chaos of the war to the peace and quiet of the caretaker's cottage in London. She had timed it once at five and a half hours, from boarding the ship in Boulogne to paying off the taxi in London at Lynn's house. This time she wasn't going back.

She had come to view her life, not as a novel, but as a series of short stories. In walking up the gangway of the hospital ship, she had ended one story and begun another. She wouldn't trade the time spent at 29 CCS for anything, but she was heartily glad it was over.

The first part of her new story was to gather as much information as she could about Manny. With Lynn to guide her, she contacted the Red Cross to find out if they had him on their rolls. If not, when they found out where he was and how he was, would they contact her?

The agency sent packages to POW camps regularly and was allowed restricted access to the camp rosters. Eventually, Manny should turn up on a list of downed pilots. She also got the names of some people at the war department, but she didn't learn much there because they didn't know much.

She had no idea what the life of a POW would be like, but she was determined to find a way to reach out to him however possible. She had the letter from the foreign office, so she'd start there. The man she talked to knew Manny from his time at the embassy but didn't even know he'd been captured and was amazed to hear he was an American civilian.

"I thought he was in the Navy," he'd said in astonishment. She doubted he'd be much help.

Once she saw Lynn, and was settled into the cottage, they caught a train to Felixstowe. She was grateful Lynn wanted to be her companion most of the time and that she had someone to talk to about all that was swirling around in her head. She'd never been to Felixstowe but wanted to talk to Cyril Porte and others about Manny's last flight. Cyril had written to her once and he knew Manny better than anyone.

"When Manny was at the academy, we'd write something in a letter before we went to bed every night and mail it once a week," she said. They were sitting in a first-class car eastbound out of London, headed for the village by the sea. "I've started doing it again. I give it to the Red Cross every week, and since, when they find him, he'll probably get them all at once, I put numbers on them so he'll know which one to read first."

Lynn smiled. "I'd like to see his face when he reads them." They talked for a while, but her friend fell into a doze. Colleen looked at her and wondered if she'd changed as much as Lynn had. The witty, wisecracking girl she'd met on the ship had become a quiet, beautiful, introspective young woman who seemed to weigh every word before she said it. She always looked sad when she wasn't smiling. While they were working together at the station, she hadn't really noticed, but here in another life, another world, you couldn't help but notice.

Manny will tell me, she thought. *He's the only one who knew me before I went over there.*

Cyril Porte was a tall, cadaverous man in his early thirties, already showing many signs of the tuberculosis that would kill him less than a year after the armistice.

"Manny believed there were problems in any new plane that would only be revealed under combat conditions. That was the last flight before we declared the F3 ready for operational use. This was his second such flight. Unfortunately, this time they were waiting for us.

"We lost four planes on that mission, and one of the F2a's had an engine shot up and barely made it home. And I lost my best pilot and someone I worked with every day. We worked on everything together." He shook his head. "With him and John Tower gone, I've got no one around here to talk to who understands what I'm talking about." Seeing where he worked and talking to some of the people he worked with was nice, but she and Lynn rode the train back to London not much wiser than when they left.

When she turned on the lights in the cottage and looked in the letter box, she found the strangest-looking letter she'd ever seen. It was a single sheet of paper covered with small, cramped writing. It had been folded into an envelope of sorts and there was a space for her name and address. The writing was Manny's. He was alive and able to write a letter even though there was an apparent lack of paper where he was.

She closed her eyes and muttered a prayer of thanks.

CHAPTER FORTY-ONE

It's called 'great' for a reason. The great pandemic of 1918-1920 was one of the most deadly single events in human history. Also known as the Spanish Flu, it infected more than 500 million people worldwide, or one of every three people on the planet. Though accurate numbers are impossible to pin down, estimates of deaths run from 50 to 100 million people in a two-year period. By comparison, fewer than twenty million people died during the four years of the war.

For reasons that are argued about, this flu didn't seem to target the very young or very old as it had in the past but was particularly virulent among young adults. So many of these, being in the military and living in close quarters like they did, probably promoted the unusually rapid spread around the world. With the armistice, soldiers infected in France and returning home carried the disease all over the world in record time.

The symptoms of infection were typical for the flu, but in addition to its lethal effects for those infected, it also opened the body to other infections and some, such as bacterial pneumonia, were just as deadly as the flu and contributed to the high death tolls.

Manny Fry was infected in the late summer of 1918 just as he moved into the new camp for captured airmen. As the war was ending, he developed pneumonia and his life was despaired of.

Manny opened his eyes and saw Colleen standing in the doorway. At least he thought he did. He was beginning to have doubts about things he was seeing and hearing. Or thought he was. He closed his eyes and when he opened them again, she was standing by his bed looking down at him with a smile.

"I believe that's the first time you've recognized me in a long time. How do you feel?"

He looked at her in silence for a long time. "Is that really you?" he asked weakly. "Or am I seeing things again?"

"It's me and I'm so glad to see you seem to be awake and alert."

"I'm hungry. My mouth is dry. Where am I?"

"I'll bring you some broth and crackers. You're at the caretaker's cottage at Lynn's house in London." This last she said over her shoulder on the way to the kitchen. She was back with some soup and crackers momentarily and fed him carefully until he finished.

"We've been worried about you. It's been touch and go for the last month, but you may finally be on the mend. There's no fever and you seem to be awake and alert."

She took the tray and set it aside. "Lynn's been helping me take care of you. You wouldn't believe what we had to go through to get you here. It took a month to get you released and home after the war was over. They wanted to keep you in the hospital."

"You mean the war's over? How long?"

"November eleventh was Armistice Day."

"What day is it now?"

"January third. Manny, you've been sick for three months. Apparently, Ian looked after you while you were in the camp. I think the only reason they released you when they did was because Lynn vouched for me. No one in England wanted to accept responsibility for an American civilian, so they just handed you around. I finally got hysterical and they relented.

"Every time we thought you might be improving, you'd get sick again. I'm hoping this will be the first step back. We have to be careful with feeding you for a while."

"I feel so weak. Keeping my eyes open is a problem. I just want to close my eyes and sleep."

"I imagine you do. I doubt you could stand by yourself. You've been in bed for three months. Your muscles are going to have to be returned to health carefully. Lynn and I will be with you all the time, but you must promise you won't try to get up unless one of us is standing by. A fall right now would be a setback you might not survive."

He looked at her in silence for a moment. "I'm tired already and I haven't done anything," he said.

"It's going to be like that for a while. Be patient and you'll get better. Don't try to do too much too fast. Lynn and I will be here to help you and make you behave.

"That's enough for now," she said from the window where she was closing the shades. "Get some rest and I'll answer any questions you have next time you're awake."

She bent and kissed him and arranged the blankets around him. "We're having trouble getting coal and it's cold in the house at night. Make sure you cover up good. No more relapses, OK? Just take your time and get better."

But it wasn't quite that simple. Three days of steady progress would be undone by the return of the fever and lethargy, and he would lie in bed sweating and tossing until the fever broke again.

Six weeks passed before he could hobble, supported by Colleen and Lynn, to sit on the porch in the late afternoon sun. As he sat there for the first time, eyes closed, breathing heavily and perspiring, a familiar voice cut through the haze in his mind, and he opened his eyes to see Ian standing on the steps smiling at him.

At first, he wasn't sure he wasn't hallucinating again, but when he felt the rough, horny hand in his, his face broke out in a smile, albeit a weak one.

"Well old man, you look better than the last time I saw you. You look like you're getting stronger."

Ian's was the face he remembered from the camp in his fleeting conscious moments before he awoke in the bedroom at the cottage.

"I don't know about that. It seems to come and go. One day I'm feeling better, the next, not so much. I've had trouble gaining weight. I'm still down thirty-five pounds from what I was when I got sick. How is it with you?"

"I'm back at home. My old dad's about ready to retire and it seems like I've got a job as a chauffeur and mechanic. Used to be two different jobs but now it's one."

He shook his head. "Lots of boys are looking for work, but things are tight. One nice thing about mine is it comes with a place to live over the garage and three squares a day. Know many who are sleeping wherever they can find a place. Makes you wonder why we went through all that stuff to come home to this."

Great Britain went into WWI as the wealthiest and most powerful nation on earth. It came out with most of its wealth in the hands of the American businessmen who had propped up the British war effort and kept the nation from starving. As far as the power end of it, their American cousins were now contesting for that title, too.

The enormous demands of war had drained British resources to the point where the nation and empire were shells of their former selves. The peoples of Europe in 1914 had been ruled by empires. Almost 400,000,000 people had lived in the British, French, German, Austro-Hungarian, Russian, and Ottoman Empires.

When the sound of guns died away, only the British and French Empires remained and both were in desperate financial straits. The rest of them were swept into the dustbin of history. The war they were so anxious to start had destroyed them.

Hundreds of thousand soldiers crashed into the British economy in 1919 and coincidentally also crashed into the British medical system with the coming of the Spanish Flu. The rising impact of the pandemic had been hidden behind the costs of the war and now the losses became more apparent and more frightening.

"When are you going back to America?" Manny had drifted off to sleep and Ian and Colleen were talking quietly.

"To tell you the truth, we haven't talked about it much." Colleen liked Ian and realized the debt she owed him. Without him, her husband would have died in that camp. "First job is to get him back on his feet."

"Lots of the fellows are talking about going out to the colonies. Not many jobs around either and with so many sick the hospitals are overflowing. If I didn't have this thing going on at home, I might like to try the colonies myself."

"If I were you, I'd get back across that ocean as soon as you can. My old dad is pretty smart, and he thinks times are going to be bad for a while."

After Ian left, she sat watching Manny snoring lightly in the chair beside her. She didn't see him being able to stand a steamship crossing any time soon. She shook her head and sighed. Besides caring for Manny, she had the problem of their dwindling resources and that situation was becoming worrisome. If he didn't begin to improve, she was going to have to seek a way to make a living and soon.

Fortunately, there was an alternative, though one she was loath to use. She could write or, better yet, wire Johnny and Annalese. She didn't have to wonder how her husband's parents would respond. They were family, but she hated to ask. What she had done was to procrastinate and wait as long as she could before she sent the telegram.

Within three days she had an answer. Funds would be available through a London bank and suddenly she could begin to plan a return to San Diego. There would be a certain point in Manny's recovery where he would be strong enough to stand an ocean voyage but he clearly wasn't there yet. Once in New York, they could rest until he was ready for the trip to San Diego.

When she went to the bank the next morning, the amount available stunned her. Now when she began to inquire about passages to New York, she could contemplate a first-class cabin, giving Manny easy access to the deck and allowing him to rest in comfort. She remembered her train travel in first-class carriages and was actually looking forward to seeing the country again from that vantage point. She believed the excitement generated by the planning and discussion about the trip would be a stimulant for Manny and might help him recover more quickly.

Now that the relapses seemed to be a thing of the past, she encouraged him to increase his activity by giving himself reasonable goals that would encourage him when accomplished. Lynn occasionally joined them on morning and afternoon walks through the Brentwood neighborhood. Each week they'd increase the distance or pace, and he was proud of his progress. He was definitely reacting to the stimulus of the trip and they talked about it and home constantly.

When they booked passage in the spring of 1919 for a crossing in late May and began to pack, they were amazed at how little they owned. Colleen had traveled during the war with everything she had in two carpet bags and that was still all she really needed. Manny's wardrobe was spare except for some of his old uniforms, but he did have a lot of books, which he went through and reduced to two boxes that they shipped before they left.

It was a nice spring evening. They were sitting on the porch, and Manny was looking at some of the books he had decided he didn't need.

"Are you going to go back to building airplanes when you get back on your feet?" asked Colleen. He was looking at a book on flying he planned to donate to a local library. "At one time flying was the most important thing in the world to you. But for some reason, I'm not sure that's still so."

"I haven't thought much about what's next for me. We've been so fixed on getting me better, and now we're excited about the trip. I haven't thought about much beyond getting home. Once we're there, it'll be time to talk about the future."

On the day they boarded the steamer, Colleen left Manny installed in their cabin and walked back down the gangway with Lynn. They embraced. "You've been so much a part of my life since the day we met on the steamer coming over here. I don't know what we'd have done without you.

"Having you as a friend has been important to me. Without you, I'm not sure I'd have made it in France."

Lynn looked at her shyly. "You know you're my hero, don't you?" She blushed a little when she said it. "When you get settled out there, I may pay you a visit. I want to go to medical school and in England women aren't allowed. So I may come to America and try to get admitted at the school where you went. I think I learned enough in France to do the work in school."

"I'm sure you did. We'd love to have you come and stay, but we live about five hundred miles south of San Francisco, which is where I went to school. But if you want to try it, I'll do everything I can to help you."

Manny was standing beside her at the railing as they waved goodbye while the ship pulled away from the pier. They stood and watched Southampton disappear and then went into the salon to celebrate with a glass of wine.

Manny had calculated that six turns around the deck would be a mile and he began at two turns. Gradually, during the six-day voyage, he increased it to six. Some mornings, Colleen walked with him, but he was feeling strong enough to do it by himself safely, so she slept in several mornings.

When they stood at the rail and watched the ship pass the Statue of Liberty, they both believed the voyage had been good for him. A lot of things had contributed to this. For one, he seemed to have passed out of the problem of relapsing, which meant his improvement could be more consistent. The daily exercise helped and the stimulation and excitement of the voyage meant he could look forward to enjoying each day. And also, they were going home.

All in all, he was improving but still needed an early bedtime and an afternoon nap. More than anything his weakness showed in his lack of stamina. So far, Colleen was encouraged by his good spirits and his interest in things when he was awake. He was gradually becoming the Manny she remembered.

The night before, they had agreed not to tarry in New York and went directly from the terminal to the station, where they entrained for Baltimore. Early the next morning, they caught the train to Annapolis.

"You're excited, aren't you?"

Manny was gazing out the window. "Yes. This train brought me to The Yard every year, and every year I was a different person. I was just thinking about how I felt the first time. That's when I met Jack. One thing I'd like to do while I'm here is track him down and Johnny Tower, too."

He paused and watched a scene passing in the window. "And CT. I hope he's alright. I haven't heard from him for a while."

The first thing they did was get a ride out to the pistol range. CT had never met Colleen, though he knew about her from talking with Manny. He greeted them warmly and they sat in the kitchen and talked.

"Well, to tell you the truth, you still look a little puny, fellow," said C.T. after they were settled into chairs over coffee at the kitchen table. The old place was gone and they'd built him a nice little cottage with a small modern kitchen.

"I'm getting better but still have a ways to go. I've been sick since September."

"Are you planning to spend any time here or are you going to hop a train and head home?"

"We've both been away for a long time, so we're pretty anxious to get home," said Colleen. "And Manny still gets tired easily, so he can't really do all the things he'd like to."

"Have you been shooting at all since I saw you?"

"We used to shoot once in a while at Felixstowe, but the only time I picked up my pistol since I was shot down, I had to hold it with both hands. I'm still pretty weak."

"I don't shoot as much as I used to." Manny had been a little surprised his old friend used a crutch now. "That leg they gave me never was much good, so I finally put it in the closet and just use this thing," he said. "Kinda hard to shoot with it."

The cottage had a spare bedroom, and he was adamant that they stay with him. "You couldn't find a place in town this weekend anyway. Probably have to go to Baltimore."

The visit to the Academy was a little unsatisfying because Manny was not able to see places and things he wanted. He was still too weak to do the walking necessary, and there were so many people celebrating commencement weekend he didn't feel comfortable looking around. Two days later, they boarded a train in Baltimore and headed west.

The one thing Colleen remembered about her transcontinental trips was the boredom, but Manny's excitement was contagious, and she found herself enjoying it in spite of herself. Though he had crossed the country many times by train he was fascinated and interested in everything passing the window, though he still napped during the long days. On the morning of their arrival, they awoke to the high hills of the coast range and, before noon, pulled into San Diego to be met by Johnny and Annaliese and other members of the family.

At dinner that night, the dining room was overflowing, and when Manny looked around the table, he realized this was where he needed to be to decide his future, their future.

CHAPTER FORTY-TWO

A sailboat on San Diego Bay is a great place to spend a late summer afternoon. Manny and Colleen were in the cockpit enjoying it in the boat Manny learned to sail in. She was sitting with her eyes closed, feeling the breeze when she felt Manny move and opened her eyes. His face was close to hers and he was leaning over to kiss her.

"You better behave and sail the boat," she said, pushing him away.

"Be careful how you treat the invalid," he said reproachfully.

She grinned at him. "It looks like Johnny has Annaliese convinced to go out to see Teressa and Bobby for a few months. Are you thinking of going with them?"

"What made you ask that?"

"A chance to spend a few months recovering on a South Sea island with your sister and your best friend? I thought you'd jump at the chance."

"He has mentioned it. He thinks it would be a good place for me to recover."

"It might be that he has ulterior motives."

Manny snorted. "No ulterior about it. He wants us to go. Says it will be good for me." He looked at her in silence for a long moment. "How would you feel about that?"

"You're asking me how I would feel about spending several months with my mother-in-law in a small house on a beach?"

"Well, from what Johnny says, it's plenty big enough for all of us and it's on a cliff, not a beach. On Maupiti, they have a house on the beach. I thought you and Mama always got along fine."

She was grinning at him. "You know how I feel about your mother. I'm joking. No, I think it's a wonderful idea. But we don't have the money to go there, much less spend several months there."

"Papa says it's his treat and his and Mama's contribution to my recovery."

"Does it bother you for him to pay our way and support us for however long we're there?"

"Not at all. That's the way our family works. They're helping take care of me and Papa and Mama know that one day we'll be taking care of them. It all works out for all of us."

"Well, I'd say let's go. When are they planning on leaving?"

"Mama has to disengage carefully from the clinic, so that will take a while. Last I heard, they were thinking about the end of October. It will take a few weeks to get there."

"Where will we be living?"

"Johnny has a map of Grande Terre. The house on the cliff is on Brony Bay at the southern end of Grande Terre. Maupiti is in the Leeward Islands, about two hundred miles from Tahiti."

"I heard Johnny say it's almost 3000 miles to Maupiti."

"Yes. It will be great for the family to be together again for a while. Johnny said the place they have on Maupiti is nice and they try to spend a few months there every year. Van loves it there."

By the time they tied up the boat, it was evening, and the lights of the city came on around them as they drove to the store. Manny had moved into Colleen's room, and it didn't take them long to fall into the rhythm of life at the store again.

At mealtime, there were usually some members of the family in attendance and it felt great to be renewing their connections with these people. Conversation at breakfast was usually just the people who lived at the store.

One morning, Johnny and Manny had ridden down to Wash's

cabin to shoot on the beach for the first time in many years and the ladies were alone at the table.

"Johnny's been dropping a few hints. He might want to retire and join Teressa and Bobby out there," said Annaliese.

"Hmm," said Colleen. "How would you feel about that?"

"I don't know. I know I want to practice medicine again, work with actual patients. Maybe I can do it out there, but I'm tired of being in charge at the clinic, tired of all the business of running things."

She paused and looked thoughtful. "I've talked to Micah and Maggie about it and they tell me they can handle it if I take off for a while to decide what I want to do." Micah was the clinic administrator and Maggie had been with Annaliese since medical school.

She gestured at Este. "That's why she's here. She's going to help Maggie with things until I see what I'm going to do."

Este and Roy had held each other at arm's length for five years before they married while she finished medical school. She had been Annaliese's first intern from the Mexican population of the city.

When they finished breakfast, Este left to see her family, and Annaliese and Colleen retired to the porch off their bedroom overlooking the city and the bay in the distance to sit and talk.

"What are the chances you might go out there to live?" asked Colleen.

Annaliese looked thoughtful, then shrugged. "Ever since he came back from Noumea he's talked about the place. He wants me to see it, so we're going. Either I'll decide to stay with him, or he'll decide to come home with me." She paused and looked at her daughter-in-law with a smile. "We'll decide when the time comes."

"Have you and Manny talked at all about the future?"

"Yes, but not much. Since he began his recovery, Manny doesn't seem to worry about anything. When he feels he's ready, we'll plan a future. Until then, he seems to be focused on getting better and enjoying the little things in life. As his doctor, that is exactly what I want him to do, but I didn't really expect him to be able to. He fooled me.

"You know Manny and I are in an unusual situation. We're going to have to learn everything about each other all over again. We came to England in 1914 and walked into a war. In the intervening five years, we've both lived through life-changing experiences, almost all of them while we were apart.

"Manny's been sick and not really himself for quite a while, so it's just in the last few weeks that we've spent any time together. We're just getting to know each other again as totally different people. Like I said, a strange situation for a couple who has been married for as long as we have."

She chuckled. "To tell you the truth, if he decides he likes me, that's enough to be going on with. For a while at least."

Johnny was standing with his hand dangling near the handle of his colt. He moved, and the pistol was in his hand, like a finger pointing. The gun roared, and a waterspout appeared several yards from where a piece of wood was floating in the ocean.

"Hard to hit it from that distance," Manny said. He was sitting on a piece of driftwood watching. He had tried the old drill of drawing and cocking the hammer, then releasing it and returning the .44 to the holster, but after three times, he gave it up.

"I guess I'm a little rusty," said Johnny, dropping empty cartridges into his hand to transfer to his pocket.

"You want to shoot some?"

Manny shook his head. "I still get tired easily. Feel good, just get tired."

"Have you thought about going with us?"

"Yes. Colleen and I talked about it and we're in. When do you plan to leave?"

"Your Mama says early November."

"It doesn't take us long to pack."

Annaliese and Colleen planned to shop in Hawaii while they were there, since their connection with an outgoing steamer gave them three days in Honolulu. Annaliese had written to Grace, and they were invited to stay at her home while they were there.

The one thing Manny had energy for was reading, and since he was living over the bookstore again, he spent a lot of time over the next month there learning about where he'd be going. He read everything he could find on the South Pacific Islands and found Melville's stories about islands he would likely see while he was there.

Manny was amazed at how little baggage they needed for so many months away from home. "We'll get what we need on the way," said Johnny. "The idea is to be comfortable, and they've lived there long enough to know what's comfortable."

"Are you suggesting we 'go native'?" asked Colleen.

"No, but I'm suggesting no one there will pass judgment on you in any way based on how you dress. Out there no one cares. So wear what's comfortable and useful."

This conversation had been at the beginning of the train trip up the great Central Valley of California, a trip they had taken many times over the years.

After a while, everyone settled into doing something, including dozing in Manny's case, while Annaliese was staring out at the unending fields of crops and not seeing a thing. She was thinking about this new adventure she was on and where it would take her.

Since she met Johnny, he had been willing to build his life around her being a doctor. Using that freedom she'd been able to build a practice, then the clinic to care for the people of San Diego. Besides that, she was also proud of the young women she sent out into the world to practice the healing arts and that half of them had come from the Mexican community in her town.

But she was no longer a doctor, no longer laid her hands on people and healed their hurts. She missed that. Instead, she was an administrator, a supervisor, someone who got things done but didn't do them herself. Her sense of responsibility had bound her to the place she had done so much to build.

Now, for the first time, she was walking away from the clinic, passing the operational responsibilities onto others and looking elsewhere for her future. She had a strong feeling she'd never return.

But now her future was in Johnny's hands, just as his was in hers all those years ago. Fair was fair. Now she would be the "tail on his kite" for a while.

Since he'd come back from his trip out there, he'd been different. She could see a look in his eye when he talked about it. She was impressed with the idea that he would take her away for six months so she could see what he loved about it. Then they would decide on where to go from there, if anywhere at all.

Fascinated though she was by the idea, she could also see she was walking away from something she'd spent twenty years building. Was she really willing to give it all up and go off to live in the South Seas with her husband?

She didn't know yet but he wasn't pushing her for an answer, and it wasn't like he was taking her to any place so terrible. This would be the first time since before the war she'd have her whole family together in one place and she was looking forward to that. From what Johnny said, they'd be living in some beautiful places and learning many new things about life.

And of course, Manny would have the time to get better. That was important. She guessed she'd make it through and she and Johnny would decide what their future was, together.

Tony, the butler, met them at the station, and they sat down to an evening meal with the large dining room table full of family. Later, when everyone had retired, they sat with Sarah and talked of old times and old friends. Madame had died several years before and the mansion was Sarah's now, though she had no idea of taking Madame's place.

"Where's Jonas?" Johnny asked.

"He's doing something in Sacramento. Should be home in the next couple of days. You'll see him before you leave."

"Seems strange not to see Lemuel when I'm at this table," said Johnny. Lemuel Waters had been Johnny's friend and business partner of many years. He too had died several years before. Indeed, many of the friends from their early years in San Francisco were gone now and the four travelers realized more would likely be gone before they returned from their sojourn.

Handy and Rebecca were there and the next morning, Johnny caught the ferry with them and spent the day at the ranch, including time in the smithy thinking about his Pa.

"So, are you really going to go out there and work on a schooner the rest of your life?" asked Handy. They were sitting on the porch talking and looking at the lights from Gray's cottage coming on in the distance.

"I don't know. I think I'd like to live out there and I love it on the schooner with Bobby and Teressa. We're all going out there. Who knows if we'll stay or maybe decide to go somewhere else. Could be we'll all decide to stay and make our life there. Anyway, we're going to try it for six months or so and then we'll decide.

"We'll miss a lot of things from back here, but it will be like it was when we came here. We'll be starting a new life in a new place. This one worked out OK, so I guess we can do it somewhere else."

"What will Annaliese do out there?" asked Rebecca. "Knowing her, she'll have to have something to keep busy."

"That's one of many questions that we'll look for answers to while we're there."

"You reckon you'll ever come back?"

"I don't really know. Maybe, but it will likely be a while. Of course, you can always come to visit."

Three days later, Handy and Rebecca were there to see them off and came aboard to sit and visit until the whistle blew.

"It'll be strange knowing you're so far away. We've spent a lot of time together over the years."

They were standing at the railing, looking down at the pier.

"Predicting the future is always hazardous. I don't know how Annaliese will feel about life there and if she's not happy, I can't be. We may be back in a year."

"You want to stay out there, don't you?"

"At this moment, I do. How I'll feel in six months, I don't know. But I know this: I'll be looking for reasons to stay and I'll show them to her and see what she says."

The whistle blew and they turned and walked to where the others were standing, getting ready for goodbyes.

The two friends shook hands, held the grip and then instinctively embraced, something men didn't do at that place in time.

CHAPTER FORTY-THREE

Teressa was writing a letter when Van and Enoah came into the dining room and sat across from each other at the other end of the table.

"What are you studying today?" she asked.

Van slid a book down the table so Teressa could read the title. "It's one of the books I had when I was little. We've tried a few of them and he's learning."

Teressa stood and said, "I'll leave you to it."

She went into the office and began going through the mail that Bobby had picked up in Noumea. She smiled when she saw her father's handwriting on one, opened it, and halfway down the page grinned, then walked back into the dining room.

"This is from Grandpa Johnny. He talked Mama into coming out here for a while. Colleen and Manny are coming too. That means the whole family will be here."

She looked thoughtful and a little stunned. "I guess we'll have room. Good thing we built the cabins last year."

She left them studying and walked out to the patio, where she stood for a moment looking down at Wind Song and thinking about the idea that four of the people she loved most in the world were about to come live with them, probably for a while.

When Bobby came out after a shower, she told him.

"It doesn't really surprise me," he said. "When he was here, I think the idea was running through his mind. I'll bet he's doing it to show her what life would be like if they came out here to live."

"So what are you thinking?" he asked. She had been standing, looking at him, a blank look on her face.

"I was just thinking about it, that's all. It will take some planning to get it ready. A letter I got from Colleen a while back said Manny had been really sick."

"I wonder if there'll be trouble with the quarantine. We need to let them know about it."

When the Spanish Flu spread across the world, several of the islands in the southwest Pacific quarantined and controlled entry successfully. Grande Terre was one of them. The fact that the island was two hundred and fifty miles long made this difficult. Because all commerce on the island passed through Noumea and almost all the non-native, mostly French, population was in and around Noumea, the authorities could control access by controlling the port. The visitors would be required to go through these controls, including quarantine, before they could come to the house on the cliff.

As they were getting ready for bed that night, Bobby suddenly said, "This thing with Johnny and them is important. I need to go to Noumea tomorrow and find out what they're going to have to do because of the quarantine."

"Are you going to take the schooner?"

"No. I'll take the launch. It shouldn't take too long. But it needs to be done as soon as we can." He hesitated, then continued. "It will mean dealing with the officials in Noumea. I wish you were coming with me." Cookie and Marie were at their home village and she didn't feel comfortable leaving the children.

"We may have to send a cable. Can we afford that?"

The quarantine had been in effect for so long she was accustomed to its presence. It had closed their business as surely as if Wind Song had sunk. She hadn't thought about it in her excitement about the family coming, but she could see the problem it presented.

The money they had saved since Wind Song was launched was disappearing a little at a time and they had nothing coming in. The situation was getting close to perilous. She thought for a moment, closed her eyes and nodded resignedly.

The next morning, she sat on the patio and watched him disappear around the headland in the motor launch. She was still sitting there an hour later, thinking about their visitors when Van and Enoah sat down.

"Good morning, boys and girls, what are you up to today?"

"We're going fishing," said Van. Enoah nodded in agreement.

Fishing was one thing they hadn't had to teach Enoah. He'd been doing it since he was a child, though the clear, unruffled waters of the lagoon were new to him. The two of them fished several times a week, and their catch was important to food supply. With that and the garden behind the house, they didn't go hungry, but there were places they did feel the pinch.

The boy was settling into the family with little trouble. On the voyage back from Nuku Hiva, he seldom left Bobby's side for the first week, after which he followed Johnny around most days. It wasn't long before he knew the name and understood the function of every pulley, rope and sail on board. He was almost a head taller than Van and with Bobby and Handy in his family tree, he seemed designed to be a very large man.

She and Bobby were very much aware of the potential for problems with puberty hanging over the family since Enoah joined them. Normal relationships between brothers and sisters develop over time and within limits and controls put on them by the societies in which they mature.

Bringing a thirteen-year-old boy with a flashing and long dark hair into a family and telling a beautiful, precocious young twelve-year-old girl, "this is your brother," does not really represent reality. Sparks of one kind or another would seem inevitable.

When she sat her daughter down to talk about it, Teressa was met with a wide-eyed curiosity that slowly turned to exasperation.

"I know all about that, Mama," Van said, her eyes rolling. "As much time as I've spent on Maupiti, I've seen it all. They aren't bashful about it."

"I understand that, but this is special because it concerns you and Enoah."

"What do you mean?"

"He is your half-brother because you had the same father. As they grow older, people develop feelings that lead them to do that sort of thing with each other. If a brother and sister have relations and produce a child, it probably wouldn't be right."

"What do you mean?"

"I mean it might not be healthy, or it could be deformed in some way. It could also be an imbecile, not able to get along as it grew older. According to the Bible, it's a sin to 'lie with your brother.' I don't know about that, but it's the kind of thing that can change your life and not for the better.

"Because he's just joined the family, you haven't grown up with him and it's easy to forget you're related. I want you to love him because he's your brother. But falling in love is a whole different thing. That's something you save for someone outside the family."

Van looked at her in silence for a while, clearly thinking about what she had said. Finally, she nodded her head. "I understand, Mama. If I begin to feel that way, I'll come talk to you." She took a deep breath and sighed. "I just wish he wouldn't smile at me so much." She looked at her mother. "I understand how much a baby would affect everyone's life, so I'll make sure we behave."

Teressa embraced her daughter, and they stood that way for a while. "I'm glad he's with us," Van said firmly.

Teressa held her at arm's length and replied, "I am too, and so is your Papa. Try to remember what my Mama told me. 'Just because you can do something doesn't necessarily mean you should.'"

Bobby made it home that evening, and after he caught his breath from the climb, immediately told her the news.

"It seems the quarantine will probably be lifted by the end of the year. They seem to think they've dodged the worst of it, and with commerce cut off, everyone is clamoring for it to be lifted. Did you know two of the town's doctors died last year, and there are only two left on the island?"

When she shook her head, he continued. "When I found that out, I pointed out that two of the people coming to visit were doctors. I sort of fudged a little and said they might be coming here to live," he concluded with a grin. "Upshot of it was, they're going to take it to the board and try to get a waiver. They'll still have to undergo an examination and probably provide some sort of statement attesting to Manny's health. I think by the time they get here, they'll be admitted alright."

"Do we have to write home?"

"Maybe, but not yet. The board's meeting the day after tomorrow. They'll fly a blue flag at the mine if the waiver is granted, a red flag if it's not. It sounds like we solved the problem. We'll know for sure in a couple days."

Marie and Cookie returned the following day with bags of fruits and vegetables from their home village. Her daughter was with them, having returned from Noumea when she'd lost her job.

"How long do you think it will take to get business back up and running once they discontinue the quarantine?" asked Teressa.

"Don't know. Never had to deal with something like that, so I don't know how to go about it. Wind Song is ready. I guess the first step is to go to some of the factors in town and see what they think. They may already have some jobs in hand. If not, we'll sail to Maupiti for a while and talk to Claude and Benni.

"They've been up and running while we've had to sit. Of course, they've had to deal with the flu. When we talk to them, we'll probably find out if the quarantine was worth what it cost."

They were sitting on the patio that evening and could see the anchor light on Wind Song below. There was also a light in the galley, and they could see shadows where Jared and Amanda were moving around. Behind them, they heard Van and Akamu talking and then laughing. "It seems he's beginning to feel comfortable with us," said Teressa. "They seem to get along well, and they do spend a lot of time together."

"Does that worry you?"

"A little. I had a talk with her and she seems OK with it. She understands what a baby would do to all our lives."

He was quiet again. The long tropical twilight had crept over them before he spoke again. "I'm glad we kept them on," he said, speaking of Amanda and Jared. "They couldn't have gone anywhere anyway, but they earned their keepa and we'd have had to replace them eventually just to get out of the bay.

"I hope Johnny and them realized if we get a job, we'll have to take it. They'll either have to come with us or stay here with Cookie until we get back. We can't afford to sit around if we can help it."

"They're all good at adapting. I think they'll understand. Is there enough room for four more people aboard?"

"Probably, but you and I may end up sleeping in a hammock."

"Does Papa know about the quarantine?"

"Yeh. He mentioned it in a letter recently. What are you grinning about?"

"I was remembering how you used to be the world's worst at answering letters."

He chuckled. "That's Pete's doing. He got me writing, keeping those logs. Keeping a diary. I wish you could have known Pete. He was an important part of my life. And yours too, for that matter.

"And Henri. I miss Henri." Bobby shook his head. "I felt like a cripple for a while after he died, but he was right. I did learn what I needed to know." He was quiet for a while. "He always knew me better than I knew myself."

"Did Papa say when they were leaving?"

"He said they'd leave in the first week of November. Probably be here in early December." He shook his head.

"What?" she asked.

"Oh, I was thinking how long it took Mirabelle to get out here from San Francisco. Of course we didn't come straight out. But still, it was eleven months before I saw the house on the cliff after we left the Golden Gate."

He pulled her into an embrace and looked down at her. "It's been a good life out here, away from the world. I'm glad you've been here to share it."

He'd always remember that kiss and especially what happened afterwards.

Organizing the doubling of the population at the house on the cliff was a big job. The first thing was sleeping quarters. To house visitors and crew members, they had built two cottages the year before. She smiled when she thought about that project.

Bobby had come up with the idea. Since there were so many people out of work in Noumea, he organized a three-day party, inviting out-of-work dockyard workers and their families to a cookout with the proviso they'd help with the building. He got the idea from the stories Handy had told him about barn-raising on the Minnesota plains when he was a young man.

There had been an amazing collection of boats in the cove below and the people proved to be such enthusiastic workers that in only two days, they had built two simple, comfortable, solidly constructed cabins that served as sleeping cabins when they had visitors. She spruced them up to welcome the family and went through the house cleaning and adjusting things to the needs of the additional people.

As much as she loved the house on the cliff, it was a decidedly inconvenient place to live. Every time Wind Song sailed from Noumea to the house on the cliff, necessities and luxuries had to be aboard, and everything had to be carried up the path to the house. Though wheeled conveniences of one kind or another had been introduced over the years, there were no stables close, so manpower alone moved needed supplies up the path.

One night, when they were sitting enjoying the evening breeze on the patio overlooking the bay, she asked Bobby why they continued to live there instead of Noumea. He looked at her strangely.

Finally, he shrugged. "I don't know. It's just home. It's Pete's place." He looked thoughtful and finally just shook his head. "I never thought about living anywhere else. Maybe if we lived here all the time, but we're not usually here more than four or five months a year. Besides, Marie and Cookie are here. It's their home."

He shrugged again. "Of course they could live here whether we do or not. I just never thought about living anywhere else.

"Why? Do you want to move to Noumea?"

"No, I just wondered why we never considered it."

He was quiet for a while, just looking out at the bay and the Coral Sea beyond. Finally, he looked at her and swept his arm around the vista. "It is worth something to have a view like this. I guess that's always been the most important thing. What it is. Not what it isn't."

When the quarantine had been imposed, their first reaction was to double the size of the garden. Clearing and preparing the new section was hard work and all hands turned out. Everyone worked to get the job done and in the end it was a success. The garden was well tended because everyone reaped the benefits of the effort they put in.

Since they had more produce than they could eat, they began to store the excess by canning it and storing it in a cellar Pete had dug years before. With the visitors in mind, they increased their efforts so that when the family came, there would be plenty to eat.

Because there was very little meat of any kind available except in Noumea, the large variety of fish in the lagoon and the abundance of enthusiastic fishermen provided Cookie and Marie in the kitchen a chance to use all the ways they'd learned over the years about how to make seafood taste special.

Beef on the island came from Noumea, but one of their problems was how to store it and they usually ate it as soon as it came up the hill. The mountains that brought the rains to the east side of Grande Terre brought a different look on the west side, a difference that produced a landscape of rolling grasslands, much like the American Great Plains, and migrant Australian stockmen introduced cattle ranching to the island.

The way she calculated, Teressa would eventually have ten to twelve people at her table most evenings. In response, Bobby and Cookie designed and built her a nice table. During the day, people used it for all sorts of things, but come dinnertime all was cleared away and the table was set.

On nights when everyone was present, there'd be good conversation to go with good company and good food. The company was Bobby, Teressa, Van, Enoah, Jared and Amanda, and Cookie and Marie. The addition of four more adults would make it a little crowded, but everyone at the table would be a part of the whole and glad to be there.

The house itself was originally an English cottage, but over the years it had been added to and expanded so that now it was more a product of its environment: low, cool, airy, and rambling.

Marie and Cookie lived in a separate part of the house. She was a healer in her clan, and people from her village would come to see her in need. She treated or counseled them on her side of the house and by tacit consent, it was not to be entered by the crew.

Teressa had long before decided that Marie was what made the house so special. She and Van loved the spicy fragrance that wafted through the house when Marie was home and lit the incense she usually burned. She had always been a second mother to Van, indeed, she cut the cord at her birth and had always given Van the same love and care she got from her mother. She was the girl's godmother in every sense of the word.

But it was more than that. The house seemed to have a power itself to make people feel comfortable and accepted, to make them feel at home. Her Papa had come for a visit, stayed for a year and was coming back, bringing Mama and talking of living out here.

There was no question the house had a pull on Bobby. This was home. The idea of home being anywhere but here had never occurred to him. It was the same with her, but the difference was, she wondered about it.

Teressa was not a spiritually oriented person, but she also marveled about this woman in her life who seemed to be connected in spirit to the house she called home.

How would she feel if the family came and stayed? Never went home, or went home and came back to live. These people were her family, not by blood but by all the other things that make a family and yet she didn't know them. In essence, four strangers were coming to live in the house with her and her family. Would they feel its pull? And if they did, what would that do to all their lives?

And Manny. Manny was her only blood relative. Was he still sick? The healthy, active boy she'd grown up with was hard to imagine as an invalid, yet Mama's last letter had said he was still recovering. She looked up at the calendar. They'd be leaving San Francisco the following week, changing ships in Honolulu, and arriving before she knew it.

The plan was to meet in Tahiti, spend a few weeks on Maupiti, then go to Noumea to deal with the quarantine and finally, home.

CHAPTER FORTY-FOUR

Manny was sitting in a deckchair on a cold November day in 1919 when the steamer passed through the Golden Gate out into the vast Pacific Ocean. The wind was brisk and biting.

"Are you warm enough?" asked Colleen. She had just come up from their cabin carrying several blankets.

"I'm fine. The breeze feels good and I feel good as well."

"Mama and Papa want to know if you'd like to join them in the salon to celebrate the beginning of the voyage."

He began to get up and she reached out to help him. "No," he said. "I'm fine. I can make it OK. I feel better the last few days. The idea of this trip has brought me out of a funk. First time since we got on the train in Baltimore I've been excited about tomorrow." She watched him stand and reach for a cane hanging on the chair.

"Let's take a stroll around the deck before we go in," he said. "We'll be at sea for three weeks and I want to make sure to walk the deck every day."

They walked in silence, careful but excited about what they were seeing, both conscious of his movements.

"How am I doing?"

She had been watching him with a professional eye while they walked, but now they stopped, and he looked into her eyes with a question in his gaze.

"You look better. Your color is better than it's been for a while and your gait seems firmer, even with the uncertain footing."

"I'm a sailor. Maybe getting back to sea was what I needed."

They entered the salon and spotted his parents sitting at a table by the bar.

"Hi there, you two," said Annaliese. Johnny raised a hand in greeting. After they had decided to make the trip, things had happened quickly and they were catching their breath after a whirlwind week of preparation. This was the first time they'd all been able to sit together and talk for the last seven days. When they all had drinks before them, they drank a toast to their future.

"You look a lot better, Manny," said Johnny. "I think going to sea is good for you."

"I just said the same thing to Colleen," said Manny. "I think maybe the excitement of going somewhere has helped. It's been a while since I've been excited."

"I'm excited about seeing Grace in Honolulu," said Annaliese. "She was my first student and she and Esty made me want to have more."

"It will take us a week to get there, and we should be able to connect with something outgoing before long," said Johnny. "Then another two weeks to Tahiti. The last cable I had from Bobby said they'd be there to meet us. I imagine we'll go right to Maupiti from there, but we'll need to get some clothes."

On Johnny's advice, they'd packed little. "Most of the clothes you have here don't wear so well out there. We'll get some things that are cool and comfortable in Honolulu."

They surprised Grace in her office. She was busy and sent them to her house to get settled in. At dinner, they talked late into the night about the past and the future. Grady invited Johnny and Manny to sit on the porch and smoke and talk.

"Don't smoke, but I'll be glad to join you," said Johnny. From the doorway, he looked at the three women doctors talking, realized he was going to be ignored anyway, and followed Manny and their host to a porch where they could sit and look out at the city and the harbor.

He sat upwind of Grady and learned a lot about the shipping business in the part of the world where he was headed. Johnny had the lifelong habit of loving to learn new things. He knew some things about the South Pacific but was keen to learn what he could about these things from another point of view. They sat for a while, and whenever it was quiet on the porch, he could hear voices and laughter in the house.

"You know the three of them have had their lives wonderfully intertwined up to now. And it looks as if, with my two, it's going to continue." He laughed and shook his head. "My life and future were pretty stable until two years ago. Then I went to Grande Terre and to Maupiti. Spent time at the house on the cliff. And I'm going back. If Annaliese decides she can handle it, we may call that place home and come back to California just to visit. We might decide to retire in New Caledonia if we can work it out."

They stayed in Hawaii for three days. The ladies shopped and Johnny came along and carried the bags. On days when the three doctors were together, Johnny loved to watch them talk, seeing little signs of affection between them. Once in a while, Annaliese caught him smiling and smiled back at him because she knew why he was smiling.

One nice thing about staying at the home of the head of the shipping line meant their voyage could be arranged easily. On the morning of their departure, boarding passes were beside their plates at breakfast. With her access to transportation, Grace's promise to visit them was more than perfunctory. She could probably pull it off.

"From what Johnny tells me, they'll be able to put you up without much trouble," said Annaliese. "The plan is to get Manny to a place where he can get better, which means we'll probably be there for a while."

When she hugged Grace goodbye, she felt again the special bond they had. Grace was family.

Colleen could see Manny improving every day on the voyage to Tahiti. He could soon walk the deck like a veteran and when the sea was a little rough, he was able to help her. In the beginning she had some reservations about this adventure they were on, but she had to admit her excitement whenever she thought about it now.

That wasn't the only excitement she'd been feeling lately. She had been abstinent for the last year, and she'd been wondering when and if Manny would be strong enough to resume their lovemaking.

That night when he came into the small bedroom of the cabin after a shave, she was lying on the bed under the covers. With a mischievous smile on her face, she said, "I'm not rushing you or anything, but whenever you feel up to it, I'm more than willing."

He sat on the bed and looked down at her, a smile playing around his lips. "Are you trying to seduce me?"

She pulled back the sheet, and she was nude. "Yes," she said. "If you feel up to it and from here, it looks like you do."

When he was naked and lying beside her, she whispered, "You take it as easy as you want. I'm not going anywhere."

He kissed her, and his hand began to roam gently over her body. "I've missed your freckles," he said. He lowered his head and began to touch them with his tongue, one at a time. In the end, they were both amazed at how much energy he had.

The next morning, they stood by the rail in light, comfortable clothes, holding hands and watched the anchor splash into the lagoon at Papeete, Tahiti, the administrative capital of French Polynesia. When they got ashore and through officialdom, they found Wind Song wasn't there yet. They decided to leave their luggage at the dock office and set out to explore the town.

As they returned to the wharf that afternoon, Johnny recognized Wind Song just dropping her sails in the harbor and let out a loud whistle.

Bobby, standing in the cockpit, waved his hand and within a few minutes, he, Teressa, and Van were on their way to the dock. Fortunately, Manny was feeling almost his old self or he may not have survived his old friend's boisterous greeting. Bobby led them into a dockside cafe he knew of, and when they were all seated and had ordered, he asked, "How long since we've seen each other?"

"I was thinking about that the other day," answered Manny. "Twelve years. I was home from school on my first leave."

Teressa was sitting beside her brother holding his hand. "How do you feel?" she asked, looking at him with searching eyes. "You look so much bigger."

"Actually, I'm just getting back to what I weighed before I got sick."

"You were a boy the last time I saw you." She smiled at him. "You'll always be my little brother even though you're taller than I am now."

"I grew about four inches at the Academy. Gained about forty pounds too."

"So how long will you be here this time?" asked Bobby, looking at Johnny.

"That depends on Manny. When he feels back to himself and wants to go on with his life, he'll tell us and we'll decide. Meanwhile," he said with a grin, "I'll show my wife why I like it so much around here."

He began showing her the next morning. They hadn't felt like sleeping that night and so did other things, always exciting in new places and new circumstances. Talking afterward was the best kind of talk.

"So, you really think this would be a good place to spend the next stage of our lives?" Annaliese asked. They were lying in a cozy alcove, and a ventilator was drawing a slight breeze across their naked bodies.

"I think it will be something to consider. It all depends on Manny. If he responds to this like we hope he will and it looks like he is, then we'll all have some decisions to make. I suggest we live our lives and see where we are in a week or a month or even six months. This is a holiday. Let's enjoy it, talk about the future, and get our son back to full health."

He looked at her in silence for a moment, then whispered, "If you don't cover up, I'm going to do strange things to you."

"You wouldn't dare." She paused and looked thoughtful. "On the other hand, I bet you would." She didn't cover up, and he kissed her and began to stroke her breast.

"What's come over you? Twice in the same night. It's been a while."

"We're on vacation, so let's enjoy it."

The next day was the kind of day you think of when you think of the South Seas. Nice weather, nice breeze, and a nice panorama around you. Johnny was up early to help get ready to depart, and they soon motored out through the reef and set sail for Maupiti. In the afternoon of the second day, they dropped anchor in the lagoon and introduced Annaliese, Manny, and Colleen to that bit of paradise.

For the next two weeks, Bobby and Johnny worked with some of the island men to pull the schooner from the water and go over the bottom to clean and repaint it. Teressa took the visitors on a tour of the island, introduced them to friends, then turned them loose to enjoy the fascinations they found around them.

For two weeks, they began each day with a swim in the lagoon, only a hundred feet from their front door. They roamed the island by day with fruit in their pockets, drinking water from streams they encountered and enjoyed dinners served island-style every evening. Manny became stronger and more relaxed as the days went by.

When the schooner was back in the water, they spent a couple of days getting ready for the voyage to Grande Terre and home, three thousand miles to the west. The long voyage gave Annaliese, Manny, and Colleen a chance to get used to life on a sailboat and they found they enjoyed it.

Sure, it was cramped and close quarters, but they found they had everything they needed and enjoyed the time spent together. Every evening after dinner, they'd sit in the galley and talk about the life they'd be living for a while.

Enoah listened and watched with bright-eyed interest at all that was happening around him. When Johnny was here before they had established a bond and he was happy to spend time with his grandfather again.

"The only time you see him with someone besides Van is when Johnny's around," said Teressa to Marie one evening. "Johnny has taken the time to teach him about the boat. He's very anxious to learn."

"I'm a little anxious about all the extra work all these people will put you to. They'll want to help with things, so let them."

"We usually work together," said Marie. "I'm sure that will not change."

"Don't be surprised if they want to help. It's just the way they are."

"I can't imagine a place more pleasant than the one we just left," said Manny. He was sitting in the cockpit with Colleen and Bobby. "I'm looking forward to seeing the house on the cliff. It must be something special."

"It's nothing like Maupiti, if that's what you mean," said Bobby. "But there's something about it that makes it home."

"I can't believe it's three thousand miles away," said Colleen. "Johnny told me something about the way you look at time and distance out here."

"It's different from back home. It's hard for me to explain, but out here, in this business, it rarely matters what time it is. No one cares. I remember what Pete said when I asked him how long it would take for me to learn all I had to learn. He just shrugged and said, 'As long as it takes.' Deadlines and schedules don't mean much out here. Everything's subject to the wind, the tides, and distance— things we have no control over."

He sat with a knotted brow for a moment. "You'll see what I mean when you've been here a while. As far as distance goes, in this part of the world, there's not much land and what there is, is separated by water. A lot of water. Sailing that much water has taught me patience.

"Wind Song and others like her are how people get around, how they communicate. And we depend on the tides and the winds. You think more in terms of days. Being somewhere on time is usually a coincidence. You learn not to expect it."

Johnny was a crew member. He wasn't really needed but an extra hand is nice to have around. He was up early, messed with the crew and was usually on deck with the dawn. Enoah followed him like a shadow and was learning enough to be a functioning member of the crew.

This left Manny and Colleen to sit with Annaliese and Teressa at the mess table in the galley and talk, which they did, sometimes for hours. Occasionally, Marie would join them, and usually she and Teressa would be answering questions about her life and her family.

None of them really had an idea about how long they would be here, but Bobby and Teressa let them know that didn't matter.

"We go on living our lives whether you're here or not. We love having you here, so stay as long as you like. Remember what Madame used to say, 'You're family. Come and go as you like.'"

Among the things the visitors learned on the voyage were how many and what items to stock in the galley. With no refrigeration, food storage was problematic, but over the years, Cookie and Marie had learned many tricks and knew how to keep the crew and passengers fed and happy.

They also learned the necessity of neatness and attention to detail as essential to smooth operation on the schooner. When there's not much space available, it has to be organized and accessible in an emergency or accidents can happen.

Annaliese noticed that, other than Jinx, Van spent most of her time with her grandfather and Enoah, who was seemingly fascinated to be on a long voyage with his new family.

"She helps me teach him English and French," said Teressa. "which means she's getting to know him pretty well. They've worked it out that he's about a year older than her and she seems to be thrilled to have a sibling. She told me she's learning as much from him as he is from her."

She asked Teressa if she was worried at all about her daughter and the problems inherent in puberty with a boy and a girl of that age in such close quarters.

"No," she replied. "I had the same talk with her you had with me when boys came into the picture. 'The things you can do are not always what you should do.' She knows a child having a child would affect not only her life, but all our lives and she understands the idea of waiting and self-control being necessary in that situation.

"Raising a child under these circumstances would have to have been challenging," said Colleen. "Just keeping her safe on a boat seems like a major accomplishment."

"We had to think about it a lot in the beginning, but now it seems to be just common sense. That and Marie. Don't know if we'd have made it without Marie. My daughter has two mothers. Between the two of us, one is always there for her."

Later that night, when Bobby and Teressa were getting ready for bed, he said, "Your Papa is thinking seriously about retiring out here. He loves working on the boat."

"Mama said something about it. How do you feel about it?"

Bobby lay down on the bed, which was barely long enough for him, and said, "Even if he wasn't family and hadn't put some money into the company, he's a good hand. I assume they'd be living with us?"

"We've got the room and they don't take up much space. I wonder what Manny will do. He's looking so much better. I think this trip is the medicine he needed."

"He told me the other day he feels back to normal. Mama told me he's probably not, but he's smiling a lot more.

"I like Colleen, but she's quieter than I expected her to be. I think she had a rough war. Mama told me a little about it, but she doesn't talk about it, at least not to me."

She turned the light down and joined him in bed. He reached for her, pulled her into an embrace, and kissed her. She smiled beneath the kiss and whispered, "We have to be quiet with all these people on board."

He grinned. "You're telling me to be quiet? You're the one that makes all the noise."

She grinned back at him and said sheepishly, "I know. Sometimes I can't help it." She thought for a minute.

"Kiss me a lot," she whispered. So he did. It helped. Some.

CHAPTER FORTY-FIVE

Just after noon on the sixteenth day out from Tahiti, they rode the tide through the reef surrounding Grande Terre and dropped anchor in the harbor at Noumea.

Bobby escorted them to the Customs House, where they began the process of entering the island's quarantine process. After conversations with several officials, they spent hours waiting while the Board of Quarantine decided how to deal with them. Ultimately, because of the isolation of the house on the cliff and their attestation that they would self-quarantine at home for two weeks, they were allowed to leave for home.

It was early evening when they dropped anchor in their cove off Prony Bay. After the hike up the hill, cool showers refreshed everyone and by common consent, all seemed to end up on the patio overlooking the cove below where Wind Song floated on the clear, bright blue water.

"When the weather's nice, this is where I start my day when we're home," said Teressa.

"What a lovely place," said Annaliese, her mouth open in awe. She was standing near the edge of the cliff, gazing at the green-covered red rock hills that ran down to the bay and at the Coral Sea in the distance. "What's that?" She pointed, and Bobby answered.

"That's the nickel mine across the bay. It's outside Prony, a village over there. With binoculars, we can see a part of it from here. They have a telephone and when they have a message for us, they raise a flag and someone goes to pick it up. If it's red, it means right away. Otherwise, it's blue. The office is behind that point you see." He pointed at the spur of a mountain that ran down to the water. "When the crew is here, we take turns going over to get the message. Sometimes we get things shipped there, but most times we just get what we need in Noumea."

Over the next couple of days they settled in. Johnny took his turn with the rest of the crew sleeping in the schooner. Bobby had no idea how long they'd be there. "When we see a blue flag at the mine, that's usually what it is. The factor in Noumea will call when he has something for us. We were getting charters for one thing or another before the quarantine, but we still carry cargo. I hope that gets going again. Claude and Benni did a lot of that."

The four of them were settled in the two small guest cottages put up the year before. They were framed with bamboo and the walls were woven mats that rolled up or down as the weather or privacy needs dictated. They were sited to be sunny in the morning and shady in the afternoon. Furniture was minimal and functional and they were nice places to take an afternoon nap with the walls adjusted to the breeze.

Meals were served in the main house or on the screened porch, and when the schooner was in port, everyone pitched in to help at mealtimes and cleanup. Everyone was usually present at the table in the early evening and it was usually a nice way to end the day.

"It feels so strange not having to worry about you anymore." Colleen was lying beside him one morning, tracing her finger across his chest. "It seems like this sojourn has accomplished its purpose much sooner than we could have hoped." She sat up in bed, assumed a cross-legged position and continued. "So, what do you want to do with the rest of your life?"

He grinned at her. "There's that Colleen girl again. Where have you been hiding this last little while?"

"I've been too busy being a doctor. Now, answer my question."

"I'm assuming you mean immediately?" She nodded. "Tell you

the truth, I'm looking forward to just living around here for a while. I mean, look at what we'll be doing while we're here." He chuckled. "Pretty much whatever the hell we want and the first thing that comes to mind is those books Papa showed me yesterday. There's fifty-two of those things. 'Pete's Logs,' he called them. I looked through a couple of them and the handwriting should be easy to read.

"I can see myself sitting on the patio in the shade, looking down at Wind Song and reading those logs. You know he's read them all? We'll have some good talks about them while I'm reading.

"Beyond that, I haven't really thought much about it." He paused and looked thoughtful. "Tell you what, we've got plenty of time and nothing else to do, so let's talk about what we're going to do with **our** lives and where **we're** going to do it."

She leaned over and kissed him. "You always say the right thing." She got up and began to dress.

"I guess the first question is, where are we going to seek our future?" said Manny. "I believe Papa is thinking about coming out here to live. How do you feel about that?"

"The first thing that comes to mind is, what would I do?" She looked a question at him. "I'm a doctor, and I've got a lot of time and a lot of myself tied up in becoming a doctor. How could I be a doctor out here? Where are my patients?"

"On the other hand, I love what I've seen of life out here. Bobby and Teressa will be here, with Van and Enoah, and there seems to be a reasonable possibility Annaliese and Johnny will also be here and those are strong attractions. I can understand them. But what would you do here? Build airplanes? Not a job in high demand anywhere close."

"I'm a college-educated engineer. One way or another, I can make a living with that in my pocket, but that's not really the issue. During the war, we talked about staying together instead of each pursuing a life like we've done in the past. What I'd like to do is for you to make a decision about what you want to do and I'll work my way around that. After all, Papa seems to be a happy man. It worked for them."

He looked at her in silence, a little puzzled by her lack of response. Finally, he said, "I believe that's the first time I've ever seen you speechless."

Next door, Johnny and Annaliese heard the laughter.

"I wonder what that was about?" Johnny was lying on the low bed in the cottage next door and Annaliese was sitting beside him on the bed brushing her waist-length hair. She was 60 years old soit wasn't all red anymore but shot with strands of silver..

"They'll probably tell us at dinner," she said. "Lots of smiling and laughing since we got here. I think that's one of the reasons you like it so much."

"How about you? How do you feel about it?"

"You're asking me if I like it enough to live here, aren't you?" He nodded, smiling. "I'm thinking about it, and when I decide, you'll be the first to know."

They had been there over a month when Bobby came in for breakfast one morning, smiling and looking excited. "Blue flag at the mine," he said. "I'll run over and get the message when I'm through eating. Bet it's the factor with a job."

"About time," said Teressa. "We were hoping to get another job before we begin the vacation charters again. Since Clyde and Benni have begun chartering vacations, we've tried a couple. They also get islanders for us who are working off island, coming and going."

They were back shortly, and everyone sat down while they discussed what they'd been given.

"It looks like a pretty standard run," said Bobby. "Up to Tulagi to deliver some mail and pick up a planter who's retiring. He'll go with us to Port Via and American Samoa. Then we drop him off in Noumea, where he picks up a steamer to Sidney, then back home. Probably take three to four weeks unless we pick up something else. Sometimes we get caught for a couple of days at Port Vila. They've got that condominium thing there, and it can get complicated occasionally."

"What is it?" asked Manny.

"They were colonized by both the French and British back in the 1840s and they have two different governments you have to deal with. It can be a pain in the butt. Sometimes we charge a little extra there."

"When do we leave?" asked Johnny.

"I think we can be ready the day after tomorrow on the morning tide. We need to go to Noumea first and clear it with them before we head north."

"I have a suggestion," said Annaliese. "Why don't you men go on the voyage and we ladies will stay here?" Everyone looked at her.

"What would you do?" asked Bobby.

"Oh, for one thing, we could get to know each other a little better. Colleen and I haven't spent much time with my daughter and granddaughter."

"Hum," said Bobby thoughtfully. "I guess I could see if Cookie will go with us one more time. I imagine he will."

"I imagine we'd sit and drink tea and talk a lot and maybe sail over to Noumea and spend a few days. There's supposed to be a nice place to have a picnic down on the cove and a little beach I've heard about that is supposed to be excellent for bathing. Things like that."

"What do you fellows think about that?" Bobby asked, looking at Johnny.

"I'm just a member of the crew, so I'm going," Johnny said. He looked at his son. "How about you?"

Manny looked at Colleen. "Can I go, Dr. Fry?"

She reached out and tapped him on the shoulder. "I hereby give you your release as a patient," she said. "Now, you're just my husband, and you can do whatever the hell you like."

He leaned over and kissed her and turned to Bobby. "Yes, definitely," he said. "I'll be packed and ready."

On the day of departure all the women were standing on the patio watching Wind Song motor out into the lagoon and set sail, finally disappearing around a headland jutting out from a dying mountain that came down into the bay.

Later that morning, they dropped anchor in the Bay of Saint Marie and spent the day in Noumea in various offices, filling out forms and talking to officials. The next morning, they got the anchor up and on the morning tide, exited the lagoon through the reef at

Bolari Pass. When they passed into the Coral Sea, they set sail for Tulagi and settled in for a thousand-mile, week-long run almost due north to the Solomon Islands.

Johnny spent the first day under sail cleaning their store of weapons. They needed cleaning because, even though they were behind glass, the ocean air bred rust, which had to be kept at bay by oil applied regularly. They were also traveling to the Solomons and usually wore pistols when they went ashore in Tulagi.

When he finished, he and Manny went to the bow and watched each other draw and cock their pistols in a drill they had done together for years and both enjoyed.

At the end, they each fired several rounds, after which Manny looked down at the gun in his hand and said, "I've been weak for so long. It feels good to hold one of those again, to be able to handle it easily again, to hit what I aim at." He raised his chin and took a lungful of air. "Colleen and Mama tell me I still need to be careful, but I feel back to normal.

"So now what? That's the question, isn't it? And it seems like it boils down to a choice between staying out here and finding ways to fill our lives in such a wonderful place, or returning to California and making a life there."

They made their way back along the deck, and when they were seated at the galley table, Johnny asked, "Any ideas about where you go from here?"

Manny took his time answering. "We've got enough saved to stay for a few months. So in that time, I'll decide where my future lies. I'll let you know when I want to talk about it."

"I understand. You decide, we'll support you, should the need arise."

They moored at a buoy in Tulagi Harbor and spent two days waiting for their passenger to arrive. David Penrod Harrington had come to the Solomons as a young man and spent his life raising and processing copra for shipment all over the world. In the process, he'd made enough to contemplate a leisurely retirement at age forty-five in his Australian hometown, somewhere outside of Sydney.

Rather than wait for a more direct passage, he chose to travel with them and see some of what he'd missed by living so much of his life in one place. He enjoyed pulling lines and working, talking and laughing with the crew. Johnny couldn't imagine him happy sitting on a porch watching the sun set over the mountains.

After leaving Tulagi, they turned south and a little east to the New Hebrides and spent two days in Port Vila shaking their heads at the complexity of dealing with the two-nation condominium that governed the small island.

From there, they went to Pago Pago, where their passenger decided he wanted to stay for a while. Their business took them to another small island of the archipelago, then Wind Song turned westward toward Grande Terre and home. They had been gone almost five weeks when they dropped anchor in the cove below the house on the cliff.

The evening of the morning Wind Song left, Annaliese and Colleen were sitting on the patio talking. "It seems like my man wants to come out here to live," said Annaliese, "and I've got to see how it will work with me if we do. All these years, he's been the 'tail on my kite,' as he says. He's lived his life around my practice of medicine and we've both been happy.

"I'm sure you know I haven't seen a patient in years, since before the war, really. Too busy running the clinic. I'm an administrator and looking back from here, I can't imagine why I'd want to go back to that job. So, now and for the rest of our lives, I'm going to be the tail on his kite. Of course, I'm a sixty-year-old tail, but fortunately, he still loves me. From now on, he's going to do what he wants and I'll work around it. Right now, he wants to crew on a schooner out of Grande Terre.

"Which brings me to what I wanted to ask. I'm going to Noumea to spend a few days there. Van is going along and I wondered if you'd like to join us. Teressa will take us over, but she has some things she needs to do here, so she won't stay. She'll pick us up on the third day."

"Sure. Why are you going to Noumea?"

"I want to talk to some of the doctors there. The quarantine was incredibly effective, but I understand they lost two doctors in the last year or so."

"You're really thinking about practicing out here?"

"Don't see why not. Noumea is bigger than San Diego was at the time we moved there and I didn't speak the language of my patients there either. It all worked out pretty well."

The next day, they found it easy to understand why this was Bobby's favorite place to sail. The passage in the lagoon to Noumea was what people see in their mind's eye when they think of the South Seas. On this day, a steady light breeze moved the small sailboat smoothly over clear water below. In the bow, Van and Annaliese were holding hands, sitting side by side, looking around at the scenery.

"Do you like going to Noumea?"

"Yes, I do. I know a lot of the men who work at the shipyard, and some of their children are my age. There's always something to do." They sat quietly for a while, watching the scene unfold around them.

"Grandmama, can I ask you something?"

"Sure, anything."

"Are you and Grandpapa going to come here to live?"

"It's beginning to look like it. Your Grandpapa seems to want to."

"Do you want to?"

"I'm beginning to think so."

"That would be wonderful."

Annaliese nodded and squeezed her granddaughter's hand. "I'm beginning to think so," she said again.

CHAPTER FORTY-SIX

Colleen started and shook her head. She had been gazing, dazed and open-mouthed, at the green beauty that rose steeply from white sand beaches and suddenly came back to herself. She turned and saw the same glazed look on Annaliese's face. She reached out and touched her friend's hand, felt her start, and saw her smile.

"So, tell me again how you plan to go about this?" asked Colleen.

Annaliese shrugged. "I don't know. Teressa has given me a name and we'll ask directions. We want to know where a doctor is. How hard could that be?"

Turned out to be pretty easy. The mother of one of Van's friends spoke English, sort of and with Van's translation after some confusion, the woman pointed them right. Eventually, they ended the day in a doctor's waiting room. They rang a buzzer and after a while, a man came out, looked at them curiously, summoned a woman with a child in and closed the door. A while later, he returned and ushered them into his office. He seated them, sat down behind a desk, and asked, "How can I help you?"

"I'm Dr. Annaliese Fry," she began. "My husband wants to retire on Grande Terre and we'll be living in the area. This is my daughter-in-law, Dr. Colleen Fry. Teressa Josephson is my daughter."

"I know your daughter. She was a patient of my partner's before he died," he replied. "I'm Dr. Hunter Morgan." He stood and shook both of their hands.

"I've been a doctor for thirty years in California, Dr. Morgan and since it looks like I'm going to be living hereabouts for a while, I thought I might see what the need for doctors is."

His face lit up with a smile. "I had heard you might be coming out here to live. You and Dr. Fry would be a godsend to us. Where in California?"

"San Diego. I was founder and chief medical officer of the San Diego Clinic. Now I'd like to try being a doctor again."

He scratched his chin while peering at her over his spectacles. "Actually, things haven't been too bad during the quarantine. It seems to have made everyone more careful about things and we've been able to keep up.

"But with the quarantine being lifted, it will go back to the way it was, so the chances are good you could build a practice here. If you're interested, we can talk about a partnership."

"Dr. Morgan, my husband just left on a voyage with Bobby Josephson and he won't be back for several weeks. We can discuss anything, but I can't make any decisions until he returns."

"I understand. But why don't we lay the groundwork for the idea so that we don't have to start from scratch when he returns?"

"You need to start from the idea that, at present, I'm living with my daughter and her husband at the house on the cliff, and I'm not really inclined to move at present. I wanted merely to assess the need for doctors in the city."

"There were six doctors in town two years ago. Now there are two of us and a fellow who's more of a researcher than a practicing physician. If things go back to the way they were before the quarantine, we'll need you sometime in the next few months. We can hold the fort till he gets home."

"Sounds like a good situation for you," said Colleen. They were sitting on the veranda at the hotel with Van that evening. "He needs help. Pretty much allows you to dictate the terms, doesn't it?"

"Yes, but it needs some thinking." Annaliese looked out at the harbor and the Bay of St. Marie in the distance and drummed her fingers on the arm of her rocking chair.

Finally, she said, "We've talked about a lot of things since you brought Manny home, but you've never mentioned the war. Have you ever talked to Manny about it?"

Colleen had stopped rocking and sat in silence for a long moment. "No, I never have. He's been sick and I didn't want to burden him with it."

"You know, a burden like that is usually easier to bear if you share it with someone. I can understand not sharing it with him, but I'm your teacher and mentor and a doctor besides. I've spent a lot of my life helping people deal with problems. I'm listening if you want to talk."

Van had stopped rocking and was listening intently.

After a long silence, Colleen began. "There was never anything like it in the history of the world. I've heard that fifty-seven thousand British soldiers were killed, wounded, and missing on the first day at the Somme. For three days and nights, we dealt with that carnage. I thought I'd go mad. If it hadn't been for Lynn and Swede, I think I would have. One or the other was always around when I needed a shoulder to cry on.

"After a while, I just stopped feeling anything, stopped being able to have any sympathy for anyone. I just did my job when I had to." She paused and sat looking down at her hands. "Did you know we never saw the patients after we operated on them? There was no postoperative care at all except in dire cases. When they came off the table, they were prepared for transport as soon as possible and were usually on a train within a few hours.

"The system was set up to save men's lives and the faster they got to a hospital, the better their chances of survival were. We were tasked with making that happen and we did. The feelings of the medical staff about a proper doctor-patient relationship were a secondary consideration at 29CCS.

"I took it for two years, then I had to leave. The day I sailed from France, I remember feeling a tremendous guilt at not being there when I knew they needed me and at the same time, an almost dizzying feeling of relief to be out of it.

"It's as though I used up all my emotions over there. They're gone. The world just looks flat and gray to me right now and I'm moved only by necessity. I don't know if I'll ever get back to normal." She paused and continued ironically. "In this world, I'm not even sure what normal is."

They sat quiet for a long time, then Annaliese said, "It would be easy for me to say they'll come back. Emotions are the seasonings of life. Without them, it can be pretty bland. But I believe whether they come back or not is in your hands. As a friend, I'd say reach out for your future. Make things happen. If you sit and let resignation take over your life, you'll never be happy."

She took Colleen's hand. "It's important to me that you're happy and not just because of Manny. I want to see and hear that courageous young girl who wrote me a letter once. I miss her."

Colleen sobbed on Annaliese's shoulder for a while, and they embraced in silence. Finally, Annaliese asked, "Have you and Manny been talking about the future?"

"Not much, but yes, we have. That's what we were laughing about the other day. He told me it was the first time he'd ever seen me speechless."

Annaliese gaped at her. "What did he say to you?"

"First, that he wants to stay here for a while and just enjoy it, and when we decide what's next for us, it will be my choice and he'll be the tail on my kite, to use a phrase I've heard somewhere. I didn't know what to say."

"I can believe that. I remember telling you one time that couldn't happen with him in the Navy."

"Well, he's not in the Navy now and I think that might have been a part of the reason he left when he did." She looked at Annaliese thoughtfully. "What would you say if I asked you if I could join you in any arrangement you make with Dr. Morgan, for a while at least?"

"I'd say, I was hoping you'd say that."

Two days later, they had thrashed out a plan. They would alternate at the office and, between them, give him a full-time doctor. They'd rent a room or apartment in Noumea for whoever was on duty and change about at times they agreed on. There were many details to work out, but they had a framework to talk to the men about when they returned.

On the day they were to return, they were sitting under a tree at the waterside, waiting for Teressa to finish running errands in Noumea. "How do you like having a little brother?" Colleen asked.

Van snorted. "Little? He's taller than I am. But I like it. Papa is teaching him about the boat and says he learns really quickly. Mama and I are teaching him how to read, too. He smiles a lot, but I wish he wasn't so pretty."

"Boys aren't pretty. They're handsome," said Annaliese. "You know one of the things an older sister does for her little brother?" Van shook her head. "She takes care of him. Your mama was like that with Manny. She always took care of him."

"Actually, he's almost a year older than me, but I'll still take care of him until he gets used to living with us. He sure looks a lot like Papa."

When they finally came back to the bay below the house on the cliff, they climbed out, helped run the boat up on the sand, then all trouped up the hill and sat on the patio to catch their breath.

"I'm glad we found him," said Van. "He wants to learn so much…" She shook her head. "It's amazing. He sure does like being around Johnny."

"Your grandfather is a natural teacher, so that doesn't surprise me."

Over the next month, Annaliese saw Dr. Morgan once more, and they agreed on a plan subject to Johnny's agreement when he returned.

Annaliese knew her husband had read all of the fifty-two logbooks, both Pete's and the ones that Bobby and Teressa had kept, and that Manny was following his father's lead. One afternoon she randomly picked one off the shelf and thumbed through it. When Teressa came in an hour later, she was immersed in it, fascinated.

"First Papa, then Manny, now you. We'll probably have a lot to talk about."

Annaliese looked at her for a moment, found a matchstick to

mark her place with and handed the book to her daughter.

Teressa glanced at the date on the book's spine and knew what she'd see when she opened it.

"Is it something you want to talk about?"

"Why would you think that?"

"Because you've never mentioned it, and we don't have many secrets."

"It's like the log says. They were blackbirders. Their method is to attack an island early in the morning, grab as many young men and women as they can handle, chain them up and sell them into a life of slavery west of here. We found out they were coming and set up an ambush."

"How many were there?"

"Twenty-seven."

"You killed them all?"

Teressa nodded slowly. "They were all killed in the ambush or on the boat after."

"Did you…" Annaliese's voice trailed off.

"Mama, I had a Henry rifle and Papa taught me to hit what I shoot at."

"I'm sorry. I didn't mean to upset you."

"I'm not upset. It's just not something I've ever talked about, and I try not to think about it. But it's like Bobby said, it wouldn't do to just run them off. They'd go do it somewhere else. If we gave them a chance to surrender, what would we do with them?" She shrugged. "We did what we had to."

"What did you do with them?"

"The islanders took them out beyond the reef and dumped them in the ocean. It was all they deserved.

"Mama, I don't regret what we did that day on Maupiti. I do regret we had to do it."

The next day they saw a blue flag at the mine, and Van and Marie sailed over and returned with the message that the men were in Noumea overnight and would be home the next day.

That night at dinner, Annaliese tapped a water glass and said, "This is the last night of our 'sisterhood,' and I'd like to say I've enjoyed it completely.”

Everyone agreed, then Teressa shocked everyone by saying, “Mama, I’ve been sick the last three mornings. I recognize the symptoms. I think I’m pregnant.”

“That’s wonderful!” exclaimed Annaliese. “Marie, pour us a little wine. Let’s have a toast.”

“Ah, Annaliese,” said Colleen with a raised finger and when Annaliese looked at her, she said, “Me too.”

“What do you mean ‘me too’?”

“I mean I think I’m pregnant too. I’ve been sick in the morning, and I’ve been around enough pregnant women to recognize what that means.”

Van was staring at her mother in disbelief. “Really, Mama? You’re going to have a baby? That’s so exciting.”

Annaliese burst out laughing and everyone turned to look at her. “Can you imagine the looks on their faces when you tell them?” The others began to smile, then grin, and finally burst out laughing themselves.

“What a coming-home present.”

A tradition at homecoming from a voyage was a celebration with all hands at a special dinner. After the table was cleared and cleanup done, the family retired to the den to sit and talk some more. When everyone was seated and comfortable, Annaliese called for attention.

“While you fellows have been gone, some things have happened around here we need to tell you about. First off, it looks like I may have found a situation with a practice in Noumea. Which means, if Johnny approves, I’ll have something to do, since it seems we’re going to be living here.”

Johnny was grinning from ear to ear. “Sounds good to me.”

“There are a lot of details to iron out, but I want to introduce you to my associate.” She held out her hand to Colleen. “We plan to work a turnaround between Noumea and here, maybe a month on and a month off. We haven’t worked out the details yet.”

Manny was looking at Colleen with a puzzled expression on his face. “Does this mean we’ll be living here too?”

"If that's alright with you. It may not be permanent. We'll have to see how it works out."

"Fine with me. Wherever you are, I want to be."

"Manny, I have something else to tell you." He looked a question at her. "I think I'm going to have a baby." She turned and looked at Teressa, who looked at Bobby and said,

"Me too. I think I'm going to have one too."

The sight of the two of them sitting there in slack-jawed amazement was too much for them. The women burst out laughing.

Later that night, Johnny and Annaliese were lying in bed talking. "As of now, the idea is for each of us to work until the other one shows up. That way, the one at home can finish up whatever she's doing and then come to relieve her. The one at home could be on Wind Song on a voyage or something. And of course, there'll come a time when Colleen will have to stop work for a while with the baby."

"It's hard to believe we'll have two grandbabies around here at the same time."

"It will be fun. They'll have all the help they need with them. I'm so glad the family is all together again. I never thought it would happen."

In the next room, they were lying on the bed after lovemaking when Manny asked, "What happened? You seem different since we're home."

"I feel different. I've been in such a daze, Manny. All I wanted to do was sleep, but I couldn't. You needed me. Your mama and I talked a lot while you were away, and she helped me see the way forward.

"Manny, ever since I got on the train that day at the Academy to go to San Diego, I've been trying to prove to the world that I belonged, that I was good enough to be a doctor. I believed I needed to be the best. To never give up because if I did, then somehow, I wouldn't measure up to what I should be. Lately, I've come to realize that's not what my life has to be.

"Now, for the first time, I think I know how to be content with who I am and that what I am is good enough. We're surrounded by family out here and everyone loves me. I don't have to prove anything to anybody, not anymore. I once heard someone say, 'you can't please everyone, so make sure you please yourself.' Now I'm pleasing myself. "So what do you think about me being pregnant?"

"I don't know what to think. It will be exciting and interesting, and I'll still have you to play with, for a little while at least."

In the house, Teressa and Bobby were also lying in bed talking.

"So, a baby." He shook his head in amazement.

"Yes. How do you feel about it?"

"Tell you the truth, I'm in shock. Every time I try to think about it, I end up thinking about something else."

"Don't worry. You'll have nine months to get used to it. It looks like we might have the family together for quite a while. What do you think about that?"

"I'm glad. It's lonely around here sometimes, and everyone will help out. With two babies on the way, we should be fine. If we have a problem getting things going again, there'll be plenty to help when you need it."

EPILOGUE

Wash was sitting at the kitchen table, smoking his pipe, and Woman was shelling peas into a large bowl when Johnny knocked on the screen door of the cabin.

He pulled it open and stood for a moment, grinning ear to ear, looking at his friend. Of course, Woman was his friend too, but Wash was special. When he was a new man, Wash had always been there to help mold what he became.

Wash's voice was still that deep, gravelly growl. "Been thinkin' about you. Wondering when you'd come back," he paused and grinned, "if you'd come back."

For the next hour, they talked. Johnny helped him into an easy chair and they sat while he talked and Wash listened. Johnny told him of how he spent his time, of the house on the cliff and the lagoon at Maupiti, of Wind Song and how he loved the feeling it gave him to be aboard her under sail.

They talked about Annaliese and Colleen's new practice, and Manny's recovery, how he was thinking of editing the logs and writing things based on them, about their granddaughter Van and new grandson Enoah, the coming additions to the family, and many other things.

Johnny could see that the back injury of his youth had crippled Wash as he aged and his ability to stand was a painful process. But nonetheless, with the help of Johnny and Woman, he managed to get upright and with the help of a cane, was able to walk with him to the door, where they stood, looking at one another with their hands clasped in one of those handshakes you remember for the rest of your life.